EQUILIBRIUM

SCATTERED STARS: CONVICTION BOOK 3

EQUILIBRIUM

SCATTERED STARS: CONVICTION BOOK 3

GLYNN STEWART

FAOLAN'S PEN PUBLISHING

faolanspen.com

This edition published in 2021 by:

Faolan's Pen Publishing Inc.

22 King St. S, Suite 300

Waterloo, Ontario

N2J 1N8 Canada

ISBN-13: 978-1-989674-17-8 (print)

A record of this book is available from Library and Archives Canada.

Printed in the United States of America

1 2 3 4 5 6 7 8 9 10

First edition

First printing: January 2021

Illustration © 2021 Jeff Brown Graphics

Copyeditor: Richard Shealy

Proofreader: M Parker Editing

Faolan's Pen Publishing logo is a trademark of Faolan's Pen Publishing Inc.

Read more books from Glynn Stewart at faolanspen.com

1

"STAND BY FOR FIRING PATTERN ALPHA."

"STAND BY FOR FIRING PATTERN ALPHA."

Commander Kira Demirci listened to the calm report as she waited. The bridge of the newly rechristened mercenary heavy cruiser *Deception* was quiet, with no one speaking except for the tactical officer. The bridge crew were faking calm competence, but Kira could *feel* the tension under it.

For six weeks, technicians had gone over every link, every switch and every breaker of the cruiser's main batteries. Even the small cadre of the cruiser's original crew weren't sure they'd found every one of the traps the ship's previous Captain had activated.

"Check charge and status on all guns," *Deception's new* Captain ordered. Kavitha Zoric had been the executive officer of the mercenary carrier *Conviction* until Kira had poached her. Now the dark-haired and dark-skinned officer occupied the central chair of the amphitheater-style bridge like she was born to it.

"Every turret is green," the chief engineer reported. Konrad Bueller was a broad-shouldered man who did dual duty as the cruiser's executive officer—he was the senior officer of the contingent of defectors from the original Brisingr crew.

He was also Kira Demirci's boyfriend, even if that role was still very fresh. He was from Brisingr, the sworn enemy of the petite, hundred-and-sixty-centimeter-tall nova-fighter commander's home-world of Apollo.

That might still wreck them, but for now he was the XO and chief engineer of the cruiser. He'd been the one who'd led the testing of *Deception*'s twenty-four heavy turrets.

"All right," Zoric said. She looked around the bridge, twisting slightly in her chair to meet Kira's gaze. She raised a questioning eyebrow and Kira nodded.

Technically, Kira Demirci was the Commander, Nova Group, for the cruiser. She was *also* the Commander, Nova Group, for *Conviction*, the mercenary carrier currently half a star system away standing guard over their employer's planet.

Of course, Kira Demirci was the main shareholder of Memorial Squadron, the mercenary entity that owned *Deception*. Zoric might command the ship while Kira led the nova fighters...but Kira was Zoric's boss, not the other way around.

But there was no point in delaying. They'd spent at least two weeks longer than they should have, in Kira's opinion, going over *Deception*'s systems—but the Redward Royal Fleet had insisted. Going over *Deception* with a fine-toothed comb had been part of their price for letting Kira keep the ship.

"Activate the drones and...fire," Zoric ordered calmly.

Almost a hundred automated drones activated their Harrington coils, leaping into motion around the heavy cruiser in preprogrammed but complex patterns. This was a test in more ways than one.

"Turrets in independent control. Engaging the targets," the tactical officer reported. Marija Davidović was a hawk-nosed Black woman from Redward, "borrowed" from the Redward Royal Fleet since the mercenaries hadn't previously needed gunnery officers.

Deception shivered as her turrets opened fire. Each pulse of plasma from the magnetic tubes was equal to the firepower delivered by a nova-fighter torpedo.

The first sequence took almost a minute, each turret firing its dual guns independently in a carefully calculated sequence that allowed Bueller to assess their problems.

"Well?" Zoric asked him as the plasma pulses faded from the display.

"All turrets still green," the Brisingr man reported. "All power-load systems are green. Everything looks like it should, Captain."

"Davidović?" Kira asked, turning *her* attention to the tactical officer. "How are the gunnery crews looking?"

"Twenty-four shots, sixteen hits against automated targets without jamming in play," the Redward woman replied crisply. "For a first firing run on a new ship, I suppose that's acceptable, but the guns and the targeting systems on *Deception* are more effective than I'm used to.

"They'd *better* improve."

"Then they will," Kira said with a small smile. Davidović was new to being a mercenary, but Kira was a twenty-year veteran of the Apollo System Defense Force, a fleet for whom *Deception* would have been barely a first-rate combatant. She could live with some of her new mercs being rather more hard-edged than her old mercs might prefer.

"With your permission, Captain, Chief?" Davidović turned to Zoric and Bueller. "Second-sequence tests?"

"Fire at will, Commander Davidović," Zoric replied. "Everything is looking good so far. Let's stress the guns and see what happens when we're a short nova from a proper yard."

Or as close as the Cluster has, Kira reflected. From the way Bueller met her eyes when she looked over at him, the engineer was thinking the same thing.

The Syntactic Cluster was on the far edge of the Rim, fifteen hundred light-years from Sol for all intents and purposes. Both of them —and *Deception*—were from the mid-Rim, almost two hundred light-years coreward.

Deception might be barely a capital ship to them...but she was the single most powerful warship in the Syntactic Cluster.

"Firing all turrets," Davidović reported. "On my mark... *Mark*."

Kira's headware flashed data across a display on her eyes as she assessed the result. *Deception*'s Harrington coils, powering her reactionless drive, had spiked to compensate for the thrust imparted by the guns.

Forty-eight plasma cannon was a *lot* of force and called for a *lot* of power. If there were going to be any problems with *Deception*'s repaired power-distribution network, they'd show up in a mass salvo like that.

"Green," Bueller said aloud, confirming what she was seeing in her headware. "All systems are green. You are cleared for sustained fire, Commander."

"Commander Davidović, your old employers gave us a nice little set of test drones," Zoric told her tactical officer. "Let's show our appreciation by vaporizing every last one of them, shall we?"

"Yes, sir!"

AS THE CRUISER continued to work through the planned exercises, Kira's attention began to drift. She hadn't been overly worried, but each test made it clearer and clearer that Bueller's teams had gone above and beyond.

If anything, *Deception* was in better shape now than she had been when Kira and a mixed team of mercenaries and Redward commandos had boarded the ship, then called *K79-L*, in orbit of Ypres. The warship had been a third party's intervention tool of choice in the civil war in that system, the gateway between the Syntactic Cluster and the galaxy beyond.

In *Kira's* hands, the warship was going to be the Cluster's answers to that third party. The Equilibrium Institute had attempted to meddle in hundreds of star systems before, but Kira's new boss was one of their former operatives. He'd made it his mission to slow and stop their plan for all humanity.

Her new boyfriend was of the same mold, a former Equilibrium operative sickened by what the Institute was prepared to embrace in pursuit of their goal. The objective "peace for all humanity" sounded good, even to Kira, but the Institute's plans to create that peace were going to drench half the galaxy in blood.

"Do we need to do any exercises for the fighter wing while we're out here at Lastward?" Zoric asked, cutting into Kira's thoughts.

Kira considered it for a moment, then shook her head. The gas giant, on the fringe of the Redward System, was a no-fly zone for civilians, a military reservation that the Redward Royal Fleet—and their retained mercenaries—used for covert testing.

"No, we've been exercising the wing while *Deception* was being gone over with a fine-toothed comb," she said. "Even the Vier pilots are familiar with their planes now."

The Brisingr cruiser had arrived in the Syntactic Cluster with twenty Weltraumpanzer-Vier heavy nova fighters. Kira had managed to hang on to a six-ship squadron of them and sold the rest to Redward.

The rest of *Deception*'s fighters were Apollo-style Hoplite-IVs, top-tier interceptors from her former home system. Most of the fourteen on *Deception* were *Conviction*-built clones using Redward-built Harrington coils and nova drives, but no one except a veteran of the Apollo-Brisingr war would ever realize that.

And all of *those* in the Cluster now worked for Kira.

"Once you're done running through the tests, we'll nova back to Redward and check in," Kira decided aloud. "Let's keep everything simple for today. RRF command is going to be pleased to hear *Deception* is ready for work."

She grinned.

"For some reason, governments don't like paying mercenaries to just sit there—though gods know they were happy to pay us to poke through *Deception*'s guts and Bueller's brain."

That worthy chuckled, clearly half-listening to the conversation.

"They moved fast on all of that, too," he told them quietly. "We don't quite have a prototype for the Twelve-X up and running, but they've started building slips and laying the keels for the ships that will hold them. A fleet carrier and a battlecruiser, to start."

Kira whistled silently.

Bueller had been the engine-gang chief on one of Brisingr's top-line battlecruisers before he'd been relegated to a desk and then recruited by the Institute for their operations here. His headware contained most of the specifications to build a ten-thousand-cubic-meter 12X nova drive—enough to build hundred-and-twelve-kilocubic warships, as big as anything Apollo or Brisingr could build.

Built with Redward's tech base, those ships wouldn't be as effective as Apollo or Brisingr's ships, but sheer size would put them ahead of anything within a hundred light-years.

"Ever wonder if that was the right call?" she asked him.

"Every hour on the hour," he replied. "But everyone I've met here has been good people, and, well, fuck the Kaiser."

Kira shivered. She wondered if Brisingr's Kaiser had realized quite what he was unleashing when he'd handed a crew of his spacers over to the Equilibrium Institute. The Kaiserreich's officers could justify atrocities committed in the name of Brisingr, barely.

But ones committed for the Equilibrium Institute's ideals and plans? That had proven a lot harder in the end.

"Sirs?" Davidović interrupted. "I have a nova signature at just over forty light-seconds. It's not on our schedules."

Kira checked the time and smiled.

"It is on mine," she told the tactical officer. "And it's part of why we're out here. Their Majesties are back exactly on time, I see."

The King and Queen of Redward had spent the last few weeks at the Ypres System, trying to negotiate both the end to that system's century-long civil conflict and the beginning of a new Cluster-wide free trade zone.

They were traveling on one of Redward's handful of cruisers, but with everything going on of late, no one was communicating their travel itinerary in advance.

"That makes sense," Davidović replied. "Biggest looks like sixty kilocubics; I'd guess that's *First Crown*." She paused, blinking at the data coming into her headware—and then visibly paled.

"New novas!" she snapped. "I have multiple gunship novas on what appear to be attack courses for *First Crown*. Multiphasic jamming engaged, and I have lost scan data on the cruiser and escorts."

"*Fuck*," Kira snapped. "Zoric, get us into motion. I need to be in a nova fighter *now*!"

2

LIKE ANY NOVA SHIP, *Deception* was not particularly large by any objective scale. Roughly twenty-five meters across, she was only a hundred and fifty meters long. She was huge by the standards of nova ships in the far Rim, but that was still small enough that it took Kira under ninety seconds to reach the fighter deck.

Her scrambling fighter pilots only barely beat her into their starfighters. She was the last to lock in, but only by a few seconds.

"All fighters, deck has the bouncing ball," she ordered. "Launch on their timing. Deck, this is a full scramble. Get us out there."

Her headware was still linking in to the fighter's software as a new gravity well was conjured in front of her Hoplite-IV, flinging the small ship into deep space and automatically bringing up her own Harrington coils.

Davidović and her second, Iyov Waxweiler, had broken out as much as they could of the arrival of their hostiles. The sixty-thousand-cubic-meter cruiser *First Crown* had arrived on schedule with two ten-kilocubic gunship escorts from the Redward Royal Fleet.

Thirty seconds after that, *twenty-four* ten-kilocubic gunships had novaed in. The timing was too close for them to have even had an agent watching for *First Crown*. They'd known the schedule.

"Davidović, do we have an ID on our gunships?" Kira demanded as her hands and implants took control of the Hoplite.

"I'm making it seventy percent that they're from the Costar Clans," the tactical officer replied. "Lot of those raiders have grudges against the Crown."

Kira grimaced. She'd had her own run-ins with the Syntactic Cluster's perennial problem children. A loosely affiliated collection of hardscrabble, borderline, or outright failing colonies and mining outposts scattered through secondary systems of the Cluster, the Costar Clans sustained the existence of their settlements by raiding more fortunate systems' shipping.

The operation seemed a bit too slick for them—but the Equilibrium Institute had used them as patsies before.

"Understood," she told the tactical officer. "Memorial Wing, form on me. Check your targets when we hit the battlespace; Redward had two gunships in play when they arrived, and we can hope they're still there!"

Ten thousand cubic meters was the default hull that anyone with a base colonial fabricator could build the systems for. *Everybody* had tenkilocubic gunships, and there wasn't that much to distinguish between them.

Kira didn't want her people to shoot down friendlies.

She took a moment to absorb the mental confirmations from her pilots and push herself into the right headspace.

"Memorial Wing...nova and attack!"

FORTY LIGHT-SECONDS VANISHED IN A HEARTBEAT, and Kira's starfighter was in the middle of the multiphasic-jamming bubble of the hostile gunships. Inside that bubble, every non-visual scanner was worthless, and even computer-enhanced optics were only reliable at limited distances.

Those optics were enough to tell her that something had already gone differently from expected. *First Crown* might only be six times the size of each individual gunship, but she still badly outclassed her attackers.

There were only nineteen gunships left in the jamming zone—but Kira's twenty nova fighters weren't the first nova strike to arrive in the battlespace. A chaotic spiral of *forty* unknown nova fighters was hurtling toward *First Crown*, and an eye trained by twenty years of war spotted the real threat.

She'd already lost coms with most of her starfighters, but she had laser links to a handful, and she tagged them all.

"Everyone who can hear me," Kira snapped. *"Target the nova bombers."*

Her Weltraumpanzer-Viers each carried two torpedoes. The heavier specialized anti-capital-ship nova craft in the heart of the hostile formation carried *ten*. *First Crown* could probably handle a salvo from one bomber.

But Kira's computers were guessing there was something between eight and fourteen bombers hidden in the enemy nova-fighter formation.

She suited her actions to her words, throwing maximum power to her Harrington coils and diving into the chaos with her guns blazing. A hostile interceptor took a moment too long to react to the presence of nova fighters, ate a full two-second burst from her plasma cannon and vanished in a ball of fire.

More of her fighters were swarming toward the enemy strike. They might be outnumbered two to one, but enough of her pilots were veterans that they didn't need her to point out the bombers. The newbies, half-trained and unblooded, were still smart enough to follow the vets.

Kira twisted her nova fighter through the strangers' escort formation and hammered another salvo of plasma into a second interceptor. That fighter novaed out in the middle of her blast—damaged and *probably* out of the fight.

Instinct dodged her fighter half a kilometer sideways, and plasma blazed through where she'd been. Threat icons flagged at least three interceptors targeting her, but she ignored them as she dove toward the bomber formation.

One of the interceptors vanished and her computers confirmed that another Hoplite had moved into position to cover her. She wouldn't know which of her pilots that was until later, but they were doing their job.

Time was everything and the clock was running out. It took sixty seconds for her nova fighter's class two drive to cool and allow for a new jump. Their opponents weren't jumping out, though. The bombers were pressing the attack—and Kira was in their midst.

Plasma flashed in the dark of space, and a bomber came apart under her guns. More of her wing was in the mix with her, but the back of her mind was also flagging something she *didn't* want to know: the enemy pilots were as good as her veterans, and she was definitely missing starfighters that had novaed in with her.

Once in the battlespace's jamming, she couldn't give orders. She focused on the bombers, shattering a second of the capital-ship killers and then cursing as the surviving nova craft salvoed their weapons—and vanished.

The gunships were still pressing their attack, and *First Crown*'s weapons were focused on them. Not that it would have mattered. A torpedo was only a physical object for about five seconds before detonating and turning into a massive plasma blast...

Plasma blasts which, in this case, ran into the armored flank of *Deception* as the heavy cruiser completed her own precision nova, dropping the big ship between the incoming threat and the monarchs of Redward.

One of the gunships was now heading directly toward Kira, their gunfire tracking far too closely for her liking, and she fell back on the first adage of nova-fighter pilots: if the battlespace is too hot...*be somewhere else.*

She novaed.

THE COMPUTERS automatically picked a rendezvous point near the battlespace, usually one light-minute away. Kira's fighter wasn't the only one of *Deception*'s parasites at the deep-space point she'd jumped to.

She could see eleven other fighters. There were almost certainly still some in the battlespace, so she hadn't lost eight planes and pilots today.

"Report," she ordered. "Convert what you can to ammo and nova back on your cooldown. This isn't over yet."

Her fighters could only hold so much energy in the capacitors for their guns, and their microfusion power plants could only recharge those capacitors so quickly with everything else demanding power. Away from the battlespace, the reduced demands allowed for far faster "reloading."

"Teach your brother to herd sheep," her second-in-command, Melissa "Nightmare" Cartman, told her. The commander of her Memorial-Bravo squadron ran the second section of Hoplites flying off *Deception*. "Who the hell were those fighters?"

"We don't know," Kira said grimly. "Not Clan, not with fucking *bombers*."

Nobody in the Syntactic Cluster was supposed to have nova bombers. The class two nova drive was difficult enough to build that there was only one plant in the cluster making them at all—and Kira had helped *acquire* that plant for Redward.

The larger version required for a nova bomber was beyond even Redward right now. The presence of nova bombers suggested someone was playing games.

"The usual suspects, Mel. Playing the usual games," she told Nightmare. "We need to save King Larry and Queen Sonia. We won't get paid particularly well if we lose our employers' monarchs *and* a third of their cruisers in one shot!"

Her old friend snorted.

"Wilco. Ten seconds," she warned. "*Deception* wasn't there when I left. Hoping?"

"She took a torp salvo meant for *Crown*," Kira replied. "She *should* be okay; her armor and dispersion networks are good. Hostile fighters novaed, but they might be back."

"Understood. Memorial-Bravo, check in," Nightmare snapped. She listened to reports Kira couldn't hear for a second.

"We're on our way," she then told Kira. "Memorial-Bravo—*nova and attack.*"

Kira's own countdown still had fifteen seconds left, and she linked in with the pilots with her. All four of her Weltraumpanzer-Viers were now there, along with two more of the Hoplites. It wasn't one of her formal squadrons, but they'd do.

"On the timer T minus ten, form on me," she ordered. "Memorials...*nova.*"

BY THE TIME Kira and her fighters returned, the battle was over. She saw the pulse of the last gunship novaing out and breathed a sigh of relief. The enemy fighters hadn't returned so far, though everyone was keeping their own multiphasic jamming up, just in case.

Even the Clans, after all, were entirely capable of building a smart missile that could cross a star system and hit its target. Multiphasic jamming would render that weapon deaf, blind and stupid in its final approach, making it an easy target, but *without* that jamming it could potentially be deadly.

The absence of immediate hostiles allowed Kira to assess the situation. The RRF gunships were gone. No real surprise there, though she didn't like it. They might be the "small" ships of the main fleets, but a gunship still had a crew of thirty.

Deception looked intact...ish. Kira's cruiser had taken sixty torpedoes. That was less than she'd estimated it would need when she was on the other side of the equation, but she still didn't like the marks her computers were picking up on the ship's hull.

Worse, while it was hard to sort out the numbers in the jamming, she was definitely missing at least two fighters. If she was lucky, the pilots had ejected and their nova-drive cores were retrievable.

If she wasn't...she'd just lost ten percent of her immediate subordinates.

On the other hand, *First Crown* appeared mostly unblemished. Kira was never happy to lose people—or lose allies, for that matter. The RRF gunships weren't her mercenaries, but she'd still mourn them.

If nothing else, a significant chunk of the pilots she commanded across *Deception* and the mercenary carrier *Conviction* were ex-RRF gunship crew.

She trained a laser com on *Deception* and linked in.

"This is Basketball," she told them. "Report."

"A bit cooked around the edges, but we're fine," Zoric replied instantly. "DamCon is sweeping the impacted hull sections, and we'll need some replacement plating and dispersal nets, but we have no casualties."

"Thank gods," Kira murmured. That was better than she'd been afraid of—*much* better. "Did you get any scans on the nova fighters?"

Zoric snorted.

"Boss, we didn't even *see* the nova fighters," she admitted. "I was novaing in to block off gunship fire, not eat a fucking torpedo strike. We got lucky."

Multiphasic-jamming fields were starting to come down, and Kira felt her shoulders tense. This was always the riskiest part. If the enemy *hadn't* retreated, her people were going to be vulnerable.

But a battle had to end sometime. It was a judgment call—and if the jammers didn't come down, no one was going to be able to tell them to take them down.

She tapped a physical switch, taking her own offline.

"Have the deck prep the ball," she ordered. "This was short and ugly, as per usual. I'm going to have to run gun-camera footage, but I think we gave a good account of ourselves."

"Only six of the gunships got out," Zoric said in a satisfied tone. "They were *not* prepared to face two cruisers."

"It's a trap," Kira said in a blatantly faked Brisingr accent. "There's *two of them*."

The humor was forced, though. As the jammers came down, it was clear she was missing three of her Hoplite-IVs. None of her Apollo veterans, but still…

"Get search-and-rescue out ASAP," she ordered. "We want our own survival pods and any escape pods from the RRF gunships." Her eyes scanned the sensor data she was receiving as well.

"Prisoners might be handy, too."

3

REINFORCEMENTS STARTED ARRIVING in short order. Lightspeed sensor delays meant the first wave was a pair of nova destroyers and a six-ship squadron of nova fighters from the Lastward security fleet. Redward was still being careful about revealing their new ability to build the drives for nova fighters, but an attack on the monarch meant *everything* was in play.

Kira watched from *Deception*'s flight control center as the new starfighters swung into formation around *First Crown*. The destroyers did the same, but they positioned themselves between the Redward cruiser and the mercenary ship.

She concealed a chuckle at that. If she'd wanted to wreck *First Crown*, there wouldn't be much *left*. *Deception* was fifteen years out of date by the standards of her home sector, but that meant she was around thirty years ahead of the Redward cruiser.

And she was almost two-thirds again the local ships' cubage. *Deception* could take on the cruiser and both destroyers and wouldn't break a sweat.

There was a reason it had taken Queen Sonia's explicit support to let Kira keep the ship.

"What's the status on our search-and-rescue?" she asked the deck boss.

Dilshad Tamboli wasn't the person she'd *wanted* for her flight deck boss, but it made no sense to move Angel Waldroup—*Conviction*'s deck boss—from a carrier now up to almost forty starfighters to a cruiser that maxed out at twenty.

Waldroup had recommended Tamboli, one of her team leads, and the dark-skinned spacer was now one of the handful of officers aboard *Deception* that held the delightfully vague mercenary rank of *Commander*.

They were focused on the screens and their headware but brought their attention back to Kira as she spoke.

"We've picked up Janda," Tamboli reported. "One beacon still in space, looks like Saari." They shook their head sadly. "We're sweeping in case Zima's beacon was just disabled, but it doesn't look like it."

One pilot lost out of three fighters destroyed. That was *good* by any standard, but Kira had still lost a pilot. Iris Zima had been one of their greenest recruits, a civilian shuttle pilot who'd leapt at the chance to fly a nova fighter.

"Keep looking for her," Kira ordered. "Any of our unknowns show up in the sweep?"

"RRF picked up the escape pods from the gunships, but we're still sweeping for fighter pods," Tamboli told her. "Either none of them ejected or they're using timed beacons."

"They didn't seem the type to fight to the death," she noted. "Too professional. Those were damn good pilots, Commander Tamboli. My guess is timed beacons."

Timed beacons triggered after twelve to twenty-four hours, in case a force didn't think they were going to be able to control the battle-space but *did* think they might be able to sneak back in and retrieve their survival pods later.

"Make sure we grab any of their class two drives we can ID as well," Kira said. "Even if we end up not using them, we can trade them to Redward. They're not making that many of the things yet."

Most of her fighters had been manufactured in the fabricators aboard *Conviction*, but the new ships' drives had come from Redward.

A class two nova drive couldn't be manufactured in zero gravity or artificial gravity, which was part of what made them so hard to build.

"Sir," a voice pinged in her headware from the bridge. "This is coms. We have incoming call for you from *First Crown*." The junior officer sounded awed. "It's the King, sir."

The awe made sense, then. Monica Smolak was a Redward native, hired for her skills with communications software and hardware. She was still getting used to the "ship without borders" nature of a mercenary crew.

"I'll take it in my office," Kira told Smolak. "Give His Majesty my apologies; I will be a minute."

DESPITE THE HORRIBLE lèse-majesté of asking both her employer and the local monarch to *wait*, King Larry didn't appear particularly bothered when his image appeared in the hologram above Kira's desk.

The office still didn't feel like *hers*, not yet, but it was the office for *Deception*'s Commander, Nova Group. It had everything she needed but was stripped down to the basic utilitarian fixtures of a metal desk and a counter with a coffee machine.

At least working for Redward meant they had *very* good coffee. It was still the planet's main export.

"Your Majesty," Kira greeted the immense smiling man on her screen. Lawrence Bartholomew Stewart, His Royal Majesty, First Magistrate and Honored King of the Kingdom of Redward, looked almost *exactly* like the kind of man who'd use the regnal name of *King Larry*.

"Sonia will be joining us in a moment," Larry told her. "She is talking to the analyst team she has with her to get their first assessment of the situation."

Kira wasn't entirely sure how many people knew that Queen Sonia was the head of the Office of Integration—or even that the intelligence-consolidation team by that name existed. Via the Office, Sonia ran the entire intelligence apparatus of the Kingdom...and it made perfect sense she had a team with her.

"I'm glad we were in position to intervene," Kira said. "We'd set it up with the RRF, but I don't think anyone actually expected it to be needed."

"Admiral Remington told us there'd be some arrangements for our security, but…as you say, no one expected trouble," Larry admitted. A second image appeared above Kira's desk while he was speaking, the tall and delicately built frame of Queen Sonia a distinct contrast to her husband.

From the fond glance the two exchanged, Kira figured they were in separate offices and hadn't seen each other much since the battle.

"*I* expected trouble," Sonia insisted. "We knew the RRF was penetrated to an unacceptable degree when we moved against the Clans last year. That battle group was sent out with sealed paper orders to cover against an intelligence apparatus we *knew* couldn't be Warlord Davies's."

"The RRF still struggles with the concept of an interstellar conspiracy specifically targeting *us*," Larry admitted. "So do I. But…" He sighed. "We have enough evidence that it exists."

"Including this," Sonia said. "Someone has the RRF sufficiently penetrated that our heavily protected and secret itinerary was leaked to a hostile force with access to both Clans-owned gunships and modern nova fighters."

"Regardless…thank you, Commander Demirci," Larry told Kira. "Or is it Captain now?"

"Commander for the moment," Kira said. "Kavitha Zoric commands *Deception* while I command her fighters…and head Memorial Squadron LLC. We, of course, work for Redward through the subcontract from Conviction Limited."

Larry laughed.

"I'm sure that all makes sense to you," he told her. "All I really need to know is that you're on our side with that behemoth." He turned his attention back to Sonia. "You may as well fill the Commander in on what your team concluded at the same time as me."

"The gunships were from the Costar Clans," the Queen told them. "We have more than enough data on the Clans' construction methods and available materials to confirm. The starfighters are more questionable. The interceptors were Veles-Four-type ships, Crest-built. The bombers aren't in our intelligence databanks."

"I can have my people go over the data we have," Kira offered. "I don't think there's anything in *Deception*'s databanks we didn't give you, though."

"I would appreciate that, Commander," Sonia said. "Right now, my analysts' best guess is that we're looking at the flight group from that *Liberty*-class ship that showed up at Ypres. We know there's a mercenary carrier working for Equilibrium in the region, and a *Liberty*-class would field forty nova fighters."

"And Equilibrium has worked with the Costar Clans in the past," Kira said.

"Indeed." Larry's voice was grim. "Our scans show you lost three fighters, Commander. Were…any of your pilots retrieved?"

"Two of them, thankfully," she replied. "We only lost one person today."

"We lost fifty-five," Larry told her. "The gunships were taken out too quickly for escape pods. We have a handful of lucky survivors, nothing more. These *people* attacked without warning and killed far more of my subjects than I can tolerate."

"We'll interrogate the prisoners on Redward," Sonia noted. "But there's no way we can keep the Clans' portion of this secret. We can probably quiet down the part about mercenary nova fighters, but…"

"What happens if people hear about the Clans' attack?" Kira asked. Sonia sounded worried.

"Parliament will explode," Larry replied instantly. "We have a working majority there, one that is loyal to us and the ideals we follow. It's made up of three parties of the eight in Parliament, but they've stuck with us through four elections at this point.

"But…" He shook his head. "Enough of my *opponents* in Parliament want the Clans crushed that it's a perennial argument. Once the people personally loyal to me start demanding we deal with the Costar Clans, we are going to have a problem."

"We will deal with that *in* Parliament," Sonia told him. "We at least have good news to bring to them as well."

"Your Majesty?" Kira inquired.

"Our mission in Ypres was a complete success," the Queen said. "For the first time in the two centuries it's been inhabited, Ypres is united. Their new Federation is going to be a kludge for some time, but it has a unified nova-warship command—and they've signed on to the Free Trade Zone."

The Syntactic Cluster Free Trade Zone was the dream the two monarchs had been pushing since before Kira had arrived. By establishing a mutual trade and security pact, they hoped to duplicate the purpose of the Old Earth European Union—economies and cultures so interlinked that war was impossible and unthinkable.

The problem was that the Equilibrium Institute, a quietly secret organization that had its fingers throughout a good chunk of human space, didn't think that kind of structure worked. So, to "save" the Syntactic Cluster from itself, they kept interfering.

"That's fantastic news," she told them. "The whole system seemed… Well, they seemed like they deserved better."

Ypres was the gateway from the Cluster to the rest of the Rim. Its division had been a long-standing impediment to all sixteen of the inhabited systems in the star cluster.

"Most people usually do," Larry said. "As monarchs, it's our job to get them that something better. As a soldier, it's your job to protect it."

"We try, Your Majesty," Kira replied.

"And you succeed," he told her. "There will be a significant bonus for your Memorials once I'm back home." He sighed. "There is also, almost certainly, going to be a lot more work coming up. If the Clans are going to provoke us, then I am left with no choice.

"If Parliament is going to demand that the Costar Clans be neutralized, then we must get ahead of those demands and make certain that it is done *my* way."

A chill ran down Kira's spine. From her interactions with him, Kira knew King Larry to be a kind-hearted man, affable and cheerful by choice and nature alike…but he was also the constitutional monarch of a system of two billion souls, who'd guided its government without notable difficulty for fifteen standard years.

She *knew* underestimating him was dangerous, and even *she* sometimes fell into that trap.

4

DECEPTION RETURNED to Redward orbit in company with *First Crown*. The two ships novaed together once the royal transport had finished cooling her nova drive. The entire point of having *Crown* jump to Lastward instead of the main planet had been to protect her arrival and leave her with a ready-to-nova drive when she got home.

In hindsight, that had been a mistake. Kira didn't bother to conceal her sigh of relief from her bridge crew as *First Crown* entered the weapons range of the massive asteroid fortresses orbiting Redward. Like almost every major human world, the planet was more than fortified enough to stand off an attack by any ship small enough to nova.

The vulnerability was in the hour between emerging from nova and entering that defensive perimeter. With the drive core cooled, *Crown* could have evaded a threat in that gap by micro-novaing. With her core heated by a full-length six-light-year nova, she'd be trapped by any enemy engaging her.

Since her course had leaked, that had happened in the far reaches of the star system instead. But Kira had been there with *Deception* and everything had turned out...mostly okay.

"Sir, we have docking clearance for Blueward Station," Smolak told Zoric. "*Conviction*'s old dock."

"Understood. We'll come in slow and careful," the Captain ordered. She didn't bother to glance at Kira for confirmation. "Davidović, where's *Conviction*?"

"I have her on the scopes," the tactical officer replied, throwing the old carrier up on their displays. "She's about three-quarters to the slip they threw together for our refit," she concluded.

"That was the plan," Kira reminded them. "Once *Deception* could take over the role of being the RRF's mercenary heavy, *Conviction* needed some tender care of her own."

A hundred and sixty-eight years old, the carrier had been demilitarized roughly on her second decommissioning, the removal of her original plasma turrets done in such a manner that she lacked the structural integrity for new ones.

"*First Crown* has launched a shuttle squadron heading for the surface," Davidović reported. "A wing of sub-fighters from the fortress is rendezvousing with them. Their Majesties are heading to the capital."

"Good," Kira said. "I have some conversations to have with Waldroup and the RRF logistics teams. We need to get three replacement Hoplites aboard ASAP."

That was going to be an argument with *Conviction*'s deck boss. The old carrier's fabricators were among the best in the system—edged out by *Deception*'s now but better set up in general for building nova fighters.

Conviction had eighteen Hoplite-IV clones aboard, and Kira wanted to steal three of them rather than waiting for new fighters to be fabbed. She'd have an easier time borrowing a pilot from Joseph Hoffman, *Conviction*'s new Commander, Nova Group, and one of her Apollo veterans, than she was going to have stealing three fighters from Angel Waldroup.

"That's your job, not mine," Zoric told her with a chuckle. She was clearly following Kira's thought process. "Did you ever think your mercenary company was going to be this much of a pain, Demirci?"

"I thought I was going to have six nova fighters forever," Kira admitted. "Not a heavy cruiser and forty-odd pilots and crews that belonged to me across two ships!"

What was going to make her life easier right *now* was that the three Hoplite squadrons aboard *Conviction* still belonged to Memorial Squadron. Waldroup ran *Conviction*'s flight deck, but those squadrons were still subcontractors.

As King Larry had said, it all made sense to *her*. Most of the time.

ONCE THE CRUISER DOCKED, Kira's headware cheerfully informed her that she had a backlog of messages at her stationside office—even though she'd been out of Blueward Station for less than twenty-four hours, saving the King and Queen included.

Instead of checking any of them, she called the man who was in charge of the Memorials' planetside affairs.

"Stipan, why is my email exploding?" she asked him.

Stipan Dirix was a former Captain in the Redward Army that she'd recruited to run her dockside office when she and her people had first arrived in Redward. There was a Brisingr death mark worth millions on her and all of her Apollon pilots, so she'd needed an intermediary.

"You have a working heavy cruiser, sir," Dirix pointed out. "While *Deception* was in dry dock and *Conviction* was doing all of the work, it was easy to redirect people to Estanza. Now that the reverse is true, people want to hire you."

"Is there anything in that pile I actually need to care about?" Kira asked.

"Are you planning on taking any jobs outside the Redward retainer?" he replied.

Kira's conversation with Larry and Sonia suggested that Redward was going to be leaning on that retainer shortly. Technically, *she* didn't even have that retainer—it was Estanza's retainer and she was merely a subcontractor.

"I'm not doing anything that isn't run through Estanza and Conviction Limited just yet," she told Dirix.

"Then you can ignore most of those emails," Dirix said calmly. "Flag 'em back to me and I'll let people down gently." The big man shrugged in the image her headware was feeding her. "I turned down everyone who was *obviously* not offering enough money, but didn't want to say no to jobs that looked half-decent or better."

"The RRF is going to need us soon enough," Kira said. "We're not going anywhere. What's the rest? Personal and ads, looks like?"

There was a message there from Hope Temitope, for example. The Redward Commando Colonel had been instrumental in capturing *Deception*, and they'd kept in contact since.

"I cleared most of the ads out based on the usual rules," he agreed, "but a few looked interesting. We don't actually have a provisioning contractor for *Deception* yet, and having one supplier makes it easier to manage safety and suchlike."

There were four different emails around that topic, Kira realized as she sorted the messages. Even *Deception*'s somewhat understrength crew was several hundred people. So far, they'd just been acquiring food and similar supplies from the station chandlery, but a contract supplier made sense.

"Fair," she said. "Do me a favor, Stipan?"

"You pay me for seven hours a day, five days a week, sir," he pointed out. "Inside that, you own me. I don't really do you *favors*."

She didn't say anything for a few seconds.

"Of course, sir," he finished.

"Throw together a request for proposal based around *Deception*'s current crew strength," she told him. "You should have the list for allergies and religious restrictions already, so you know as much of what we need as I do.

"Get me at least four proposals and I'll try to find time to talk to the two best ones." She looked at her schedule. "I'm keeping things relatively open because I'm expecting to get called into a Fleet briefing sooner rather than later.

"I've got some work to sort out around the nova fighters, but I also need your backup list. We lost a woman today. Iris didn't make it back from rescuing the King."

"All right," Dirix said, his tone more subdued. "I'll have you three names and files by the end of day."

"Thanks, Stipan," Kira told him. "I'll be heading over to *Conviction* shortly, probably with both Zoric and Bueller. Let me know if you need anything more immediate."

"Wilco."

5

CONVICTION'S FLIGHT deck made *Deception*'s look like the squeezed-in compromise it was. Cramming twenty starfighters into a K70-class cruiser had taken impressive ingenuity on the part of the ship's designers.

Conviction was built around her flight deck, capable of serving up to sixty starfighters. It also fit in search-and-rescue craft, transport shuttles and a landing place for visiting shuttles like the one carrying *Deception*'s senior officers.

Kira was the first one off the shuttle, taking in the familiar scent of a working flight deck with a deep inhalation. There was no greeting party waiting for them—the mercenaries might run warships, but they didn't run anything resembling a proper military.

"Demirci, welcome back," a familiar deep voice boomed. Angel Waldroup, the broad-shouldered and muscular deck boss, emerged from behind a moving cart of supplies. "Hearing all kinds of crazy shit about what went down at Lastward."

"Most of it's probably true," Kira replied, glancing behind her to check in on her boyfriend and Zoric. "Clan ships tried to jump the King and Queen's transport—backed up by a bunch of Crest nova fighters that no one outside the fight ever saw."

"Shit," Waldroup cursed. "Work for us?"

"Almost certainly," Kira agreed. "But for you? I lost three Hoplites and I'm expecting new work from the RRF within the week at most. I need to steal three planes."

Waldroup drew herself up and glared.

"I've only barely got the squadrons up to strength as it is," she said. "I haven't even managed to get the replicator pattern for the Viers working yet."

"They're my birds," Kira pointed out. "And *Conviction* is in dry dock for weeks, at least."

"Argue it with Hoffman, I guess," the deck boss said grouchily. "He's sacked out right now, but I can get someone to wake him."

"I sent him a message," Kira said. "But if he's asleep, yeah. We've got a meeting with Estanza and we need the top hands.

"Things might be about to get messy."

"Things haven't *been* messy?" Waldroup asked. "The man getting off the shuttle behind you used to be a Brisingr officer!"

Bueller stepped up beside Kira and gave the woman—native of a Fringe system at least six hundred light-years away—a broad grin.

"Switching to a mercenary made things *much* less complicated for me, I'll admit," he told her. "But I'm not sure that's Kira's point."

"Things have *been* messy, but not of late," Kira told the others as Zoric stepped up on the other side of her. "After we drove off Equilibrium's mercenaries in Ypres, things have been pretty calm. The King and Queen apparently even got the factions to agree to a system-wide government, somehow."

"I've been in the Syntactic Cluster for five years," Waldroup noted. "I find that harder to believe than the interstellar conspiracy part!"

"The Yprian Federation," Kira said. "A new light for the future, I guess."

She shook her head.

"Anyway, we need to get to that meeting. I'll ping Hoffman's headware again—but you need to start prepping Hoplites for transport over to *Deception*."

"Fine, fine." Waldroup shook her head. "I guess they are your planes, after all."

29

WHEN KIRA HAD FIRST MET John Estanza, she'd only really known of him as Gold Cobra, one of the pilots of a near-legendary elite merce- nary squadron from the outer Fringe and Inner Rim. Her own late CO had been Jay Moranis, *White* Cobra.

When she'd first arrived in the bridge-attached office she and her officers now entered, she'd found the man drunk as a skunk, with an impressive wet bar spread out along the wall behind him.

There was no trace of that drunkard in the solidly built older man sitting behind the desk today—and even less trace of the wet bar. The wall of booze had turned out to be mobile and was replaced with a small table with a coffee machine.

Today, Estanza's heavy desk had been pulled closer to the wall to allow for a half-dozen seats to be set up in a rough circle that included the desk. Only one of the chairs in front of Estanza's desk was occu- pied, the gaunt black form of Akuchi Mwangi leaning backward as he studied the new arrivals.

Mwangi was *Conviction*'s new executive officer, replacing Zoric after Kira had stolen the woman to command her cruiser. He was a long-standing member of the mercenary crew, though not one Kira had met much before he'd risen to second-in-command of the carrier.

"Hoffman is on his way up," Estanza told her. "As is Hersch. I got the impression that we were going to be having some interesting discussions."

Joseph "Longknife" Hoffman was the man Kira had picked to replace her as *Conviction*'s acting CNG, but Ruben "Gizmo" Hersch headed up the Darkwing flight group, the pilots who flew the PNC-115 fighter-bombers that provided *Conviction*'s heavy punch.

"I'll wait until they're here, then," Kira said. "Basic summary is that the Clans jumped the royals, and the Cluster is going to get compli- cated again. We lost three fighters and a pilot. I'll be *borrowing* three Hoplites to fill the hole, since *Conviction* is in for repairs."

"That makes sense," Estanza told her. "Though..."

The door slid open to reveal *Conviction*'s two senior fighter commanders standing together. Joseph Hoffman was just as gaunt as

Mwangi, but only of average height and pale-skinned from a life aboard spaceships. Ruben Hersch was equally pale, but his eyes and hair were far darker than Hoffman's Aryan features.

"Have a seat, gentlemen," Estanza said, indicating the remaining chairs. "Kira, you may as well go back to the beginning, and we'll talk about your fighters at the end."

"All right." Kira glanced around the group. Outside of Mwangi and Bueller, she'd known everyone in the room for at least a year and regarded them all as friends. She was still getting to know Mwangi, too. Bueller, on the other hand, was her lover and she was more comfortable with him than the time she'd known him might suggest.

"*Deception*'s exercises were intentionally scheduled to put us in the region of the short-stop that *First Crown* was using for her return nova," she explained to the three *Conviction* officers who hadn't known that. "We were about forty light-seconds away when she arrived, in position to see when she was jumped by a flotilla of Costar Clans' gunships."

"The FTZ is going to need to deal with those people," Hoffman said grimly. Neutralizing pirates was one of the key requirements to claim that a power was "in control" of a region. The point of a mutual-trade-and-protection pact like the Free Trade Zone was to make an area safe for trade.

"They'll get to it," Kira agreed. "The biggest problem today was that the gunships were as much a smoke screen as anything else. My wing were not the first nova fighters in the jamming zone."

She had everyone's attention now.

"Someone had launched a full nova strike on *First Crown*. Thirty-two interceptors, tentatively identified as Veles-Four-type fighters from Crest, and eight bombers," she listed off. "The bombers were Uglies, assembled from parts from a dozen systems, but they were fully functioning proper torpedo platforms. *Deception* ending up taking most of their salvo, but her armor and dispersion networks are enough better than Redward's that we're really just looking at surface damage.

"We got lucky. The same number of torpedoes could have done a lot more damage if they'd been properly sequenced, but they thought they were shooting at *First Crown*."

Deception's armor diffused sixty-five percent of the impact energy of the first plasma bursts that hit it. That ratio degraded noticeably as more hits came through, but not as much against simultaneous impacts.

First Crown's armor, on the other hand, was only rated for a dispersal of somewhere between thirty and forty percent. Kira had never got a solid number out of the RRF on that metric.

"The nova fighters retreated in good order after we and *First Crown* took out a quarter of the bombers and a third of the interceptors," she continued. "The gunships continued to press the attack until over three-quarters of them had been destroyed, then bailed as well.

"They were focused on *Crown*," Kira concluded. "We only lost three fighters and one pilot, but the attackers were pros."

"Any idea who?" Hoffman asked. "The Clans definitely don't have forty Crest-built fighters."

"A few Brisingr ones from the Institute's meddling, but that's it," she agreed. "Redward Intelligence is noting that the flight group would be exactly right for a *Liberty*-class strike carrier—and the Institute's mercs had one of those at Ypres."

"That would fit with the Crest-built fighters," Hersch agreed. "Assuming someone wasn't playing games."

"There's an RRF destroyer and a gunship division sweeping the battlespace for their survivors, so we should have some answers on that front soon," Kira said. "Joseph, I need you to sign off on moving three more Hoplites over to *Deception*. I don't like stealing your fighters, but we're going to need a full deck on *Deception* sooner rather than later."

"And we are back to where we were when you gentlemen arrived," Estanza interjected. "May I make a suggestion, Kira?"

"You're the man in charge around here," she said. "I'm just a subcontractor."

"*Just*," Estanza echoed. "The subcontractor with the most powerful warship in the Cluster. I feel a bit outclassed here."

He grinned to remove any bite from his words.

"But my thought is that *Conviction* is in dry dock for at least sixteen weeks and *Deception* is going to get called up for whatever the RRF does next," he reminded everyone. "I suggest we rearrange the fighter wings again. Move the greenest pilots from *Deception* to *Conviction* and send the vets who aren't commanding squadrons the other way.

"That way, we can run exercises here with the pilots who need them, and you have old hands on *Deception*. Not just a full deck but an experienced deck."

"There's only one way to *get* an experienced deck," Kira warned, but she nodded. "We'll go over it." She gestured to Hoffman and Hersch. "See who we can best move."

"What happens next?" Mwangi asked, his voice soft.

"The nova fighter part of the attack is almost certainly Equilibrium-backed," Kira said. "The Queen thinks that the Institute has their fingers back into the Clans—but it doesn't really matter."

"Why not?" the carrier XO asked.

"Local politics," Estanza and Zoric said simultaneously, in a chorus that reminded Kira that Zoric had been the old man's XO for a long time. Estanza leaned back and gestured for the newly minted cruiser Captain to speak.

"Redward's Parliament has long been divided into three camps on the Costar Clans," Zoric explained. "Basically: contain them, ignore them, destroy them. The theory behind containment has always been that humanitarian efforts in the Costar systems will remove the underlying desperation that drives their raids.

"So, they destroy any Clans forces that attack shipping on the one hand and try to lift the actual home stations out of their desperate poverty on the other." Zoric shook her head. "My own impression is somewhat uneducated and biased by the RRF's prejudices, but it does appear to be *working*.

"But the cost is too damn high. It requires more patrols and countermeasures to engage the Clans in the act of piracy than to eliminate their anchorages." She shrugged. "The 'Ignore' grouping is pretty small, basically the last bastion of Redward isolationism, and very much an 'I've got mine' movement.

"Basically, they hold that doing more than protecting Redward shipping is a waste of money, and the Clans should be ignored if they're not bothering us. It's a bloody stupid position, especially given the creation of the SCFTZ and the definite policy and plans of the King and government."

"So, they've been following containment as a policy?" Mwangi asked.

"Exactly. But 'Destroy' has always been a powerful force in Parliament, not least because it's the preferred choice of many of the RRF's senior officers. Different levels involved, but they want to move against the Clans' home stations and colonies and destroy them as anchorages.

"Since most of the Clans' bases are also their homes and are marginal at best, this isn't a..."

Zoric trailed off.

"It's genocide," Kira said bluntly. "Which is why King Larry and Queen Sonia hate it as an option. There are people in the 'Destroy' grouping who recognize the consequences of what they're suggesting and have ideas for reducing the impact, but in the main, they see pirate bases as legitimate targets.

"Regardless of whether those bases are home to thousands of innocents who are one system failure away from starvation or asphyxiation."

"But the Clans keep attacking," Estanza said grimly. "And while the King holds together a coalition in Parliament, much of that is personal loyalty. A lot of people who'd follow him on the current plan because it's *his* plan are going to see this attack as spitting in the face of their help."

"That was what he told me, yes," Kira agreed. "I don't think they're going to be able to keep their plan as it is. He said something about 'getting out ahead' of the demands, so I hope he can come up with a *better* plan."

"Either way, he's probably going to be hiring *Deception*," Estanza told her. "But..."

"It depends on the plan," Kira said bluntly. "I have enough money that I can and will pay back my bloody retainer if they want to contract me for genocide."

She felt as much as heard Bueller shift uncomfortably next to her. She didn't think anyone was explicitly looking at *Deception*'s ex-Equilibrium executive officer, but the thought had to be on everyone's minds.

The reason Konrad Bueller and dozens of his shipmates were now part of *Deception*'s mercenary crew was because the ship *had* committed genocide under Institute orders. That had been a step too far for many of them, and they'd joined her after she'd taken them prisoner.

Their help was the only reason *Deception* had managed to be involved in the Battle of Ypres at all...but they'd all been aboard her and involved when then-*K79-L* had murdered thousands of innocent people in the DLI-O54 System.

"I can't see King Larry signing off on any operation that would count as that," Estanza admitted. "Though he may well end up counting on our refusing an immoral contract as part of his argument against it. The RRF is stretched damn thin at the moment."

"Their two new cruisers are still at least a year from completion, even *after* their shipbuilders and I went through everything I could think of to improve their construction time," Bueller said quietly.

Most of what he'd contributed, as Kira understood, was schematics for more efficient equipment. The actual processes and people involved were already effective. He'd just helped them build better gear.

"The big ones are going to be at least twice that," Estanza agreed. "So, for the foreseeable future, Redward is running around with three cruisers and three carriers plus us. Including *Deception*, there's only seven cruisers in the entire sector."

"If my being unwilling to commit war crimes for Redward helps keep things stable, I'll call it a win," Kira replied. "Details are messy, though. It's not like I'm going to go sit in their Parliament and listen to the arguments."

"RRF will brief us when the contracts come up," Zoric said calmly. "Unless the Queen decides to invite you to another private party."

Kira snorted. Queen Sonia had a tradition of holding small private parties with carefully selected guests that she felt would do well out of knowing each other. The first of those parties Kira had been invited to, though, had been to recruit her for the covert op that had ended in her ownership of *Deception*.

"She probably will, but I doubt I'm getting another covert-operation briefing at a party," she told them. "The last one I went to was just a party."

"The contract should technically come through me," Estanza noted. "I'll keep an eye on the terms and plans—though if it's just *Deception* being deployed, I'm leaving the final call to you, Kira."

"Of course, sir," Kira said. "I'm looking forward to *Conviction* not being quite as vulnerable. The refit specs I saw looked promising."

"I haven't had a yard I trusted that was capable of doing the work needed before," the carrier's Captain admitted. "Redward's earned that trust, at least, even as we've helped them get to the point where they can do the work.

"*I'm* looking forward to flying something with actual guns again."

The gathered officers chuckled, but Kira spotted the moment where Estanza froze and flicked his eyes upward—an almost-universal tic of people receiving an unexpected headware message.

"Link to the office audio and repeat, please," he ordered aloud.

A moment later, the voice of one of *Conviction*'s com techs echoed through the room.

"Sir, we have an unknown shuttle on approach to *Conviction* and requesting docking clearance," the young man reported. "They have no identity or authentication codes the system recognizes, but we're only detecting one person aboard.

"He has identified himself as 'Platinum Cobra' and says he's an old friend of yours, Captain."

Kira inhaled sharply. Moranis had sent her out to Redward with his old White Cobra handle as a key to get into Estanza's presence, but she'd had a few other points in her favor: not least, six nova fighters in the time before Redward had acquired a class two nova-drive factory.

"That's..." Estanza trailed off. "I was going to say *impossible*, but I suppose I don't *know* that Lars Ivarsson is dead. Send my headware whatever imagery or audio you got, son."

He paused again, watching a video only he could see, then swallowed hard.

"The decades haven't been as bad for him as I figured," he admitted. "That's Ivarsson. That's Platinum Cobra."

"Sir...Cobra were Equilibrium," Kira warned quietly. Everyone in the room knew that both Konrad Bueller and John Estanza were former Equilibrium Institute operatives. Their experiences made the existence of the organization inarguable to their comrades.

"We deserted," Estanza argued. "But...you're right. I'm not sure why he'd be here." He exhaled.

"Mwangi, get back to the bridge," he ordered. "Scan that shuttle for everything." He looked around the office. "Kira, could you and Bueller join me in a meeting room by the flight deck?

"We'll brief everyone else after, but I think we want this quiet and private—but bringing both of the ex-Equilibrium agents and my second-in-command makes sense to me!"

6

ONE OF THE disadvantages of a carrier having a massive flight deck was that the designers had seen no reason to provide the ship with an additional shuttle bay large enough for the incoming shuttle. Every spacecraft of that size arriving at or leaving *Conviction* came through the flight deck, which also gave strangers a potential look at the carrier's fighter wing.

Kira watched a video feed via her headware as the "Platinum Cobra" shuttle touched down in a designated spot. A squad of mercenary troopers in intentionally mismatched armor immediately surrounded the spacecraft—but almost more importantly, several of the flight deck's mobile carts swung large white screens closer to it.

Those screens had been between the shuttle's scanners and the fighter wing from the beginning, Kira presumed, keeping the unknown vessel from having a perfect count of *Conviction*'s fighter strength.

It wouldn't be a perfect block, but hopefully this Ivarsson was still partially in the dark. If they were lucky, he wasn't an enemy...but something about the situation didn't leave Kira thinking that.

The shuttle's sole occupant took the presence of the armed guards calmly as he exited the spacecraft. He was a tall man with almost translucently pale skin and pure white hair.

"Guards will search him and bring him here," Estanza told her.

They'd taken over a tiny office next to the carrier deck, usually used by one of Waldroup's team leaders, and removed everything they could. All that was left was four chairs, three of them facing the fourth.

Kira watched Ivarsson the entire time as he was searched, and shivered when she saw his eyes. They were a piercing unnatural golden color, suggesting either cosmetic surgery or long-standing genetic modifications—and his movements as the guards brought him across the deck spoke to *other* modifications.

Soldier boosts were rare, even among mercenaries like those on *Conviction*. From a distance, she couldn't tell if Ivarsson's boosts were genetic, cybernetic or organic, but he moved like an angry cobra.

Of course, the mercenaries around him wore armor that could duplicate anything his boosts could do. That was *why* soldier boosts were rare—but it said something that a presumed *fighter pilot* had them.

Kira just wasn't sure what that *something* was.

Estanza waved the door open as the mercenaries escorted their guests over, and all three of the officers watched as Ivarsson walked into the office like he owned it and took a seat in the empty chair.

"John," he greeted Estanza with a nod. "It's been a long time." He looked at the others. "I know Em Bueller, by reputation at least, and this must be Kira Demirci."

Still sitting, he bowed slightly to Kira.

"You have made quite an impression in a single year, Commander," he told her. "Apollo is poorer for your leaving."

"Their choice, not mine," Kira said flatly. Too many of Apollo's ace pilots had died mysteriously for her to believe that her government hadn't *allowed* Brisingr's assassins to operate in Apollon space.

"You've managed to track me down across about six hundred light-years and three decades," Estanza said quietly. "Somehow, Lars, I don't think this is a social call."

"No," Ivarsson agreed. "I owe you my life, John. We both know that. At least four or five times over, so I felt obliged to make a call once we were in the area."

Kira swallowed her response and looked over at Bueller. Her lover looked unsurprisingly nervous and she realized there was only one way Ivarsson could know him *by reputation*.

"*We*, Lars?" Estanza asked.

"Cobra Squadron, John," the stranger said. "Not all of us failed to find the moral fiber necessary to carry through on our ideals and our missions. We lost a lot of people to your little propaganda coup, but Cobra Squadron survived.

"We've been working our way across the Rim, just like we always did," Ivarsson continued. "Legends proved a pain in the ass, so we've tried to draw less attention to ourselves, but we've helped a dozen sectors find equilibrium and peace."

"Betraying allies, breaking contracts and committing atrocities along the way?" Estanza asked, his voice icy.

"Where that was what was necessary to bring peace to a dozen star systems, yes," the Institute operative agreed. "You and Bueller both understood that once. When the future peace and prosperity of a hundred billion people is on the line, the qualms of the moment are meaningless. The hard calls must be made."

"Everyone here has heard the pitch, Lars," *Conviction*'s Captain noted. "What's to stop us from turning you over to Redward for interrogation? That would be one of those *hard calls*, wouldn't it?"

"I suppose," Ivarsson said. "Of course, the three-hundred-megaton fusion warhead in my shuttle will object if I'm not back aboard in an hour. I don't think this ship is in good-enough shape to survive that, do you?"

"You fucker," Kira snapped.

"I'm here to offer you and your people a chance, John," the man continued as if he hadn't heard her. "Cobra Squadron is here now. I'm not going to tell you who we've been contracted with, but you know we work for the Institute above all.

"Everything here has proceeded along the projections of the Seldonian calculations," Ivarsson said. "The Institute's attempts to divert the psychohistorical projections have been countered at all turns by you and your Redward friends."

"Because you keep funding pirates and coups, perhaps," Estanza growled. "How many people have died because of the Institute's meddling?"

"I have no idea," the golden-eyed man said calmly. "But I've seen the projections, John. If the SCFTZ takes shape as planned, without any intervention, it will slowly degrade into two factions: one centered on Redward and one centered on Ypres.

"Without a central power with both the economic and military might to keep the Syntactic Cluster from splitting in two, your much-vaunted Free Trade Zone will dissolve into warring factions in twenty to thirty years, splitting the Cluster into an interstellar war that will claim millions, maybe even *billions*, of lives and set the cultural and technological development of the region back decades.

"The Institute will do everything in our power to prevent that, John, and if you keep getting in our way, I will have no choice but to destroy your carrier and kill you," Ivarsson admitted. "I don't want to kill you. I owe you my life, so I'm here with a warning.

"Leave the Cluster, John. Take your ships and your people and get the hell out."

"Not going to happen," Estanza replied. "The Institute has broken more worlds than it's ever fixed. You've never even *tested* the damn projections, just assumed they are true and killed millions to stop them."

"The fundamental math and analysis have been tested a thousand times," Ivarsson countered. "Given the projections, we cannot stand by and allow the societies we have seen flourish across human space fall and burn."

"Even if it means destroying everything that makes them flourish? I can't believe that anymore, Lars. I won't. Redward's leadership has a dream, a plan that worked on Old Earth, and I won't let the Institute tear it down based on *math*."

To Kira's mind, they were more fighting *against* the Institute than *for* anyone, though she'd admit that she liked the people of Redward—

and that she trusted King Larry and Queen Sonia more than she'd ever trusted the Council of Principals on Apollo.

"You used to understand," Ivarsson said. "People like the leaders of Redward are too busy trying to do what's 'right' to realize they need to do what's *necessary*. Again and again we have seen it: the only answer for peace in a given region is a single unchallenged hegemonic power able to *enforce* that peace.

"If Redward won't become that power here in the Syntactic Cluster, then the alliances they have built will fracture into fire and blood," he concluded. "Which means that if Redward won't become that power, the Institute has no choice but to make sure someone *else* does.

"Unfortunately, that requires breaking Redward's power. But so long as King Larry will not do what is necessary, we have no choice."

"You always have a choice, Lars Ivarsson," John Estanza told him. "That was why we deserted. When I realized that the Institute would find ways to justify *everything*. The math might be wrong. It might not be.

"But I won't let you shape all of humanity into a single mold because you think it's safer."

The room was quiet.

"The ends justify the means," Bueller said into the silence after a moment. "It's a seductive belief, Em Ivarsson. Especially when the end is as glorious an image as the Institute likes to project. But I wonder if you have ever spent time in the sectors you have supposedly made *better*.

"I was only with the Institute for a year. In that year, I saw more bloodshed than I did in three years of a goddamn *war*. There are means that cannot be justified by any ends. If your goal is peace, there is only so much bloodshed that can be stomached in its pursuit."

"The goal is peace *for all time*," Ivarsson reminded Bueller. "For *that* goal, I will sacrifice anything."

He rose.

"It seems I have wasted my time, but old debts required the effort," he told them. "John, I'd far rather be on the same side again, but I knew that wasn't possible. I beg you to reconsider. A single eighth-rate heavy cruiser and a carrier that barely qualifies as *ninth*-rate anymore can't turn back what's coming."

"That depends, in my experience, on the crews and pilots involved," Estanza said. "Get off my ship, Lars. Platinum Cobra or no, the next time we meet, I'm going to kill you."

The old mercenary's voice was calm, collected...and utterly frigid.

"You can try," Ivarsson told him. "But you're not facing random mercenaries gathered from three hundred light-years of the Rim anymore, old friend. You're facing Cobra Squadron...and *you*, of all people, should remember what that means."

"TRACK THAT SHIP," Kira suggested quietly as the Cobra Squadron shuttle drifted out of *Conviction*'s hangar. "That might give us some clue as to where he's going."

"Mwangi's already on it," Estanza said calmly. "I don't expect it to do us much... Yeah, there he goes."

Kira linked her headware into the sensors and blinked. The shuttle was gone.

"It had a class two nova drive," Estanza told her. "I didn't recognize it until I realized he was still with Cobra. *Fuck.*"

"How bad is it going to be?" Bueller asked. "Last I heard of Cobra Squadron, they weren't even in the Rim."

"That pretty much tells you the problem, doesn't it?" *Conviction*'s Captain said grimly. "When I last flew for Cobra, we were uniformly equipped with Banshee-Nine-class heavy fighters. They were older planes, but they were from the *Periphery*, not even the Fringe."

He shook his head. The Fringe was roughly the worlds from seven hundred to a thousand light-years away from Sol. The Periphery was the worlds from *four* hundred to seven hundred light-years away. The nearest Periphery System was *eight hundred* light-years from Redward.

"Thirty years ago, we were flying fifty-year-old fighters from a fifth-rate power in the Periphery while dealing with Fringe states," he told them. "That meant those nova fighters were still *better* than most of the ones we fought.

"Even if Cobra hasn't upgraded their gear since, well..." Estanza shook his head. "Those fighters were from a world six hundred light-years from Sol. We're *fifteen* hundred light-years from Sol. Even an eighty-year-old Periphery nova fighter is probably equal to or better than the Viers aboard *Deception*."

Kira sighed. It was generally considered a safe rule that for every ten light-years farther you were from Sol, technology was, on average, about a year and a half further behind. *Especially* military and other restricted techs.

It was almost two hundred light-years from Apollo and Brisingr to the Syntactic Cluster, and the Cluster's wealthiest systems were easily thirty years behind her home world in military tech.

From six hundred light-years closer to humanity's homeworld? The Banshees might be eighty years old, but they were still probably *decades* more advanced than anything her people had.

Multiphasic jamming was a great equalizer in the battlespace, but those fighters were still going to be an ugly handful. If they'd upgraded to newer fighters, even birds from the Fringe, Kira's people could be in serious trouble.

"How many?" she asked.

"We had two covert carriers thirty years ago," Estanza said grimly. "Each carried fifty fighters. So...at least a hundred, plus they definitely seem to have that Crest carrier running around for another forty."

"At least that one seems to be flying Crest fighters," Bueller said. "Not stuff that's going to make us look like cavemen in rowboats."

"The differences aren't going to be *that* severe," Kira countered. "But if we throw my Hoplites and PNCs up against Banshee-Nines, the odds aren't in our favor...and that's not considering that most of our pilots are still green."

"And Redward's pilots are worse," Estanza agreed. "Their production of the Sinisters and Dexters will help make up the numbers, but... we're facing a disadvantage in both experience and quality of hardware."

The Dexter interceptors and Sinister fighter-bombers were clones of *Conviction*'s Hoplite-IVs and PNC-115s, respectively. The Escutcheon-type heavy fighters were still in prototyping, but they would be clones of the Weltraumpanzer-Viers taken from *Deception* once they hit commission.

"We'll have to brief the RRF," Kira said grimly. "I'm not sure we know enough about what Cobra Squadron has today to provide solid data, but just their presence in the Cluster is a major change."

"The Institute is pulling out everything if they've moved Cobra here," Estanza told her. "Cobra Squadron has always been their most capable active arm. We've drawn their attention and they've sent their best."

"Thank god we have *Deception*, then," Bueller concluded. "But it sounds like we need to train up the crew even faster."

"We're already out of time," Kira replied. "We're just waiting for the call that Redward has signed off on whatever Larry and Sonia's plan for the Clans is. I don't expect us to spend more than a week here."

"I'd say the same," Estanza agreed. "I hope the two of you enjoyed what time you've had to relax. Things aren't going to slow down from here, I don't think."

7

UNLIKE THE MERCENARY CARRIER, *Deception* did have a separate shuttle bay. Despite that, the next day saw Kira and Zoric standing on the cruiser's flight deck, watching a shuttle maneuver its way carefully into the ship.

Off to the right, three Hoplite-IVs were being gently ushered into bays while their pilots dismounted, laughing as the trio of old hands dodged around the deck crew with the ease of long practice.

Kira was paying more attention to the spacecraft with active engines and missed who the three pilots were until Zoric cleared her throat carefully.

"Sir, I thought Hoffman was staying on *Conviction*?" the cruiser's Captain asked.

Surprised, Kira turned to assess the two men and one woman walking across her flight deck toward her. Sure enough, Joseph Hoffman was in the lead, accompanied by his boyfriend, Dinesha Patel, and Evgenia Michel, one of his squadron commanders.

The three were all veterans of the Apollo System Defense Force, the survivors of the old 303 Nova Combat Group she'd brought out to the far end of nowhere with her. Her own squadrons included Abdullah

Colombera and Mel Cartman, which meant that all six of those survivors were now aboard *Deception*.

"The gang is all here, it seems," Patel said brightly as the trio reached them. "Are Nightmare and Scimitar around?"

The dark-skinned pilot, callsign Dawnlord, didn't seem to think there was an issue with all six of the core Memorials being aboard the same ship. If nothing else, the six of them made up the entire shareholdership of the mercenary company!

"They'll be out as soon as the shuttle is safe," Kira replied absently, glaring at the heavyset form of the man she'd left in charge on *Conviction*. "I wasn't expecting to see *Conviction*'s Commander, Nova Group, here today."

"*Conviction* isn't going anywhere and you're going into the teeth of it," Hoffman said calmly. "I'm a pilot, sir. I'll fly under you; I'll fly under Mel. No issues either way. Whatever you need."

"How generous," Kira replied. "Except I left you with a forty-fighter nova group to train up, didn't I?"

The shuttle finished landing and an echoing chime declared the flight deck clear.

"Hersch and I flipped a coin," Hoffman admitted. "It was his coin, even. If anyone rigged it, blame Gizmo."

Ruben Hersch—callsign Gizmo—was the most experienced of the PNC-115 pilots from *Conviction*'s crew. Kira had hoped that *both* of the two senior officers would remain behind, but she kept her expression level as she turned to see the pilots trooping off the shuttle.

Deception might carry fewer nova fighters than *Conviction* did now, but when Kira had arrived, her six fighters had brought *Conviction*'s wing up to *fourteen* nova fighters. With losses along the way, there were only eleven true veteran pilots across the combined mercenary company.

Including all of her Apollon pilots, it looked like she had ten of them. Gizmo had remained behind, but that still gave her a solid core of experienced hands. The rest of the six pilots transferring over had been PNC *copilots* when Kira arrived…which still put them ahead of most of their new recruits.

"None of my people even argued about being sent back to *Convic-*

tion," she murmured to Hoffman. "The green pilots *know* they're green. The more time we can give them in sims and exercises, the better."

"They weren't supposed to be facing off against anyone with comparable gear, let alone experience, for a while yet," Zoric agreed. "The hope was that Redward's pilots and ours would have the experience edge by the time anyone else out here had nova fighters."

"We didn't count on Equilibrium," Mel Cartman said, *Deception*'s second squadron commander sliding into the conversation as she joined the crowd. She quickly gave the three other Apollon pilots hard hugs before stepping back to study the crowd.

"All of the Memorials, huh?" she asked.

"I'd like to send Longknife back," Kira admitted, but she sighed and shook her head as she looked at Patel and Hoffman holding hands and grinning shamelessly at her. "Not going to split up the wonder boys, though. You both are under Mel. Play nice."

She turned to Michel.

"Sorry, Socrates, you're flying for me," she told the blonde woman, the youngest of the surviving Memorials. "Step down from squadron command, I know."

"If you think I'm holding on to my squadron over backing up the Memorials in the shit-show we've found, you're wrong," Michel told her. "Plus, doesn't Scimitar fly for you?"

For a moment, Kira almost reconsidered. Then Colombera followed Cartman out of the ready room and embraced his usual partner in crime gleefully.

"Yes, yes, I do," the second-youngest of her pilots announced. "We'll have to see what kind of trouble we can get into!"

Scimitar and Socrates had earned a reputation for practical jokes and trouble in the Three-Oh-Three. The deaths of three-quarters of the old squadron had ground some of that out of them, and Kira didn't have it in her to step on them.

"Keep it clean," she ordered, then turned to salute the approaching *Conviction* pilots. "Indigo. Good to see you. How are you feeling about heavy fighters today?"

Rosalinda "Indigo" Navratil was a PNC-115 pilot and had spent the entire time Kira had known her in the fighter-bombers. But since

Kira didn't *have* any experienced pilots for the Weltraumpanzer-Viers...

"The Vier looks damn shiny," Navratil said quickly. "Is that where you want the Darkwing hands?"

"Exactly," Kira confirmed. "Purlwise is already heading up the squadron, so I have a neat alignment of six heavy fighters and six fighter-bomber pilots."

Akira "Purlwise" Yamauchi was currently on the planet, spending time with a local girlfriend Kira hadn't met. He was on-call and they were keeping him up to date, but it made him the only squadron commander not already on the ship.

"It's a party," Cartman said brightly. "Should I be planning on booking a room for an *actual* party, sir?"

Kira gave her second a cautioning glance. It had been at a party of that style where she'd ended up confessing her feelings for the former commander of the Darkwings—a man who was now dead.

"We don't know how long we have until we ship out," she warned everyone. "We play it carefully. Sims and real-space exercises until we're certain we can go against people just as experienced as us...and with better nova fighters."

That earned her several grimaces.

"Do I *want* to know what's going on?" Navratil asked.

"I'll brief you on some of it later," Kira promised. "For now, I think I need to actually make some announcements.

"Hey, everybody!" she shouted.

She might be one of the shortest people in the room and was almost certainly one of the lightest, but she had a *lot* of practice at making herself heard. The conversations outside the small circle of Apollons and senior officers died down.

"Clear a circle, people," Kira ordered. "Everybody get over here!"

She wasn't at all surprised to realize she now had seventeen pilots on the flight deck and gathering around her. Only nine had arrived, but the existing pilots she hadn't sent back to *Conviction* had trickled out of the woodwork while she'd been talking to her friends.

That had been part of the point in having those conversations, after all.

Looking around, she identified the missing pilots and grinned.

"All right, so I know Purlwise is MIA getting laid, but what happened to Galavant?" she asked.

"She had a date last night," Cartman told Kira. "Headed onto the station when you went over to *Conviction*."

"So, am I sending search parties or congratulations cards?" Kira asked.

"She has leave and she warned me she might not be coming home, so I'm guessing she's *also* MIA getting laid," Cartman replied. Annmarie "Galavant" Banderas had been a PNC-115 copilot Kira had co-opted to fly a Hoplite before she'd had her full squadron.

She'd earned both her spot in one of the Hoplite squadrons *and* the right to stay overnight on the station with a date. Assuming she checked in, which it sounded like she had.

"All right, so that leaves me just you lot!" Kira looked over the crowd with a grin. "You all know some of what's going on. We moved everyone we thought needed more experience before being thrown into the fire back to *Conviction*.

"Captain Estanza has put the old girl in dry dock for upgrades. That means her nova group gets to spend the next few months doing exercises and training with Redward's new nova squadrons.

"Everybody needs that time, but somebody's got to do the real work, so you're all here. With me." She grinned. "All of you have seen enough of *my* training regimens to know that you're not winning that exchange."

"What do we exercise against this week? SolFed?" Shun "Sword-heart" Asjes asked. Asjes was one of Kira's pilots, the other copilot who'd been recruited alongside Banderas.

"If I had sim files for SolFed, you know I would put you up against them," Kira warned.

The Solar Federation was one of the few multi-stellar nations in existence, consisting of Sol and about half the star systems in the Core —the space within a hundred light-years of the home system. It was the most technologically advanced society known, to a nearly legendary level from this far away.

The nearest SolFed system was fourteen hundred light-years away, after all.

"As it *happens*, I may have picked up some sim files from the Fringe," she continued. "Sold under the table from the Breslau Principality's system security forces, as I understand it, then illegally copied a few dozen times.

"But hey, the files are only ten years old and have the Principality's best simulations of their own ships and a decent guess at the Star Kingdom of Griffon's!"

Everyone groaned at that. Griffon Sector might be where John Estanza had made his legend—but it was also a Fringe sector six hundred light-years closer to Sol and almost seven hundred light-years' actual distance from the Syntactic Cluster.

Their fighters were a *lot* better than her people's gear, which was some of the best they could steal from Apollo or Brisingr.

"But this time, it's not just me wanting you ready for everything," she warned. "We have data, data I can't share details of yet, suggesting that we'll be running into nova fighters of about that vintage and quality.

"We're unlikely to have the edge in numbers facing them, and they're going to have the edge in tech," she said grimly. "Which means, pilots, we need to have the edge in *skill*. We need to be better than they are.

"And I have *complete* faith that we can do that! Do you?"

She was asking nova-fighter pilots. She already *knew* the answer they were going to give her—and the shouts were still rattling the metaphorical rafters as she began handing out squadron assignments.

8

THE SUMMONS WAS a surprise when it came. Not so much that Kira was being asked to report to *somebody*—she'd been expecting that from the moment she'd returned to Redward orbit.

But the request she'd received wasn't to report to an RRF ship or station or even a surface military base. What she received was a true *summons* in the classical sense, a formal request calling for her to attend the monarchs of Redward at their palace.

That meant she'd dug up the dark-teal dress uniform used by officers of Conviction Limited—she hadn't managed to draft one up for the Memorials yet—and loaded herself, Zoric and Bueller onto a shuttle.

Of the three of them, only Zoric wore any insignia—a standard stylized gold rocket marking her as a starship Captain—though all three of them wore the identical uniform: a long jacket in their specific dark teal green over a white turtleneck and black slacks. The outfit could fit handily over a shipsuit, though it would have problems with a proper pilot's suit.

Bueller probably looked the most awkward in it. The Brisingr Kaiserreich Navy went for a shorter jacket and a black turtleneck, but *their* version of the jacket was much heavier and carried a lot more gold embroidery than the mercenary version.

"I'm not used to being summoned to royal audiences," Bueller admitted. "I never even met the Kaiser."

"King Larry is a bit less formal than the Kaiser, as I understand," Kira said with a chuckle, watching their approach through her headware. Their course was taking them directly over Red Mountain, the planet's capital city, toward the titular mountain. She could pick out the tower with her rarely used planetside apartment as they flew over it, but their destination was around the side of the craggy peak.

There was a clear delineation where the luxury condo towers with mountain views ended and the security zone around the palace began. Designed from the beginning as the planetary capital, there was a full ten-kilometer zone where no residential construction was allowed that surrounded the administrative center of Redward.

That zone was a carefully maintained park, gorgeous even from above, where not a single plant was tall enough to block anyone's line of fire. There were no *visible* defenses on the interior of that circle of parkland, but Kira knew they'd be there. Concealed bunkers with ground troops and automated guns were probably the least of it.

Behind those invisible defenses rose another series of towers. These were all office buildings, a series of fifty-story buildings designed to be decorative as well as functional. Those towers contained a significant portion—though not all as that would be *too* tempting a target—of the system administration.

On the north end of the complex of office towers was a structure that looked like a theme-park escapee, a scaled-up fairy-tale castle of red stone whose turrets almost certainly contained real weapons.

Kira was enough of a newcomer to Redward that she thought that structure *was* the palace for several seconds. Then the shuttle curved around toward the other end of the complex and she queried her headware.

Apparently, the Hóngsè Chéngbao was the home of Redward's six-hundred-member Parliament. The King and Queen of Redward only spoke to Parliament at preagreed times, usually twice each local year—three times a standard year.

The *palace*, it turned out, was a sprawling, overgrown bungalow on the south end of the complex, surrounded by another block of mixed high and low parks—for privacy and security, respectively.

Their immediate destination looked to be a landing pad at the center point of the E-shaped building, in clear view of the only *unconcealed* defensive installation Kira had seen on the entire approach: a decorative-but-clearly-functional three-story bunker that loomed over the road and landing pads necessary to reach the Palace.

Redward took no chances with their monarchs, it seemed.

———

THE REDWARD PALACE was only extravagant on the outside in its scale, and that pattern continued in its interior. A pair of guards in pristine crimson uniforms led Kira and her people into the building, which proved to have ordinary-looking tile and drywall.

The security officers led them to a small room off a large hallway in the central wing and opened the door.

"Their Majesties are in scheduled court at the moment," the woman in charge told them. "They will join you here in about ten minutes."

Kira led the way into the plain room, registering the weight of the door only due to the sound as it *thunk*ed shut behind them.

"Welcome, welcome," John Estanza greeted her with a wide grin, the mercenary Captain waving a coffee cup at them. He wore the same dress uniform as they did, with the same Captain's insignia as Zoric. "Mwangi's in the bathroom. Try the coffee; it's fantastic."

Kira shook her head at the man as she crossed the room to a rolling table with a coffee machine. Everything in the room looked like it could be easily moved except for the heavy wooden bookshelves that covered the interior wall. A set of dark burgundy couches formed a rough square in the middle of the room around a heavy-looking but wheeled table, and a second rolling table held an array of small sandwiches.

As she took a cup of the coffee and inhaled its familiar scent— Queen Sonia had served her Redward Royal Reserve, the royal family's personal coffee blend, before—she studied the room.

The west wall *appeared* to be three giant windows opening on to a carefully manicured grove of trees between the central and western wings of the house. Kira's practiced eye picked up the lie, though—all three windows were actually extremely high-fidelity screens. They almost certainly showed what the room's occupants would see if they *were* windows but also covered what were likely armored walls.

It wasn't until she looked at the bookshelves that Kira realized that the room wasn't necessarily for show. The contents of the shelves were not the carefully matched sets of leatherbound books she'd expect to see in a show space. There definitely *was* one of those sets, an Encyclopedia Galactica, it looked like, but most of the rest were a mismatched collection of textbooks on half a dozen subjects.

"At least they gave us the good coffee," she observed as she turned back to Estanza. "Have you been here before, sir?"

"Yes," he confirmed. "So has Zoric." He gestured to *Deception*'s Captain. "Four or five times, though Larry does prefer to do a lot of business away from the palace."

"Everyone who comes here is monitored," Mwangi told them as he stepped into the room through a semi-concealed door. "That we are here will be on the news feeds within the hour. *Mercenaries summoned to meet the King; what plans are in the offing?* type articles, I'm sure."

"So, if we're here, His Majesty *wants* people to know about it," Kira concluded. "That makes sense. He wants to be seen to be doing something about the Clans."

"And so long as we're on retainer, we do what they ask," Estanza agreed. "Even if your subcontract is starting to look more and more strained by the day."

"If I'm not subcontracted by Conviction Limited, deintegrating the crews and fighter groups would be a nightmare," Kira pointed out. "And this way, I mostly get to leave negotiating to you."

She looked around the room again before taking a seat next to Bueller and Estanza and sipping her coffee.

"Mostly," she repeated. "Somehow, I get the feeling today is going to be busy."

9

ADMIRAL VILMA REMINGTON was the first person to enter the room after the mercenaries, followed immediately by a trio of other uniformed RRF flag officers—and a group of Redward Palace staff who quickly refreshed the snacks and coffee while the burgundy-uniformed officers filled their own coffee cups.

The straight-backed Admiral gestured her own officers to seats on one of the couches but remained standing herself as she drank her coffee.

"You're lucky, you know," she told the mercenaries. "*You* didn't get called in front of Parliament to talk about all of this bullshit."

"The joys of the mercenary life," Estanza agreed cheerfully. "We just get to drink coffee, fly where we're told and collect a paycheck. We also have to pay for our own ships, though," he added thoughtfully.

"And you have to pretend you don't care," Remington said, her gray eyes leveled on Estanza.

"That can be harder some times than others," the Captain agreed. "I'm guessing things are in motion?"

"Have some patience, John," the Admiral said. "The King wants to make his own announcements."

"And not letting the King have what he wants is treason," a loudly cheerful voice said from the door as King Larry stepped in. Sonia was a step behind him, and two of the crimson-uniformed Palace Guards were in front, peeling off to flank the door.

King Larry walked over to the snack table first, filling a plate before he took a seat in one of the chairs. He took a sandwich in his fingers and surveyed the room.

"You don't actually have to be silent when I walk in, you know," he reminded them. "I'm going to eat this before I brief *anyone*."

"Regular court, for the strangers to our world, is a scheduled affair where any of our citizens can apply to come before the Royal Us," Sonia told them all. She had grabbed coffee while her husband had been grabbing food, and passed him a cup while she took one of the sandwiches he'd acquired.

It looked like long-practiced teamwork, in fact.

"In truth, it's a mix of a lottery and a waiting list," she continued. "But we do our best to make sure that everyone who applies gets into Court sooner or later."

"And some days they're useful," Larry added. "And some days they're trying to get us to implement dog-breed bans."

He shook his head and inhaled the rest of his sandwich.

"The science and logic—or *lack* thereof—around that isn't what we're all here to discuss, though," he told them after swallowing. "What we're here to discuss is the nightmare some idiots in the Clans have decided to create for all of us."

"Yes, Your Majesty," Remington said, her tone long-suffering.

The King made a vague, probably joking, dismissive gesture. Then he leaned forward in his chair and his countenance completely changed.

"The situation is much what I predicted when we spoke after the attack, Commander Demirci," he told her. "For the Clans to dare to enter the Redward System and directly attack myself and Sonia is a drastic change.

"We know that the Equilibrium Institute is probably behind this, but they're little more than a conspiracy theory to my Parliament. Enough of my MPs have wanted to see the Clans wrecked that the current anger leaves us little choice."

"There is also a legitimate argument to be made that neutralizing the Clans as a long-term threat is the best way to meet our commitments under the Free Trade Zone agreements," Sonia added. "Of course, those same agreements only give us an avenue for requesting assistance in specific situations.

"An invasion of what are technically sovereign systems is not one of those situations."

"Fortunately, we have ambassadors and such here on Redward for most of the major players," Larry noted. "I've met with them all and we have commitments for ships and resources to wage this campaign. *A coalition of the willing*, I think, is the term."

Kira winced. That was not a term with a positive history over the last few thousand years or so.

"The simplest way to deal with this situation, and the way I'm sure some of our MPs would like us to handle it, is the destruction of the Clans' stations and colonies," Larry said quietly. "Few of them are more than marginal, and most of them are easily exposed to vacuum. The destruction of their mobile forces would easily enable...extermination.

"This will not be our strategy."

It was clear from the expressions of the officers sitting with Admiral Remington that at least some of the RRF thought it *should* be —but no one was going to argue with King Larry when he made his orders clear.

"Our commitments under the SCFTZ require that the Clans be defeated," Sonia said into the silence. "The morals and ideals that we uphold require that the Clans *survive*."

"Neither *Conviction* nor *Deception* would be available for hire for a campaign of extermination," Estanza said levelly. "My own morals may be more flexible than yours, Your Majesties, but I will not participate in wholesale murder."

"Nor will the Kingdom of Redward," Larry said firmly. "The units are being selected as we speak, but major Redward Army detachments are being prepared to occupy the four primary Clan star systems."

"Each has significant economic potential," Sonia reminded everyone. "That's why the various abortive efforts at outposts and colonies that became the Clans existed in the first place. Given a committed external partner—Redward initially, but hopefully the entire SCFTZ in the end—those systems can and should become able to support their populations at a high standard of living.

"Without piracy."

"They lack the seed capital to become more than they are," Larry noted. "Theft has only ever kept them alive. The closest they got to what they needed was when Equilibrium was trying to turn them into our local space Mongols."

"So, what is the plan?" Kira asked.

"Vilma?" Larry gestured to the Admiral.

Remington gestured a holographic map of the Syntactic Cluster into the air above them.

"The Cluster," she said unnecessarily. "Sixty stars, sixteen systems with habitable and inhabited worlds. And then these four systems."

The inhabited systems—now all members of the Syntactic Cluster Free Trade Zone—were highlighted in blue. Four systems, scattered through the Cluster but mostly sitting between multiple inhabited systems, were flashing in red.

"KDC-15RT, KLO-32DE, KSR-92RR and KLN-35XD," Remington reeled off. "Arti, Klo, Kaiser and the Kiln. Each lacks a truly inhabitable world, though Kaiser does have Wilhelm, which is...marginal at best."

Kira's headware brought up the specifications of KSR-92RR's second planet. The central star was a cold dwarf that would burn forever but didn't create much heat. Wilhelm had an annual average temperature barely above freezing in most latitudes and had basically *no* freshwater. Most of the surface was covered in shallow seas of brine and the planet's life had adapted to that heavily salted water.

The planet had an unpleasant but barely breathable atmosphere. That was all it had going for it.

"All told, the four systems have a shared population of just under fifty million human beings, mostly living in abject poverty," the Admiral noted. "They have access to the basic colonial fabricator setup and have assembled a couple of small shipyards in each system, sufficient to produce the small freighters that keep them alive—and the gunships we have grown all too familiar with in the Cluster.

"The RRF and the RRA have spent most of the last century trying to game out ways to neutralize the Clans in one way or another," she said. "Without destroying the Costar Clans' ability to survive at all, we can't remove their ability to build more gunships.

"Without a major commitment of troops from somewhere, occupying four star systems and an estimated three thousand habitats is an exercise in impossibility. We now, thanks to His Majesty and Parliament, have that troop commitment."

"Roughly sixty percent of the Redward Royal Army," Larry agreed. "The first wave alone is four corps. Two hundred and forty thousand soldiers."

"Which would be barely sufficient for us to put a couple of platoons on each habitat," Remington warned. "We have instead selected a list of one hundred habitats in each system that will receive anything from a company to a pair of battalions, depending on need.

"Those four corps represent the *entire* troop transport capability of the RRF." She shook her head. "If we could bring more troops in the first wave, we would.

"As it is, the plan is simple: we are concentrating a new fleet, designated the Coalition Fleet, at the trade route near the Arti System. Redward will be contributing a carrier with a fully operational novafighter group, *Perseus*, along with both *Last Denial* and *Guardian*. Bengalissimo is committing a cruiser, and we will have a total of ten destroyers and thirty corvettes or gunships from assorted systems.

"We want to contract *Deception* to provide the fourth cruiser for the fleet," Remington concluded. "While you shouldn't be required to deal with the Clans' forces, we have every reason to expect Institute intervention."

"Especially with Cobra Squadron in the region," Estanza said grimly. "Putting that large a chunk of the Cluster's military forces in one place..."

Kira nodded her unwilling agreement. That was half of Redward's capital ships and a third of Bengalissimo's. With *Deception* along and

Conviction under refit, they would have half of the Cluster's active capital ships in a single fleet.

No one else *had* cruisers or carriers, after all.

"Part of the logic is to assemble a force that has a decent chance of going toe-to-toe with a Cobra Squadron detachment," Remington agreed. "Our odds in that situation are always going to be difficult. Even including *Deception*, the Coalition Fleet will only muster a total of about eighty nova fighters."

"Having *Deception* and the other cruisers for fire support will even the odds," Kira noted. "Everything we've seen suggests that the Cobras are drawing on the same mercenary fleet as we saw at Ypres for support. The only real change is the addition of two new carriers and fighters with a major tech edge over ours."

"While we must prepare for their intervention, we must also complete the mission before us," Remington said. "Can we count on *Deception* for the job?"

"Yes," Kira confirmed. "You can sort out the pay scale with the purser."

King Larry snorted.

"We'll pay you what you're worth," he told her. "We've always paid *Conviction* generously and I see no reason to change that. Captain Estanza has always been worth it."

"You realize, Your Majesty, that this is a trap?" Estanza said softly, his first words since Remington had started her briefing. "The Admiral has allowed for the possibility of intervention, but it's not a *possibility*. It's a certainty. The fighter strike on the cruiser carrying you and the Queen was intended to create this exact response.

"They will ambush you. This Coalition you've assembled... Even with *Deception*, I'm not sure they can face off against Cobra Squadron."

"We have no choice," the King replied. "To create the SCFTZ, we promised we would secure the trade routes as a group, but the lion's share of the work was always going to fall on us and Bengalissimo.

"To hold the FTZ together, the Clans must be neutralized sooner or later. My Parliament is determined that now is the time and that this attack on our space cannot be allowed to stand."

"Even if we revealed everything we know about Cobra and the

Institute, we would still be pressured to move forward on this," Sonia told them. "And we've put too much in play assembling this Coalition.

"If we back down now, we sacrifice both internal and external political capital we cannot afford to lose. Without the proof that Redward will defend our own space, let alone the rest of the Cluster, the Trade Zone agreements themselves might be in danger."

"That seems unlikely," Zoric said, *Deception*'s Captain looking thoughtful. "The Trade Zone is about money, isn't it?"

"And safety. And if we can't provide safety to our own, no one is going to trust us to protect others," Remington countered. "You are correct, Captain Estanza. This is almost certainly a trap—but it is a well-laid one. One we have no choice but to walk into."

"Assembling this Coalition is a risk as well," Larry admitted. "But if we start acting alone, throwing our military weight around without partners, we become exactly what Equilibrium wants us to become.

"Some of our MPs would be more than okay with that. Control is always more reassuring than cooperation—but that it is the harder path helps reassure me that it is the right one."

The King spread his hands wide, smiling as his wife took the one closest to her and squeezed it.

"We *will* remove the threat of the Costar Clans," he said firmly. "We will do it with our allies at our side and the general agreement of our neighbors that it is necessary—and we will do it in a way that preserves their culture while helping them out of the hole fate handed them.

"If we do anything less than all of these, we are not the beacon of hope that I insist Redward become."

10

"WHAT NOW?"

Bueller's question hung in the quiet restaurant, and Kira raised a questioning eyebrow at him. They'd been scheduled to have this date since before the summons to the Palace, though they'd barely made it back to Blueward Station in time.

The quiet sushi restaurant wasn't as perfect as she'd hoped, but it at least lived up to the promised ambience if not the quality of the food. Each of the low booths was wrapped in sound-deadening foam, reducing both the sounds of the other patrons and of the station in general.

"Well, we do have another order of sushi coming," she pointed out. "And then a hotel room booked just down the hall with a nice big bed. I did rather think that part was obvious."

The big engineer flushed, still easily teased despite the several weeks since she'd first dragged him to bed.

"I meant..." He paused, considering his words. "With the Clans."

"Four days," Kira said. "That was the timeline in the downloads Remington sent us. Then we move out with the Redward capital ships. This isn't a work dinner, so I won't ask if you know a problem with that."

He chuckled and took a sip of his tea.

"Not really thinking about work, I guess," he said. "If the Institute really brought the Cobras all the way out here...are we as badly outgunned as I think we are?"

"Maybe, maybe not." Kira waved a hand in the air as the second round of sushi arrived. She waited for the waitress to leave before continuing. "There's no question their fighters are going to be better. No idea what they're flying today, but Estanza flew fifty-year-old Periphery fighters thirty years ago. Even *those* fighters would be better than ours.

"But they're not flying off cruisers or true carriers. They're flying off glorified freighters with almost no onboard weaponry. Cobra Squadron's *carriers* aren't a factor, just the fighters. If they're using Rim mercs for their major ships, *Deception* will even the odds."

"So, we fight the Institute," he said. "Again."

"What were you expecting? You did defect to the people who have the biggest grudge against them," she pointed out.

"Fair. I just..." He sighed. "It's not like I didn't buy their ideals at one point. I see what King Larry's trying to do here and it makes sense to me, but what if the Institute's right? They've done the Seldonian calculations; this Ivarsson said things were proceeding as expected."

"Estanza once told me he'd handed a copy of Equilibrium's calculations to a non-Institute psychohistorian," Kira said. "*They* told him that the calculations were flawed. Variables taken as constants and similar assumptions.

"That, as I understand, is just as dangerous in psychohistory as it is in engineering. How accurate are your reactor efficiency numbers going to be if you assume hydrogen flows the same at every temperature?"

Bueller swallowed the last of his rice roll and shook his head.

"Not great," he admitted. "I don't pretend to understand Seldonian math. It's an entirely different path of super-complex math than I learned. I just... Well, I'm an engineer. I trust math by default."

"I'm a historian by education," Kira told him. "Not that it really ever mattered. ASDF officer training gave you one of six degrees, depending on your course selection, but we got a grounding in everything.

"And using trade pacts to avoid war has a long and successful history. Just as successful, I think, as having a superpower playing interstellar cop. Equilibrium says only one of these works, but *history* disagrees with them.

"I understand that Seldonian calculations and psychohistorical projections supposedly work, but I can't help but feel that people aren't that predictable. They're too messy, too argumentative, for it to be that easy."

"The math is supposed to predict societies, not individuals," Bueller argued. "King Larry's plans and ideals still have to exist inside the pressures and restrictions of the Syntactic Cluster's economics and structures."

Kira shrugged.

"I get that, but I still think people like the Institute put too much weight on it because it *is* math," she told him. "And since they've been stirring the pot in every sector you or I have ever lived in, it kind of ruins the examples, doesn't it? Isn't the principle that once you observe a thing, it's changed?

"So, once they observe these potential futures, they act to change them. They never see them come to pass and they reassure themselves that it's because of their actions. Or maybe, just maybe, the situation they predicted was never going to happen in the first place."

Her date raised his hands in self-defense.

"All right, all right," he said with a chuckle. "It doesn't matter, I suppose. The Institute was prepared to go too far for me to support them, even if I still trusted their math. Some means *cannot* be justified."

"Which is why there were versions of this mission *Deception* would never have participated in," Kira agreed.

She looked down at the remaining sushi. Both of them had been slowing down, and it wasn't entirely due to being full.

"Do you really want to finish the rest of this?" she asked. "Or should we go check into that hotel?"

11

DECEPTION'S BRIDGE WAS LARGE, designed to hold up to eighty working spacers at any point in time. With only a single shift on duty, roughly twenty-five people were scattered through the workstations, throwing holograms and virtual representations around and onto the screens as the big cruiser made her way out of Redward orbit.

She wasn't alone. While Kira's mercenary company didn't stretch to escorts for their heavy cruiser, the RRF was moving enough ships for this operation that Remington had assigned several to *Deception*.

Two destroyers and six gunships made up a neat cube around the cruiser as they accelerated toward rendezvous. The screens around Kira showed other ships moving with them as well, though *Perseus* and her escorts were farther away.

Redward was providing most of the capital ships and half of the lighter warships that would make up the Coalition Fleet. All of those ships were moving from various stations throughout the Redward System

"Make a note, Zoric," Kira told the cruiser's Captain quietly. "I'd really like to get some escorts of our own. *Deception* is a decent jack-of-all-trades, but she'll be safer with a destroyer or two of our own."

She was standing behind Zoric's chair. There *was* an observer seat on the bridge—for that matter, there was entire separate flag bridge for a squadron commander—but Kira liked standing. It helped remind everyone that she wasn't actively part of the cruiser's bridge crew.

"Would be nice to have some that could keep up with us," Zoric said drily. "But I don't think Redward will sell us *Serendipity*-class ships."

A glance at the reports floating around them confirmed Zoric's complaint. Scans showed the destroyers were moving at full standard acceleration, roughly eighty percent power. *Deception*, on the other hand, was accelerating at roughly sixty-seven percent power.

The cruiser could have easily left her "escort" behind.

"Who knows," Kira said. "Resources and money are definitely a limit for them building new ships. If we can come up with the kroner to fund the construction of the yards as well as the ships, they might just let us buy ships they wouldn't sell most people.

"They trust us, after all."

"You're still new to being a merc," Zoric pointed out. "You have no idea how weird that feels."

"*Conviction*'s been here for what, three standard years?" Kira asked.

"Three and a half. We've earned that trust and collected a lot of retainers over the years, but still." The Captain shook her head. "I've worked for Estanza for almost fifteen years now. Mercenaries aren't trusted, Demirci. *Anywhere*."

"Given that they're the major component of the fleet the Institute is throwing at us, I can see why," Kira acknowledged. "If our fellows can be hired for conquests, invasions, piracy and murder...yeah."

"Not everyone can be, but it's hard to tell which companies won't sign on for atrocity," Zoric said. "That's why the boss likes Shang—and why Redward helped Shang rebuild and replace his ships, even though he bases out of Exeteron. He's a long-standing merc of good rep here.

"We *know* he's not going to show up on the wrong side of this fight."

"Do we?" Kira asked quietly. "The Institute has a *lot* of money."

And Commodore Shang, thanks to the money and assistance Redward had provided him after the Battle of the Kiln—the *last* time a

Redward fleet had gone into one of the Clans' systems—now commanded three modern-by-Cluster-standards destroyers. If Equilibrium was going to hire anyone…

"I guess we don't know with anyone who isn't us," Zoric conceded. The icons and images on the screens were starting to converge at the rendezvous point.

Kira had spent enough time in the Syntactic Cluster now that it looked like a lot of ships, but it was still hard for her to really process the fleet gathering as being impressive. All three of the Redward capital ships were sixty thousand cubic meters.

They *wouldn't* have qualified as capital ships in Apollo's fleet. Worse, the carrier was a "junk carrier"—a refitted freighter with no guns. *Perseus* had been built to carry sub-fighters, the nova fighters' sublight and vastly inferior siblings. Recently refitted to carry nova fighters, she only had fifty of them aboard.

Bengalissimo was supposed to bring the last half-dozen fighters aboard the cruiser they'd refitted to have a small flight deck. All told, they'd have under eighty planes. It would have to do.

"Are we waiting on anyone?" Kira asked Zoric.

"I see two cruisers, us, a junk carrier, six destroyers and ten gunships," Zoric listed. "That's all Redward was bringing. Well, that and the twenty-four troop transports 'hiding' behind the carrier!"

"Sirs, incoming transmission from *Perseus*," a com tech reported.

"Command screen, please, Liselot," Zoric ordered.

The small screen directly in front of Zoric's chair lit up with the image of a tall blonde woman in the RRF's burgundy uniform.

"Captain Zoric, Commander Demirci," Admiral Ylva Kim greeted them. "It's a pleasure to be working with you both again. *Deception*'s refit is complete?"

Kim had commanded the task force that had gone into the Battle of the Kiln to deal with an Equilibrium-equipped Costar Clans warlord. She'd only been a *Vice* Admiral then, but there'd been rewards and compensation aplenty to go around after that fight.

"That it is," Zoric confirmed. "We are fully functional up to the standards her original Navy would expect."

Kim glanced sideways, as if making sure no one could hear her on her end.

"So, you could take out the rest of this battle group, couldn't you?" she asked quietly.

"It would probably depend on how close we got and who launched fighters first," Kira said. She was probably giving the RRF too much credit. In hostile hands, *Deception*—then *K79-L*—had intimidated the Cluster into assembling a massive joint fleet.

That fleet would *probably* have been enough, but it had also been larger than the Coalition Fleet they were taking against the Clans.

Kim's smile suggested she picked up on Kira's diplomacy, but she didn't argue.

"Everyone on our side is ready to nova out," she told them. "I'd like to bring *Deception* into the battle group tactical net. Your sensors are enough better that I can use that as an excuse to anyone who complains about linking in mercenaries."

At the Battle of the Kiln, *Kim* had been the one to refuse to link in mercenaries. Kira and her people had clearly earned some respect there.

Zoric glanced at Kira for confirmation before saying anything, and Kira nodded. It wouldn't matter once the multiphasic jamming went up, but prior to that, it could be useful for everyone.

"Of course, Admiral. We are standing by to nova on your command."

"Thank you, Captain." Kim blinked, distracted for a moment as she sent headware messages. "I also want to make one thing clear, since we had confusion about it prior to the Kiln: while my CNG has more fighters than you do, he and I are agreed that *you* are the Coalition Fleet Nova Group Commander, Commander Demirci."

She smirked.

"You probably should pick a new title. Most *Commanders* don't own heavy cruisers, after all."

12

THREE DAYS and three novas later brought the entire task group to their destination, a trade-route stop four light-years from the KDC-15RT System. Like most trade-route stops in the Rim, it was empty, with nothing visible to mark it as one of the heavily mapped regions of space considered safe to nova to.

The maximum range of a class one nova drive was six light-years, requiring a twenty-hour cooldown. Even out there on the edge of the Rim, there were lines of trade-route stops positioned six light-years apart spread between the systems.

Travel consisted of novaing to the nearest trade-route stop, then following the route. The risk of piracy using the premapped points was more acceptable than the risk of vanishing when jumping to unmapped locations.

Kira's nova fighters would require forty hours' cooldown for the six-light-year jump, though they could make it independently if they needed to. Their main advantages were their smaller size and shorter minimum cooldown. A class two nova drive was only thirty cubic meters and could cool down in a minute after a short-enough nova—versus the ten-minute minimum cooldown for a class one.

The class twos could also be mass-produced once the various

complicating factors had been handled. Redward had only had a class two plant for about nine months and had manufactured over a hundred of the drives.

It was the products of that manufacture she was watching from *Deception*'s Flight Control as they swept out into a standard Carrier Space Patrol. A six-ship squadron of Dexter interceptors was now orbiting the collection of ships, while a pair of two-ship detachments of Sinister fighter-bombers were novaing away to sweep the edge of the trade-route stop.

"We're not seeing anything around," Davidović reported from the bridge. "Just the RRF contingent."

"Keep your eyes open," Zoric ordered. "The Costar Clans are just as stuck with the trade-route stops as anybody else. If they're heading out on a raid, there's a good chance they'll come through here."

The Clans *probably* had other mapped points around their systems to make intercepting them harder, but there was a reason blockades worked. Kira had encouraged the RRF to establish backup nova zones around Redward to give them escape routes, but that was a work in process.

The maximum safe nova to an *unmapped* target was around one light-week. It could take months to travel six light-years without a target zone. Once you were there, establishing a solid-enough map of the gravity of an area to classify it as a safe nova zone took weeks.

Her understanding was that there were a couple of ships doing that scouting as they spoke, but they weren't done yet. Unlike Arti, which was only within jump distance of two trade routes, Redward was a convergence point for the maps and had six ways out.

But still only six.

That thought was bothering her now, especially with so much of Redward's firepower here. An outright invasion of a system like they were attempting was rare, but blockading a system to contain its military and merchant shipping?

That was how wars were fought.

"Nova signatures on the scopes," Davidović reported. "Escorts and fighters are maneuvering to intercept."

"Stand by the scramble team," Kira ordered. That was Purlwise's

Memorial-Charlie and the Weltraumpanzer-Viers at the moment. If the nova signatures were hostile, Purlwise's people would reinforce *Perseus*'s CSP while the rest of the fighters from the cruiser and carrier got into space.

"Scans suggest six ships: two destroyers and an escort," the tactical officer continued after a moment. "Beacons mark them as Ypres Federation Space Fleet."

"That's got to be *all* of the destroyers they have left," Zoric said. "But they're friendly, right, boss?"

Kira snorted.

"If the Federation is here to cause trouble, this Coalition is already fucked," she told the other woman. "Yprians are ours. We're still expecting four more destroyers, mostly along with the Bengalissimo cruiser, and an assortment of lighter ships."

"My timeline says another twenty-four hours for everyone to show up?" Zoric asked.

"Mine too. I've scheduled a meeting for all of the fighter squadron commanders in twenty-six hours," Kira said. "Hopefully, the Bengalissimo actually bring their nova fighters and their squadron commander isn't an asshole."

"If they're a rocket-jock, what's the chance?" *Deception*'s Captain replied.

"Decent." Kira glared at the image of the cruiser's CO. "Not all rocket-jocks are arrogant and troublesome."

"I was XO of a carrier for ten years, Kira," Zoric pointed out. "My experience suggests otherwise."

"Behave, Captain," Kira murmured. "This isn't going to be a fighter-focused campaign, but you still need my people."

"Always, sir," the other woman agreed. "Teamwork is the key, after all."

THE NEXT ARRIVAL was a surprise but a pleasant one. They'd only been expecting one destroyer from the mid-tier powers of the Cluster.

When *three* arrived, accompanied by a dozen gunships, alerts woke Kira from a much-needed night's rest.

"Report," she demanded as she rolled away from Bueller and onto her feet.

"Fifteen new contacts, three destroyer-sized," Waxweiler's voice told her grimly. The Brisingr defector was Commander Davidović's second in tactical, a position he'd earned by handling the entire tactical workload in Ypres after they'd stolen the ship.

"Still assessing beacons, but *Perseus* is scrambling."

"Get the scramble wing up," Kira ordered. "I'll be in my fighter in—"

"Wait," Waxweiler cut her off. "ID codes coming in. I'm flagging… Damn."

"Chief?" Kira asked. Technically, Waxweiler's job title was *team leader*, but he'd been a chief petty officer for the Brisingr Kaiserreich Navy, and habits died hard.

"I've Otovo codes, Exeteron codes and New Ontario codes," he reported. "Destroyers are transmitting mercenary codes. Does *Commodore Shang* sound familiar to you, sir?"

"*Grumpy Cat*, *Twister* and *Compensation*?" Kira asked, reeling off the names of the mercenary Commodore's three destroyers.

"Those are the IDs I'm seeing, yeah."

She exhaled.

"Stand down the scramble, then, Chief," she told him. "We were expecting those three systems to put up New Ontario's solitary destroyer and then a dozen gunships, but it looks like they hired Shang instead."

"That's good, right?" Waxweiler asked.

"*Twister* and *Compensation* are a generation behind *Serendipity*, but they're Redward-built destroyers, solid ships." She paused. "By Cluster standards, anyway."

Shang had lost a destroyer at the Kiln and seen *Grumpy Cat* badly damaged. Redward had repaired his flagship and helped him buy and upgrade two destroyers they were decommissioning as compensation for his losses—hence the names.

"An extra pair of destroyers aren't going to go amiss," she

concluded. "And I'm glad to see locally available mercenaries on *our* side instead of with the Clans. So, yeah, that's good news."

She considered the situation for a moment, then shook her head.

"I'm going back to bed, Chief," she told Waxweiler. "Hopefully, any other surprises will be just as pleasant!"

Killing the com channel, she turned around to see that Bueller had also been awakened by the emergency alert. He was sitting on the bed, his head tilted, as he'd clearly been listening to the conversation.

"Everything seems in hand," he noted. "We good?"

"We're good," she confirmed, eyeing the Brisingr man's uncovered muscular torso. "And since we're both awake, I suddenly have plans to be even *better*."

13

DECEPTION'S BRIEFING room was intended to hold all twenty of her pilots. It wasn't really intended to hold them all *comfortably*, but it at least had the space to fit all of Kira's new squadron commanders in hologram form.

Cartman and Yamauchi were the only people physically present, the two *Deception* squadron commanders seated in the front row like particularly eager students. The eight squadron commanders from *Perseus* were arrayed behind them, their holograms nearly perfect.

Kira suspected that the hologram of her aboard *Perseus* wasn't nearly as perfectly life-like as the ones she had from the carrier. The recorders were much the same, but the projectors on *Deception* were significantly better than those available to Redward's fleet.

"Colonel Sagairt," she greeted the carrier's Commander, Nova Group. "It's good to see you again."

The slim, copper-haired RRF officer grinned at her. He was at least five years her junior, but that *still* left him the most experienced and senior nova-fighter pilot the Redward Royal Fleet had to offer. He'd commanded the grand total of six battered secondhand medium fighters the RRF had possessed before they'd captured an Equilibrium fabricator capable of manufacturing class two drives.

"Likewise, Commander Demirci," Sagairt replied. "I didn't even have to argue with Admiral Kim about who the fleet CNG should be this time."

She returned his grin. When they'd taken a fleet to the Kiln, Kim had tried to insist Sagairt command the nova fighters. Sagairt, realizing that Kira had three times his fighters and four times his experience, had insisted she take command instead.

"As of our last update, everyone, the Bengalissimo force has not yet arrived," Kira told the squadron commanders. "Despite that, they're only supposed to be bringing one fighter squadron, so I figured we'd go ahead with this meeting.

"First, introductions." She gestured to her two officers. "Commander Mel 'Nightmare' Cartman commands Memorial-Bravo, a squadron of six Hoplite-IV interceptors. Commander Akira 'Purlwise' Yamauchi commands Memorial-Charlie, a squadron of six Weltraumpanzer-Viers."

Kira would rather fly an interceptor over a heavy fighter any day, but she had to admit that the Viers were the most advanced starfighters available to her and her allies.

"You presumably all know who I am," she said to a chorus of chuckles. "I fly under the callsign Basketball and directly lead our Memorial-Alpha squadron, which has eight Hoplite-IV interceptors."

Brisingr used a ten-fighter squadron but Kira was used to the Apollon system, where four six-ship squadrons were combined into a Nova Combat Group. *Conviction*, prior to her arrival, had operated with a squadron strength of "we only have eight nova fighters."

When they'd needed a more divided structure, Kira had set it up based on her own experience.

"Equally, everyone knows who I am," Sagairt said. "I command *Perseus*'s nova group and, like Commander Demirci, also run *Perseus*-Alpha—a squadron of eight Sinister fighter-bombers."

He gestured to his officers.

"*Perseus*-Bravo and *Perseus*-Charlie are both six-fighter Sinister squadrons, under Major 'Witch' Vanhanen and Major 'Crown' Herrera." A dark-haired woman and a shaven-headed man both nodded as they were named.

"We then have thirty Dexter interceptors, in squadrons *Perseus*-Delta, -Epsilon, -Fox, -Gamma and -Hotel," he reeled off. "Those are respectively, under the command of Majors 'Priestess' Church, 'Windmill' Muller, 'Toybox' Macauley, 'Nemo' Filep and 'Barnstorm' Lowe.

"Each squadron has six interceptors. Only *Perseus*-Alpha is over-strength, because it turned out we could only fit fifty nova fighters into a space designed for sixty sub-fighters."

Including Sagairt, four of the eight squadron commanders had been the pilots of the single squadron of nova fighters Redward had owned when Kira had arrived. Some of the others were dead and at least one was commanding an entire carrier group.

Even the *squadron commanders* on *Perseus* were so green they smelled like mint.

"Let's get one thing out of the way first," Kira said after a moment of silence. "Admiral Kim and Colonel Sagairt are perfectly fine with a mercenary officer acting as CNG for the entire fleet. Even once Bengalissimo's ships show up, a quarter of the destroyers and cruisers in this fleet will be merc ships, *and* I'm the most experienced nova-fighter officer here.

"I can list off my kills and accomplishments, but truthfully, the only objection I see you having to me *is* that I'm a merc," she concluded. "So. Anyone going to have a problem?"

There was an extended silence until Sagairt chuckled.

"I don't think so, Commander."

"All right." Kira skimmed her gaze across the ten officers in the room. "Theoretically, the only opposition we're going to face in this operation is from the Costar Clans. We know most of their lineup: ten-kilocubic gunships, twenty- to twenty-five-kilocubic corvettes."

The RRF officers nodded. Regardless of how they'd made it into the nova-fighter wings—mostly from the *sub*-fighter wings—they'd all been on the wrong side of the Clans' raiders.

Kira raised a hand with three fingers upright.

"But there are three known jokers in this deck and one of them is a trump card," she told them, mixing her card game metaphors terribly.

"The first two jokers are both in the hands of the same asshole. Anthony Davies got the hell out of Dodge when we went after him at the Kiln. He isn't dead…and he's got at least one Brisingr-built D9C heavy destroyer in his hands, plus an unknown number of Weltraumpanzer-Fünf heavy fighters.

"Intelligence is pretty certain he's been able to repair the D9C and that at least six Weltraumpanzers survived the Battle of the Kiln," she counted out. "That's our first two jokers in the deck.

"The D9C is forty thousand cubic meters of Brisingr warfighting tech of the same generation as *Deception*. The repairs the Clans will have been able to do might have cost her some capability, but she's still likely capable of going up against any cruiser in the sector *except Deception* on an even keel."

Kira shook her head.

"I'm sure RRF Command would *love* to capture her, but despite my recent track record, capturing starships is actually quite difficult," she said drily. "If she shows up, she's our primary focus until she's debs, people. Same with the Weltraumpanzers.

"The third joker in the deck is the trump card, though," she continued. "It's the same trump card that almost screwed everybody at Ypres. There's a third party out here with deep pockets and a grudge against Redward and the SCFTZ.

"We're reasonably sure at this point that the mercenary fleet we saw at Ypres remains intact and under contract to that party," she told them. She wasn't going to name the Equilibrium Institute, though most of the people here had probably been briefed on it.

Too many people were willing to dismiss a galaxy-spanning conspiracy as just a conspiracy theory. That was probably *healthy* in Kira's opinion, even when she was one of the people with proof.

On the other hand, she didn't need to say who their third party was for people to accept that a rogue mercenary fleet had shown up at Ypres and might show up again here.

"For assorted reasons I can't go into, we know that fleet has been reinforced with some serious sucker-punch capability," she continued grimly. "I'll be downloading some scenarios for simulations for you to run your squadrons through, and we'll try to set up a full-fleet nova group simulated exercise before we move on Arti."

"Is this an exercise I should expect my people to survive?" Sagairt asked carefully.

"Not the first time," Kira replied. She appeared to have a *reputation*...but on the other hand, no one seemed to mind her throwing them into near-impossible virtual situations anymore, either.

"We will do what training we can as a group, but my understanding is that we will be moving within twenty-four hours of the Bengalissimo cruiser group arriving," she told them all. "That should be enough for *Perseus*'s squadrons to run through a few iterations of the updated scenario deck I'll be providing."

She'd spent most of the time she hadn't been in a fighter on the trip there working on the new deck. It should run them through what they needed to expect.

"How bad are we expecting, sir?" Major Church asked. She was a soft-spoken woman with wispy blonde hair and watery blue eyes, but she seemed present enough as she spoke. "What's the worst case, I suppose?"

"Around a hundred and forty modern Inner Fringe standard fighters," Kira said bluntly. "Nova fighters and bombers easily eighty years ahead of ours technologically."

"No one would let mercenaries have planes like that," Herrera said, the shaven-headed officer looking perturbed.

"It depends on who's doing the buying for the mercs—and from where," she replied. "I don't know exactly what we're looking at, people, but that's our worst case. The tech level of the fighters in the simulations I'm providing is closer to our mostly likely scenario." She forced a grin. "So, of course, there are *more* of them."

That got her chuckles again, which slowly died into silence as everyone considered her words.

"Sir," Cartman asked, Kira's friend being more formal than usual. "One question, I guess."

"Of course."

"How long are we going to wait for Bengalissimo to show up?" she asked. "If they don't, that is."

"Thirty-six hours," Kira told her. "We've already seen civilian shipping come through here. It says good things about the RRF that that shipping has tried to get *closer* to this fleet while it's been here, but it also means that the Clans will shortly know we're coming.

"We can't avoid that, but if we move in the next thirty-six hours, we can be reasonably sure we won't meet any reinforcements from the other Costar Systems."

"What the heck could delay an entire cruiser group?" Herrera asked. "Bengalissimo was sending what, eight ships?"

"Seven," Kira told him. "Per the last update we had, anyway. A cruiser, two destroyers and four corvettes. Second-heaviest contingent after the RRF, and the only other one with nova fighters.

"Lots of stuff could have delayed them, so we'll wait. I don't think anyone is overly worried that the Bengalissimo component of the fleet has gone missing, after all."

Well, anyone except Kira. She'd been running fully automated simulations that she wasn't going to share with her subordinates just yet...simulations that said she didn't need to get anywhere *near* her worst-case scenarios of Cobra Squadron's strength to allow them to punch out that cruiser group.

14

DESPITE THE EXERCISES, the wait for the rest of the Coalition Fleet to assemble was the quietest time *Deception*'s crew had had since they'd rearranged the fighter wings. There might be a pall of concern beginning to spread over the Bengalissimo detachment's absence, but it was still safe and quiet.

That meant that Kira wasn't entirely surprised to exit her starfighter after a grueling round of exercises—throwing *Deception*'s wing, with the cruiser's support, against their counterparts and *their* cruiser from the Royal Griffon Navy—to find that the deck crew had assembled a party around her while she'd been working.

She landed on the deck as the freshly printed banner proclaiming 303RD REUNION unfolded across a table that threatened to buckle under the weight of sandwiches and pastries.

"Just what is this?" she asked, loudly enough to be heard but not loudly enough to be objecting.

"A party," Cartman told her, her old friend having left her own fighter earlier. Probably so that she *could* intercept Kira. "I cleared it with the Captain and everything."

She grinned.

"So long as you insist you're *just* the CAG, some things aren't your call, Kira."

"Fair," Kira allowed. "Who got invited to this mess?"

"Pilots and officers and...well, everyone," Cartman replied. "Milani, Bueller and Zoric should all be here—yeah, there's your boyfriend!"

Bueller and Zoric were making their way through the slowly thickening crowd toward them. Kira gave her lover a small wave and turned a smile on Cartman.

"Mostly your doing, then?" she asked.

"You need the break and so does everyone else," Cartman replied. A few abortive guitar chords echoed across the deck, and Kira looked up to see that Janda had gathered several of the deckhands around her as the pilot started testing her instrument.

"I'm not arguing," Kira said. "Just...scoring up the points, Commander Cartman."

The cruiser's two senior officers joined them, with Bueller pausing about a meter away.

"No rank in the mess and no protocol at the party," Kira told them. "You'd *better* be planning on kissing me, Konrad."

The big man laughed—and then swept her off her feet, picking her up off the ground and delivering one of the more *thorough* kisses Kira had experienced in her life before putting her back down.

"Yeah," she said breathlessly. "That'll do."

She pulled him to her side and leaned against him as she eyed the crew. The original Memorials were already converging around her, Hoffman and Patel only releasing each other's hands long enough to give her lazy salutes.

"Just a small warning, since you're the senior officers and all," Michel said quietly as she and Colombera joined the group around Kira. "Watch the blue and purple punches. They may be, ah, somewhat stronger than is appropriate."

"What did you do?" Kira asked. She wasn't *overly* worried. The pair had clearly done *something* to the punches, but she doubted they'd done enough to completely take someone out—and in the worst-case scenario, *Deception* was inside the defensive perimeter of *Perseus*'s fighter wing.

And the medbay had a solid stockpile of dealcoholizers, for that matter.

"Blue punch just has three times as much vodka as expected," Colombera said cheerfully. "Purple *may* have acquired some liquid cannabinoids."

"Anyone starts tripping, it's on you two," Kira told them. "So, keep an eye on things. So long as there's no harm, there's no foul. Am I clear?"

"Yes, sir," the two junior Memorials chorused.

Another figure, this one in full body armor with a drunken red dragon frolicking around the exterior, joined the group.

"Same goes for my troopers," Milani told the two pilots. "I can *smell* the cannabinoids from in here, remember."

Milani had never left their armor in Kira's presence. She wasn't sure it was personal preference, habit, religious commandment or what, but she'd only ever seen the mercenary trooper in armor decorated with an animated dragon.

They were good enough at their job that she'd stolen the squad leader from *Conviction* and put them in charge of *Deception*'s ground team. They didn't have the two hundred weltraumsoldats the cruiser had carried in Brisingr service, but the sixty mercs Milani commanded were still enough for Kira and them to cause *plenty* of trouble.

"We're watching," Colombera confirmed, tapping his head. "Live headware feed of a camera I left by the bowls. No one is overindulging yet."

"I figured you had a handle on it," Kira replied. "Trust but verify, as always."

She was still leaning on Bueller as she looked over at Zoric.

"You approved the party, they tell me, Kavitha."

"She's my ship, last I checked," Zoric replied.

"She is," Kira agreed. "Not complaining. It was the right call."

"I'm going to tell you again what everyone's been telling you for weeks, though," the cruiser Captain said. "You can't be a Commander and act as the flag officer, even if we're talking a squadron of one."

"I'm not the flag officer. I'm the *owner*," Kira said. "I also fly starfighters."

"Even Apollo had flag-rank fighter pilots," Hoffman reminded her. "I don't know what the rank for a *mercenary* nova-fighter flag officer is, but it might avoid some confusion if you started using it.

"Right now, you're the CNG for the fleet while having the same title as two of your squadron commanders. Everyone here knows what's going on, but the more strangers get involved, the worse it gets...*and* Zoric answers to you."

"And in an actual battle, Kavitha answers to herself," Kira argued. "I'm not giving orders to *Deception* from a starfighter."

"In a battle, rank is irrelevant," Bueller said. "Outside of a battle, your current rank is already causing you trouble; it's just been small and controlled so far. *Admiral* Kira Demirci is going to have a lot fewer arguments than *Commander* Demirci."

"Et tu, Konrad?" Kira asked, looking up at her lover. "I am *not* hanging a fucking Admiral's stars on my uniform. Not when I still answer to Estanza and *he's* only wearing a Captain's rocket."

"Colonel, Brigadier, Marshal, Big Kahuna." Milani reeled off suggestions as their dragon laughed. "Or just *Commodore*, I suppose. That's always a nice vague one."

"*Commodore* would make sense, I think," Zoric said. "Covers the vague placement of *person the warship Captain answers to* while still keeping you in the cockpit."

"Do I even get a call in this?" Kira asked.

"Well, I think we have every shareholder of Memorial Squadron LLC here, don't we?" Patel said. "All in favor of promoting Kira Demirci to the title and rank of Commodore? It's not like we're giving her a *raise*."

Kira did not point out that she owned sixty-five percent of the company. The other five original Memorials owned seven percent apiece—a seventh survivor had cashed out his shares to buy a freighter and avoid any chance of being called to combat again.

A chorus of ayes surrounded her anyway and she jokingly glared at her friends.

"Fine," she conceded, still using Bueller as a prop. "I'm blaming you for this, Konrad," she told him.

He chuckled, the same warm, velvety sound that had first attracted her to him.

"We'll add it to the list that starts with our home systems being mortal enemies," he replied. *"Commodore."*

Kira sighed and nodded.

"You've all got a point. You all got your party. Now, if you'll excuse me, some of that beer is calling my name—assuming our jokers haven't done anything to it?"

"I DON'T THINK we're getting the Bengalissimos."

Kira wasn't sure who'd spoken. She'd been heading toward the pickup basketball game someone had started on one the side of the flight deck when she heard the comment.

Konrad Bueller was happily ensconced next to the dessert table, talking nova drives big and small with Tamboli, the deck chief arguing the virtues of the class two drive while Bueller cheerfully nodded along but pointed out their errors.

She'd heard the bounce of a basketball and been drawn like a moth to the flame, but the half-heard comment was probably worth interrupting. Bidding the game she hadn't even managed to *see* yet a sad mental goodbye, she turned to survey the crowd around her.

It took her all of ten seconds to pick out Marija Davidović talking to several of the locally-recruited pilots. The Redward hands made up a good half of the crew at this point, though they were generally careful to keep from forming cliques.

"Overdue is overdue, not missing," Iyov Waxweiler, the tactical chief, replied to his boss. "All sorts of things can hold up a nova ship. Easy enough for them to misjudge static discharge and have to make a detour. That would add two days at least."

One of the factors of the nova drive that helped keep stopover systems like Ypres wealthy was that a full-size starship could only make six novas before they needed to attach themselves to a significant gravity well to discharge a buildup of assorted exotic energy forms.

The class two drives didn't suffer from that to the same extent, though the longer cooldowns more than made up for it over an extended journey.

"Forgive me, Iyov," Davidović said, "but you're not local." She gestured to the other locals. "Folks, what're the odds that a Bengal fleet cruiser would muck up their discharge estimate and end up forty-eight hours overdue?"

Kira stepped into the group with a small smile.

"Outside my experience, Commander," she told the tactical officer. "I only saw the Bengalissimos at Ypres, and that wasn't a fight in the end. So, what do you say?"

She gestured for the Commander and others to speak.

"The Bengals are either the second or third most powerful player in the sector," one of Bueller's new engineering team leads said. "Third, I guess, with Ypres united now. Their fleet is smaller than Redward's but just as professional. Just as competent."

"And just as well-led," Janda agreed, the pilot looking a bit more hesitant. "An RRF cruiser group wouldn't be two days overdue without something serious happening. Neither would a Bengalissimo Fleet group."

"So, you figure they're not going to show up in the next twelve hours, huh?" Kira asked. "I'd really like to have that fourth cruiser."

"If they're this late, they're not coming," Davidović said quietly. "I've known too many Bengal officers. Did a couple of joint ops with them in the RRF. Something's happened. I don't know what Admiral Kim is thinking, but either we're going without them or we're not going."

"I appreciate the honesty, Commander, people," Kira told them all. "I don't know the local fleets well enough to make that call, so I need your insight sometimes."

She shook her head.

"I don't like it, but I can tell you one thing for certain: if they're not coming, the Coalition Fleet is going into Arti without them."

15

"ALL SHIPS, stand by for nova. All ships, stand by for nova."

Commodore Hajna Fini was Admiral Kim's operations officer, and her voice echoed across every ship and starfighter in the Coalition Fleet.

Kira was in her Hoplite. Her headware was feeding her updates from every one of the sixty-nine starfighters under her command. It was the largest force she'd ever commanded—though not even in the top ten for forces she'd been part of.

The standard Apollo fleet carrier had four or five twenty-four-starfighter nova combat groups aboard. She'd occasionally flown off cruisers or smaller carriers, but it had been common enough to see starfighter strikes of well over a hundred ships.

A map of the Arti System was projected in front of her, with a large green icon marking their intended destination. There might be over four hundred stations and asteroid habitats scattered across the system, but over half of them were concentrated into six clusters.

The entire Coalition Fleet was going to *visit* the largest cluster to begin with, clearing the way for the Redward Army transports. Sixty thousand soldiers were earmarked for this system, and the Fleet's job was to make sure they got to their destinations safely.

"All nova fighters are clear to scramble," she told Fini. There was no verbal acknowledgement, but a checkbox on the prep list in her headware turned green. Other checkboxes changed color as Kira relaxed into her starfighter, ships checking in one by one.

"All ships confirmed green. All ships prepared for nova."

A moment's pause caused Kira to suck in her breath.

"All ships nova...*now*."

Reality *pulsed* and the Coalition Fleet was somewhere else. The trade-route stop had been empty space, its every minuscule gravitational effect and particle density mapped. Novaing into a star's gravity well was actually *easier*, using the star's gravity as a guide.

Three cruisers, a carrier, twelve destroyers, ten corvettes and twenty gunships emerged in a surprisingly well-synchronized flash of bright-blue Cherenkov radiation.

"New contacts, new contacts," Davidović chanted. "On the screens, jammers up!"

"Launch fighters," Kira ordered, still processing the data. There'd only been a few seconds of live data before the multiphasic jammers had encased the fleet. The jammers rendered them just as blind as their enemies, but the data Davidović was feeding her said they were barely a million kilometers from the enemy.

The defenders were lighter than she'd been afraid of. A trio of corvettes led thirty gunships, backed by a mere two dozen weapons platforms. It was nothing compared to the fixed defenses that covered most inhabited systems—and spoke to the same mind-crushing poverty that had driven the Costar Clans to piracy in the first place.

The world flashed around her for the second time in a few moments as her fighter blazed into space. The status listing for the fighter group was still *mostly* updated in the initial moments, as the mother ships maintained laser links with each other through the jamming and tried to hold links with the nova fighters.

Her own computers were using that data to line up laser links with her combat group as the fighters drifted into a standardized formation. The Clans' ships hadn't entered the Fleet's jamming bubble—but they also weren't her job today.

There were *three cruisers* in the Coalition Fleet. They didn't need nova fighters to handle corvettes and gunships. The defensive weapon installations, however, had a scale advantage over systems mountable inside the strict size limits of a nova ship. Even the Clans could build a one-shot plasma cannon that could gut a destroyer in one hit.

But the tracking on those big guns was never good...and nova fighters could always be somewhere else.

"This is Basketball," she said. "All squadrons, check in."

The last few orange icons flickered to green as a chorus of replies filled her mental ears.

"All fighters. Target is the weapons platforms. Let's do this by the numbers and come home clean. Coalition Fleet Group...nova and attack!"

A MILLION KILOMETERS or six light-years, a nova took the same amount of time every time. Kira and her squadrons emerged into the midst of the Clans' defenses. Multiphasic jamming from seventy nova fighters rendered the area chaos in the moment of their arrival. The corvettes and half the gunships were already moving out toward the Coalition Fleet, sweeping to see if they could assess their enemies.

Sixteen gunships had remained with the fixed defenses, probably as a countermeasure to exactly the strike Kira was leading. Unfortunately for them, the Hoplites and Dexters could carry a torpedo apiece—but it slowed the interceptors down, and the RRF pilots had already picked up the attitude of *every* interceptor pilot ever handed a torpedo: *Get rid of this damned thing.*

Thirty Dexter interceptors salvoed thirty torpedoes at sixteen gunships. Three ships survived to nova out, an escape that would leave them out of the fight for at least ten minutes.

Kira was already losing links to most of her people, but she nodded in satisfaction as she saw that none of her Hoplites had fired their torps. That had been the plan if there'd been defensive ships. With the core Memorials there, she had the best interceptor pilots in the Cluster —and some of the defenses *were* capable of targeting starfighters.

Plasma blasts were already filling the space around her as she led the Memorials forward. Her fourteen fighters had one objective, and part of it required them to draw fire. Kira was tracking as much of the flak as she could as she danced her fighter through it.

"There," she said aloud, haloing one of the closer platforms. It wasn't big enough to carry one of the big antiship guns, but it had an impressive collection of lighter guns. There in the Cluster, they were probably intended to target gunships, but they'd make a mess of her heavier fighters and greener pilots if she let them.

A mental command deployed her torpedo, and she dodged around the plasma flak as she opened fire with her own guns. An asteroid with surface guns couldn't dodge.

The torpedo's fusion blast swept most of the installations off the smallish rock, and she dove in behind the wave of plasma, her own cannon spitting fire as she targeted the remaining guns.

Forty seconds had passed since her arrival, and one of the installations was dead to her guns alone. The squadron of Weltraumpanzers flashed past her, heading toward the heavy antiship cannon her target had been protecting.

Explosions were lighting up across the battlespace, diffused by the jamming but still clear to her scanners as she popped up to search for threats. Platform after platform was disappearing from her computer's estimates as torpedoes struck home.

She spent ten seconds attempting to locate a target before the timer flipped green and she did what nova pilots did best: she vanished.

ICONS in her head flickered from orange question marks to green confirmed dots as nova fighter after nova fighter appeared out of nothingness at the rendezvous point and shut down their jammers. Kira watched the list run down and then blinked as the last Sinister fighter-bomber appeared.

"Squadron leaders, check in," she ordered. "I see everyone. Confirm."

They'd just punched out the fixed defenses of a cluster home to a million and a half or so people *and* knocked out two squadrons' worth of gunships. They couldn't have done it without losses...could they?

"I confirm, Commodore," Cartman told her. "All *Deception*-Bravo fighters are present."

"All Charlie fighters are here," Yamauchi agreed.

The *Perseus* officers took a few moments longer, but it quickly confirmed her surprise. They'd taken seventy fighters, most of their pilots green, into the teeth of a major settlement's fixed defenses, and brought them all out.

The Costar Clans were poor, but there wasn't much wrong with the hardware built into their defenses. The crews just hadn't been ready for this...and they'd paid for that lack of attention with their lives.

"Stand by for group-wide nova recharge," Kira ordered. They were a light-minute away from anyone right now, though it would be a few more minutes before the battle between the Coalition Fleet and the defenders opened up.

It probably wouldn't last very long once it *did* start.

A few more seconds passed as the last fighters reported cooldown.

"All ships, nova to the fleet on my command," she said. "Hold defensive positions and establish laser links with the motherships. Maintain defensive maneuvers and keep your eyes open; the Clans might be outclassed, but a lucky hit can take down anyone."

She took a breath and nodded firmly to herself. It wasn't a lucky hit she was worried about—but if Cobra Squadron decided to get involved, her people weren't going to need torpedoes.

Which was good, since they'd fired them all at the local defenses.

"All ships...nova."

16

THE BATTLE WAS ALREADY OVER. The sortieing defenders had worked out the rough outlines of what was waiting for them before they'd traveled far enough to enter the multiphasic-jamming bubble around the Coalition Fleet—and promptly novaed the hell out.

Kira pulled her fighter into a position between *Deception* and *Perseus* and established laser links to both ships. The enemy may have fled the battlespace but the jamming remained.

"Basketball reporting," she greeted *Perseus*. "I need Fleet-Actual."

"Fleet-Actual here," Admiral Kim replied immediately, linking into the channel with barely so much as a blip. "Status report, Commodore?"

News of that "promotion" had spread quickly enough.

"Fixed defenses around the settlement cluster are down," Kira reported. "No losses, but the fighter group is out of torpedoes. As expected. Do we proceed to stage two?"

"The Fleet is advancing; ETA to deployment point fifteen minutes," Kim told her. "Did you pick up anything in your sweep to suggest against stage two?"

"Negative."

Stage two was the deployment of the first wave of Redward Army troops. This cluster was earmarked for an entire twenty-thousand-soldier division. Even assault shuttles were vulnerable to defenses that a nova fighter would dance around, which was why the nova group had cleared those defenses out.

"If the corvettes and gunships are out of play for the moment, this may just be over, Admiral," Kira pointed out. "Permission to send the fighters in to rearm."

"Granted. We'll be lowering the multiphasic jamming shortly. Always takes a bit for that message to transfer, and I want to keep an eye open. Allowing our enemy an impossible level of perfect information, the next twenty minutes are when we are at our most vulnerable.

"But per Their Majesties' instructions, I have to talk to these people."

"Makes sense to me. I'll have the flight decks make contact and bring everyone in. We'll be ready to defend the fleet."

"Appreciate that, Commodore. This has been all too easy so far."

"Basketball out." Kira turned to giving orders to the flight decks and lining up her own return to *Deception*, but Kim's final words hung in her.

All too easy.

It could be a trap. Given the presence of Cobra Squadron, Kira was *expecting* a trap...and yet. They'd brought overwhelming firepower to bear on the Costar Clans there in Arti—and while she expected the Institute to intervene, she also expected them to wait for just the right time.

They weren't there yet. Kira wasn't sure what *there* was going to be, but she was sure they hadn't reached whatever trigger the Institute was waiting for.

And that when they reached it, they were going to know very, very quickly.

"GET the torpedoes on everything and get them back out into space," Kira ordered as her fighter linked to a transfer cart on *Deception*'s flight deck. "The pilots don't even need to stretch their legs yet, and the Admiral feels like we've got a bull's-eye painted on us."

"Even the Hoplites?" Tamboli asked.

"Even the interceptors," Kira confirmed. She didn't like having a torpedo on her Hoplite any more than her pilots would, but the mission parameters weren't dictated by her preferences. "We'll dump if we only face nova fighters, but the odds are in favor of more gunships and corvettes."

"Your call, sir, but I'll remind you that a torpedo is expensive," Tamboli pointed out.

"I'll charge Redward for them if we shoot them or drop them," Kira told the deck officer. "Load us up."

Tamboli laughed, but they were already directing their people as they switched channels. More starfighters were following Kira's in, the mix of interceptors and heavy fighters calling for careful spacing on the retrievals.

The Hoplites were much more maneuverable than the Weltraumpanzers, especially in confined quarters like this. The Weltraumpanzers could accelerate just as quickly on a straight line, but they had a small but noticeable delay in changing direction compared to the interceptors.

Everything was flowing according to plan and practice, allowing Kira to turn her attention to the exterior battlespace. The last of the multiphasic jamming was down, and the Coalition Fleet was advancing on the settlement cluster they'd flagged as Arti-One.

She wouldn't have wanted to be on the wrong side of that advance. *Deception* might be the only ship in the fleet she'd call *modern*, but four capital ships and dozens of escorts was still a real fleet by any standard.

A ping in her headware informed her that Admiral Kim was transmitting, and Kira linked into the message. As the Fleet CNG, she needed know what they were telling the locals.

Stage two called for her interceptors to escort the army shuttles in. If Kim said the wrong things, that was going to be a more unpleasant experience. The Clans didn't have much left to cause trouble with, but no space station was ever *entirely* without ways to make approaching ships' lives difficult.

"Costar Clans of the K-D-C-One-Five-R-T System," Kim greeted her captive audience. "I am Admiral Ylva Kim of the Redward Royal Fleet, leading an allied Coalition force operating under the authority of the Syntactic Cluster Free Trade Zone.

"This system has been the home base for continuing raids and piracy against the trade of the Syntactic Cluster. Your choices and actions have made you enemies of all peaceful worlds in this region."

Kim was silent for a few seconds to let that sink in.

"But. The SCFTZ recognizes the nature of your settlements. The abandonment and betrayal of your ancestors by the systems and governments of the Cluster. You have my word that the end of your predations will not be the end of your people or your homes.

"As of now, the K-D-C-One-Five-R-T System is a protectorate of the Kingdom of Redward. We will not permit further raids or theft...but my monarchs will also take direct personal responsibility for your well-being.

"*If* you lay down your arms and surrender now. Units of the Redward Army will be launching within the next few minutes to commence the occupation of key stations and settlements across the system. Major General Mazhar Costantini is now the military governor of this system in their Majesties' names.

"Our troops are under orders to minimize harm, but they *will* use whatever force is necessary to secure control of critical systems and facilities. We will not embrace collective responsibility, but resistance will be neutralized.

"Work with us, and the Costar Clans will become something new. A name that you can use with pride in the future. Oppose us, and my monarchs will drag you into the future kicking and screaming.

"The choice is yours."

It wasn't the tack Kira would have taken, but it was certainly *an* approach.

New icons flickered across her headware and physical screens as the fueling umbilicals disconnected and the torpedo slotted into place.

"You're good to go, Commodore," Tamboli's voice said in her ear. "Things should be quiet now, yes?"

"We can hope," she told them. "It's down to the Clans now...and whether they believe King Larry's promises!"

17

AFTER THIRTY-SIX HOURS in the cockpit, all Kira wanted when she finally got out of her fighter was a shower. The nova fighters hadn't been able to take a break for a day and a half, with the Arti Clans having *just* enough firepower left to make even taking possession of surrendering stations dangerous.

"Kira, Admiral Kim wants us at a senior officers' briefing in five minutes," Zoric's voice greeted her as she hit the deck. The cruiser Captain was probably on the bridge, though *she* had almost certainly slept in the last day.

"Okay," Kira said in a swift exhalation. "I… I might be late, because by starfires and deep space, I am going to shower before I do anything else."

"I get it," Zoric agreed. "I'll cover for you. I doubt Sagairt is going to be any faster. He isn't even aboard *Perseus* yet."

"Thanks." Kira looked around the deck for Cartman and gestured the other woman over to her as she started for the ready room.

"Mel, I have a briefing with the Admiral," she told her friend. "I'm going to shower and get political, I suspect. Make sure everybody else in the squadron gets their asses to a rack. Things are looking under control for now, so let's take advantage of it."

"No CSP?" Cartman asked.

"Gunships have it for now," Kira replied. "We'll launch fighters to back them up in six hours, but the group's been running since we got here. They *have* to rest."

"Not arguing, but wanted to be sure," her subordinate said as they reached the showers. "What about you?"

"Rank hath its privileges," Kira said dryly. "In this case, meetings on four hours of naps in the last forty."

AT LEAST KIRA was able to take the meeting from her office. She initially joined the virtual conference with an avatar as she was dressing, allowing her to hear the briefing even if she couldn't easily participate.

"Officers, I appreciate you joining me," Admiral Kim greeted everyone. "I know a few of you have been run more than a bit ragged since we arrived here, but there are updates everyone needs to hear.

"First, and most critical to the moment, we are now fully in control of the Arti System," she said firmly. "Major General?"

Major General Mazhar Costantini took over the focus of the virtual conference's camera. He was a tall and heavyset man with dark skin and hair and a level, calm expression.

"Thank you, Admiral," he told Kim. "As of twenty minutes ago, we have established communications with every station in the Arti System. I suspect that most of the promises of cooperation from settlements outside the core clusters are nominal at best, but since we now control the shipyards, it'll do.

"Our current estimate is that there are approximately four hundred settlements of various types in the Arti System, with an average population of under fifteen thousand. Only about a hundred of these settlements were originally constructed by other Cluster powers, which means that a large chunk of them are..."

He paused thoughtfully.

"Potentially hazardous to their occupants," he concluded. "Once I have more resources from home, my first order of business is probably going to be inspection and repair of those habitats. But…as of now, we have also taken control of the remaining gunships and weapons platforms in the system.

"The full presence of the Coalition Fleet is no longer required, though I have asked Admiral Kim to provide some level of security detachment."

"That was part of the plan," Kim confirmed. "The destroyers *Armed Sedation* and *Nightmare* will remain here with the Thirty-Third RRF Gunship Flotilla. The Thirty-Third will also be responsible for examining the captured gunships and seeing if any will be brought into our service.

"The key point for everyone is that we have succeeded in our mission in the Arti System," the Admiral told them. "If nothing else comes of this operation, that is six million people who will shortly be more than one system failure from death.

"We can feel good about that, even if the price is always too damn high."

Kira was carefully *not* doing the math about the gunships and weapons platforms their initial nova strike had taken out. The gunships alone would have each had at least twenty people aboard. The defensive installations could have been anywhere from a dozen to several hundred.

"Unfortunately, we also received an update from several of our governments," Kim continued after a moment's pause. "Our mail came on the RRF courier some of you may have seen, and I'll be releasing it after this meeting, but I wanted to make sure that all of our senior officers received the news at the same time and the Coalition Fleet was able to approach it as a team.

"We will not be receiving our Bengalissimo Fleet contingent," she told them all firmly. "Battle Group *Civet* was assembled as planned but instead of leaving to support us, Admiral Rossella Gaspari made a different choice."

That was never a good sign. When a fleet officer in command of a battle group chose to do something other than their orders, the possibilities *started* at treason.

"As of our best intelligence, King Isidoro is dead," the Admiral concluded. "Admiral Gaspari's battle group made a dangerous short nova into orbit of Bengalissimo itself and their marines stormed the orbital fortresses before anyone knew what was happening.

"Redward Intelligence presumes that this was prearranged with multiple parties," Kim noted. "There was insufficient resistance on the orbital fortresses or in the capital city. Plus, many of the marines from the fortresses joined Gaspari's troops when they stormed the Parlamento Bengalissimo.

"The exact final nature of the affair is still being established, but the government of Bengalissimo has been overthrown," she concluded. "King Isidoro was executed on a planetwide broadcast. Prime Minister Petit's fate is unknown, but the information we've received from the Redward Embassy is that there has been at least one round of mass executions of Members of the Parlamento."

The virtual conference was dead silent. Kira had read up on the history of the Cluster. *Most* of the governments represented in the Coalition Fleet had seen coups in the last century—the Yprian Federation was brand-new, but the events leading to its formation had involved both coups and forced annexations.

Still. Bengalissimo had been one of the bright spots of the Cluster, up with Redward as one of the stable and powerful systems everyone looked up to. No one had expected to see a military coup there.

"Does this impact our mission?" Shang asked, the mercenary asking the question everyone was wondering.

"Hopefully, it does not," Kim said grimly. "But that depends on the messages and orders your governments have sent you. *My* orders from Their Majesties are to continue the operation and to move on the KSR-92RR System as soon as we can.

"My intention is to wait two more days to see what updates arrive from your governments and to make certain that Major General Costantini's governorship is solidly in place," she continued. "The Coalition Fleet will then move against the Kaiser Clans.

"Understand that if you do receive recall orders from your governments, I will not hold that against any officer here," she told them all firmly. "While I would prefer that all of your ships remain with us, I understand duty comes first."

Kira's headware told her that the conference was alive with side channels linking officers to each other. She could easily open one to Zoric or Sagairt—though she noted that the RRF fighter officer was *still* present via avatar.

"Do we have other questions?" Kim asked. "I want to make sure we all understand as much of the situation and the potential consequences as we can."

18

KIRA WOKE from an extended twelve-hour collapse feeling notably more human and refreshed. Another shower finished the job, and she considered the news from Bengalissimo as she dressed.

She'd never met Admiral Gaspari, though she understood that the woman had been in command of the Bengalissimo detachment at Ypres. Somehow, watching the coups and civil wars in Ypres hadn't been enough to convince her this was a terrible idea.

Going through her messages, she found a short note from Bueller asking her to meet with him once she was awake. It *looked* like work, though a no-longer-tired part of her certainly took a moment to consider the option of being bent over the desk in one of their offices.

Shaking that off in favor of professionalism, she pinged his head-ware for a voice call.

"Konrad. I'm awake and handling paperwork while I consider where to start my meetings," she told him with a chuckle. "My *usual* plan would be to sit down with Tamboli and see how our fighters are handling after a thirty-six-hour series of sorties. Since they don't know I'm awake yet, I can put that off."

"Can you grab Zoric and swing by my office?" he replied. "I think we want to talk about this news, and I think Zoric probably needs to be in on it."

That was a no on getting bent over a desk. Shame.

"Yeah, I can do that," Kira confirmed. "What do you think is going on?"

"I don't know, but I've got some pieces of the puzzle I want to share," he told her. "And then we can put all of our brains on working out how much trouble we're in. Something smells."

"Something always smells," she said. "And the fact that everything smells like Equilibrium makes me feel like I'm paranoid."

"You're only paranoid if you're wrong," her boyfriend said. "And believe me, I know *exactly* how you feel. I'm half-considering fabricating string and a corkboard."

Apollo and Brisingr shared enough popular media that Kira got the reference and grinned.

"Well, let's all get together and put our conspiracy-theorist hats on before we get that far. That way, we all *agree* on what goes on the conspiracy board!"

BUELLER WAS STARING off into space, studying something in his headware, when Kira entered his office. She took the moment to pour herself coffee from his machine, sniffing it in surprise before tasting it.

"You know this ship has a full stock of several very good Redward coffee varieties *and* the Queen gave me a pallet of the royal family's personal blend I keep for the senior officers, yes?" she asked as she took another sip.

"You've *seen* me drink coffee," he said, gesturing toward the cup on his desk without changing his focus on empty air. "Why would I subject *good* coffee to cream and honey?"

"How are you a spacer again?" Kira said, noting the pale brown color of his drink. "I thought black coffee was a requirement?"

"Only for fighter pilots," Zoric told her, the cruiser Captain carrying a thermos in her hand as she joined them. She poured herself a coffee from the thermos and grinned at Kira. "Our engineer executive officer always had access to a fridge, after all.

"*I*, on the other hand, spent too long on a carrier to not pick up bad pilot habits. I've learned to bring my own coffee to meetings with Konrad."

Kira chuckled.

"When I finish this cup, I might steal some of that," she admitted.

Bueller refocused his gaze on the two women and shrugged, taking a sip of his coffee-cream-and-honey beverage.

"I'm not going to subject good coffee to the way I drink coffee," he repeated genially. "And I wouldn't torture myself with black coffee... Especially not black coffee from *Brisingr*."

"Oh, is that the reason? Your homeworld's coffee is awful?" Kira asked.

"Pretty much," he agreed. "Even during the war, we never managed to stop people smuggling Apollon coffee. I don't think anyone even tried very hard."

"So, some of your people are sensible. Good to know."

He shrugged.

"I could say the same about Apollo," he noted. "We at least don't have a cash requirement for the voting franchise."

Kira grimaced. To vote for the Council of Principals on Apollo, you had to have paid a minimum amount of average tax over the last five years. That minimum amount was, roughly, what someone who'd just entered the top tax bracket would be paying. Since certain minimums on that bracket were set in the constitution, it was supposed to provide the wealthy *some* sense of public obligation.

She'd never qualified to vote in anything except municipal elections —and nova-fighter squadron commanders were paid well.

"I'd argue that we don't have a hereditary ruler, but I suspect it washes out," she admitted. "Plus, our current employers have the same system."

"Don't be *that* generous to the Kaiser," Bueller replied. "He has a lot more direct authority than King Larry does. Larry built a political coalition to achieve his objectives. The Kaiser didn't need to."

"Fun as watching you two snipe about your homeworlds is, we were here to talk about Bengalissimo?" Zoric said dryly.

"That's actually where this coffee comes from," Bueller noted, taking another drink.

Kira finished the rest of the aggressively mediocre coffee and gratefully took a refill from Zoric's thermos.

"You had thoughts," she told Bueller. "You want to lay them out? I think we're all kind of in the same direction."

"Gaspari is an Equilibrium patsy," the engineer said. "Quite possibly an active agent. It would fit with some of the bits and pieces I saw before we took the ship. There were definitely several other irons the Director had in the fire outside Ypres.

"I suspect he had them set up so he could pull the plug easily enough on them all, but there were more strings to their bow than Ypres."

"I'm getting really sick of clearing up one Institute scheme and finding another one waiting for me," Kira said. "First the Clans. Then Ypres. Now Bengalissimo?"

"They're fond of military dictatorships and sovereign-tilted constitutional monarchies," Bueller noted. "*Stable* ones, at least. Establishing a military dictatorship is always a mess, but a solidly run one can last the lifetime of the dictator—or longer, if they're smart about the succession plan or have a council of generals backing them up."

"Because those dictatorships are so much better for the average citizen," Zoric grumbled. "These people piss me off, Konrad. How the hell did you end up with them?"

"I come from a constitutional monarchy where the Kaiser holds the balance of power," he pointed out. "*Exactly* the Institute's preferred government." He shrugged. "I don't have any proof that they helped tilt the scales against Apollo, but the Kaiser was certainly willing to do them favors afterward."

Like sending a K70-class cruiser to the far end of nowhere, Kira knew. That was how they'd ended up with their heavy cruiser, after all.

"And the ideal they sell is powerful," Bueller reminded the two women. "Peace and prosperity. It's easy to accept when someone tells you that the math says exactly what sacrifices are required to get there. Especially when you're in a field where *math* controls everything you do."

"He's with us now, Kavitha," Kira said. "So's Captain Estanza, for that matter. Our little mix-up of mercenary companies has plenty of ex-Institute guilt to go around."

"Sorry, Konrad," Zoric apologized without further prompting. "You think Gaspari is Institute, though?"

"If she's not, the Director has his hooks into her closest advisors and supporters," Bueller said. "The descriptions of the coup I can find read like a laundry list of standard Equilibrium assets. On the other hand...even if she *wasn't* Institute, the Director will have latched on to her within days."

"So, she's not just going to have the Bengalissimo Fleet," Kira concluded grimly. "Every one of those mercenaries we saw at Ypres, plus Cobra Squadron, is probably contracted to her by now."

"Exactly." The engineer shook his head. "I'd be surprised if the Institute hasn't already installed a class two nova-drive fabricator somewhere in Bengalissimo. If they're far enough along that their asset is seizing power openly, they've probably upgraded the BF more than we're counting on."

"I *think* we'd know if the BF was building new capital ships," Zoric said.

"Zoric, how big is a star system?" Kira asked.

"Touché," the cruiser Captain allowed. "A lot of places to hide a shipyard. Redward's building four cap ships at the moment. Do we think Bengalissimo got ahead of them on cap-ship building?"

"They haven't shown their hand on new ships yet," Kira observed. "Redward Intelligence thinks they're still at the same three cruisers they've had for twenty years, but I don't think anyone had any reason to look for secret construction programs."

"Gaspari is independently wealthy," Bueller told them, his gaze focused on thin air again. With a wave of his hand, he transferred the file he was looking at to the air above his desk. The hologram was the Bengalissimo system-pedia entry for the woman.

"She comes from money, the top tier of Bengalissimo's unofficial aristocracy if I read between the lines," he continued. "That probably helps her case for control right now...but probably more relevant is this."

He highlighted a section of the text. *Rossella Gaspari is the only sibling of Luigi Gaspari, primary shareholder of Victory Star Manufacturing.*

"Do I dare guess what Victory Star Manufacturing does?" Kira asked.

"I didn't know, so I checked," Bueller told her. A new article popped up into the hologram. "As it turns out, Victory Star Manufacturing is the primary contractor that builds the Bengalissimo Fleet's warships.

"VSM, in fact, built two of the three cruisers that currently anchor the BF and carried out the twenty-year refits on all three ships," he concluded. "They have both the funds and the resources to have built warships, even *capital ships*, without involving the Bengalissimo government.

"If the Institute helped underwrite the costs, the BF could be about to dramatically expand under their new military dictator."

"Starfires and horseshit," Zoric cursed. "That's bad. That's *really* bad."

"Bengalissimo already had as many cruisers as Redward," Kira said. "That Redward had the sub-fighter carriers and *Conviction* on retainer was the only thing that made the RRF the premier navy of the Cluster.

"Once *Deception* came into the picture and Redward replaced the sub-fighters with nova fighters, the balance of power was clearer...but if Bengalissimo even has another three sixty-kilocubic cruisers, that balance is in question."

"Throw in that mercenary Crest carrier and Cobra Squadron, and Redward is outnumbered and outgunned," Bueller agreed. "I just feel like if they had this in play, it would have been a problem for both of the plans we collided with earlier."

"That depends," Kira admitted. "If they were holding back the class two drives, then it makes sense. Deceiver and the Clans with a nova-fighter fleet would have been able to arrange the destruction of even six cruisers. Or they could have had an arrangement where

Gaspari's family were compensated with power and wealth for the cruisers suddenly up in Ypres's hands after the system's forceful unification.

"But now that Deceiver is a shadow instead of a warlord and the Ypres Federation is solidly onside with the SCFTZ, they'll pull out all of the stops. If VSM was building cruisers for them and now Gaspari runs Bengalissimo, they're only, oh, a *mercenary carrier fleet* away from *having* their hegemon.

"They just need to convince the rest of the Syntactic Cluster to fall in line."

The three of them stared at the hologram, currently focused on a listing of warships built by Victory Star Manufacturing.

"What do we do?" Bueller asked.

"We stick with the Coalition Fleet for now," Kira told them. "Right now, enough of the Cluster's warships are concentrated here to represent both a strength and a weakness. I don't think the BF can break enough ships free, even with merc backing, to take on the Coalition Fleet just yet.

"They need to break it up, get the individual components to go home, and defeat us in isolation," she continued. "They need to do what Brisingr did back home: demonstrate that no one can travel the trade routes without paying for their protection.

"They can't do that while we're out here with the largest concentration of ships the Cluster has ever seen. Plus, securing the Clan Systems is a solid counterargument: a proof that the FTZ *can* provide security for the Cluster."

"So, we do what we were already doing?" Zoric nodded slowly. "Seems like it leaves us open."

"It does," Kira agreed. "But it's the best plan we've got. We watch the news that comes by courier and we keep our options open. Worst-case scenario, I'm pretty sure Kim will listen to me if I tell her we need to get back to Redward ASAP."

19

DESPITE THE LONG-STANDING cultural links between the Costar Clans, the four star systems they controlled were surprisingly far apart. The Coalition Fleet's course resembled a giant circle, beginning and ending at Redward.

KSR-92RR was the farthest of the four systems from Redward, and still four novas from Arti. One out to the trade route, two along it, and one to the Costar Clans Systems.

It was at the second trade-route stop that the fight she'd been waiting for started. *Deception*'s crew was made up of four entirely distinct and separate contingents, after all.

"Senior officers to the deck six mess," an alert rang in her headware. "*Somebody* to the deck six mess, *please.*"

Kira's headware happily informed her that the speaker was Shyam Bartolomeo, a new recruit whose main prior qualification had been rising from barista to manager at a chain coffee shop. He was now the manager of one of the cruiser's four crew mess halls.

Fortunately for Bartolomeo, Kira was on deck six. The mess hall was only a few dozen meters away, and she was the first senior officer to reach the doors to the large room.

Pausing at the entrance, she heard shouting and a crash of furniture

—and brought up the security footage before she charged in. A quick glance confirmed that a contingent of Redward hands and a contingent of Brisingr defectors had come to screaming and blows.

The older mercenary hands from *Conviction* appeared to be standing off to the side, taking bets, which did *not* help.

With a sigh, Kira slapped the control panel for the door. A headware protocol she'd coded years ago took control of the room's speakers and proceeded to induce a brutally loud feedback.

The scream served its purpose, stunning the brawlers into a moment of silence and frozen motion as she walked in.

"Sit your asses down," Kira barked into that shocked silence. "All of you."

One of the old *Conviction* hands started to get up to head for the door—and she mentally commanded it to lock behind her.

"*All* of you," she reiterated, pointing at the merc.

It took a few moments, but no one was apparently stupid enough *not* to listen to the diminutive woman who owned their ship.

"Now. I don't think *anyone* here thinks brawling on a warship is remotely appropriate, so just what the fuck happened here?" she asked.

"They're murderers—"

"They called us murderers—"

At least seven or eight people started speaking, but the words were close enough that Kira could pick out both sides of the argument. She gestured them to silence.

They didn't obey.

She glared.

The shouting kept getting louder.

She triggered the feedback loop again.

Everyone shut up.

"Really?" she finally asked. She pointed at the Redward crew. "You all know *damn* well what brought the Brisingr members of this crew here. They signed on in good faith to serve their Kaiser. They were supposed to be making the galaxy a better place—even the ones who didn't know about the Institute thought they were expanding human knowledge and explored space.

"They were *lied* to and *used*. When they realized that, they helped us capture this ship and turn it on the very people who brought them here. To do the right thing, they gave up their right to go home. *Ever.*"

Kira turned to the Brisingr crew.

"You've earned your homes here on *Deception*," she told them. "That said, there's a reason this damn fight came up today and not a month ago, isn't there? This ship, while you were her crew, killed twenty thousand innocent people.

"We aren't forgetting that. Not ever. But there haven't been mass fistfights over it yet, so…someone care to explain?"

The mess hall was deathly quiet, and then the same merc who'd tried to leave stood up and spread her hands.

"I think that was me, boss," she confessed while Kira's headware brought up her information. Tijana Roy was an environmental tech for *Deception*. She'd been an environmental tech for *Conviction* for over a decade before that, and her home was a system Kira had never heard of in the Inner Rim.

"And just *what* did you do?" Kira asked.

"Sorg over there burned his toast well and good," she said, pointing at one of the Brisingr hands. "I made a joke about it being DLI-style toast. That went down like a broken antigrav plate and, well…"

She shrugged.

"Too soon, I think," she conceded. The DLI-O54 System had been where *K79-L* had destroyed dozens of civilian outposts to cover her destruction of a Redward ship in a testing engagement—killing tens of thousands along the way.

Kira leveled her flattest gaze on the mercenary tech.

"Yes," she agreed, then turned the same gaze on the brawlers.

"Really?" she said to them. "You started a fight over a tasteless joke?"

Both contingents looked sheepish.

"It…went downhill from there," one of the Redward techs admitted.

"So it did." Kira surveyed them. "Everyone in this room is docked a half-day's pay," she told them. "This ends now and is forgotten. Mostly. If it happens again…"

She drew her finger across her throat in an ancient and evocative gesture.

"Am I clear?"

"Yes, sir!"

"Now. You are *all* going to help Em Bartolomeo clean up his mess and then report to your duty stations before I decide that's not enough. *Am I clear?*"

"*Yes, sir!*"

THE CAPTAIN'S private dining room was significantly smaller than the main crew mess halls, though it was larger than was needed for the three officers sitting around the table, watching the recording of Kira's little speech.

"Well, that was inevitable," Bueller finally said. "Ugh. I need a drink."

In answer to a wordless command from Zoric, a panel in one side of the dining room opened and a flat-topped robot trundled out. The artificial stupid crossed over to Bueller and popped up a fifty-centimeter hologram of an androgynous-looking bartender.

"What can I mix for you, sir?" the artificial stupid asked cheerfully.

"I forgot Captain Sitz had that," he noted. "I'll have a screwdriver."

The robot happily chirped. A few seconds of whirring later, a glass emerged from a panel with what Kira *presumed* to be the mixed vodka-and-orange-juice drink he'd ordered.

"Beer," she told the robot as it rolled over to her. "Redward Black Bear if you have it."

"Of course," the AS replied. "Captain Zoric has provided me with data on the preferences of key officers, and I make certain to have them on hand."

A frosted bottle of the dark ale emerged from the robot as Kira laughed. She took it—and Zoric didn't even bother giving the robot instructions. It produced a gin and tonic for her without asking, then returned to its cubby.

"I'm honestly surprised we've made it this far without an incident," Kira admitted after taking a swallow of the beer. "DLI-O-Fifty-Four was an inevitable spark point, an atrocity no one in the Cluster is likely to forget."

"I know," Bueller said quietly. "Least of all the Brisingr hands on this ship. We were there, we were *responsible*, but we couldn't do *anything*. No one left aboard this ship gave those orders. No one here had a chance to even intervene."

"If I remember the report correctly, you blew Sitz's head off yourself," Zoric said. "I'm guessing that was satisfying."

The big engineer grimaced.

"First and only person I've killed with my own hands," he admitted. "And in her case, fuck if it wasn't easier than I expected. Most of what happened in DLI was her call. The Director added some extras, but the plan was hers."

Sitz had been *K79-L*'s Captain, the woman with her finger on the self-destruct button when Bueller had disabled the system and shot her.

"I think if we distribute this little recording, it will remind people of where our Brisingr hands stand," Zoric suggested. "Though...seriously, Konrad? Your people can't go home?"

"Nooo." Bueller shook his head and swallowed a probably over-large mouthful of the cocktail. "*Definitely* more me than the rest, but *treason* is the word you're looking for. That's the description of handing a Brisingr capital ship over to a *mercenary squadron* working for a ninth-rate power on the edge of the Rim.

"That's excluding the fact that all of us were entirely open with the RRF shipyard people as we went through the ship. The RRF now knows almost as much about the K70 class as anyone in the Brisingr Kaiserreich Navy.

"Even the most junior of the crew who stayed is guilty of at least two types of treason—and then we factor in that all of the *spacer*s were still active-duty BKN personnel, seconded to the exploration company. So, add *desertion* to the list.

"Desertion in time of peace, but all we'd get back home is a jail cell," he reminded them. "That's how pissed the people who are left are at the Equilibrium Institute, Kavitha, Kira. They made us murderers and we will never forgive them for that."

The dining room was silent, and Kira took a long drink from her beer bottle.

"Distribute the speech if you think it will help," she told Zoric. "For now, though...I believe this was a dinner invite?"

"Yeah. Let me call David," Zoric told them. "I figured we'd get this out of the way first. The tension between my old mercs, Bueller's ex-BKN hands and the new Redward recruits... It's a pain in my ass."

"If we've only had one fistfight, I think we're doing just fine," Kira replied. "That's what I'd expect from an actual professional military... which we are most definitely *not*."

20

"I READ the database entries on that planet and looked at pictures, and I *still* think it's uglier in person."

Davidović's observation summed up Kira's feelings on Wilhelm. The planet was on the small side, with barely sixty percent of Earth's gravity, with a barely breathable atmosphere, no potable water, and an average temperature that would turn any potable water to ice.

Somehow, it still had plant and animal life. None of said life was edible to humans, but it did provide the barely breathable atmosphere.

"About a third of the population of the Costar Clans lives on Wilhelm," Zoric replied. "Twelve million people, with another four million stretched across the system. The asteroids here are worth mining, and I think *every* inhabited system in the Cluster has made a go at colonizing Wilhelm."

"And ran out of resources to ship food," Davidović said. "I'm familiar with the history."

"More importantly," Kira cut in, "what are we seeing for threats?"

She was in her Hoplite, but the Coalition Fleet hadn't launched their fighters yet. She wasn't seeing *anything* in terms of mobile threats on her own feeds, which made her nervous.

"There are fixed orbital defenses above Wilhelm, but they're trash,"

Davidović told her. "We had a plan to actually use missiles against them."

Kira blinked.

"They can't be *that* bad," she argued. The stations would have multiphasic jammers aboard, even if they hadn't come online yet.

"Orbital dynamics are orbital dynamics," Davidović said. "They don't have the Harrington coils to maneuver much, so smart missiles can nail down their positions with a decent degree of accuracy before they enter the jamming zone."

"They still have plasma guns," Kira pointed out. "I'm not sure the missiles are *that* cheap."

Even if the stations were completely unable to move themselves from their fixed orbits, they'd be able to shoot down missiles by the dozen in the final light-second, where the artificial stupids would have to basically fly straight.

"Cheaper than dead ships," Zoric said. "Scans are clear of ships, Basketball. Looks like even the freighters have left the system. It's creepy as hell and worrying."

Kira's headware pinged on the fleet command channel and she switched over.

"Basketball.

"Demirci, it's Admiral Kim. Are your people seeing what we're seeing?"

"If you mean *nothing*, yeah," Kira agreed, reviewing the data in the virtual display in front of her. "We're making seven fortresses and about two hundred defensive satellites in orbit of Wilhelm. One of the asteroid habitat clusters has two fortresses and thirty or so satellites. Everything that can nova appears to be gone."

"That's exactly what I'm seeing," Kim said. "We fabricated around a thousand smart missiles to use against the Wilhelm fortresses. Analysis says we'll lose ninety percent of them, but it doesn't take many big nukes to mission-kill fortresses that small."

"That wasn't in the plan dockets I went over," Kira said. "When did that happen?"

"This was somewhere around Plan N, Demirci," the Admiral replied. "We were expecting to have to clear gunships and corvettes.

What's making me think twice is that they haven't raised their jammers. They're waiting to see what we do."

"They might be thinking about surrender," Kira said slowly. "That would fit. We shredded their fixed defenses without losses at Arti, and enough ships left Arti that they know what we did."

"Agreed." The Coalition Fleet commander was silent for a few seconds. "I trust your judgment, Kira. Most of the rest of our subcommanders have blood going back years with the Clans. What do you think?"

Kira hadn't even considered that, but Kim was right. The Costar Clans had been *the* primary opponent of any significant military force in the Cluster for a century—and the honors, by and large, had been pretty even.

Every senior officer in the Coalition Fleet had killed Costar Clans raiders and lost crews to them in turn. Even Kim, who was bending over backward to follow her King's orders.

"I think it costs you nothing to talk and could save lives on both sides," she finally said. "If we can get the Kaiser Clans to surrender without a fight, that's half the population of the Costar Clans under Redward protection. Half their systems."

"Only about a third of their industry and their raider construction," Kim countered. "The Kiln is the biggest source of their actual ships. But you're right. A chance for a bloodless victory.

"Thank you."

"You're the one who has to talk them down," Kira said. "Good luck."

———

FOR THE SECOND time in a week, Kira watched as Admiral Ylva Kim sent a mass transmission to the Costar Clans. This time, an entire planet was getting the transmission—a planet that had been settled and abandoned at least fourteen times. Each colony had left behind a small cluster of determined homesteaders who wouldn't give up their new farms.

Those farms and the assorted abandoned miners had built a series of hardscrabble communities across the planet. Twelve million people sounded like a lot, but it was nothing versus a planet. The largest settlement any of the Coalition Fleet could detect was maybe half a million people.

"Kaiser Clans, I am Admiral Ylva Kim," Kim introduced herself. "From the absence of nova-capable shipping in the Kaiser System, I assume you are aware of the existence and mission of the Coalition Fleet.

"It is my task, as mandated by the monarchs of the Redward System and by the leadership of the systems of the Syntactic Cluster Free Trade Zone, to bring an end to the threat of the Costar Clans' raiders.

"When the dust settles here today, the Kaiser System will be a protectorate of the Kingdom of Redward," she said firmly. "Ulli Novak is already preparing their divisions for an assault landing on Wilhelm and hostile boarding operations on the stations and habitats throughout this system.

"We have a plan in place to neutralize your orbital defenses. You lack the industry and technology of a major inhabited system and so you lack the traditional invulnerability of a home system.

"We are aware of the situations and problems that you have faced here in Kaiser. We of Redward are as guilty as anyone else of failing to provide the support you needed to survive. That changes today. As a protectorate of the Redward crown, King Larry and Queen Sonia will take direct responsibility for your situation.

"Tomorrow will be a better day for us all," Kim told them. "But today you must decide if that tomorrow is one you will accept peacefully. Stand down your defensive stations and turn over control of your armories to Major General's Novak's people, and this transition can happen with a minimum of bloodshed—hopefully none.

"Fight me and I will break your defenses with fire and steel. I have fought the Costar Clans for my entire professional career. I will not weep to send more of your raiders to hell—but that is the past that we must all put behind us if the Syntactic Cluster is to rise above what we have been.

"My King, my Queen, they see a future where we stand together. I will work toward that vision until my dying breath. Your children will benefit from that vision no matter what you do today...but if you stand down, so will you."

The transmission ended and Kira studied her scanners. The orbital forts' jammers were still down. Everything looked very quiet.

"Helmet," she hailed Sagairt. "Get your interceptors into space for assault-shuttle escort duty. Hold back the fighter-bombers for now but have them prep for mass launch."

"What are you thinking, Commodore?" Sagairt said.

"I think the Admiral's little speech might have an effect. I'm also thinking that I trust the Clans and the Institute as I far as I can throw that planet over there. So, let's be very, *very* paranoid."

"I can live with that. Interceptors launching. Standing by for updates from the Admiral."

Kira cut the channel and turned her attention to the gray and ill-looking world ahead of them.

"Well?" she murmured. "Are we playing games?"

"Commodore, we have a signal from the surface," Davidović reported. "The orbital stations have deactivated their sensors and appear to be commencing an evacuation."

"Signal is for the Admiral?" Kira asked.

"It's broad enough that we're getting it too," the tactical officer reported. "There's a lot of hedging around the fact that nobody actually *runs* all of Wilhelm, but they're ordering the stations to stand down."

"Everyone who wants to fight loaded up and ran," Kira guessed. "Those forts aren't worth anything, so they're concentrating forces for an old-fashioned slugging match with the Coalition Fleet somewhere."

"My guess, too," Davidović agreed. "And given everything I know about the Clans...it's going to be at the Kiln."

"Wonderful," Kira said. "That's our next stop."

21

THE REDWARD ARMY was going to have a busy few years, Kira suspected. The initial landings and boardings had gone unopposed so far, but the people left in Kaiser had been abandoned by their supposed champions.

Taking the Costar Clans Systems was proving easier than she'd feared so far, but *holding* them was going to be another problem. Given time, she had faith in Queen Sonia's ability to keep Redward's promises, but…she didn't necessarily think the Clans were going to give their occupiers that time.

That was the army's problem, though. Her attention was locked on an RRF fast courier making a rapid approach to *Perseus*. She had just poured herself a cup of coffee—some of the Royal Reserve Sonia had given her—when the ship had novaed into Kaiser, and now she was waiting to hear what the news was.

She *had* work to do, but she suspected the courier's cargo was more important than going through the engineers' assessment of whether Wilhelm's orbital forts could support a squadron of Sinister fighter-bombers.

The ping on her headware wasn't really a surprise. A ship-to-ship coms request from *Perseus*.

"Commodore Demirci," she answered it, her gaze still locked on the tactical display. The courier was now physically docked to the carrier, which meant she was well inside the defensive perimeter of the Coalition Fleet.

"Demirci, you can imagine how much crap is on one of our fast couriers right now," Admiral Kim greeted her gruffly. "But there's a My Eyes Only message from the Queen as head of the Office of Integration, and she's requested that I bring you in as well."

"Don't you have senior subordinates of your own?" Kira said with a chuckle. "I'm not objecting to the Queen's trust—or yours, Admiral —but I'm not RRF."

"That's part of why I'm leaning on you, Demirci," Kim told her. "Plus, you have an outside perspective that's valuable. Regardless of whether *I* trust you, Her Majesty clearly does. Shall we see her message?"

"I am at your and Her Majesty's service until the transfers start bouncing," Kira replied. "Link me in."

She flicked the channel to her desk, replacing the tactical display with the image of the blonde admiral. A moment later, the image split, moving Kim into the background as the image of Queen Sonia appeared.

The slim Queen sat behind a massive desk, half-covered in data chips. Her hands were laid flat on the aged wooden surface and her eyes were level...and tired.

"Ylva, Kira, we received your reports from the Arti System," she told them. "It sounds like things went as well as we could hope, though I've bad news for your mission: I need you to accelerate your operations.

"As of my recording this message, our allies supporting the Coalition Fleet are staying in, but I don't know how much longer that's going to last," the Queen said calmly. "I would not count on keeping all of your ships for the full operation. The international situation in the Syntactic Cluster has...clarified but not in a good way."

That sounded bad to Kira. Sonia's Office of Integration was the group responsible for bringing all of the data from the various civil and military intelligence services together under one roof and assembling the best possible view of the outside galaxy from them.

"We have received some formal communication from Bengalissimo since the coup," Sonia told them. "And I have learned that there is apparently a school of thought on Bengalissimo that because the first two monarchs were Queens, Queen Ilaria's eldest daughter should have inherited the throne instead of her eldest child, her son.

"Since no one challenged King Celestino's ascension, *his* daughter's ascension or her son's ascension, that has mostly remained a purely theoretical argument for a certain type of historian or royalist.

"King Isidoro was unquestioned in his rightful claim to his mother's throne," she noted. "Except now he's dead and we have no idea what's happened to his two children. And under that esoteric and forgotten school of thought, the supposedly rightful heir would the eldest daughter of the eldest daughter of the eldest daughter of Queen Ilaria."

Kira realized where this was going and grimaced.

"Which, as it turns out, is Her Royal Majesty Queen Rossella the First, formerly Admiral Rossella Gaspari," Sonia said levelly. "We have received formal notification of her ascension to the throne of Bengalissimo.

"We have *also* received formal notification that Bengalissimo has withdrawn from the Syntactic Cluster Free Trade Zone." Sonia shook her head and sighed. "That's all the formal communication we have received, but I do have sources in the Bengalissimo System."

The whole mess stank of Equilibrium to Kira, but it sounded like Gaspari had kept that inheritance in the back of her mind for a while. Not many people woke up on the wrong side of fifty and suddenly decided that their vague claim to the throne was worth killing a bunch of people for.

"Those sources tell me the tone of Queen Rossella's story so far," Sonia said grimly. "She is claiming that the Yprian Federation is a false front for a Redward occupation of the Ypres System, pointing to the Coalition Fleet campaign against the Clans as proof of our sudden aggression and expansionism.

"I'm not sure of exact numbers, but roughly half of the Parlamento members have been executed for treason for cooperating with the FTZ," the Queen said. "Politicians who strived to make the entire Cluster a better place are now dead, murdered for having not somehow put Bengalissimo above all others."

Sonia looked at the recorder.

"I am finding it difficult not to be spectacularly angry at Queen Rossella," she admitted. "But we cannot make decisions that turn the fates of stars and millions of souls based on our personal feelings.

"We will attempt to negotiate with Rossella, but I expect that her anti-FTZ position will make many of the smaller members of both the FTZ and the Coalition Fleet nervous. We will see them withdraw their ships to secure their own systems and nearby trade-route stops.

"While it feels hypocritical, I urge you to move against the next system as quickly as possible. We must secure as many of the Clan Systems as we can while we have the resources. We will not hold those systems and ships to their promises when they are afraid."

A simplified three-dimensional map of the Cluster appeared in front of Sonia, showing the positions of Redward, Ypres and Bengalissimo. The three stars formed an even-sided triangle, with Redward at the center of the Cluster, Ypres at the inner coreward side, and Bengalissimo sitting north of them at the "top" of the Cluster relative to old Earth.

"Given our general lack of communication from the new Bengalissimo government, we're mostly guessing on what they're going to do next," the Queen reminded them. "That said, most of my analysts are agreed that they're going to have to move against Ypres, given their propaganda. We expect to see some attempt at blockading the Ypres System in the near future...and with it, the entire Syntactic Cluster.

"Until Bengalissimo moves, the Costar Clans remain the largest known threat in the Cluster. If at all possible, we want them neutralized *before* we need to move against Rossella. In all honesty..."

Sonia sighed.

"In all honesty, I can't imagine that will be possible. Even if the Equilibrium Institute wasn't involved in Rossella's coup, their usual policies would almost certainly lead to them putting their resources in our region at her disposal. Given what we know about Cobra

Squadron, she will shortly have the resources to court a full war with Redward and Ypres.

"A war we may well not be able to win. A war we definitely will *not* win if we are fighting the Clans on the other front. Finish your mission, Kim, Demirci. The entire Cluster's fate may depend on it."

Sonia's image froze and Kira exhaled a long sigh.

"No pressure, I see, Admiral," she told Kim.

"Or something like that," Kim agreed. "Your thoughts, Commodore?"

"Gaspari is an Equilibrium asset and probably has been in their pocket for at least as long as I've been in the Cluster," Kira replied. "Another backup plan—or potentially the original main plan. If they've been quietly helping her get ready for this all along, it's entirely possible the Clans were always intended to fail—but against *her*."

"Thankfully, she's limited to the resources of the Bengalissimo Fleet and whatever the Institute can put at her disposal," the Admiral said. "That gives us some advantages."

"Her brother runs the company that built Bengalissimo's cruisers," Kira pointed out.

The channel was silent for several seconds.

"Fuck." Kim met Kira's gaze. "You're sure."

"We don't know the Cluster, so we did the research," the merc said. "Victory Star Manufacturing is publicly traded, but a majority of its voting rights are held by members of the Gaspari family—with Luigi Gaspari, Rossella's younger brother, holding thirty-five percent and acting as chairman and CEO."

"You think they've built more ships."

"I think the Gasparis could have funded entire cruiser groups out of their own pockets," Kira admitted. "And I think that the Institute has likely been funneling them money for years.

"I don't know how she's going to explain it when she produces her new ships, but I'd guess that the BF is going to double in strength in the next couple of weeks. *And* she has that entire mercenary fleet from Ypres *and* Cobra Squadron."

Kira shook her head.

"If it's war, Admiral Kim, we might just be outgunned. Even with *Deception* and *Conviction* and the new nova fighters—because if Rossella has been an Institute agent, *they* may well have nova fighters too."

"How can the Institute bring so many resources to bear out here?" Kim asked. "We're nothing, the edge of fucking nowhere. All we want is to make the Cluster a better place."

"And they think your plan will destroy the Cluster," Kira said. "I don't know where their resources come from, Admiral, beyond that they come from much closer to Sol. The amount of money they're throwing around out here is *nothing* to a Meridian interstellar corporation.

"They're ruining the FTZ with their pocket change."

Kim echoed Kira's earlier sigh but nodded firmly.

"Well, there's only one thing I can really do with all of this," she admitted. "Tell Captain Zoric to get *Deception* ready to nova, Commodore. My gut feeling is that the Clans will fight us at the Kiln— and that was next on my schedule anyway.

"Let's get this fleet moving."

22

"ALL RIGHT, EVERYONE, LISTEN UP."

Kira's pilots and senior officers were scattered around the briefing room in a semi-organized chaos. The room wasn't really designed to handle *both* the ship's officers and the pilots, but she wanted to make sure everyone was on the same page.

That meant they'd crammed a collection of folding chairs in around the fixed seats for the fighter wing, and several people had clearly decided to stand instead of risking them—including Bueller, who was holding up the wall next to the exit.

"Some of you have already been to the Kiln," she continued. "Specifically, some of us have *vivid* memories of Cluster Sixty-Five-X-Nine and the construction base belonging to the Costar Clans' Warlord Anthony 'Deceiver' Davies."

They'd lost friends there when it had turned out Davies's support from the Equilibrium Institute had included multiple Brisingr-built D9C heavy destroyers capable of taking on Redward-built cruisers and a swarm of heavy fighters.

"In six hours, we're going back," Kira said calmly. "Our destination today is Cluster Forty-Two-K-Seven, the site of the very first attempt by a Cluster power to exploit the Kiln. It failed, for much the same reasons as the rest of them: a lack of political will and financial support to provide food and replenishables for an interstellar facility.

"No one in the Cluster really understood what maintaining facilities in another star system was going to take in terms of resources, time and money," she concluded. "I was honestly surprised by how much extra the current Redward plan for the system has baked in. I half-expected them to underestimate the cost of uplifting these star systems."

She made a throwaway gesture. That she was actually impressed by and confident in Queen Sonia's plan for the Costar Clans wasn't relevant to today's briefing.

"But the repeated and consistent failures in these systems are where the Clans were born," she reminded everyone. "Cluster Forty-Two-K-Seven, while not necessarily the richest or most powerful set of habitats in the Kiln, is the oldest. Home to roughly three million people, the habitats act as the closest thing the Kiln—or the Clans in general, to be honest—have to a central capital.

"We are novaing in ten million kilometers from the Cluster and will move to reduce its defenses as quickly as possible," she continued. "We do not expect the Kiln to have been abandoned the way Kaiser was. Our estimate, in fact, is that the warships from Kaiser will be here —and, with some confidence, we expect them to be in place to defend Cluster Forty-Two."

A mental command brought up what information they had on Cluster 42K7 in a holographic display in front of her. It wasn't much.

"Given how limited our intelligence is, the first stage of the plan is a testing attack," she told them. "We're going to open up with the missiles we fabricated to use against Wilhelm."

She shrugged.

"They're not going to *achieve* anything, but they will give us a better idea of what's out there. Once that is completed, the Sinisters from *Perseus* will launch an initial fighter strike. With the squadron we left in Kaiser under Major Herrera, that's only fourteen fighters. Again, it's a test, and their orders are to prioritize survival and information."

Kira was grimly sure they were still going to lose several of

Sagairt's fighters, but they *needed* the information the multiphasic jammers were going to deny them.

"Once we have that information, we will assess whether or not to launch a general nova-fighter strike prior to the main engagement," she continued. "Most likely, we will go in shortly—as soon as the Sinisters have rearmed—targeting the enemy corvettes and any nova fighters they have.

"We expect to be encountering both a D9C heavy destroyer and a small number of Weltraumpanzer-Fünfs," she reminded them. "We don't know for certain that Davies lives, but one of his destroyers did survive our last trip here, and we can assume she'll show up for this.

"Even so, we expect the weight of metal and firepower to be heavily in our favor. Our biggest concern is third-party intervention." She looked around the room, assessing how much her people truly believed that.

Despite everything, she knew that not even all of her *pilots* truly believed that the Equilibrium Institute existed.

"I expect, at a minimum, the arrival of a contingent of mercenary destroyers to try and sucker-punch us," she told them. "We can also be reasonably sure we're going to see the survivors of the nova group that hit the King and Queen's transport in Redward.

"Normally, I would press the initial attack with our fighters and try to neutralize as many of the enemy's light and medium ships as possible prior to the clash of the main fleets," she noted. "Given the expectation of a stab in the back, however, we will be holding our positions inside the Coalition Fleet as much as possible.

"We are not the striking sword today. Today we watch the Fleet's back and make sure we don't get shanked."

She looked around at her people again.

"Questions?"

———

AS HER PEOPLE DRIFTED OUT, Kira was somehow unsurprised that all five of her old Apollon hands remained. Bueller was one of the last to leave as well. He looked like he was waiting for her, then looked at the five still seated and shrugged at her before heading out.

Finally, there were only the original Memorials left, and Kira leaned on the lectern and looked them over.

"Well?" she asked. "What's the trap this time?"

Cartman laughed.

"I dunno; is this a trap?" she asked, then produced a case of Black Bear beer from under her seat. "Seems like a good chance for us all to grab one last drink together."

"We should probably try to avoid being too much of a clique, you know," Kira observed. She took a beer anyway. "On the other hand, I guess we are the shareholders."

"And the old Memorials are special and everyone knows it," Colombera told her, taking a beer of his own. "We've been through a lot in your wake, Basketball."

"And we might not all make it through what's coming tomorrow," Patel added grimly. "If Cobra Squadron jumps the fleet, we'll be outnumbered two to one by people with better nova fighters."

"But not better pilots," Kira said. "You've all done a good job of working with the old Conviction hands and the best of the Redward pilots. The Coalition Fleet's nova fighters might not be what I'd like them to be, but there is a shortage of perfect demigods in the world."

"Yeah, just six of us," Hoffman replied with a chuckle. "Probably should have kept Konrad, but even he knows we're a special lot."

"He's getting laid before we nova; he doesn't get to complain," Kira told the older pilot with a grin. "I made sure there was a gap in *both* of our schedules for it."

Her subordinates—her *friends*—laughed at that.

"But yes. If you want to pull a party like this, we should probably be pulling Konrad in," she told them. "Maybe even Kavitha and Milani, too. They're almost as good with us as we are with each other. And we need them."

"I can't say I ever expected to command a squadron flying off a Brisingr heavy cruiser on the ass end of nowhere," Cartman said after draining half of her beer. "We've made more new friends out here than

I was afraid of when we left home, but I'll be damned if I wasn't terrified when we came out here."

"Those of us that made it made it one step ahead of assassins and bounty hunters," Kira said quietly. Several of the old Three-Oh-Three pilots had died *in* Redward when people chasing the Brisingr death mark had caught up to them.

They hadn't seen any bounty hunters in a while. They had a *reputation* out there now, and no one wanted to tangle with them.

"To absent friends," Michel said, raising her beer. "Never forgotten, for all that happens."

"Absent friends," Kira agreed. "Absent friends and new homes. Redward has been good to us, but so has *Conviction* and now *Deception*. I don't know about you lot, but this ship is more home to me than anywhere else now."

Hoffman chuckled and gestured around at the other pilots. He had to wave vaguely over Patel, as his boyfriend was well inside his personal space.

"Home to me isn't a ship or a planet anymore," he admitted. "It's you lot. We went through one war together. I'm not afraid of what Bengalissimo is bringing. I'm not afraid of the Equilibrium Institute.

"Not so long as we're together."

"Hey, be careful with jinxing us like that!" Colombera snapped. "This isn't going to be easy and we can't afford bad luck when we're going out there later."

"Didn't say it would be easy," Hoffman countered. "I agree with you, in fact. It's going to be ugly and it's gonna be messy, but I see two definite upsides to all of this."

"Oh?" Kira asked.

"First, that we're going in together," her most senior subordinate told her.

"And second, that if Anthony Davies survived the last time we came to the Kiln, *this* time we are *definitely* going to scatter his ashes across the star system," Joseph Hoffman said grimly. "If that fucker is still breathing, I don't think any of us or the old *Conviction* hands are done with him yet."

Kira bared her teeth in what was definitely *not* a smile. Her first encounter with Anthony Davies had ended with Daniel Mbeki, a man she'd been rapidly falling in love with, dead in space.

Konrad Bueller was growing on her by the day, but Mbeki's loss was still a sore spot.

"Fair," she allowed. "If Davies is still alive, we're *definitely* going to have to finish the job."

23

THREE CRUISERS, a carrier, eight destroyers, ten corvettes and eight gunships novaed in a single pulse of blue light. Kira had every datafeed she could access feeding to the cockpit of her Hoplite, her mental finger hovering over the *scramble all fighters* command.

Cluster 42K7 was a million and a half kilometers ahead of them, but there was no missing the gathered Costar Clans fleet. Kira had agreed with Kim that the Costar Clans were likely to make a stand at the Kiln, but they'd also clearly identified 42K7 as the most likely target for the Coalition Fleet.

She activated the command, exhaling as *Deception*'s gravity generators flung her starfighter into space. *Perseus* was deploying as well, and within moments, sixty-four nova fighters were forming up in a defensive formation in front of the fleet.

Kira had them linked up in laser coms without even thinking—and then realized the fleet hadn't brought up their multiphasic jammers. Neither had the Clan fleet, which had to know they were there by now.

"We have resolution on the defending fleet," Davidović reported from *Deception*. "One D9C heavy destroyer, fourteen corvettes, one hundred and forty-five gunships. We're still resolving defensive installations, but it looks like half a dozen armed asteroids that don't deserve the title of *fortress* and fifty or so weapon satellites."

"Do you see nova fighters?" Kira asked. "If the D9C is here, there should be Weltraumpanzers."

"I don't see any, but they could be aboard the asteroid forts or docked at a habitat," the tactical officer replied. "They wouldn't be in space, would they?"

"Maybe not," Kira allowed, then switched to the laser-com web. "Coalition Fleet Nova Group, form on me! Make sure your laser links hold up and stand by."

The plan called for the missiles to be salvoed first, but Kira was surprised by the complete lack of jamming in the battlespace so far. The Clan fleet was definitely maneuvering on her feeds now, forming up with the heavy destroyer in the center.

Cubic meter for cubic meter, the D9C was the second-most powerful unit in the battlespace. The Clans' corvettes and gunships, however, were the least powerful units by the same metric. Quantity had a quality all its own, though, and a hundred and sixty ships made for a *lot* of quantity.

Then the artificial stupid that helped run her fighter's coms informed her that the Clans were transmitting. It was a broadly directional unencrypted message the entire Coalition Fleet was going to receive.

With a sigh, Kira started it and then glared at the image of a man she'd hoped she'd already killed. She'd never actually met Anthony Davies in person, but she was familiar with file footage of the man.

He'd aged a lot since then, she noted with a certain degree of schadenfreude. A new, ugly scar rose from the right side of his neck, wrapping across his face in a way that suggested they'd come damn close to killing him last time.

But he was alive, wearing a plain black shipsuit with a golden vulture emblazoned across his right breast as he faced a holorecorder.

"Coalition Fleet, I am Anthony Davies," he told them. Kira *had* heard his voice before, when he'd deceived *Conviction* into maneuvering most of her fighters out of position by pretending to be a beleaguered freighter Captain.

"I have been many things to you and to my people," he continued, and if his voice was just as gruff as it had been when she'd first heard it, there was a gravelly edge to it. The scar had clearly done something to his vocal cords.

"Today, I am charged to speak with you as the new Marshal of the Costar Clans, tasked with the defense of our homes and our culture." He spread his hands wide. "Today, I am not a raider or a pirate. Today, I am a man standing between my home and those who would crush all that we are."

He shook his head.

"I could make a grand speech about your crimes, but we all know your mission here. You seek to end us and wrap that truth in pretty lies of future dreams.

"We will not lay down and die for your shining future," Davies told them. "We are the Costar Clans, born in adversity and abandonment, forged in the fires of your neglect and betrayal. This is *our* star.

"Leave or be destroyed."

The transmission ended and Kira glared at the space where the pirate had stood. She didn't want to *sympathize* with the bastard, but she had to concede his point. The Clans had been born out of the rest of the Cluster walking away from the systems they now controlled. They had every reason to distrust Redward's promises of help and a better future.

Even *Kira* wasn't sure that Redward would be able to afford to fulfill those promises in the long run. She trusted that they would *try*, though, and that was all anyone could ask.

In the end, though, Davies had also spoken to *why* the Coalition Fleet was there: he might be defending his people today, but he *was* a pirate, a raider and a murderer. Without some guarantee that the Clans would stop stealing from everyone else, the SCFTZ couldn't tolerate their existence.

"All ships, this is Admiral Kim," the Admiral's voice cut into her thoughts. "I don't see a reason to reply to the Deceiver, but I wanted to remind you all what kind of man we're facing.

"Anthony Davies is directly linked to the capture or destruction of over a hundred and fifty freighters in the Cluster," Kim reminded them all. "Thousands of dead, billions of kroner in theft and destruction.

"And remember that the man who speaks of defending his culture and people killed thousands of his *own* people to destroy the shipyards he'd built when it looked like Redward would capture them. Those were civilians, not pirates or soldiers, people we meant no harm— people *he* killed.

"*His* people."

Kim paused.

"Anthony Davies was named the Deceiver for good reason. Do not let his claims of being a grand defender allow you to forget what he is and what he does. Men like him are why we are here, because we cannot trust the Clans to honor any deal that called for them to give up piracy.

"The age of pirates like Anthony Davies must end. He knows this and he will fight us till the end, no matter how many of the people he says he will protect get killed along the way.

"The point of today's mission is to *end* the dying, the piracy, the raids and counter-raids, the violence and destruction," Kim concluded. "I won't claim we are here to *save* the Clans. We are here to crush the Clans' piracy.

"We hope that the Clans' *people* will benefit from this, but our priority is to protect the Cluster from monsters like Anthony Davies."

There was a grim silence.

"And on that note, raise jammers and prepare for missile launch."

EVEN AS THE multiphasic jammers turned Kira's sensor feeds into a chaotic mess, she still turned a curious eye and her fighter's optics toward the clouds of small spacecraft taking shape around *Last Denial* and *Guardian*.

In twenty years of service with the Apollo System Defense Force, she had *never* seen anyone use missiles. They were so vulnerable to multiphasic jamming that they were entirely useless. Anything that was slow enough that it could be easily targeted by something that couldn't localize it inside the last light-second of the approach had more than enough defenses to vaporize an almost-infinite number of incoming weapons.

Since the Coalition Fleet had *built* the weapons, however, Admiral Kim had seen no reason not to *use* them. For the first time in Kira's entire career, she watched over a thousand sets of Harrington coils light up simultaneously.

They blurred out of the jamming zone in short order, and Kira lost immediate track of them. She was still receiving updates via a serial laser link to a set of sensor probes positioned outside the jamming field.

Those probes and laser links wouldn't hold up to the serious maneuvering of a real fight, but right now the Coalition Fleet was holding position while they studied their enemies—and Davies clearly had no inclination to start the fight sooner than he had to.

That made Kira suspicious, but it wasn't like they weren't expecting a trap.

Even through the multiphasic jamming, it was clear that the Clans had no idea what they were even looking at. Kira was a fully trained military officer with a background in military history. She was entirely familiar with smart munitions and their limited use in deep space combat.

The crews aboard the Costar Clans' warships didn't have that education. Their ships' anti-meteor systems could handle the incoming fire on their own, Kira suspected, but the Clans' warships were trying to expand their formation, visible in an expansion of the multiphasic-jamming bubble.

She wasn't sure what they thought they were achieving, though she could see a logic to it. The ships could be trying to open up lines of fire and make it easier for them to engage missiles targeting the other ships.

Of course, the vast majority of the missiles weren't *aimed* at the ships. It wouldn't take much maneuvering to render the missiles' targeting solutions on the ships useless. Most of the missiles were aimed at the handful of fortified asteroids defending Cluster 42K7.

Once the missiles entered the Clans' jamming field, they were lost to the sensors of their launching ships. Long-range optics on the remote probes could establish *some* details of what was going on inside a multiphasic-jamming field, but not enough to track a smart munition barely three meters long.

They *could* track the asteroid station that came apart under a dozen hundred-megaton warheads, to the shock of everyone who'd been involved in the decision to fire the missiles. Their optics could roughly pick out explosions when the warheads actually managed to detonate, and the computers could interpolate multiple sets of data to estimate the presence, if not the location, of ships.

Out of over a thousand missiles, fired at a force that had *no* idea of how to handle the weapons and no doctrine for antimissile defense, twenty-six of the Coalition Fleet's weapons had survived to detonate and taken out one asteroid fort.

That was twenty-six more detonations and one more kill than Kira had actually expected. She waited for the computers to make their final assessment and then checked that she still had a laser link to Colonel Sagairt.

"Helmet, stage two is go," she told the Colonel. "Fly carefully."

"Got it," Sagairt replied. "*Perseus*-Alpha, *Perseus*-Bravo...nova and attack!"

EVEN A FIVE-LIGHT-SECOND NOVA had a full minute's cooldown. They could see the moment that the two squadrons of fighter-bombers emerged, and Kira had to keep herself from holding her breath as the seconds ticked away.

Several explosions were visible through the jamming as she counted, too big to be nova fighters, and Kira let the cheers on the fighter network go on for several seconds.

"Belay that," she finally ordered. "We don't know what's happened until they're back."

Normally, there'd be a rendezvous point in deep space where they'd lower their multiphasic jamming for updates. With the potential threat of Cobra Squadron, Kira had set the rendezvous point directly behind the Coalition Fleet.

If someone jumped the capital ships, the fighters would all be available. It delayed her update when they did nova back, which meant she *was* holding her breath after the sixty seconds elapsed.

Eleven seconds after the nova strike was completed, the laser comlinks were reestablished.

"Helmet reporting in," Sagairt greeted her. "Strike complete; downloading data on enemy formation and positions to the Fleet." He paused. "Two ships down. I *think* Bravo-Six managed to eject the pods for both crew. I...don't think Alpha-Four did."

"Damn," Kira murmured. "We'll retrieve them, Helmet. You have my word."

"Understood. Mark up two corvettes and four gunships for *Perseus* wing, sir," Sagairt concluded. "We didn't even get near the destroyer. That's what got Alpha-Four killed."

Kira could look up the callsigns and names of the four people on those two starfighters, but she held off. There would be time for that later.

"Take the Sinisters back to *Perseus* to rearm and hold for further orders, Helmet," she ordered. "We're still playing games with these people."

The Coalition Fleet was still declining to advance and the Clans were refusing to come out. The worst part, from Kira's perspective, was that the Clans' force could *afford* to trade gunships for fighters at two to one. They'd still have gunships left afterward, though probably not enough to stand a chance against the Fleet.

"Commodore, it's Kim." The Admiral linked to her again as she reviewed the data from Helmet's strike. "Your assessment?"

"About what you'd expect," Kira replied. "The Clans have put their best on the decks today. They're short on anti-fighter experience, but they've got enough firepower to make up for that. If we launch a mass strike, it'll be more effective than sending in two squadrons but we'll leave the Fleet unprotected.

"We're reasonably sure Davies has at least half a dozen

Weltraumpanzers of his own, but we haven't located them yet. If we uncover the fleet, those ships could do a lot of damage."

"Because we don't have much more anti-fighter experience than they do," Kim concluded. "Understood. We'll go with Plan Cataphract, then, Commodore Demirci. Once the Sinisters are rearmed, we will commence the advance.

"I have faith in our cruisers to handle corvettes and one destroyer that outclasses us."

"We'll watch the Fleet's back, sir," Kira promised. "That's what we're here for."

"I have full faith in the nova-fighter group under your command, Demirci. I'm not releasing you for an independent strike, but beyond that...nova-fighter operations are at your discretion. I do not expect you to remain with the battle line if you see an opportunity or a need."

"Understood, Admiral."

Kira turned her attention back to the feeds from the drones and the ships around her.

"All fighters, this is Basketball. Plan is Cataphract. Assume defensive formation around the Fleet, but keep your eyes peeled," she ordered. "We're watching for Davies's Weltraumpanzers and we're watching for Cobra Squadron.

"The Fleet can handle a bunch of raggedy-ass corvettes and gunships. *We're* here to handle the fuckers with the nova bombers who jumped King Larry. They *don't* get to the Fleet."

24

PARTLY DUE TO her own specializations and partly due to the nature of the war between Apollo and Brisingr, Kira had never been present for a straight-battle-line slugging-match fight between nova ships. Her involvement in that kind of fight had usually been preliminary, with the nova fighters softening up enemy cruisers and then withdrawing to cover the carriers as the Apollon battle cruisers moved in.

Today that wasn't an option, and she held her Hoplite near *Deception* as the two multiphasic-jamming zones merged and the battle was joined. Communications were already growing spotty, even the largest capital ships maneuvering heavily to avoid incoming fire.

Deception was the first of the ships to open up. Her targeting optics were better and her guns were bigger and more modern, giving her a small but slight functional range advantage over even the D9C destroyer in the Clans' formation.

The D9C design was of the same vintage as *Deception*, even if this one was probably newer than the heavy cruiser. She was the second ship to open fire—but *Deception* tagged her before she did, heavy plasma bolts hammering into the smaller ship's armor.

More ships joined the fray as they ranged on each other, evasive maneuvers sending the majority of the bursts of plasma spiraling off into deep space. Kira was holding a fragile com network together with her fighters as they hung back out of the fight, their eyes open.

Then the gunships made their move, a wave of over a hundred smaller ships charging forward at maximum power to try and overwhelm the Coalition capital ships.

"Nova fighters, target the gunships," she snapped as soon as she spotted the maneuver. "Break and attack."

It was a trade-off. If they gave up the fragmented but mostly functional com network, the fleet was more vulnerable to a surprise fighter strike—but if the gunships overwhelmed the fleet, there wasn't going to be anything left to protect.

Kira matched her actions to her words, flaring her Hoplite's Harrington coils to full power and lunging forward. She picked a gunship at random, firing careful two-second pulses of plasma fire at the larger ship as she charged.

The gunship didn't see her coming until her fire had torn off one of its turrets. Whoever was in charge was still *good*, and the ten-kilocubic vessel twisted in space, standing on her engines to dodge the next salvo of Kira's fire.

The bigger ship's main guns couldn't really track a nova fighter, but that was why a gunship even *had* turrets. There were still three of them left spitting fire at her as she lined her interceptor up and released the torpedo slowing her down.

A flash of plasma filled the space between her and the gunship. She'd pulled close enough that the larger vessel had no chance to dodge, and a blast equivalent to *Deception*'s main guns hammered into the middle of the gunship, burning a hole bigger than Kira's fighter through the ship.

Power signatures fluctuated for half a second and then the gunship blew apart as her fusion reactor lost containment.

One down.

Kira flipped her fighter instinctively, dodging a stream of fire from another gunship as she searched for targets. Even without the multiphasic jamming emerging from every vessel, the battlespace would have been a chaotic mess. She couldn't track the course of the battle from behind the stick of a starfighter—that was why she'd hired Zoric to command *Deception*, after all.

She was just one more pilot, with her naked eye and some computer-enhanced optics to pick out threats. The gunship shooting at her had earned her attention, and she twisted across its fire, drawing its attention as the *other* spacecraft she'd spotted surged in.

Kira didn't know which of her Weltraumpanzer pilots was on her flank, but their timing was perfect. The Weltraumpanzer-Vier had *much* heavier blaster cannons than her Hoplite-IV did, and the pilot didn't even bother with their torpedoes.

The gunship's attempt to shoot down Kira proved fatal as the heavy fighter's guns blazed in the void. Their torpedoes might have been faster, but the Weltraumpanzer's pilot held the gunship in their sights for a full five-second burst that tore the larger ship in half.

Kira flashed a *thank-you* via laser coms and jetted away, hunting new targets. The tempo of the battle was obvious to her—the Clans had more ships, but the Coalition Fleet's ships were just *that* much bigger and better.

The D9C destroyer was reeling, a defenseless hulk battered to wreckage by *Deception*'s guns. She might be rebuildable—and Kira flagged the hulk as a possibility for retrieval later—but she was out of this fight.

Despite the cubage ratio being heavily in the Costar Clans' favor, it was becoming rapidly clear that they couldn't stand against the bigger ships the Coalition had brought *at all*.

And in the moment Kira thought things were finally decided, the nova fighters arrived. Even through multiphasic jamming, nova emergences were clearly visible, and she cursed herself.

She'd *known* they were going to be ambushed, but she'd grown so used to only dealing with gunships, she hadn't held back any interceptors to defend the capital ships.

On the other hand, she was assessing the situation even as it took shape. There were only twenty flares, and she was already maneuvering toward them. While some of the Redward pilots had let themselves be lured away from the battle line, all of her veterans from *Deception* were still in position to support the fleet.

Kira couldn't give any orders through the jamming, but she didn't *need* to. She knew that even as she was turning her own fighter toward the newcomers, her old ASDF hands and the ex-*Conviction* pilots were doing the same.

So, she noted absently, were about a quarter of the RRF pilots. The rest were catching on as the first fighters changed their course, but many of the Redward pilots definitely had the right instincts.

Kira reached the first nova fighter just as the Weltraumpanzer-Fünf —presumably one of Davies's fighters—pulled straight for a moment to launch their paired torpedoes at *Perseus*.

The nova fighter didn't live that long, her guns tearing into the heavy fighter from below and detonating one of the torpedoes just as it cleared the fighter's hull. A flash of ignited hydrogen and more super-heated plasma tore the spacecraft apart, and Kira flashed on to her next target.

There were more Weltraumpanzers. Almost twice as many as she'd allowed for, and all too many of them *had* launched their torpedoes. There was nothing her people could do to stop the weapons that were already converting into plasma blasts, but the half of the fighters that hadn't launched when her people arrived didn't survive to do so.

Twenty torpedoes still savaged *Perseus* and *Last Denial*. The cruiser weathered her hits decently enough, but *Perseus* was a converted freighter.

Kira looked at the leaking atmosphere her computers were identifying, and a chill ran down her spine. The RRF had done a good job of refitting the ship, but she still had the bones of a sixty-kilocubic bulk hauler.

And the heavy fighters were pressing their attack, charging at the carrier with their heavy guns while her own fighters tried desperately to bring them down.

A Costar Clans fighter died under Kira's guns. Two more to her compatriots. The RRF fighters were in the mix now, desperately trying to salvage their home base as plasma fire savaged the already-damaged carrier.

Then it was over, the surviving heavy fighters novaing out in a series of blue flashes as Kira exhaled a sigh of relief. *Perseus* was battered, probably a write-off, but she looked intact enough to bring her people home.

She pinged *Deception* with a laser.

"Did anyone get a vector on those novas?" she asked.

"Negative," Davidović replied. "We're a bit busy, sir."

The remaining corvettes and gunships were making a hard push at Kira's cruiser. They were paying for the privilege, with multiple ships dying every time the heavy cruiser opened fire, but they were pressing her hard.

Kira was watching the time. She wasn't sure how many of the Weltraumpanzers had escaped, but they had a sixty-second cycle until they could return. They weren't going to get a second pass at *Perseus*; she was grimly certain of that.

But there were twenty-three seconds left on that timer when the second wave of nova flashes lit up across her screens...and it wasn't a mere half-dozen survivors of Davies's squadron coming in now.

Fear froze Kira for a critical second as at least a hundred nova fighters arrived in the battlespace.

25

KIRA'S FEAR gave way to her training and professionalism quickly enough, and she cursed multiphasic jamming as virulently as she ever had. The sheer number of hostile nova fighters was bad enough, but the key was obvious to a twenty-year veteran of nova-fighter warfare: the thirty bombers at the heart of the formation.

Thirty nova bombers charging directly toward the crippled *Perseus* and her two undersized cruiser escorts.

If she'd had coms, she could have coordinated a counter. If she'd had a full nova group of veterans, she wouldn't have *needed* to coordinate anything.

In the realities of the battlespace, all she could do was go after the bombers herself and hope that enough of her people saw the same threat for them to save the capital ships. Her Hoplite whined as she pushed her Harrington coils into overdrive, flashing across the chaos of the jamming to engage the enemy.

The nova fighters turned to meet her, a pair of interceptors flipping out of their formation to protect the bombers from her. Blasters flashed in the void, and Kira barely dodged the incoming fire—and her own went wide.

She'd badly misestimated the maneuverability of the hostile interceptors, and a rock settled into her stomach as her computer analyzed the data it was bringing in. They had at *least* a thirty-percent edge in acceleration on her.

The Hoplite-IVs were supposed to be the fastest fighters in the Syntactic Cluster, top-line ASDF interceptors stolen and covertly shipped two hundred light-years to the fringe of human space. Very few nova fighters in the Rim could match Apollo's finest, and the handful that could exceed those planes were from the very Inner Rim.

To have her outclassed this badly, there was only one possible source for the starfighters coming at her.

Cobra Squadron had finally made their move—and Kira Demirci had no way to tell anybody else what was happening.

She twisted her Hoplite through space, her attempt to reach the bombers secondary to pure survival now. She still needed to get through the defensive formation, though, and only seconds remained.

Measuring the distance and the speed, she fired again—and this time, she *did* hit her target, the more-advanced starfighter proving only slightly more durable than her own as a two-second burst of plasma fire ripped it in half.

Kira charged through the sudden gap in the enemy maneuvers, leaving her second challenger trailing in her wake as she reached her targets.

There were other Coalition nova fighters with her, a scattering of her Hoplites and the Redward Dexters and Sinisters…but not enough. Maybe ten fighters joined her in a desperate strike on the hostile nova bombers.

Plasma fire washed through the hostile formation. Kira watched her own target come apart under her fire with its torpedoes still unfired, but had to twist over the nova bombers as the interceptors came around after her again.

Some of the bombers died. Others novaed out, choosing to preserve their fighters over completing their mission—but Kira was out of options. With Cobra interceptors swarming in on her from multiple angles and every escape cut off, she fell back on the oldest escape of a nova-fighter pilot.

She novaed.

KIRA WASN'T the only one at the secondary rendezvous point. She took a second to throw her fighter's entire power generation into refilling her guns' capacitors and then checked in on her people.

"Report," she ordered.

A cascade of callsigns and status levels came back at her, all of them sounding a bit shaky.

"We're holding our own against those people," she told them. "Get back in there when you can and focus on any remaining bombers. Several of them novaed out with full torpedo loads; those are the key threat.

"Cover the capital ships and watch your asses. We need to get as many people home as possible."

The responses sounded a bit more reassured, but Kira's attention was focused on the minute-old data she was getting from the battle-space. The jamming shredded any chance of really useful data, but she could at least see novas and the loss of capital ships.

It didn't look good. The seconds ticked away toward the moment she'd novaed out, and she realized she'd missed *Perseus* dying. The converted freighter had never been intended to be in the middle of the fight. She should have been left with the troop transports, but that would have required the nova fighters to travel to the Kiln on their own, leaving their drives on cooldown and rendering them useless.

Instead, she'd delivered her starfighters and stuck with the other capital ships because Admiral Kim had figured the carrier was safer with cruisers in company. Now the ship was wreckage, torn apart by Cobra Squadron torpedoes along with a crew of over a thousand.

Fighters were cycling in and out of the rendezvous point as she waited, providing limited updates from their own view of the battle, but Kira paused as Hoffman emerged and downloaded his data.

"Longknife, can you confirm this?" she demanded.

"Yeah. The last of the new fighters novaed out shortly after the Weltraumpanzers returned. I think Davies's people are still in the fight, but the modern bastards are out."

"They'll be back," Kira said grimly. "I'm heading back in. Watch our lost chicks?"

"Always, Basketball," he confirmed. "Shoot straight."

THREE OF THE Redward fighters novaed with her, giving her a formation of four interceptors she could direct for a few seconds. She emerged to find a wing of six Weltraumpanzers charging toward *Deception*—while being the last hostile nova fighters in the battlespace.

"*Perseus* wing, target the hostile Weltraumpanzers. Break and attack!"

The three Dexter interceptors followed her orders and her example, lunging toward the remaining hostiles.

Part of Kira's mind was watching the entire battlespace. *Deception* had moved forward to position herself between the Clans' ships and the Coalition Fleet. There were *far* too few ships left in the latter force and too many left in the former, but her job was the nova fighters.

The heavy fighters' pilots were maneuvering as they closed, trying to evade both *Deception*'s fire and the other nova fighters. They didn't see Kira's wing until it was too late—and that gave her time to assess their maneuvers and work out which two fighters still had torpedoes.

Those were the focus of her initial fire, one of them blowing apart before they even knew they were under attack. The rest of the Weltraumpanzers scattered, the one torpedo-equipped plane trying to get closer to *Deception*—but Davidović's gunners had been paying attention.

A heavy cruiser's main turret wasn't *generally* the right tool for taking out a heavy fighter, but it had the pulse size and rate of fire to make any nova fighter pay if their attention slipped.

The torp-armed heavy fighter *vanished*, the plasma burst that hit it almost as large as the fighter itself.

With a mental salute, Kira spiraled her fighter in space and went after another Weltraumpanzer.

There were only three left and their drive cooldowns had them pinned. She did *not* want to give them a chance to rearm. The Coalition

Fleet was battered enough, with *Deception* the only capital ship still in the fight.

Kira couldn't tell where the RRF cruisers were through the jamming...or even if they were still there. Thirty bombers had hit the Coalition formation. It was entirely possible all three RRF capital ships were gone.

Unfortunately for the Clans, *Deception* remained. The Costar Clans were out of heavier warships, only gunships remaining as they tried to tangle with the massive heavy cruiser. *Deception* was taking a beating, but she was *built* to take a beating.

Kira's guns tore apart the last Weltraumpanzer and she turned her own attention to the gunships. There were maybe fifty left and their formation was chaos. Whatever command-and-control network they'd set up was long gone, probably lost with the bigger ships that anchored it.

The remaining gunships were still dangerous, even to *Deception*. The cruiser might be ten times the size of the smaller nova ships, but there were still *fifty* of them.

She turned her fighter back into the fray. Her guns were at half-charge, which was more than enough to take out a gunship or two if she was careful. The problem was the nova fighters.

If Cobra Squadron came back, the battle was over and she knew it. She didn't know *who* was dead yet, but she could only pick up thirty or so starfighters in the battlespace.

That meant thirty other fighters were gone and at least that many people she was responsible for were dead. Add in the lost carrier and the cruisers... It was a bad day for Redward.

Her focus *had* to be more immediate and she yanked her attention back to the gunships as she blazed toward them. The Clans' warship's focus was mostly on *Deception*, and she wasn't the only nova fighter charging to the big cruiser's aid.

Kira's guns blazed as she closed with one of the light nova warships, hammering plasma into her target's turrets as they tried to bear on *Deception*. Around her, the cruiser's big guns hammered half a dozen of the gunships to debris, and fighters tore into the others.

For a few seconds, the battle still hung in the balance—and then the gunships broke. *They* hadn't novaed to this fight—so they novaed out of it.

Kira had no idea how many of the Clans' ships had survived to run, but she suspected over a hundred of the Clans' nova ships had died in the battle. The Costar Clans could probably have replaced them once, given time, but with three-quarters of their systems and eighty percent of their manufacturing capacity in Redward hands...it looked like piracy in the Cluster might just be over.

The only remaining question was the price, a harsh reality still concealed by multiphasic jamming as Kira maneuvered to watch for returning nova fighters.

While the multiphasic jamming remained, the battle appeared to be over. Nova fighters were slowly falling into formation with each other as they orbited the fleet, searching for the potential of Cobra Squadron's return.

Only silence answered that patient wait, and the jammers slowly began to come down. Kira's systems were slowly able to identify who was left, of both the capital ships and the fighters, and she hated herself for the sigh of relief that escaped when she realized all of her Apollons had once again beaten the odds.

"All jammers down," Zoric's voice said quietly in her as coms reestablished. "I'm... I'm not sure who's in charge, Commodore. Kim was aboard *Perseus* and her second-in-command was aboard *Last Denial*."

Kira knew what Zoric had to mean, but she looked at her scanners to confirm. *Guardian* remained, but the Redward cruiser's energy signature was worrisome. *Perseus* and *Last Denial* were gone. One of Shang's mercenary destroyers was missing, and the rest looked barely better than *Guardian*.

Their gunships were gone. Only three of the corvettes remained, clustering with the remaining destroyers like terrified puppies.

"Someone needs to make contact with Major General Westley," Kira said quietly. Reese Westley was the officer designated to serve as the Kiln's governor. "He might be the best option to take on overall mission command."

She shook her head.

"I'm not sure we even have the firepower to reduce Forty-Two-Kay-Seven's defenses enough to allow for a landing, but I think we have to try," she admitted. "Get Tamboli on the deck and thinking fast. I haven't crunched the numbers yet, but my money says we can fit thirty-four fighters into the hangar if we leave the RRF birds on the deck itself."

She shook her head.

"And I know what these birds are worth to Redward. We're not leaving any of them behind."

26

KIRA WAS on *Deception*'s bridge, unable to sleep or even walk away from the sensor displays, when the Royal Army transports arrived. Major General Westley had clearly picked up the right tone from her message, as the transports' defensive sub-fighters started spilling out the moment they were in the Kiln.

"Okay," she said in a long, exhaling sigh. "Kavitha, can we set up some kind of virtual conference with everybody? Who the hell is in charge now?"

Her cruiser Captain chuckled sadly.

"You're the only one giving orders, Kira," Zoric pointed out. "*You're* in charge."

"Well, fuck."

Kira stared blankly at the sensor displays for a moment while that sank in. Her half-serious Commodore title put her on par with the remaining surviving officers, and given that *Deception* outclassed the rest of the fleet combined…

"All right," she said, repeating the long sigh. "Then we definitely need to pull together that virtual conference. Westley, Shang, senior officer from every national contingent, whoever the *fuck* that is at this point."

"I'll get Harrel on it," Zoric promised. Stef Harrel was the cruiser's communications officer, though Kira's own interactions tended to go through the tactical team. "Any idea what we're planning?"

"Securing Forty-Two-K-Seven to start," Kira replied. "After that..." She shook her head. "We secure the Kiln and then I guess we talk about what happens next. This was Kim's job."

But Ylva Kim was almost certainly dead along with *Perseus*'s crew.

Kira swayed from exhaustion and then carefully took a seat in the observer's chair next to Zoric.

"What a mess," she murmured.

"We survive, we pull through, we get the job done," Zoric told her. "May I make a suggestion, Kira?"

"Sure."

"Activate the flag bridge," the cruiser Captain said. "We haven't really made any use of it since we took the ship, but Bueller and the RRF made sure everything worked. It's got the tools for the kind of conference you want and is the best place to command a task force from."

Kira grimaced. *Task force* was definitely a solid description of what was left of the Coalition Fleet.

"Good call," she admitted. "I'll head there...in a minute."

"I'd say take a nap, but Stef's already on that conference," Zoric told her. "Twenty minutes. Shower?"

"Also a good call," Kira conceded. "I need everything we have on what's left of Forty-Two-K-Seven's defenses forwarded to my head-ware, Kavitha. I know roughly what we've got for resources, so... someone's got to make a plan."

TWENTY MINUTES LATER, Kira was refreshed and sitting in the flag officer's chair on *Deception*'s flag bridge. The K70-class ships had been built as task-group flagships originally, so the working space was more extensive than she'd expected.

Like most spaces on a cubage-limited nova ship, it could always have used extra space, but it was still large enough to feel very empty with only Kira in the room.

Holograms fixed that a moment later as she activated the conference, linking in the assorted officers left of the Coalition Fleet. She surveyed the images silently for a moment, waiting for the last handful to pop in, then smiled as calmly as she could at them all.

"Greetings, everyone," she said. "This is a bit of a mess, and I know damn well that the Coalition Fleet's chain of command didn't go past Rear Admiral Armbruster on *Last Denial*." She gestured around.

"If we want to get technical, we have four Commodores left," she reminded them. "Myself and Commodore Shang are mercenaries. Commodore Shinoda is from the Yprian Federation, but—apologies, Commodore—you have two destroyers left. Commodore Lyon speaks for New Ontario, but..."

"I showed up with a corvette and I'm lucky to still have her," Jackie Lyon said, the dark-haired officer shaking her head. "Commodore Shang's ships were the real contribution from Otovo, New Ontario and Exeteron."

"Technically, Major Generals Westley and Simmons outrank the naval officers here," Kira conceded, gesturing to the two Redward Army officers.

"Neither of us is going to attempt to take command of the naval portion of this operation," Westley said grimly. The dark-haired and lightly bearded man looked like he'd just eaten a lemon, but that appeared to be his constant expression. "Based off what you've just said, I suspect there's only one real choice to command the Coalition Fleet, but that's not my call."

"It's ours," Commodore Shang agreed, the heavily bearded Asian mercenary looking around at the other holograms measuringly. "My friends, *Deception* is operating under the auspices of the RRF, who we all acknowledged as being the premier force of this fleet.

"I propose that we all accept Commodore Demirci as the acting commanding officer of the Coalition Fleet. She was the only one organized enough to bring in the Redward Army ships and assemble this meeting.

"In the face of an enemy with a major nova-fighter force, I think our best choice is the only veteran of a true nova-fighter war we have. I will follow Commodore Demirci's orders until this contract is up."

Kira felt the way the attention of the dozen or so people on the call immediately shifted to one man. Captain Mahmoud Hodzic was a soft-spoken, dark-skinned man who hadn't said much in any of the Coalition Fleet briefings, but he was still the commanding officer of *Guardian*, the last remaining RRF cruiser in the fleet and the only capital ship Kira didn't directly control.

"I hesitate to trust a mercenary, no offense," he said. "But I know Admiral Kim did, so I am content to yield operational command to Commodore Demirci."

Kira hadn't actually expected everyone to go along that easily, but the nods through the holographic crowd suggested that no one was actually opposed. She concealed a dry swallow.

"Thank you for your trust," she told them. "General Westley, General Simmons, the next stage of this operation is still primarily yours. Securing the Kiln is *probably* within the capabilities of our remaining force, so long as those nova fighters do not return."

"Do we even know who those people *were*?" Shang asked.

"Yes," Kira said flatly. "Collating the data from everyone's optics, we have a solid identification on the nova interceptors used. They are Griffon-built Manticore-Sevens. I have simulator files on them but not true detailed specifications…but they were just beginning to be phased out of the Star Kingdom of Griffon's active service ten years ago."

"What the hell are *Fringe* fighters doing out here?" the other mercenary Commodore demanded.

"Our best guess is that they're in the hands of Cobra Squadron, which appears to be operating under contract to the same people who hired a mercenary fleet to support the coup in Ypres," Kira told them. "We *know*, for reasons I won't go into, that Cobra Squadron is currently operating in the Syntactic Cluster.

"They appear to currently be equipped with last-generation Griffon-built fighters, but those ships are significantly more advanced than our own nova fighters. We didn't drive them off, people. They were only here to launch one strike."

"And that strike killed two RRF capital ships," Westley said sourly. "What happens if they come back, Demirci?"

"We fight," Kira replied. "But the way we currently have the remaining nova fighters loaded aboard *Deception* limits our abilities. It will take us at least ten minutes to get the nova fighters into space now, a vulnerability we can't avoid without giving up on bringing the RRF's fighters home."

"Your rescue and retrieval of our fighters and people is appreciated," Hodzic said quietly.

"Search-and-rescue continues through the wreckage of our ships and fighters," Kira pointed out. "We have retrieved, at last count, ten class two nova drives and twenty-two pilots and copilots.

"But right now, we have thirty-four nova fighters, two cruisers, five destroyers and three corvettes," she listed. "We have about thirty-six more hours in which we expect to be able to find survivors, and my intent is to continue the sweep until that time is up.

"We are also retrieving the Clans' survivors, which may offer General Westley some options."

"It should," he agreed. "I intend to demand Forty-Two-K-Seven's surrender before I request the Fleet engage in combat operations. It may be possible for us to secure the Kiln without further combat.

"What I have seen suggests that the spaceborne firepower of the Costar Clans has been shattered. We can hope that defeat will be enough to prevent stubbornness on their part."

"Once we have secured as many survivors as possible and are in control of the Kiln, we will need to consider what happens next," Kira told everyone. "Technically, my contract and our mission call for us to proceed to the Klo System and secure the last of the Clans' holdouts for General Simmons.

"Despite the losses inflicted on the Clans, I'm not sure we have the strength for that," she admitted. "We will have to reassess the state of our repairs and our estimates of the Clans' strength over the next two days.

"I suggest we focus on S&R first, then repairs, then securing the Kiln System," she told them. "Then... Then we'll see what happens."

27

THE AVERAGE SHIPSUIT was designed with forty-eight hours of oxygen. Most ships had survival kits and bunkers scattered throughout the hull, allowing for that to be extended to at least a week —and including beacons to guide search-and-rescue crews to the survivors.

The Coalition Fleet's people did everything they could inside those forty-eight hours and swept up every beacon they detected. Fifty-five hours after the battle was over, Kira knew *exactly* how many people had died and been saved in the Second Battle of the Kiln.

Too many and *not enough*, respectively. Of her *Deception* pilots, she'd lost nine fighters, but five of the pilots had been retrieved.

The RRF wing had been hit even harder. Sagairt lived, but he'd lost his own fighter—along with twenty more of his planes. Half of them had been the two-person Sinister fighter-bombers, and they'd only pulled eighteen of his people from the wreckage.

For being outnumbered by superior fighters, Kira was grimly aware that the loss of thirty nova fighters and sixteen pilots and copilots was a damn miracle. The loss of *Perseus*—crew of thirteen hundred —and *Last Denial*—crew of nine hundred—counted heavily against that. Between the capital ships and lighter units lost, they'd pulled a thousand survivors from their own wreckage.

Which meant they'd only lost *two* thousand people to the black.

The Clans were worse off. Kira's new fleet had done their best, but they'd only pulled about a thousand of the Clans' survivors from the chaos. With over a hundred of the Clans' warships reduced to wreckage in the fight, she couldn't even guess at their losses.

"It's over," Westley told her in a private conference. "Some of the other clusters may stick it out, but Forty-Two had a front-row seat to you annihilating their fleet. We've been arguing for a day and a half, but it was clear from the beginning how it was going to end."

"Your troops are going in?" Kira asked. She was on the flag bridge. She hadn't *left* the flag bridge since heading in, though the flag officer's chair at least reclined enough for her to sleep.

"Shuttles launching in ten minutes. We could use nova-fighter escort as we move transports to some of the other clusters," he admitted.

"Give me a list, I'll get you fighters," she promised. "Might take more than ten minutes. Fitting thirty-four fighters on a deck designed for twenty lends itself to inefficiency."

"I get that," Westley said. "We did it, Commodore. Three of the Costar Clans Systems are now protectorates of Redward. That's... That's a lot. That's more than anyone's ever done."

"Pat yourselves on the back in thirty years if you manage to keep all of your promises," Kira told him grimly. "I've read the projections. If the FTZ doesn't make as much extra money as your analysts think, the Clans' systems might just bankrupt the Redward Crown."

"That's the risk we have to take," Westley agreed. "I understand the urge to destroy a long-standing enemy, but, speaking as a soldier and a student of history, violence only begets more violence.

"Diplomats might write checks that only soldiers can cash, but we only truly *win* when we make our enemies our friends."

"I'm a mercenary, General. These days, anyway. I have to at least pretend I'm only concerned about one kind of check," Kira told him.

"Rumor says that peace might leave you unemployed, but unemployment wouldn't exactly leave you bankrupt, Commodore," he replied. "If you get me those fighters, we might actually be on the edge of finishing up your role here."

"I'm waiting on a courier," Kira admitted. "Too much is going on in the Cluster for me to want to commit the Coalition Fleet to a move on Klo. We're in better shape post-self-repair than I'd dare hope, but..."

"I understand, Commodore. The work remains."

"Good luck, General," Kira told him. A chime in her headware informed her she had the list of missions that would require nova-fighter escort. "I'll have those fighters for you in fifteen."

ROUGHLY HALF AN HOUR LATER, the flag bridge door slid open to admit Konrad Bueller. The broad-shouldered Brisingr man crossed the space silently, laying his hand on Kira's arm without a word.

"There should be a chair somewhere around here that moves," Kira suggested. "Though I suppose most bridges don't have those."

"Not generally, no," her boyfriend agreed. "We tend to design spaces like this with fixed seats with safety belts. Just in case."

She snorted, studying the big display in front of her. It was an interesting mix of media, combining flat screens, a hologram, and data feeding to her headware. She gave a mental command, allowing Bueller access to the headware feed.

"That's a lot of green," she murmured, gesturing to the map of the Kiln System. "A few oranges still, clusters and stations that are being difficult, but the system is basically under our control."

"So, what happens now?" Bueller asked. The question sounded familiar, and she shrugged.

"We wait for word from Redward," she told him. "The situation with Bengalissimo is complicated enough that I don't want to risk the Coalition Fleet without more data—especially when Cobra Squadron already jumped us."

"My math says they've upgraded," he murmured. "Estanza said they had two fifty-plane carriers. That could launch a hundred nova fighters, but I feel like they wouldn't have risked everything here."

"Some of the extras could have been the survivors from the Crest carrier," Kira pointed out. "I don't know if they had ten bombers after they ran into us in Redward, but I'm not going to assume that *every* fighter out there was a Manticore."

"Or Cobra Squadron has three carriers now," Bueller pointed out. "Or two bigger ones. Either way, you're right to wait for word. What I have to *question* is whether you're right to wait here on the flag bridge without resting."

"I'm sleeping," she countered. "Some."

He chuckled.

"Kira, wearing yourself out doesn't serve anyone. You're right that the flag bridge is your post right now, but that doesn't mean you're needed here twenty-four hours a day."

She sighed and he moved around to start massaging her shoulders, taking advantage of the privacy.

"You're not actually going to move on to Klo, are you?" he murmured.

"No," she admitted. "I'm expecting most of the Coalition to be recalled...and their home systems to be horrified at their losses. This *hurt* a lot of Redward's partners and if they're not careful, it's going to look like a lot of their partners got hurt for their benefit."

"Because Redward now theoretically owns three giant holes they're going to pour money into for the next twenty years?" Bueller asked.

"Basically. Territorial expansion always makes people nervous," Kira replied. "And Redward hasn't set themselves up as an unquestioned hegemon that everyone is too scared to challenge. That would be what the Institute wants."

"I see the point, some days," he said. "But could I impose on you to see the point from your actual *bed*, Kira? It's more comfortable than that chair, and I promise we'll wake you when the cour—"

"Nova emergence," Davidović's void reported through a speaker. "IDing as *Kenobi*, one of the RRF's fast couriers."

"Never mind," Bueller said with a long sigh. "I don't think we're going to need a chief engineer for a few minutes. Need company, or is this going to be too classified for the XO?"

"Stick around," Kira ordered. "I suspect I can use the moral support."

28

THE FIRST MESSAGE flagged for Kira was from Queen Sonia. It was also for Admiral Kim, which sent another spike of guilt down her spine. Pushing that aside, she started the message and met the holographic gaze of Redward's junior monarch and head intelligence officer.

"Demirci, Kim, I'm going to play the message we received from Gaspari before anything else," Sonia said bluntly. "I'll then give you the intelligence rundown on what's going on, and then there are formal orders attached to this message from Admiral Remington and RRF command."

She shook her head.

"This is a nightmare and I hope you have some better news out of the Clans' Systems than we have," Sonia told Kira. "First, though... 'Her Majesty' Queen Rossella."

Sonia's holographic image faded, replaced by another woman. Both had the posture and bearing of a proud leader, though Sonia *definitely* had looked more tired. Where Queen Sonia wore a plain suit, Queen Rossella wore her Admiral's uniform with the stars replaced by a small golden crown.

Rossella was a tall woman with well-kept shoulder-length black hair and warm-toned skin and eyes. Her face was marked with the lines of someone who smiled easily and often, but there was a darker edge to her expression today.

"People of the Syntactic Cluster," she greeted the camera. "I am Rossella Gaspari, the rightful Queen of Bengalissimo. While an erroneous theory of succession put someone else on my homeworld's throne, I was prepared to accept that for the benefit of Bengalissimo... until it became clear that not just Bengalissimo but the entire Cluster was suffering for my cousin's blindness.

"I have taken my rightful throne as Queen Rossella the First and begun the process of ensuring the security of my system and my people."

She held up a hand palm-up.

"You have all seen, I think, the greatest threat. The one I see, the one that forced me to action at last," she said calmly. "The Free Trade Zone sounded like a brilliant idea when it was first presented to me, but time has proven it for the lie it is.

"Redward ships have been everywhere of late, enforcing Redward's rules, convincing people to follow Redward's lead," Rossella continued. "But it was in Ypres that Redward finally showed their true colors. They called on the mutual-defense agreements of the Free Trade Zone to *attack* a system that wasn't part of their FTZ and forcefully intervene in their politics.

"The result? The puppet state calling itself the Ypres Federation. The closest thing I've ever seen to conquest of a system in the Cluster, as the Federation takes its cue from Redward. Proud and mighty nations humbled to the power of Redward's ambition."

Rossella shook her head, her eyes sad.

"But this wasn't enough for King Lawrence. Instead, he bribed and blackmailed and imposed his will on the nations of the FTZ again to create his Coalition against the Clans—but who benefits when the systems the Clans control become Redward protectorates?

"The piracy might stop, yes, but when the resources of the Clans' systems fuel the Redward war machine, we will all pay for our blindness, for our failure to recognize what Redward has become."

She spread her hands in a shrug.

"King Lawrence and his fleet have become aggressively expansionistic, using the cover of this so-called Free Trade Zone to bend the entire Syntactic Cluster to their will. It is not enough that Lawrence commands the most powerful fleet in the Cluster. The rest of us must call him King as well…and I will not permit it.

"Bengalissimo is a free and independent system. We have rescinded our participation in the farce that is the SCFTZ and taken the measures we feel necessary to secure our safety."

She smiled thinly.

"For the rest of the Cluster, I promise that we will not let Redward's aggression go unanswered. We will shortly move to protect the Ypres System and assist them in separating themselves from Redward's control.

"Bengalissimo is and always will be a beacon of hope for the Cluster. In this dark hour, as Redward attempts to impose their will on all of us, trust that we will stand up for your freedoms. Bengalissimo will fight this expansion.

"I give you my word, as Queen, that Redward will be stopped."

The image froze for a moment, and Kira reached up to cover Bueller's hand on her shoulder.

"That all sounds very familiar, doesn't it?" he said, his voice flat. "Do you think she borrowed the Kaiser's entire speech or just the speechwriter?"

"What?" Kira asked, pausing the message as Sonia's image reappeared.

"I take it you never watched the Kaiser's appearance before the Brisingr Diet to ask for the declaration of war against Apollo?" her boyfriend asked. "Because swap out the names and it feels like the same damn speech."

She felt him shake his head.

"It's not as exact as it feels," he admitted, "but I'll be damned if it isn't the same message."

"The Institute at work," Kira suggested. "We know the Kaiser felt he owed them enough to give them *Deception*."

"I'm trying not to believe that my home country bought into their nightmare, but I keep hitting things like this," Bueller said. "Finish the message, Kira; my...concerns about home aren't going to change anytime soon."

She nodded and Sonia's image resumed.

"You can guess what kind of measures Bengalissimo is taking," Sonia told them. "We have confirmed some of our worst-case scenarios. At some point—we're still trying to establish when—Bengalissimo built four new cruisers. That brings their strength up to seven, and it looks like they also doubled their destroyer strength.

"Some of those ships are definitely mercenaries, as our agents have confirmed older Crest designs being quite common," the Queen noted. "So far, we haven't confirmed any carriers or nova fighters, but we suspect that both Cobra Squadron and the strike carrier we saw at Ypres are under contract to Queen Rossella.

"Nothing has been officially announced, but we have evidence to suggest she's already moved elements of either the BF or her mercenaries in around Ypres. A partial blockade is in place and will almost certainly become a full blockade shortly. No one in, no one out, until the Federation concedes to her.

"I don't even know what kind of concession she'll want from them," Sonia admitted. "It'll be hard for them to stop being a puppet state when they aren't one."

She shook her head.

"I am over ninety percent certain that the courier carrying this message will also be carrying recall orders for every ship in the Coalition Fleet that isn't Yprian, Redward or mercenary. I do not expect to see contact from the Federation shortly, but I would recommend that their ships come back to Redward with you.

"Your formal orders will follow, but you can guess what they look like. Secure whatever Costar Clans Systems you have already taken... and then let the Fleet dissolve. We will make no attempt to force our allies to continue this campaign in the face of Bengalissimo's threats and claims."

Sonia shook her head.

"It appears the Equilibrium Institute had at least one more string to their bow and we badly underestimated how many resources each level of their plans had in play. Several of my analysts are already looking into theories that suggest that Rossella was always their secondary target.

"If they couldn't convince Larry and me to become their military hegemon by arming the Clans against us, Bengalissimo was their best second choice.

"For an organization supposedly attempting to *prevent* a Cluster-wide war, it very much looks like the Institute may have just started one."

29

KIRA GAVE the officers of the Coalition Fleet's various contingents six hours to digest the news and whatever orders they'd received from home before convening a second all-hands virtual conference.

"Officers," she greeted them all. "My understanding is that everyone has received the news updates and at least some orders from home, correct?"

The only officer who *didn't* nod was Commodore Shinoda. The Yprian officer looked worried, his face a frozen death mask amidst the sheepish concern of most of the rest of the Fleet's officers.

"Let's make this easier, then," Kira said. "Does anyone *not* have a recall order?"

The holograms surrounded her shuffled uncomfortably. She smiled mirthlessly.

"I don't," Commodore Shinoda replied. "On the other hand, the message I have from the Federation Embassy on Redward suggests that Ypres has been blockaded and any attempt to communicate will have been interdicted."

That chilled what little humor the meeting had.

"I also do not," Commodore Shang noted. "I in fact have a request from the syndicate contracting my services to remain with the Coalition Fleet...while they withdraw their own forces."

Kira nodded.

"Nobody anticipated the losses we took here," she reminded everyone. "But the overall political concerns of the Cluster are clear. The orders *I* received were intended for Admiral Ylva Kim."

Everyone was silent, waiting.

"I am interpreting the silence from everyone except Commodores Shinoda and Shang as evidence that you all have at least partial recall orders," Kira said. "I actually discussed this possibility with Admiral Kim prior to her death.

"Neither I nor the RRF have any intention of expecting you to ignore those orders. You are all released to follow whatever orders you have received from your home governments," she told them. "Given what limited authority you have all given me and those prior discussions with Admiral Kim...I don't see any reason to try to do something stupid."

"What about the Kiln?" Westley asked. The new Governor was, correctly, concerned about his area of authority.

"There are two remaining RRF destroyers with the Coalition Fleet," Kira told the Major General. "Between myself and Captain Hodzic, we have the authority to detach *Providence* and *Repose* to provide support for the RRA occupation.

"*Guardian* and *Deception* will join the rest of the Coalition Fleet in returning to our home system," she concluded. "Commodore Shang, Commodore Shinoda, I believe I can fairly speak for Redward when I say that your presence would be both welcome and appreciated while Redward works out their response to this new state of affairs."

She looked at the rest of the officers.

"We have achieved great things together," she reminded them. "Three star systems and forty million people are being given a second chance because of the Coalition Fleet. We have broken piracy in the Cluster for years, buying your homes time to build new answers and new hopes.

"But the situation has changed and our losses already suggest against moving against the last of the Costar Clans' systems. The dissolution of the Coalition Fleet is the next logical step.

"On behalf of my employers, thank you," Kira told them. "For myself, thank you. We've fought together and won together. We are called to different duties faster than we expected, but the Coalition Fleet was only ever a temporary formation.

"Go home, people. Watch your people's backs. We made the Cluster safer in one way…but it seems like fate had a different chaos in mind than we feared."

SOMEHOW, Kira wasn't surprised that Hodzic, Shang and Shinoda remained on the channel as the virtual conference dissolved. A few mental commands to her headware changed the presentation of the "room" to bring the four of them into a more intimate meeting space.

"Shang, I can't guarantee that Redward will be able to hire you," she pointed out. "It seems very likely, but I have zero authority to actually commit them."

"I have some authority," Hodzic murmured. "Enough to guarantee you are paid for bringing us home."

"There is a point, Commodore Demirci, where even a mercenary must consider just whose money they are *willing* to take," Shang said primly. "I will not work for a military dictator imposed by coup d'état. That leaves me with one choice in what is about to happen, and I do believe in the depths of Redward's bank accounts."

"What Redward won't fund, Ypres will," Shinoda stated. "If my system has been blockaded, my ambassador and I will shortly be emptying our interstellar accounts to fund whatever counter-operation we can.

"My ships…" He exhaled and shook his head. "We have built no new warships since the establishment of the Federation, my friends. My two destroyers are all the nova warships left to my home system.

"The monitor fleets render Ypres unassailable by any rational enemy, but they cannot break a blockade by a nova-capable enemy. And while Ypres is blockaded…"

"The entire Syntactic Cluster is blockaded," Kira finished. "Anyone coming from the rest of the Rim will almost certainly attempt to come through Ypres and collide with the Bengalissimo blockade.

"Redward Intelligence expects them to have moved a minimum of two cruisers and a dozen destroyers to impose the blockade," she continued. "The destroyers may or may not be mercenaries; as of them sending my latest update, they weren't certain how many destroyers Bengalissimo had built in secret."

"We *have* confirmed that Bengalissimo has built four new cruisers," Hodzic said.

Shinoda's face was a frozen death mask again as he nodded.

"Ypres cannot defeat that," he said quietly. "The Federation Fleet was just in the process of reviewing the combined tech base of the five factions to assess how large a cruiser we'd even be able to build. The monitor slips can be repurposed, but a nova warship has a far more complicated set of requirements than a sublight defender."

"Bengalissimo would have started building their new ships years ago," Kira said. "Someone has been preparing for this for a long time."

"I was never a believer in Estanza's little conspiracy theory," Shang observed. "But I'll be damned if reality isn't determined to bring me onside. I'll follow you back to Redward, at least."

"As will my ships," Shinoda agreed. "We need to escort the Redward Army transports anyway. I wouldn't put it past our old friend to set up an ambush for them."

"Anyone expecting to ambush transports with a few dozen sub-fighters between them is going to have a rude awakening when they collide with two cruisers," Kira reminded them. "I almost feel like we should be escorting the rest of the Coalition Fleet home."

"Gaspari can't risk pissing off everyone just yet," Shang said. "Not while she's trying to pretend she's the protector of the Cluster against Redward. Her propaganda requires her to focus her efforts."

Kira nodded her agreement. That focus was probably their only real advantage—it meant that Bengalissimo couldn't move against anyone except Redward or Ypres without risking the moral high ground she was trying to claim.

"On the other hand, she knows her propaganda is bullshit," Kira pointed out with a sigh. "It's going to be a mess. The sooner we're back to Redward, the better."

Not least because once she was back to Redward, the mess stopped being entirely her problem.

30

THE TASK FORCE that novaed out of the Kiln System a week after arriving was a pale shadow of the Coalition Fleet that had arrived. Two cruisers and five destroyers were still a powerful force by the standards of the Syntactic Cluster, but they'd started with a *lot* more ships than that.

The numbers were filled out by the empty army transports the warships were herding. The remaining army corps had been deployed in the Kiln to reinforce Westley, leaving Kira's ships with only empty hulls to bring home.

Those empty hulls were still valuable enough that she'd prefer not to lose any of them, and a flight of nova fighters flashed green on the screens around her moments after they emerged into the trade-route stop.

"Scans show the area is clear," Davidović reported.

Kira was back on the bridge now, keeping a mental eye on the route to her starfighter. She might technically be in command of the task force, but she was certain she'd better serve everyone in a nova fighter.

"Helmet has his wing out and flying patrol," Kira told Zoric. "Anything else going on we should be watching for?"

"Nothing," the cruiser Captain replied. "Twenty hours, then we nova again. We'll be back to Redward soon enough, boss."

Kira nodded.

"There is a very spiky itch in the middle of my back," she said. "I can't help but feel that we're vulnerable right now—and while we've bruised Cobra Squadron, they're still in the fight."

There were prisoners aboard *Guardian*, but so far, they'd proven surprisingly closed-mouthed. From the reports Hodzic had forwarded, they weren't even getting name, rank and serial number out of the nova pilots.

"You wrote the patrol schedule," Zoric replied. "Anything else you think we should do?"

Kira studied the tactical display. The five warships were assembled into a rough cone around the transports, close enough to support each other if needed, with half a dozen nova fighters circling the entire formation.

"No," she admitted. "Unless someone can conjure a fleet carrier out of nothing, we stick with each other and head back to base."

Deception was lightly fried around the edges from her encounter with Cobra Squadron, but most of the other ships were showing mild to moderate damage despite their repair efforts.

"I'm going to go rest," she finally decided. "Wake me if something comes up. We'll be ready for anything."

"We always are," Zoric agreed. "And we're *readier* if the Commodore isn't running on a sleep deficit."

Kira snorted.

"What, are you and Konrad on the same team or something?" she asked.

"I wasn't going to push you while we were in the Kiln, but I *know* you didn't get enough sleep," the Captain murmured. "Now we're on our way home, we can wake you if something comes up, and you need to rest."

"Already heading to bed, Kavitha," Kira promised. "See you on the other side."

"THE OTHER SIDE" turned out to be almost twelve hours later. Kira always woke up quickly, but this time, it was almost a struggle for her to emerge from her rest.

She could have pushed it, but no one had triggered an alert, and long experience told her that if she was having trouble waking up, she'd truly needed the sleep.

Finally getting up and showering, she checked over the reports. Sagairt and his fighters had returned aboard, replaced by her Weltraumpanzers under Yamauchi. She only had four of the heavy fighters left now, though they'd retrieved enough class two drive units from the wreckage that Tamboli would be able to fabricate replacement fighters.

Once the decks were empty, anyway. They could fabricate components, but they had nowhere to put whole nova fighters. The sub-fighter bays on the army transports were both full and too small for proper nova fighters.

The trade-route stop had been quiet while she slept. The cooldown timer said they were eight hours from novaing, and the sensors said that their battered fleet was in control of the situation.

Once dressed and ready to face the day ahead, she checked her messages and decided the best thing she could do was check in with the cruiser's chief engineer—and if that happened to also let her visit with her boyfriend, well, she wasn't going to turn down that bonus.

THE ENGINEERING SECTION was surprisingly quiet, with only a handful of the techs present watching the reactors. Kira made her way through the narrow confines of *Deception*'s beating heart, taking a moment to study the nova drive itself.

Even thirteen hours into the cooldown, the radiators were glowing red behind their protective shields. Most of the actual heat venting was taking place outside the ship's hull, but not all of the "cooling" was actually heat.

Two long transparent tubes were positioned next to the drive, clearly visible from everywhere in the Engineering section. Blue and white sparks flashed up and down them, arcs of electricity drawing from the electrostatic buildup on the nova drive to act as a warning sign.

A thousand computer systems and sensors measured every aspect of the buildups and cooldowns inherent to the nova drive, but one of the biggest dangers in the system was trying to nova with too much static built up. The levels of electrostatic buildup were a leading indicator for other types of buildup the human eye couldn't see, which made those two tubes a key tool for the chief engineer.

When she knocked on the door of Bueller's office, he was watching the static tubes through the one-way window of his office wall.

"Concerns?" Kira asked, taking a seat across from him. She'd brought her own coffee this time, pouring it from a thermos into the cup he half-consciously slid across to her.

"Couple of the hits left a few things more fragile than I like," Bueller admitted. "Nothing unfixable, but we need to take the ship fully cold to do so."

He shrugged.

"That means a thirty-six-hour cooldown on the drive core and a full shutdown on all of the main reactors for at least eighteen hours," he said. "We're not doing that until we're in Redward, under the guns of their defensive fortresses."

"Agreed," Kira replied. "Anything I should worry about?"

"Nah." He shook his head and turned to look at her. "We're not venting as much tachyon static as we should, but we've excess margin built into that system, anyway. We'd probably be clear for a full six novas, and the trip to Redward is only five."

"We took a few knocks," she said. "Are we okay?"

"*Deception* is designed for this. On the heels of that bomber strike in Redward, I'd *like* to pull her up for a full review again, but I don't have the impression we'll have time."

Kira grimaced.

"Who knows? Bengalissimo has seven cruisers...and Redward now has two. Three with us."

"And Cobra Squadron and the rest of the mercs put them at three or four carriers to our three, even with *Conviction*," her lover agreed.

He shook his head. "I knew that the Institute had vast resources by even Brisingr standards, but they just keep fucking coming."

"Queen Sonia suggested that Gaspari might have been their real plan all along," Kira said. "If they couldn't get Redward to build up their fleet and enforce their will by blockades and force, well, they had a fleet at Bengalissimo ready to go."

"And everything else was just setting up to give her an excuse?" Bueller asked. He sighed. "I think that assessment puts a bit too much weight on any given option, from what I remember of the Director."

She nodded slowly. It was easy to forget that Bueller had met and worked with the unnamed man who was heading Equilibrium Institute operations in the Syntactic Cluster.

"What do you think?" she asked.

"I think the Director had four bloody plans moving in parallel with every intention of letting them fight it out for dominance," he guessed. "They were arming the Clans, they were pushing for Yprian unification under their terms, and they were arming Bengalissimo. *Any* of those would work for their ultimate objective."

"And the fourth plan?" Kira said.

"Convincing Redward to become Brisingr," Bueller said. "I don't think they even planned to overthrow Larry. If enough of his Parliament got sick of compromise and diplomacy, they could force his hand."

She grimaced.

"Yeah, that would do it. He's tried to keep a balance of building new ships and not pushing too hard on the smaller powers," she said. "I could see the Parliament pushing to fund new ships by some suitably euphemistic tribute payments from the smaller powers."

"The label *Free Trade Zone* has covered that in the past," he agreed. "I don't think that's what Larry and Sonia are doing, or we'd be arguing a lot more, but I suspect it might be Gaspari's plan."

"Between us and Redward, at least the Costar Clans and Ypres plans are spiked," Kira noted. "But Bengalissimo is in play with a lot more firepower than anyone expected. We're months away from any expansion to the RRF."

"What does the RRF even *do* in the face of a challenge like Bengalissimo's?" Bueller asked. "I guess...break the Ypres blockade?"

"That's how the war between Apollo and Brisingr was fought," Kira agreed grimly. The struggle between the two powers had been a series of blockades, counter-blockades and blockade assaults. "But if Bengalissimo really has seven cruisers and that entire mercenary fleet, the numbers Sonia gave me for the Ypres blockade make me nervous."

"Why?" She had Bueller's attention now.

"If they only sent two cruisers and a dozen destroyers to Ypres, the rest are going somewhere else," Kira told him. "And there's only one other target on the board."

She half-consciously looked around to confirm they were alone in the private office.

"I *think* we're moving fast enough that we'll get into Redward before the gate drops," she said grimly. "And we've got enough firepower, we can hopefully blast our way in if we need to, but..."

"You think they're going to cut off Redward as well as Ypres?"

"They have to," she told him. "And if they do, they win." She shrugged helplessly. "If Redward can't even secure their own exits, who's going to look to Redward for protection? With the losses they've taken and the timeline for their upgraded ships..."

"This could all be over before their first wave of new cruisers commissions, let alone the Twelve-X ships," Bueller finished grimly. "What do we do, Kira?"

"We get two cruisers back into Redward," she told him. "I haven't seen specifications on the BF's new cruisers, but I'll bet *Deception* can take them one-on-one easily. With *Guardian* backing us, I'm betting we could take two."

"Neither we nor *Guardian* are in perfect shape," he warned. "And if they bring decent escorts, well..."

"We have nova fighters, and their cruisers don't. If they bring one of the Cobra carriers alone, well." She sighed. "There's only so much we can do, Konrad. Your old friends have put us on the wrong side of the firepower differential again."

"I would love to go back to having an infinite budget," he said. "What a mess. So, we fight?"

"Like I said, I think we can get back into Redward without a fight," she told him. "After that…our only advantage is that they don't know where and when the RRF will try to break out. We can throw the entire nova-capable fleet at one chunk of the blockade."

"Except…" He swallowed.

"Finish your thought, Konrad," she told him. "It's not like you can make me *more* stressed at this point."

"Redward is sufficiently penetrated by Institute or Bengalissimo agents that they knew where the King and Queen were novaing into," he reminded her. "They might well be able to anticipate a breakout."

Kira exhaled and bowed her head, closing her eyes as that sank in.

"Then we deal with that when it happens," she said firmly, with a certainty she didn't feel. "Fortunately, *that* isn't my problem.

"I just have to get seven warships and thirty-plus army transports back to Redward."

31

EVERY BONE in Kira's body ached to be in a starfighter as the countdown to their second-to-last nova ticked through her headware. If they
were going to run into any trouble on their way home, the trade-route
stops accessible directly from Redward would be the place.

"Nova in one minute," Zoric said calmly.

Kira was back on the flag bridge. This time, she wasn't alone,
having commandeered Chief Waxweiler to act as her "staff" while she
managed the glorified convoy that remained of the Coalition Fleet.

"All ships confirm ready and timeline," Waxweiler reported.
"*Guardian* and the destroyers are all at battle stations; transport sub-
fighters are ready to launch."

Kira just nodded. If Cobra Squadron were present, launching the
sublight fighters aboard the army transports would be basically
murder. Those experienced pilots and advanced nova fighters would
obliterate the raw recruits flying the transport defense craft.

The real key to getting to Redward was *Deception* herself, still the
largest and most powerful warship in the Cluster, and the now-battle-
hardened veteran nova pilots on her decks.

"Helmet, Nightmare, Longknife, check in," she ordered. Each of
those three now led a mixed squadron of mercenary and RRF pilots.

The need to put Sagairt in a fighter had been the final mark against Kira flying herself—he was borrowing her Hoplite today.

"All starfighters are ready to go," Nightmare told her.

"I'll be in space with all ten fighter-bombers the moment we're out of nova," Sagairt confirmed. "I believe your deck crew when they say sixty seconds for the rest."

Sagairt would also launch with four interceptors. Hoffman would follow with the heavy fighters and more interceptors, and then Cartman would launch a full interceptor squadron.

"I hope this prep is for nothing," Kira said, watching the seconds tick away. "But the target on my back is itching like crazy. Stand by for nova."

"All hands stand by for nova," Zoric's voice echoed her order on the public announcement. "Five seconds. Four. Three. Two. One.

"Nova."

The universe flashed and one section of empty deep space was replaced with another chunk...that was *not* empty.

"Multiple contacts," Waxweiler reported crisply. "Still resolving; I'm eyeballing at over fifty individual contacts. Is this trade stop this busy?"

"No," Hodzic said grimly. "There should be a few corvettes and maybe a dozen freighters."

"Most of the contacts are in one location," Davidović said. "Looks like corralled transports with a warship guard force. I'm flagging a destroyer and six corvettes playing guard dog on at least forty transports."

Data was flowing to Kira's headware, but the details didn't matter. She knew what an interstellar blockade looked like, and there was no question in her mind.

"I'm not seeing nova fighters," she barked. "Confirm?"

"Confirmed," Waxweiler said a moment before Davidović could. "Enemy strength is four destroyers, twelve corvettes. No gunships, no nova fighters."

"Good." Kira smiled coldly. Those sixteen warships were a significant fighting force by the standards of the Syntactic Cluster—and they didn't stand a chance against her battered command.

"Launch all nova and sub-fighters," she ordered. "Set your course for the freighter corral. Helmet, punch out the corral guards ASAP. Longknife, Nightmare, follow up behind him and secure those ships."

"And the sub-fighters, sir?" Davidović asked.

"Sub-fighters will split in two. Odd-numbered squadrons will remain with the army transports. Even-numbered squadrons will form on *Deception*, as will the other warships. Your course is for the corral, Captains.

"If these sons of dogs think they're going to hold on to civilian shipping while we're in the system, they're going to learn *very* differently!"

MULTIPHASIC JAMMING LIT up space moments after Sagairt's fighter squadron vanished into nova. Kira's capital ships were moving forward, the two cruisers forming the tip of a wedge of lighter warships.

They were already initiating evasive maneuvers to make sure the strangers didn't get any lucky long-range shots in, but they'd once again deployed drones outside their jamming bubble with laser links to *Deception*.

The details Kira had half-dismissed earlier updated as they closed. There were forty-six freighters under guard in the impromptu holding zone the blockaders had assembled, varying from ten-thousand-cubic-meter tramps to fifty-kilocubic bulk container ships.

Even the big ships looked small to her eyes, but there was still the best part of a million cubic meters of shipping interned under the guns of the Bengalissimo ships—or at least, what were *claiming* to be Bengalissimo ships.

"IFF codes flag them all as Bengalissimo Fleet warships, but we know diese Arschlöcher," Chief Waxweiler told Kira. "Every one of them has a direct match in our files. They were *all* at Ypres. These are Institute mercs, Commodore."

"I always appreciate the confirmation on just who we're blowing into tiny pieces," Kira replied. "Thanks, Chief. How long until we have an update on the nova-fighter strike?"

The nova hadn't even been a full light-minute, but they hadn't lost sight of the holding pens yet. That would change as soon as—

"Now," the Brisingr Chief replied. That portion of their data had now dissolved into multiphasic jamming as the fighters emerged.

Their sensor feed was forty seconds out of date there. Kira had to trust Sagairt and her own people to handle rescuing the trapped merchants. *Her* attention was on the rest of the mercenary force.

Three destroyers and another six corvettes were scattered across the trade zone, their positions more concerned with intercepting freighters than engaging in an actual fight. The closest units had detected *Deception* and her friends and were now maneuvering to rendezvous with their compatriots.

"Commodore, all of them have the speed to outrun our escorts," Zoric said from the bridge. "If we leave the Cluster ships behind, the sub-fighters and *Deception* can catch them."

"No," Kira replied. "Let them run. Let them consolidate and realize that we're not afraid of them at all." Her smile was cold. "If they're smart, this battle is already over."

"Return nova from the freighter corral," Waxweiler reported. "One of Helmet's interceptors, downloading data by laser com. Hostiles are destroyed but the freighters appear to have enemy troops aboard."

"Damn," Kira murmured, then turned her attention to her senior RRF officer. "How many troops are left on those army transports, Captain Hodzic?"

"They're mostly empty but...they've got at least a battalion or so worth of support troops that know which end of a blaster goes toward the enemy," Hodzic said. "They can retake the merchant ships."

"All right." Kira considered for a moment. "Commodore Shinoda?"

"Commodore Demirci," the Yprian officer replied calmly. "Would you like us to escort the Redward Army to deal with some wayward pirates?"

"They're a military unit engaged in merchant interdiction, Commodore," Kira pointed out. "We may not like what they're doing, but they *are* accorded respect under the laws of war.

"But yes, that is what I was going to ask."

"Much as I want to kick some Bengal butt, I think we might be more valuable with the RRA," Shinoda said. "Adjusting course to fall back on the transports."

"I'll pass on the orders," Hodzic confirmed. "What about the mercs?"

"The rest of us keep hunting," Kira replied. "But…they'll run. No one is going to fight two cruisers with three destroyers."

Much as she might want them to.

"NOVA SIGNATURES," Waxweiler said, his tone satisfied. "Remaining Bengalissimo ships have withdrawn. Orders, Commodore?"

"Bring everyone about to support the transports in securing the merchants," Kira replied. "We'll secure them and help with whatever repairs they need to nova into Redward. Anyone heading away from Redward gets our best wishes, but our destination is set."

She considered the big tactical display—larger than it would normally be on the flag deck, with only two of them there—and shook her head.

"We'll keep the full fighter force out for now," she decided. "It's possible those guys went for reinforcements and Bengalissimo has enough cruisers out there that they could bring a few to tangle with us."

She *hoped* they didn't have enough cruisers around Redward to want to tangle with *Deception* and *Guardian*. That would suggest that either the cruisers were more upgraded than they expected or that the BF had sent a lot more ships to Redward than the mercenaries' presence suggested.

"Multiphasic jamming is phasing down," Waxweiler reported. "Reestablishing full communications with everyone."

Laser com-links could often be maintained between larger warships during a battle, but they were limited in how much data could be transmitted reliably through multiphasic jamming and required precise calculation.

Plus, even the sub-fighters were almost impossible to maintain coms with inside the jamming zone. Anything smaller than a destroyer couldn't maintain even unreliable coms during a battle—and anything more than a few hundred thousand kilometers, barely outside the jamming bubble, was a lost cause.

"It'll take a minute or so before we have coms with the nova-fighter group," Waxweiler warned.

"I know," Kira reminded him with a chuckle. "I'm used to being on the other side of it, but I know."

The warships swept toward the corral and she sighed.

"I was hoping things hadn't gone this far yet," she admitted. "But if Bengalissimo has mercs blockading Redward, it's war."

"It wasn't before?" the chief asked.

"Oh, it almost certainly was," Kira said. "But if they were blockading *Ypres*, then they hadn't directly moved against Redward yet. Redward and Bengalissimo could still potentially talk things down from the precipice. The blockade would be a problem, but we wouldn't already be in a shooting war."

"If they moved in on these trade-route stops, they either ran off or destroyed the RRF lookouts," Zoric said. "That's been the main use the RRF has for gunships and corvettes, so it could be worse, but…"

"But the shooting has started," Kira finished. "I doubt the RRA is going to have any problems securing the merchant ships, so we should be ready to move on as soon as our drives have cooled down.

"I'm looking forward to being back in friendly space."

"Last time I checked, this particular chunk of void was supposed to *be* friendly space," Zoric said.

"And that, Kavitha, is the problem."

32

DECEPTION AND GUARDIAN emerged into the Redward System at the tail end of a massive train. Dozens of Redward Army transports and merchant ships had led the way, novaing half a dozen at a time while Kira slowly retrieved her nova fighters.

"Make a head count, Kavitha," she told the cruiser's Captain. "Let's make sure everyone is here, and then I am officially surrendering this mess to higher authority."

"Marija is on it," Zoric confirmed. "We do have multiple nova-fighter squadrons flying escort."

"Damn," Kira muttered as she took in the details. "I guess Redward decided that secret was out of the bag."

There were at least five six-ship fighter squadrons circling the merchant ships she'd brought back with her—and she could see a pair of destroyers rushing out toward them at maximum power as well.

"Let's check in with the RRF as soon as we have that head count," Kira told her friend.

"Everyone is here," Zoric replied. "Any last words to our traveling companions?"

Kira snorted, but she opened a channel to Hodzic and the two Commodores.

"All right, everybody, this is where I loose you to your own devices," she told them. "*Deception* is going to head for Blueward Station until someone tells me differently. Shang, Shinoda, I suspect you'll both want to check in with Admiral Remington as well as your usual local contacts.

"I doubt Redward's going to take the news we're delivering well, but that's our job."

"That it is," Hodzic agreed. "I already have orders to report to Green Ward for a shipyard assessment of *Guardian*'s damage. Thank you, Commodore Demirci."

The Redward officer dropped off the channel.

"I have sent a message to our ambassador and to check in with Redward orbital control," Shinoda said. "I'll take your advice and contact Admiral Remington. It's been... I won't call it a pleasure, but you've done right by me and mine. I owe you a beer, Commodore Demirci. Fly safe."

And then there was only the other mercenary Commodore on the channel, and Shang chuckled.

"You did good, Demirci," he told her. "I wouldn't have backed you if I didn't think you would, though I was going on faith in Estanza as much as you. But you did good. I appreciate the backup—and the getting my people out intact.

"I suspect we'll be seeing each other again soon. Good luck, Commodore."

The command channel dissolved for the last time, and Kira exhaled a long sigh. Back to her regular duties—well, at least once she found a home for the extra starfighters on her deck and briefed the commanding officer of the Redward Royal Fleet on just what the *hell* had happened.

———

"SIR, we have an incoming shuttle that just adjusted course toward us," Davidović reported in Kira's ear as she was entering her flight deck. "No prior communication, nothing; they're just vectoring toward us."

Deception was almost in Redward orbit and barely twenty minutes from her usual dock. They were in the middle of the planet's orbital traffic, which meant there were enough shuttles around that someone *could* sneak up on them.

She just didn't like it.

"Get an ID," she snapped.

"On it," the Redward officer replied, then swallowed hard. "Okay," she said in a small voice. "Redward Crown One is on approach, sir."

Redward Crown One was the call signal for the spacecraft carrying the King. Kira *fully* understood Davidović's choked response—and Kira wasn't even one of Larry's subjects.

"Understood," she said. "Inform Zoric and vector their shuttle to the main flight deck. I'll handle things on this end."

Somehow.

"Milani," she pinged her ground troop commander.

"Here. What's up?" they asked.

"King of Redward is landing on our deck in seven minutes. I need an honor guard."

"Done," Milani replied. "But with that kind of warning, I'm leaving the dragon on *extra* terrifying."

Kira snorted.

"Sounds good to me," she told them. "Pulling Tamboli in. Tamboli, King Larry is landing in six minutes. How clear is the deck?"

Tamboli audibly *squeaked* at the question.

"I just cleared twenty-three RRF nova fighters out," they replied. "We've got parts for assembling replacement birds starting to move in on cargo dollies so we can at least *start* to plan for having a full fighter wing!"

"Move those dollies back," Kira ordered. "At least they're still on wheels and nine of our bays are empty. Shove whatever you can in the hangar bays and clear everything out. I can't imagine we're going to have many people hanging out on the flight deck for long, but we need to at least look *half*-decent when the damn local monarch shows up."

"Right." Tamboli muttered something Kira carefully didn't hear. "We'll do what we can."

"We all will," she told them. "I'll be there in two."

KIRA ADDED another entry to the mental checklist of things she owed Milani for as she watched the plain RRA assault shuttle sweep onto *Deception*'s hangar deck. Somehow, they'd produced a dozen merceñaries for an honor guard in clean and respectable armor.

The armor didn't *match*, but Kira didn't really care about that. Her people were mercenaries.

Between Milani's people and Tamboli's, they even managed to clear enough space for the honor guard to take up formation safely as Kira and Kavitha Zoric waited for it to land. There was no way someone was going to mistake the flight deck for that of a true carrier or for anything resembling *clean*, but there was at least space for the shuttle—which there wasn't even in *Deception*'s proper shuttle bay right then.

The spacecraft settled to the metal on well-maintained antigrav coils, and a ramp extended. Crimson-uniformed Palace Guards marched down it in perfect lines, joining Milani's formation like the two units had trained for this exact maneuver.

Somehow, Kira wasn't surprised to see John Estanza walk out of the shuttle one step behind King Larry. The large-girthed monarch walked quickly enough that the mercenary Captain was clearly surprised, but the pair reached Kira and Zoric in swift order.

"Commodore Demirci, welcome back to Redward," Larry told her. "There have been better times for you to come back to, but you have also done us a greater service than we would have dared ask."

His smirk was clearly somewhat forced.

"As mercenaries, you will be rewarded in the usual manner of mercenaries who do grand things: with more money," he said loudly. "For the truth, though, you're also going to get the usual reward for a job well done."

"Another job," Kira guessed.

"Exactly. Do you have a space where the four of us can meet in private?" Larry gestured at Estanza and Zoric. "The situation before us is…"

"I think you should leave off finishing that sentence until we're in private, Your Majesty," Kira suggested grimly.

33

"THIS IS A FUCKING DISASTER," Larry snarled as the doors closed behind them. The Commander, Nova Group's office was still Kira's main retreat aboard *Deception*, and the ship's systems readily produced chairs for everyone.

A gentle shove from Kira's foot and a mental command from her headware sent her desk rolling back against the wall as she and Zoric got everyone seated with coffees in their hands.

That process left the King's curse unanswered in silence until they were all seated.

"I sent a canned report to Admiral Remington," Kira said. "Do you want the short version?"

"It can't be worse than most of the reports I've seen the last few days," he replied. "Lay it out."

"The Coalition Fleet's mission was fundamentally a success," she told him. "Arti, Kaiser and Kiln are all under the control of your army, with two destroyers with either gunship or nova-fighter support in place in each system.

"We can't guarantee they will hold in the face of active assault, but the Clans' ability to engage them is nonexistent," she concluded. "I can't see any strategic value to Bengalissimo in moving against them, especially as we have no ability to recall those ships.

"Unfortunately, we were ambushed at the Kiln by what appears to have been Cobra Squadron. Advanced-by-Rim-standard nova fighters and bombers. *Perseus* and *Last Denial* were destroyed along with a significant portion of the Coalition Fleet.

"Admiral Kim died with her flagship, but she and I had discussed her intentions with regards to recall orders for Coalition Fleet members." Kira sighed. "When those arrived on *Kenobi*, we let the ships go home. Several of those systems are still underwriting Commodore Shang's fees, though he's as out of touch with them as we are, I guess."

"Thank you," Larry said quietly, staring down at his coffee cup. "That's better than I was afraid of, if worse than I'd hoped. That we still have the ships and people who were missing from your formation is reassuring. At least they're not *all* dead."

"To absent friends," Estanza murmured, making a toasting gesture with his coffee cup. "Ylva was a good officer."

"To absent friends," Larry agreed, finally taking a sip of the coffee. "She was. She knew her duty and she did it well. More, she understood that just because she disagreed with a mission didn't mean it wasn't the right thing to do."

"Your Majesty?" Kira asked.

"She didn't tell you?" Larry asked. "Kim was a major advocate of repeating the last Kiln strike. Destruction of shipyards and industrial nodes with no attempt at follow-through. In theory, the Clans' habitats can survive without trade."

"In practice, though..." Kira trailed off.

"I think she knew that. I think she felt she had to present the most militarily sound option, even if it was of questionable morality," the King concluded. "She's not the only good officer we've lost."

"The last updates I had were the messages on *Kenobi*," Kira told him. "What's the situation?"

"Well, *Conviction* is busy being sealed up with barely a tenth of the planned work done," Estanza told her. "We got about a third of the flak turrets in, but that's all. We're going to need her before this mess is done."

"*Perseus* is lost, and *Achilles* is either in Ypres or lost," Larry admitted. "*If* Admiral Chen Ling got our message, she was supposed to take her carrier group to Ypres to help protect the people there. She should have had the firepower to do what you did here, but she didn't have a cruiser."

"What's the RRF down to, then?" Kira asked. She was running the math, but it didn't sound good.

"*Theseus, Guardian* and *First Crown*," Larry laid out. "Four destroyers in-system, all of them *Serendipity*-class, thank God, and about a hundred nova fighters."

The *Serendipities* were Redward's latest construction program and their most advanced ships. They were still toys compared to *Deception*, but they could hold their weight better than most Cluster ships.

"The RRF has lost or is cut off from half their capital ships and four-fifths of their destroyers," Estanza concluded. "That you brought Shinoda and Shang here might be the best news we've had since the *Ypres* blockade started."

"Obviously, we have limited news in the last few days," Larry said. "Sonia's best guess is that the blockade started four days ago and was fully sealed by forty-eight hours ago."

He shrugged.

"It will only take them a day or so to reclose the trade-route stop you cleared. We do know that there are least two Bengalissimo cruisers supporting the blockade, though our intel suggests that most of the blockade are mercenary ships."

"That was our conclusion from what we saw as well," Kira agreed. "They hesitated to commit suicide against two cruisers." She considered the situation. "*Deception* with two of your cruisers can easily handle two of Bengal's, I suspect."

"Don't be so certain of that," Estanza said grimly. "Your Majesty?"

"You may as well brief her," Larry said. "You know the language better than I do."

Kira's headware informed her that Estanza was trying to take control of the room's holoprojectors. She gave him access and swallowed down a mouthful of coffee.

She was glad to be able to set the cup aside as the holographic image of a nova ship started taking shape in the air above them. It was a *lot* bigger than she'd expected.

"I'm not going to pretend I know *how* Sonia's people got this," the mercenary Captain said, "but we have near complete specifications for Bengalissimo's new *Tabby*-class cruisers."

The hologram glimmered amidst them, at least a third again bigger than Kira had expected.

"About the only *good* news is that they don't have an organic nova-fighter force," Estanza told her. "Eighty kilocubics, twenty dual heavy plasma turrets. We're not sure on dispersal rating for the armor, but probably inferior to *Deception*. The guns are slightly lower-power than *Deception*'s as well, but…"

"Given what we lose in cubage for the fighter wing, they're better than the Cluster should be able to build," Kira finished. "Cube for cube, those ships are probably *Deception*'s match. We're enough *bigger* to make up the difference."

"But *Deception* is the only ship that can fight them one-on-one," Zoric said. "Do we have a plan?"

"Not as much of one as any of us would like," Larry told them. "We need to borrow your executive officer again, Captain Zoric. Your Commander Bueller and Estanza's Commander Labelle are the two most knowledgeable engineers in the star system, and we are prepared to pay significantly to hire them both.

"We need *our* two new cruisers, and we need them tomorrow, not in eleven months," the King concluded. "We're hoping that between our people, Bueller and Labelle, we can accelerate their construction and find ways to upgrade the ships we have.

"I've already ordered the emergency conversion of several modular container ships into escort carriers. We don't have time for the level of conversion done on *Achilles* and *Perseus*, but we can at least have something to haul nova fighters to the field."

"*Conviction* will be clear for action in a week at most," Estanza told the King. "But I don't have full decks of fighters."

"I'll speak with Remington," Larry promised. "We'll provide you with as many drive cores as you need to fabricate new fighter craft. If we don't have enough time, we may end up filling your decks with RRF birds, if that is acceptable?"

"We'll charge you rent, but that could work," Estanza agreed. "But...bluntly, Your Majesty, your pilots are undertrained and outmatched by Cobra Squadron."

"What choice do we have?" the King said.

"None," Kira said grimly. "We were able to identify the Manticore-Seven as the main interceptor in the formation that hit us. There were heavier fighters, but we didn't get enough visual data to allow for warbook confirmation."

"That's bad enough," Estanza replied. "Your Majesty, the Manticore-Seven is a reasonably modern interceptor by *Fringe* standards. We've brought your nova-fighter fleet up to Mid-Rim standards, but you're still badly outclassed.

"Worse, Cobra's pilots are going to be battle-hardened veterans. They've paid for the strikes they've launched, but...I'd want a two-to-one edge at least before going up against veterans in Manticores with newbies in Sinisters."

"I know," Larry said grimly. "Sonia had a solution for that. It's not perfect, but I agree with her on its value."

"Sir?" Kira asked.

"You need to expand your own fighter-pilot strength and we need to expand the RRF's fighter-pilot strength," Redward's King told them. "I want to hire you two, plus as many of your own veterans as you think will be helpful, to launch a crash training course for *all* of our pilots.

"I'm *hoping* to get the cruisers accelerated, so I can give you eight standard weeks to give as much training as possible to a class of three hundred pilots," he continued. "The course, the curriculum, the tools... *Everything* is yours to decide. If it can be provided, it will. Fifty of those pilots can be yours, recruited to fly off *Conviction*, but two hundred and fifty will be mine."

Kira traded a glance with Estanza. Two months to train three hundred pilots—and those pilots would be complete newbies; the

RRF had already run out of gunship and sub-fighter pilots to cross-train.

"It's doable," Estanza said quietly. "Demirci and I will need at least a week to put together a plan. I have some ideas, but if you want sixty-day specials, I need time to assemble the program."

"I don't *want* sixty-day specials," King Larry told them, his voice equally quiet. "I *want* to put my pilots through a detailed four-year training program that gives them a breadth of education that provides value to a post-service life and produces elite pilots.

"But what I want is irrelevant. What I *need* is a fleet that can punch through Cobra Squadron two months from now. I can hope and pray that our reputation and efforts will buy us those months," he said grimly. "But I can't delay longer."

"What about the Costar Clans Systems?" Kira asked. "We just left a quarter-million troops and half a dozen warships behind."

"There are contingency plans in place, prearranged with several of the other members of the Coalition," Larry told her. "Money and food and supplies will flow in our absence. *Quietly*, I have to hope, but we have little choice.

"Redward is besieged. I will not waste lives and ships to break out until we have the best chance we can put together." He shook his head. "There will be prices to pay for delay. But delay we must.

"I hope that your engineers and mine can get us a fleet worth the name in two months—but I *believe* that you can get me a nova-fighter corps worth deploying by then."

"We will do everything within our power, Your Majesty," Estanza promised. "But our enemies have caught us on the wrong foot this time. I don't think any of us expected to suddenly be facing an Equilibrium-funded enemy with a superiority in capital ships."

"But here we are," King Larry replied. "If we can accelerate those cruisers, we'll have five cruisers and four carriers to make the breakout with. I'd love to have the hundred-twenty units, but those are too far out.

"We go to war with the ships we have. Or"—he grimaced—"the ships we'll have in a few months, because we literally cannot go to war with what we have today."

34

THE KING and his Palace Guards left eventually, leaving John Estanza behind in the small conference room. Bueller joined them after a few minutes, taking a careful seat next to Kira, while Estanza and Zoric set up a channel to bring Labelle and Mwangi into the loop.

"I think everyone has the basic briefing on the shit-show we're in now, right?" Estanza asked. "Long and short of it: Bengalissimo's new queen has seven cruisers, four of them eighty-kilocubic units built to much the same standard as *Deception*. Plus a destroyer fleet, plus mercenaries—including a carrier fleet based around Cobra Squadron that appears to be able to field at least a hundred nova fighters."

Every one of the five mercenary officers was silent as they processed.

"Redward is down to two cruisers and a carrier, plus us," Estanza told them. "They've got four more destroyers, two seventy-five-kilocubic cruisers, and a pair of hundred-and-twenty-kilocubic units under construction. They've also begun emergency conversion of a pair of bulk carriers into forty-fighter escort carriers.

"Labelle, Bueller, they want to hire you as technical consultants," he continued. "If at all possible, they want you to help turn around the seventy-fives and the escort carriers inside two months."

"We already did everything that was rational to compress the construction schedules on the seventy-fives," Bueller replied. "I can try, but..."

Kira squeezed her boyfriend's hand, not really caring that everyone could see. If there was anyone in the entire mercenary company that didn't know about the two of them, they were deaf and had broken headware.

"This is now the time for more desperate measures, Konrad," she told him. "We can't fight seven cruisers with three. Given the way they've divided their forces, we *might* be able to pin them down in pieces and fight them with five."

Bueller exhaled a long sigh and squeezed her hand back.

"Lakshmi?" he asked Labelle. "I... There might be a few things, but I think the best bet is to put us and some Redward engineers in an office with a whiteboard."

"Anything we do will be risky," Labelle replied, their eyes dark. "Do they realize that compressing what was originally a twenty-four-month construction cycle to ten means they risk losing a ship? They *will* lose people."

"I suspect King Larry knows both of those things," Estanza admitted. "And if he doesn't, his engineers do. But every day that Redward remains blockaded, Bengalissimo inches closer to permanent dominance of the sector.

"While Redward is blockaded, the Free Trade Zone is dead. They'll have to rebuild *everything* once the dust settles, but the less time Larry and his people are out of the loop, the better chance they have to fix things.

"He's put the marker on two months—nine weeks, really. He might be being optimistic there," the mercenary Captain told them. "But in terms of what's needed, nine weeks is pushing it."

"We're clearing our slip for a merchant conversion job," Mwangi reported. "That's limiting how much work we can do, but I suspect we'll get more use out of a junk carrier than out of *Conviction* getting her four heavy turrets back."

"Agreed," Estanza said. "I'm going to have to leave that on you, Akuchi. Just like Kira's going to have to leave *Deception* and the fighter wings to her people. We're being hired to assemble and run a sixty-day fighter pilot curriculum."

Kira and Estanza were the only two fighter pilots in the room, but they set enough of the tone of the combined mercenary organization that *everyone* in the meeting winced. They knew how much training a nova-fighter pilot needed.

"My current inclination is to move the four of us who will be working locally down to the surface to get us out of the way of the people up here and put us closer to the locals," Estanza continued.

"We can use my apartment," Kira replied. "It's got enough bedrooms for that." She paused. "Um. I think it has ten?"

"That you don't even know is part of why you are my favorite business partner," Estanza said with a chuckle.

"I'm your only real business partner," Kira said. "I'll want to go over the list of senior pilots with you for the people we're going to need to grab for instructors. We need to leave some people up here to keep things running and keep training the non-newbies."

"Agreed. I suggest you put Hoffman in overall command of the nova group while we go be teachers," Estanza told her. "It's him, Cartman or Hersch. I *know* Hersch will be a better teacher."

"He and Cartman could both do either role but I'm thinking to leave Patel in space and I don't split the pair up if I can avoid it," Kira said. "Konrad, Lakshmi, are you okay to crash at the penthouse until we sort out what we're all doing?"

"Are we okay to *crash at the penthouse*, she asks," Labelle replied. "I've seen photos of the place Moranis left you. I think we will be okay to stay in your luxury apartment you barely use...even *before* we realize we don't need a bedroom for Konrad."

Kira smirked as she caught Bueller's blush. Despite his age and experience and everything, he was still surprisingly teasable. It was *adorable*.

"We have a plan, then," she said. "I'll check in with the pilots and see what we can get sorted out. Konrad—I'll need you to make sure that everything is set up to take care of our own damages and that tachyon-static problem."

"Already in place, boss," he confirmed. "We can rely on the local forts to keep us safe for now, so we'll begin the process of cooling *Deception* off to open up the core pretty quickly here."

"All right." Estanza shook his head. "We're all going to stretch our specialties for the next nine weeks, but if everything goes *well*, we'll help our employer pull off the impossible."

"And if we do that, we fuck Equilibrium while they're not expecting it," Bueller noted. "I'm looking forward to that part!"

"Agreed. Let's get to work."

35

KONRAD BUELLER, it turned out, was the kind of man whose attention to detail was carefully rationed to his working hours. This didn't manifest itself as a particularly large problem aboard a nova ship, where the engineer was arguably *always* working, but it did result in annoying habits when someone was sharing a master bedroom and en suite bathroom with him.

From specks of depilatory cream to drops of forgotten toothpaste, the self-cleaning function of the sinks wasn't enough to keep the entire vanity surface clean—and the cleaners were only coming in every week.

It was an annoyance to Kira, though hardly one worth having a fight over. In many ways, that the man had annoying self-care habits was almost a good thing—a reminder that she didn't know as much as she could about her lover.

She had, for example, known his taste in coffee was execrable, involving creamers and sweeteners to a level she wouldn't tolerate. It had been a surprise, then, to discover that Konrad was not merely capable of making drinkable black coffee but actually *good* at it.

The two engineers staying in the penthouse had farther to go in the mornings and so were the first up. By the time Kira, usually the first of the pilots, made her way into the main living area, Konrad had several pots of coffee going to cover the needs of the ten people living in the luxury apartment.

Thanks to Queen Sonia, he had Royal Reserve to work with, but he still was doing *something* slightly different that brought out the rich flavor of the beans...which he then smothered with cream and a local sweet syrup in his own cup.

Two weeks of living on the surface was bringing a certain degree of routine to them all. Kira traded Konrad a kiss for a cup of coffee and eyed the autochef in the corner of the kitchen. They had everything to cook properly, but none of them had the time.

"Two more minutes," Konrad told her. "Waffles this morning. I'll bring them out to you; go grab a seat."

Kira snorted and hooked a tall stool over so she could sit next to the island and watch him putter around the kitchen.

"So wonderfully domestic we all are," she murmured. Labelle had presumably grabbed their own coffee already—*Conviction*'s engineer was the one programming most of the meals into the autochef, the machine's code no longer recognizable to anyone else—and the pilots were still waking up.

"We get up, we share breakfast, we go off to the impossible tasks before us," Konrad said with a chuckle. "How's the training?"

"Seven days into sixty," Kira said with a shrug. "Encouraging so far, but we're not even into simulators yet. They're *promising* me enough nova fighters for practice maneuvers in three weeks, but I'm not counting them until I've put pilots in them."

"That's fair," Konrad agreed. "We're robbing Peter to pay Paul with the construction right now. The one-twenties are just...sitting there, which hurts to see."

Kira nodded. She'd give a *lot* to have the battlecruiser and fleet carrier for the breakout, but they were little more than a keel and a rough prototype for their Twelve-X nova drives. There was no way they could finish the big ships in time for it to matter.

"How's the rush construction?"

A shadow passed over her lover's face and he sighed.

"Two worker pods crashed yesterday," he told her, an explanation, she supposed, for why he'd been the last one home the previous evening. "Ten people aboard. Four are dead...two are crippled for life.

"And I'm in an office playing with computer models that I *know* are going to result in more deaths," he growled. "We're accelerating again and we're well past what's safe. Gods, give me two years, and I think we could put together a program that would be rolling out a destroyer every thirty days...but right now, we need to finish two cruisers and a bunch of freighter conversions in two months."

"Did they sign off on the extra conversions?" Kira asked. There wasn't much she could say about the dead yard workers, so she just squeezed Konrad's hand.

"Yeah. If everything works out, we'll have a grand total of *five* junk carriers for the breakout," he admitted. "The new ones don't carry as many birds as *Theseus*, but an extra hundred and sixty nova fighters..."

"We need two-to-one odds against Cobra Squadron," she said quietly. "I don't like what that means from any perspective. These volunteers we're training..." She shook her head. "It's going to be feeding broiler chickens to a wolf pack."

"That bad?" Konrad asked. "I know the training is abbreviated, but some of the pilots on *Deception* never had any formal training."

"It's not just that," Kira explained. "They'll get the best training eight veterans can give them, and I have faith in that training. But they're only getting two months of it, and then we're putting them into fighters that are thirty years behind what their most likely opposition has and throwing them up against hardened veterans equal to their *instructors*."

"Ah." Konrad looked down at his coffee, then crossed to open the autochef as it chimed at him. Plates of steaming waffles came out—and the rest of the mercenaries started drifting in, cutting their conversation short.

"What's on the plate today?" Cartman asked as she grabbed her food. "At work, I mean."

"Waffles?" Estanza replied, intentionally ignoring her clarification. "Come on. Let's debrief with a view."

Konrad joined them in the main seating area, where the officers collapsed into comfortable chairs looking out over Red Mountain,

Redward's capital city. There were a few moments of silence as everyone tucked into the waffles.

"Today we're going over types of warships," Estanza finally answered Cartman's question. "Starting with gunships, all the way up to the battlecruisers and fleet carriers they're not going to see anytime soon.

"Basic divisions between types, general likely armament, counter-measures and approach tactics..." The old mercenary shrugged. "We're cramming a lot of data into their heads, but we'll come back to it in exercises once they're in simulators. Today is just establishing a baseline."

A baseline that should have taken a week all on its own, Kira knew. She—like Cartman—had helped write the curriculum. There wasn't much time for questions or review with that kind of compression.

"Speaking of bigger ships," Hersch said, the *Conviction* pilot turning a look on Konrad. "Bueller, is it looking like we're actually going to have those cruisers?"

Kira hadn't been quite so blunt, but she'd also been derailed by his discussion of lost workers. It was an important question.

"When Labelle and I first started working with their people two weeks ago, I would have told you that you were going to have an extra month at least for your training," Konrad replied, gesturing toward the other engineer with his plate as they joined the crowd.

"I would have said two," Labelle noted. "Bueller had worked more closely with them than I had and had a more accurate assessment of what they could do."

"And?" Estanza asked.

"We're now up to a definite *maybe*," Bueller told him. "It's not... easy. In two weeks, we've already lost almost forty people, dead or maimed. The kind of pressure we're putting the yards under isn't safe, and neither are some of the things we're doing to put those ships together."

"It's also hurting the ships," Labelle pointed out. "The RRF'll have two seventy-fives...for about three years. Then they're going to have to either scrap them or rebuild them. We're sacrificing internal stability for weapons and armor. They'll still be able to take a hit and give a hit, but they won't stand up to long-term service."

"For comparison, *Deception* was designed to operate for twenty years without a major overhaul and as many as fifty without the kind of rebuild we're talking about for the revised *Baron*-class ships," Konrad said. "My understanding is that they'll be laying one-twenty keels in the yards as soon as we move the *Barons* out."

"What about the carrier conversions? Or escorts?" Hersch asked.

"You'll have carrier conversions, but they are more truly junk carriers than anything I've ever seen," Labelle warned. "And I've seen some *shitty-ass* carriers in my life."

"They'll be freighters that can launch fighters," Konrad agreed. "Nothing more. They won't be able to maneuver like a warship; they won't be able to take a hit like a warship. But they'll bring a hundred and sixty nova fighters to the fight."

"And it's our job to make sure those fighters have pilots," Kira reminded the rest of the trainers. "What's your time looking like, Konrad?"

"Pretty much gone," he admitted. "Labelle?"

"Meet you in the hall," the other engineer agreed.

KIRA TOOK a moment to walk Konrad out to the elevator and give him a hug.

"Are you all right?" she asked.

"No," he admitted. "This kind of rush construction program is hell. I can't imagine the training is any better, though."

"No," she agreed. "We at least aren't going to see many of our students die in training, but we'll be sending a lot of these kids to their deaths."

"And I'm sending people to their deaths right now, working them too hard and cycling processes too close together," Konrad said with a sigh. "But what can we do? I'm not surrendering to Equilibrium."

"*Redward* isn't surrendering to Equilibrium, whether we help them or not," Kira told him. "Do you think they'll succeed as well or lose less people without us?"

"They won't get the ships and they'll lose more people trying without Lakshmi and me," Konrad said grimly. "And they'd lose a lot more of those pilots without you training them. We do what we can, save as much as we can."

"Exactly. But that still doesn't make you all right, does it?"

"No. You?"

"No. It's just what we've got to do."

Labelle's emergence from the apartment cut the conversation short again, though Kira didn't rush to release Konrad from her embrace.

"We're all in rough shape and I don't want to rush you," the older engineer told them after a moment, "but the RRF aircar is only two minutes out and we *are* on the fifty-eighth floor."

"Go," Kira said, stepping back. "I've got work to do as well."

36

"TRAINEE GROUP ONE, ATTENTION!"

Kira used Milani for many different tasks, but the dragon-armored mercenary also did a *fantastic* job of projecting their voice through the suit, bringing a semi-chaotic slurry of twenty-year-olds to a halt and focused toward the podium.

Kira gave her friend a nod and stepped up onto the stage, gesturing her other instructors up with her. Cartman, Hersch, Colombera and Michel brought her to five mercenaries. Another five RRF officers spread out around them.

With the intensity and compression of the training course over the last four weeks, she'd barely had time to pick up the names of the *trainers*, let alone the three hundred recruits she was responsible for. They were a blur of names and ID numbers and test scores—but the top one hundred of them by test score were gathered in front of her.

"All right, people. Welcome to Shadow Ward Station," she told them. "Thanks to your test scores, you've all been assigned to Group One. The overall training cohort has been split into three groups because we have pushed live flight exercises back as far as we can."

A mental command transformed the wall behind her, changing what had appeared to be plain rock into a transparent window out onto one of the many craters on the surface of Shadow Ward—it was an eight-kilometer-wide asteroid, after all.

This crater had been repurposed and paths of artificial gravity plates led out onto the field, allowing access to the rows upon rows of nova fighters.

"Despite assorted promises, we only have one hundred Dexter-type interceptors to train you on," Kira told her trainees. "Plus ten Escutcheon-type heavy fighters for your trainers to fly, since I think your government hates me."

That earned her a few chuckles, as expected. She'd made her preference for the interceptor-style nova fighters clear over the last thirty-five days.

With only twenty-five days left in their training—and only twenty-eight until Bueller and his colleagues said they could deliver mostly functional cruisers—Kira had drawn a line in the sand. They needed as many fighters to put the recruits in as possible, even if that meant stripping the active squadrons supporting the defensive stations.

That had earned her one hundred and ten nova fighters... Enough, she hoped.

"Now, today is *not* a live-fire exercise," she told them. "The main thing we're testing today is that you can actually get a starfighter off an asteroid and back onto it. A landing plain is honestly *easier* than a carrier deck, because you only have one surface to hit instead of four!

"Both the weapons and nova drives on your starfighters have been disabled, but you will go through a full version of your checklist regardless," she continued. "Deactivated items will run by local simulator—your headware will interface with the fighter's hardware. Trust it.

"Anybody who fucks up the checklist doesn't fly today," she warned. "But...remember that for all the simulated components and disabled systems, these are very real nova fighters in your hands. Redward only *has* two hundred of these babies at the moment."

Which was still hopefully more than anyone else, even including Cobra Squadron. With the blockade, Redward—and by extension, Kira—knew *nothing* about what was going on outside the system.

It would fall to these kids to help change that.

"Your headware should be receiving your fighter and squadron assignment as I speak," she told them. "They should also guide you to the right bird. You're all suited up."

She smiled at the crowd, tapping her helmet against her hip.

"This is your first chance to do something only a tiny handful of people *anywhere* ever get to do, people. Don't fuck it up for me.

"Trainee Group One! Board your fighters!"

THE ESCUTCHEON COULD HAVE BEEN WORSE, Kira reflected. It was at least roomier on the inside than the Hoplite or its Dexter clone, though that wasn't saying much.

She and the instructors had completed their checklists and lifted off on their antigrav and Harrington coils before the first students finished their own once-overs. They might be unfamiliar with the particular starfighters they'd been lent, but all ten of the trainers spoke fluent spaceship.

"Any red flags, Cartman?" she asked her subordinate as she skimmed through the checklist reports. In training mode, the fighters were happy to tell her *everything* about what their pilots had done— something no active-duty pilot would ever tolerate.

"Nothing... Wait... What the fuck?" Cartman flagged the second checklist complete. "Never mind; someone just pinged a counter-hack flag."

"Someone *hacked* their checklist?" Kira asked, making sure she was hearing that correctly.

"Charlie Squadron, Fighter Three," Cartman confirmed, flipping the data over. "Pilot-Trainee Neha Bradley."

The name was meaningless to Kira on its own, so she brought up Trainee Bradley's record. She was consistently the second-ranked or third-ranked...at everything. Never first, never the best, never enough to draw attention to her, but enough to make sure that she was going to get her choice of posting when this was over.

Assuming she had actually learned *anything*.

"Locking down C-3," Kira announced. "Hack alert triggered. Milani—secure Trainee Bradley."

"Yes, sir," the mercenary replied instantly. "Hold the rest of the fighters?"

"They're not launching till I give the word," Kira said grimly. "I'm *hoping* we're just dealing with someone determined to look good, but she overrode her checklist and trainee-monitoring software."

Kira flipped a mental switch and brought her nova fighter's guns online. If Bradley could override the trainee-monitoring system, she might be able to override the trainee lockdown systems, too—and Kira would rather leave an expensive starfighter strewn across Shadow Ward's surface than let a potential spy escape.

"C-3 is secured," Milani reported after a moment. "Trainee Bradley has been detained. No resistance; she's…very upset."

"Take her back to Shadow Ward's brig," Kira ordered. "We'll hand her over to Redward Intelligence. Might have been innocent enough, but we *cannot* have a cheater in this program."

She exhaled a long sigh.

"Let me know when you're clear of the landing field," she told the merc. "This show still needs to get on the road for the other ninety-nine trainees."

THE TAKEOFFS WERE ROUGH—BUT Kira had frankly seen worse. The extra five days of simulator time over what had been planned seemed to have helped, and all of the fighters made it up to deployment altitude without problems.

"Wobbly but acceptable," Cartman said, echoing her thoughts. "Stick to the plan?"

"Exactly. Instructors, you have a designated squadron," Kira reminded her trainers. "Pick them up and take them for a run around the region. Don't get more than half a light-second from Shadow Ward, and have them back in three hours.

"We're getting them comfy with the birds, not running an endurance trial."

She waited for acknowledgements and then flicked to her own channel.

"Alpha Trainee Squadron, report in," she ordered.

Ten young-sounding voices replied. They were more nervous than she'd expected, and she grimaced as she realized that they'd all just watched armored mercenaries march across a landing field and drag one of their compatriots from her fighter.

"Form on my wing and follow me out," she told them. "Don't waste your attention worrying about things you can't control. Pay attention to what you *can*—right now, getting used to the cockpit and controls of a Dexter-type interceptor."

Five nova fighters formed on either side of her in a shallow V. It wasn't as even as it could have been and it wasn't as intentionally chaotic as a combat formation would be, but it would do. She studied it for a moment, then shrugged.

"We're in parade-ground mode today," she warned. "By the time you leave my tender care, you'll know how to maintain a formation while maneuvering enough to frustrate long-range fire. Right now, however... Six, move up and toward me three degrees and increase accel by ten percent for six seconds. Eight, move down and toward me seven degrees; increase accel by three percent for ten seconds."

She watched as the two trainees followed her instructions, slotting into their positions in the line. Nine made a quick adjustment on their own before she gave an order, and all ten of her trainees were in perfect parade formation.

"All right, not shabby," she told them. "Not up to *my* standards, but people tell me my standards are unreasonable. Now. *Stay* in formation and let's put these birds to work."

37

A THREE-HOUR PATROL in a nova fighter was nothing to Kira or the other trainers, but by the end of the loop, she realized it was potentially too much for the first time she'd put the trainees in a real spacecraft.

The formation in her squadron was getting sloppier as she brought them in on approach to Shadow Ward. They were still holding it well enough with a few corrections here and there, but she could see fatigue in their maneuvers.

"Group One Trainers, report in," she ordered. "Positions and status."

The reports were trained and automatic on the part of her people. All of them were still over ninety-five percent fuel and they were all in various approach vectors to the landing field.

"Understood. India, Juliet, adjust your vectors back; you'll have to come around on a second loop," she told them. "Hotel, Golf, increase your deceleration by twenty percent. Foxtrot, Echo, increase your decel by forty percent. Charlie, Delta, increase by twenty. Bravo, form on my Alphas."

A hundred-plus starfighters swung through space to answer her orders. Increasing the deceleration meant that the various sets of squadrons would come to a halt away from the station, requiring further maneuvers to bring them into landing after Alpha and Bravo had landed.

The trainers were adjusting their own fighters immediately as they passed on their orders—and some of the pilots were matching the trainers' changes without waiting for the order.

Some weren't, and Kira's stomach lurched as she realized that two of Golf Squadron's fighters were still coming in on a hard approach, the pilots lost to tunnel vision of their existing plan.

"G-Three, G-Seven, report," she snapped. Then she swore as she realized the fighters weren't directly linked to her channel—she was linked to the trainers and Alpha Squadron. "Golf-leader, get those planes in formation!"

The two fighters were still hurtling forward on landing vectors—and four entire squadrons of starfighters in front of them were now decelerating hard. There *should* have been enough space...except that they'd all been on a course for a landing field barely two kilometers across.

Golf-Three finally broke off, the pilot slamming their deceleration to full as they finally caught up with what was happening. They'd screwed up to get where they were, but they reacted correctly once they realized what was going on. Their vector went sideways relative to the rest of the training group as they accelerated away from the other planes.

Golf-Seven's pilot woke up and flipped their fighter, going to maximum acceleration—just as Charlie-Four realized there was a problem and tried to maneuver out of the way.

Space should have been too big for them to collide, but the Devil Murphy plays no favorites. Charlie-Four dodged *into* Golf-Seven's new vector, and the two Dexter interceptors slammed into each other at several hundred kilometers per second.

Pieces of starfighters went flying as one fighter cut through the other, and then containment failed on *both* fusion reactors. Two of Kira's trainees vanished in a single blue-white fireball.

"ALL PLANES, MAX DECELERATION *NOW*," Kira barked. "Move away from the danger zone; clear a path for search-and-rescue."

"I've pinged search-and-rescue," Cartman promised, her voice sounding ill. Charlie was *her* squadron, even if all of this was Kira's problem. "Shadow Ward is launching support shuttles, ETA five minutes."

"Thank you, Nightmare. Everyone, get the trainees clear and sweep for survival pods," Kira ordered her trainers. "They're automated. There's... There's a chance."

Two of Redward's multi-million-kroner starfighters were gone, but there was still a chance that the *pilots* had lived. Not a large chance, but a chance.

The trainees were following orders exactly now. Kira and her trainers were issuing *exact* courses and she was seriously considering taking direct control of the fighters—there was more reason than one that no pilot would voluntarily fly a nova fighter with a training module installed.

For now, though, the trainees seemed to be awake. Fear and adrenaline burned away fatigue. Grief sharpened attention.

Even as the S&R shuttles arrived for the fruitless chase, Kira was forcing herself to remember who the two trainees had even *been*. With three hundred students, few of them registered as more than a file and maybe a face...but these two, she was going to have to remember.

Charlie-Four had been Kyauta Maina, a name Kira *did* have associated with a face. The young woman had been the darkest-skinned person Kira had met across a dozen worlds, with pitch-black hair and warm brown eyes. She'd been eager and intelligent, but that covered all three hundred of the trainees.

Golf-Seven had been Lucja Colt, a dark-haired and sharp-featured woman who Kira had barely encountered. She knew nothing about Colt except what was in her file and image, and she hated herself a little for that.

She'd watched the accident. There was no way either pilot had survived. There were no survival pods on her heavy fighter's scanners. No life signs. Just debris and radiation.

38

"SIRS."

"Sit down, Kira," Admiral Vilma Remington ordered. The gray-eyed commander of the Redward Royal Fleet gestured Kira to a seat in front of her desk, next to John Estanza.

"I assume there will need to be an investigation," Kira said quietly. "I am prepared to take full responsibility and withdraw from this contract. I…"

She swallowed. She'd lost people before, but rarely in training. In the six hours it had taken her to get her fighter back to the surface and end up in Remington's office, she'd gone over all of it in her headware.

They'd pushed too hard and two of their pilots had died. That responsibility was hers.

"I was in command of the training exercise and wrote the parameters," she finally finished. "Someone has to be punished for this."

"No," Estanza replied. "No one has to be punished for this, Kira. It was an accident. A shitty, awful, *tragic* fucking accident that claimed two young women who didn't deserve to die, yes, but still an accident."

"We owe it to them."

"You do not," Remington said, firmly. "At this point in time, I would prefer not to change up the command structure of the training program. While the RRF cannot *force* you to complete your contract, we have no intention of releasing you from it, and the break penalties are…significant."

Kira inhaled sharply and nodded. She could *pay* those penalties, she was sure, but she hadn't paid as much attention to them as she should have.

"What do we do?" she finally asked.

"We give the students one day to grieve," Estanza told her. "Today, the three of us"—he gestured to include Remington—"go over the high level of what happened and how to avoid it. Tomorrow, we go over it with the trainers and we readjust the parameters of the curriculum so we don't lose people to *this* particular error again."

The office was quiet.

"I have researched nova-fighter training programs as best as I can from here," Remington said after a moment. "Having never flown a fighter myself and working from documentation that is redacted at best, it's difficult to identify best practices.

"What is not, unfortunately, difficult to realize is that even best-practice training programs lose students. You are training children to handle some of the most powerful hardware in existence on their own. Accidents can and will happen."

"I've never been in charge of an entire training program before," Kira admitted. "I've worked as a trainer but not as one of the two people running the whole damn thing."

"I *have* and I'll remind you that *we* wrote the training program," Estanza told her flatly. "This isn't the first time I've been hired to train up an entire system's nova-fighter corps. It *is* the first time I've been asked to do it in sixty days.

"These kids had fifteen days of classroom training and twenty days of simulator training before we put them in nova fighters. That's a *quarter* of the time they should have had," he noted. "We have twenty-five days to put them through mixed training with actual nova-fighter time. They're not getting the breathing room, the digestion time, *anything* that they need to really have it all fit together in their heads."

"We knew this would be a problem when we gave you the time-line," Remington said. "Bluntly, Commodore Demirci, I expect to lose thirty of those trainees before we're done. I hate myself for it, but I *need* those pilots.

"Redward needs those pilots."

"I..." Kira swallowed. "I hate it, sirs."

"We all do," Estanza told her. "So, we do everything we can to minimize the impact."

He gave himself a full-body shake and leaned forward, studying Kira.

"Now, you saw what happened. What was the biggest mistake we made?"

"We assumed they could do a three-hour patrol as their first flight," she said instantly. "To you or me, three hours is nothing. We do seven hours in space as a standard non-combat patrol. To these new trainees, kids with no spaceflight experience, just a standard flight is as draining and adrenaline-intensive as full-on combat.

"We're used to, at worst, training shuttle pilots and gunship pilots to be nova-fighter pilots," Kira concluded. "They know how to fly and we're just adjusting their habits and skills to the new hardware. These kids are learning to fly for the first time.

"I think we need to cap them at an hour live flight time per training session for at least the first ten days," she said. "We'll ramp up rapidly after that, we only have twenty-five days, but we need to do multiple smaller sessions for that first week and some."

"If you move the entire training cohort onto Shadow Ward, you can cycle them more quickly and get about the same amount of training as you were planning," Remington pointed out. "Mix simulator, class-room and live flight training in a single day, rather than having one day of sim and classroom followed by a day of live flight."

"We can do that, if you'll give us the space on the Ward," Estanza agreed. "I'll miss the penthouse."

Kira managed a small chuckle. It was somewhat forced, but it was real. She suspected that the pressure of the training program was going to wear down her humor over the remaining days...and it would have been a lot easier with Bueller to support her.

"We'll make do, sir," she told Estanza. "I can hope that Shadow Ward's transient officer quarters are better than some of the places I served Apollo in."

"You may well be disappointed," Remington warned. "But we will do what we can."

39

THEY GAVE the students a day to rest and grieve. Kira and the rest of the trainers spent that day moving everything to a new space on Shadow Ward. One of the advantages of an asteroid battle station was that it had a *lot* of space to work with.

The area they'd been given was basically a surface apartment building with some attached conference rooms, a few minutes by transit tube from the landing field they were storing the training fighters at.

By the end of the day, Kira even had an office to collapse into in a half-exhausted state. The students would be shuttled up in the morning, and then they would be back to work.

There'd be no chance to pause for grief if there were more losses. The timelines were already tight—and they had no way to judge if they were getting tighter for external reasons. Ypres could have fallen already, and they wouldn't know.

Local politics, on the other hand, were definitely a factor. The news playing on a hologram above her desk was *painful*.

"One does not wish to impugn the wisdom of our King," an MP was saying. "But I have to question what we are fighting for. Without interstellar trade, there is no Free Trade Zone. Have we even made an attempt to communicate with the blockaders? Surely, they must have some demands we can negotiate around!"

"Someone doesn't know how this works," a dry voice said from Kira's door. Kira looked up to find Milani standing just inside the entrance, the dragon on their armor looking *very* unimpressed with the politician.

Kira turned the news report off with a wave of her hand.

"I'll admit the lack of communication makes *me* twitchy," she told the merc trooper. "It's been a month and we haven't seen a single ship from outside. No demands, just a complete blackout."

The *good* news was that the ships the RRF had sent out to map secondary exit points would be returning in another month. That would at least give Redward some options for communication.

They would need a visible and clear victory to break the blockade and get shipping to start coming back, though. Once the RRF had secondary exit points, communications could be reestablished, but only defeating the Bengalissimo force would actually change anything.

"Says the Institute is playing an ugly game to me," Milani observed. "One where Redward disappearing is more useful than a Redward brought to heel."

"Or they don't think they can bring Redward sufficiently to heel, and blockading keeps them in line," Kira said. "If they think we're still on the old construction timelines, they may think they have time. I don't quite believe that, given how badly we've been penetrated in the past."

"On that note, sir, I have someone who wants to talk to you," Milani told her.

"Who?"

"Neha Bradley," the merc told her. "The one we grounded for cheating and passed onto the RRF for interrogation. I'm guessing you haven't had a chance for an update there?"

"Not yet," Kira admitted. "Buried in my email somewhere."

"She's Equilibrium," Milani said bluntly. "Made some interesting offers to Redward Intelligence but insisted on talking to you. Alone."

"That sounds like a trap, Milani," Kira replied.

"I was planning on chaining her to a chair and giving you a

blaster," her subordinate said brightly. "She seems straightforward enough, but…it's your call."

"What's she offering?" Kira asked.

"The man who recruited her, her handler, and the woman she thinks runs the Institute's intelligence on the planet," Milani told her. "But she won't make a deal with Redward. She wants to make it with you."

Kira sighed. She needed six hours of sleep and a shower, but…that was probably worth it.

"All right. Bring her in."

NEHA BRADLEY WAS, without question, gorgeous. A lithe young woman with athletic curves and raven-black hair, even in a prisoner's jumpsuit she was catching more than a professional gaze from the two RRF Military Police who escorted her into Kira's office.

Milani was true to their word, though. Bradley was handcuffed to a heavy steel chair before the MPs left, and the mercenary visibly paused to put a large hand blaster on the desk in front of Kira.

"If you shoot her attempting escape, no one's going to blink much," the merc told Kira—clearly enough for Bradley to hear. "She might be useful, but I suspect Redward thinks you're more so."

The dragon-armored mercenary stepped out the door of the plain office, leaving Kira alone with the prisoner.

"Em Bradley," Kira said, studying the young woman. "You cheated your way through half of my training program and apparently work for the people who've been making my life misery since before I even knew they existed.

"Milani tells me you insisted on talking to me before making any kind of deal," she concluded. "I'm…not enthused. So talk."

"I can finger at least three key Institute agents on Redward," Bradley said quietly. "I'd think you'd be more interested in neutralizing them."

"Oh, I'm interested; I'm just not sure why you're talking to me," Kira replied.

"Because everyone who knows anything knows that the RRF is riddled with informers," the woman said. "So, if I want actual *help*, I need to talk to someone who can do things without them. Plus"—she shrugged—"I want back in the training program."

Kira laughed.

"You cheated your way as far as you did," she pointed out. "If the program you'd been using was just a *bit* more sophisticated, you might have kept cheating all the way through. I can't trust that you know any of what we taught, I can't trust an enemy agent, and you want me to put you back in a nova fighter?"

"Yes," Bradley said firmly. "Because these sons of bitches have my daughter."

Kira's spine straightened and her feet slammed onto the ground as she held Bradley's gaze firmly for an assessing ten seconds. The woman's file said she was twenty-two standard years old and she looked it, which meant Kira had been a military officer and a leader of people for as long as Bradley had been alive.

There was a hang to the other woman's eyes, an anger to her tone, that spoke to the truth of her words.

"She'd be what, six months old?" Kira said levelly. It was a guess, but an older child would have been hard to excise from the younger woman's file—and there was *nothing* about a kid in Bradley's file.

"Nine months," Bradley said. "A foolish accident the father wanted nothing to do with, but Jessica is my baby girl. And I will do anything to protect her and make sure she gets the life she deserves."

"What happened?" Kira asked. She still half-suspected she was being played, but she would let it play out. A young single mother... She could see a dozen ways that the Institute could have co-opted her.

"I..." Bradley inhaled a deep breath, then nodded firmly to herself. "I had a hard pregnancy and had to drop out of the shuttle-pilot training program I was in. With half a qualification, I couldn't do much, and it was hard to find the time around a baby and keeping us both fed to earn any more qualifications.

"But the RRF was in recruiting mode, and they've always had a reputation for good mental-health and family support," she admitted.

"Didn't even realize they had a fighter pilot program until they offered me a place in it.

"And then the next day, a man I didn't know started walking next to me on my way home from work." She shivered. "He was polite, but he made it clear he knew far too much about me. He offered me a *lot* of money to help him *keep an eye* on the training program, enough that I wouldn't need the RRF's family-support program."

She spread her hands.

"I...heard him out," she admitted. "More than I should have, but once he started talking about serving the greater good and saving the galaxy, I realized things were going far weirder than I could deal with. Threw him out of my place before my roommate got home with Jessica.

"Next day, someone broke into the apartment and kidnapped Jessica."

Bradley said the words without emotion, but the pain her flat tone concealed only confirmed Kira's initial assessment. The lack of a child in Bradley's Navy files was both a point against her story...and a point in its favor, if her blackmailer was who Kira thought it was.

"They somehow edited my application to take out the family-support request," she continued. "I was *allowed* to visit my daughter and they promised to continue paying me, so long as I kept them fully in the loop.

"I met the third woman at the house where they were keeping my girl," Bradley noted. "I don't think I was supposed to—she was *furious* with my handler and I never caught a name, but...I have headware footage."

"Of all three, yes?" Kira asked.

"Yes," the young woman confirmed. "I will give details, headware recordings, whatever is needed...so long as you get my little girl back and let me fly."

Kira looked down at her hands.

"Neha, you're a traitor," she said bluntly. "The RRF is going to cashier you. I can't change that; I'm just a merc."

The woman inhaled and nodded slowly. Kira watched her for a few seconds. What she'd said was *true*, but Kira Demirci had options the RRF didn't.

"If you save Jessica, I'll…give you everything anyway. I'll go to jail. I just need to know she's safe."

"Give me what you can on that safe house," Kira told her. It seemed Bradley had passed her test. "We'll see what we can find. And if what you give us is worth what you say it is, I will *gently* remind the RRF that fifty slots in this program are *mine* to do with as I please.

"If you're telling the truth, we might have to see how well you fit the mercenary life."

40

THE OFFICE OF INTEGRATION operated out of a nondescript office building tucked away in Red Mountain's main business district. Kira took a certain degree of amusement in Bradley's confusion as the aircar parked in an underground garage and their mercenary escort was met by a group of youths in black suits.

To Kira, the security handoff between Milani's troopers and the plainclothes Palace Guard was obvious. She suspected it was less obvious to Neha Bradley, the gorgeous brunette sticking closer to Kira than before as they followed their escort to the elevator.

Unlike Bradley, Kira knew what was waiting for them—and what Milani's strike team had found at the Equilibrium safe house the young woman had sent them to. She was still irritated enough with the contrite spy to let her squirm as they made their way to the thirty-third floor.

The lobby they entered was plush, decorated in well-balanced shades of blue and orange, and announced itself as a private wealth management company.

The young woman behind the reception desk was *supposedly* a sign of the wealth of the financiers behind her security doors, since only the richest of clients expected to deal with humans instead of artificially stupid holograms.

In truth, Kira could tell she was cut from the same cloth as the guard ushering Kira and Bradley deeper into the intelligence agency's office.

"Why are we *here*?" Bradley whispered to Kira. She was still hand-cuffed and had—correctly—guessed that Kira had the keys for her manacles.

"You'll see," Kira promised.

A security door slid open and their guards ushered them into a more plainly decorated corridor that still reeked of expensive interior design. Their destination was an even more heavily secured door, though the corridor door took them past several open-plan office sections. Those desks were full of analysts even at this early hour in the morning, though their data exchanges had automatically gone full-headware when strangers entered the office.

The secured conference room door belonged in a bunker, not on the midlevel floors of an office tower, and Kira could see Bradley's nervousness as they approached. It swung open and Kira's amusement broke into a full grin as she recognized the woman standing in the door.

Brigadier Hope Temitope was now the second-in-command of the *entire* Redward Commando Corps, the elite special forces Kira had worked with to seize *Deception*. The golden-eyed woman had been a Colonel then, but victory shared many rewards.

Most importantly for Kira's companion, however, was that the whip-thin, dark-haired Black woman was holding a child with equally dark hair, the baby curled into Temitope's shoulder as the commando held her prize with extreme delicacy.

"You found her?" Bradley gasped, lunging across half the distance to the commando officer before pulling herself up short.

"And seven other children of various ages," Milani's voice told them, the armored mercenary stepping up next to Temitope with a duplicate of the control Kira had tucked in her pocket.

They tapped a command and Bradley's cuffs unlocked, falling to the floor forgotten as the young mother completed her aborted lunge and gently took her baby from Brigadier Temitope.

"Other children?" Bradley said, her voice choked with tears as she rocked her child.

"Let the poor woman sit down," Queen Sonia ordered. "We still need quite a bit from her this morning."

Kira let Milani, with uncharacteristic gentleness, take Bradley by the shoulder and guide her to a seat around the conference table. Like the rest of the office, the conference room kept up the illusion of being a private finance company for wealthy clients, providing comfortable seats and absolutely up-to-date electronics.

Well, up to date for Redward, Kira reflected.

Bradley collapsed into the seat, clutching her baby to her. Kira would freely admit that she didn't have much of a maternal instinct, but the sight twinged even her heartstrings.

Despite her tears, she managed to transfer a file to Kira's headware.

"Everything I promised," she told Kira. "Faces, names, locations… Everything I was able to learn while I was working for them."

Kira flipped the file to Sonia, who smiled.

"Thank you, Em Bradley," the Queen told the young woman. "Brigadier, we need to move on this quickly."

"That's why we have an office full of analysts outside and I have a battalion of commandos I trust on standby," Temitope replied. "I'm on it."

With a sharp salute, the woman bowed her way out.

"We are currently identifying the parents of the other children at that safe house," Sonia told Bradley. "I took the liberty of ordering the officer responsible for your recruitment detained as well. They might be innocent, but it seems…unlikely."

"I will give you anything I can," Bradley promised. "I… I understand I committed treason. But…" She looked down at her daughter's face. "I didn't know what else to do to protect her."

The room was silent and Sonia sighed.

"Do you know who I am, young lady?" she asked.

Kira couldn't help but smirk at the shocked look on Neha Bradley's face when the woman finally looked at her Queen and realized who she was talking to.

"Yes, ma—Your Majesty."

"We cannot permit you to remain in the RRF after your actions, but there will be no further consequences after your discharge without prejudice," Sonia told the young woman. "The files on this matter will be sealed. Kira?"

"You already retested on what I could test you on tonight," Kira pointed out. "You passed all the tests, so I have to wonder just why you kept using the cheat program. I'm forced to conclude that you were *trying* to get caught."

"I... I wasn't sure," Bradley confessed. "I was trying... I needed to keep her safe, but..."

"I understand," Sonia told her. "I have a daughter of my own, Em Bradley. Not much older than your Jessica and my only child. I *understand*. But I also have to protect Redward."

"I understand," Bradley echoed. "So, what happens now?"

"The records are sealed," the Queen repeated. "You will need to remain in protective custody for at least a week while we clean up as much of the Institute's network as we can, as much to keep you safe as anything else."

"I would prefer if she was able to keep up with at least a simulator routine in that week," Kira said. Both women looked at her in confusion. "*If*, of course, Em Bradley is still interested in being a nova-fighter pilot and is prepared to become a mercenary."

"I don't know," Bradley admitted, looking down at Jessica's face. "I need... I need the money and it's the only thing I've worked toward qualifications on. But I don't want to leave Jessica, either. I don't know."

"That's fair," Kira allowed, looking over at the Queen. "I know she's safe with you for now. If the Queen is willing to let me recruit you, I can give you a few days to make up your mind."

"It seems a reasonable solution for everyone," Sonia agreed. "If you don't think her fellow trainees will be a problem?"

"Believe me, Your Majesty, I can make sure they aren't."

"Then I believe the decision is entirely Em Bradley's," Sonia noted. "For now, though, rest assured that you and your child are under the protection of the Crown of Redward."

41

SEVEN DEATHS. Thirty-one withdrawals. Sixteen injuries severe enough to require more than a few days' recovery, washing those trainees out.

On the final day of the sixty-day program, Kira stood next to John Estanza on the edge of the Shadow Ward landing field. They'd *eventually* received enough nova fighters for all their pilots to train at once—even including Sinisters and Escutcheons.

Now the trainers were lined up in their spacesuits, watching almost two hundred and fifty nova fighters make their approach, six at a time. The spacing was greater than Kira would have wanted for veterans, but it was closer than she'd have expected even ten days earlier.

Starfighter after starfighter swept in to soft landings on the low-gravity field. Squadron after squadron took shape over the course of about fifteen minutes while the mercenary and RRF trainers alike stood at attention.

"They're not what I'd want," John Estanza admitted on a private channel to Kira. "But they're better than I'd dare hope."

"Agreed." Kira watched the "lucky" pilots who'd drawn the heavy fighters today bring up the end of the formation. "The irony is not lost on me, either, that one of our best students was the Institute spy who cheated her way through half the course."

Estanza chuckled.

"You know she's going to be lucky if she manages to avoid getting stuck with *Traitor* or something similar as her callsign, right?" he asked. "I'm glad we gave her another chance, her situation was horrific, but no one is going to let that go any time soon."

"Everything we see suggests her defection *shattered* the Institute network on Redward," Kira pointed out. "We came out ahead for her being a 'traitor.'"

"And that is why she'll be flying for you," Estanza agreed. "Still seems weird to have a *Commodore* answering to a *Captain*."

"We're business partners; I only answer to you sometimes," Kira replied. "I figure we're adults and can handle it."

"That we can." The last squadron edged toward the ground. "Speaking of being adults, how's Bueller?"

"Exhausted and stretched to paper-thin, like everyone else involved in ship construction right now," Kira said. "On the other hand...they did it."

"I hadn't heard that officially yet," Estanza murmured. "Where are we at?"

"*Baron* and *Duke* are just closing up plates today; they're done," she told him. "They officially launch tomorrow. The destroyers were finished a week ago, and the last of the carrier conversions was done yesterday.

"We didn't lose a ship in the process, though..." She sighed. "Konrad stopped talking about the death numbers with me weeks ago. Official death toll is over three hundred."

"I know," Estanza said. "That's going to hurt him. Fuck, I'm torn up enough about the kids *we* lost."

"Me too. They were volunteers and they knew the risks, but *fuck* if I don't feel like I killed them," Kira agreed. "And I swear, the ones that lived through it all... I'm not feeling much better about sending them into a goddamn war."

"Not much choice," the carrier Captain agreed. "But for now, we graduate them and we send them to get a drink."

"And us?" Kira asked.

"*We* have a briefing with Their Majesties," Estanza reminded her. "And unless I miss my math, that means the first covert couriers are back and we have some idea what the Cluster looks like today."

BRIEFINGS and the future would wait. Kira and the rest of the trainers split to lines on either side of the path as their graduating trainees made their way back into the underground segments of Shadow Ward and the marshaling ground where Estanza would give the final speech.

It took less time for the pilots to enter the asteroid than it had taken for the fighters to land, and the trainers followed them in at the end. Kira accompanied Estanza to the podium at the front of the big room and stood at his right hand as he removed his helmet and looked out at the class.

"Pilot Trainee Class One," he greeted them. "You are no longer trainees."

That earned raucous applause, made louder by the flight suits the pilots were wearing. Armored hands smacked together loudly, echoing in the large man-made cavern.

"As of today, you are graduates of this rush training program," he told them. "We all know this program was more compressed than any of us would like. You rose to that challenge and exceeded our expectations.

"The price has been high," he said grimly. "Don't forget those we lost to get here, but you all know why we were rushing. An enemy fleet blockades this system. You will not go from this training program into easy peacetime service.

"You will go from this training program into war. Within days, weeks at most, you will pilot your fighters in a breakout attempt against the best that Bengalissimo could muster in mercenaries and loyal patriots alike.

"I wish we could have given you more time," Estanza admitted. "We have given you all we can. I have faith in you to rise to your training and your gifts. To become more than we dare hope.

"I have faith in you to save Redward and the Syntactic Cluster—and I remind you all that I will be right with you the whole way, as will most of the pilots who've trained you.

"Forty-two of you are officially mercenary recruits and will be joining me aboard *Conviction*," he continued. "You've received your orders and contracts with Conviction LLC already. Shortly, I will be delighted to welcome you aboard my ship.

"The rest of you aren't going to dragged all over the galaxy by my ancient ass," he continued to a loud series of chuckles. "Five carriers, four cruisers, and a dozen stations like Shadow Ward itself call for your services. If you have not already received your orders from the RRF, you will be receiving them shortly.

"For all of you, mercenary and royal officer alike, your next set of orders is the same: you are being given thirty-six hours' leave. Shuttles are awaiting to return you to Redward for a final visit with friends and family to celebrate your graduation."

He smiled at them, but Kira could *feel* the shadow behind the old pilot's eyes.

"Make the most of it," he told the graduates softly. "Because very soon, we are all going to war."

42

THEY HIT THE PENTHOUSE FIRST, rendezvousing with Zoric and Mwangi as well as Bueller and Labelle. Pilots and engineers and XOs and Captains filled the main living room of the luxury apartment in a chaotic swarm that was rapidly going to turn into a party.

Not for all of them, of course, but Kira wouldn't begrudge her friends the break. Patel and Hoffman had come down with *Conviction*'s XO, and all of the old Memorial hands were gathered.

She took a moment to join them in looking out over Red Mountain, the lights of the town *still* seeming somewhat provincial to her.

"Hell of a task ahead of us," Hoffman said grimly, his beer in his hand. "But we're here together, and that means a lot."

"Despite everything Brisingr and the Institute has thrown at us, here we are," Kira agreed. "They can't kill the Three-Oh-Three, my friends. We were a spark thrown into the tinder, and an entire nova-fighter corps has risen from the ashes.

"I don't want to take *all* of the credit for the RRF's new fighter wings, but we were the ones who captured the class two drive manufacturer. We were the ones who captured *Deception* and scared off the mercs at Ypres…and now we were the ones doing the training of their new pilots.

"Without the Three-Oh-Three, the Syntactic Cluster would be going somewhere very different today." She toasted the city outside the window with her coffee cup. "No regrets, my friends. I mourn our friends and miss our home, but I'm glad we ended up here."

"Together," Cartman added, raising her own beer. "This Cluster was never ready for us."

"Together," Hoffman agreed. "These're good people. I'm glad to fight for them—and I like their money."

"The correct mercenary mindset!" Michel cheered. "To the Three-Oh-Three, standing together!"

"Together!" the six of them chorused.

Kira took a slug of her coffee and then spotted Konrad leaning on the breakfast bar in the kitchen. He was staring blankly at the window, not even looking at her or the others.

"Excuse me," she murmured.

"Go," Cartman said instantly, following her gaze. "He's gonna be okay, boss, but he'll be okay faster if you're there."

Kira dipped her head in a nod to her friends and crossed the apartment to her lover.

"Hey," she said when he didn't react to her approach. "Are you all right?"

"No," he admitted. "But you knew that."

"I did." She came around the bar and pulled him into an embrace. "Estanza and Zoric and I need to get to a briefing soon, but I have time. You want to talk?"

"Not really," he admitted.

"Will it help?"

He snorted.

"Probably." He sighed, leaning into her. He had a good fifteen centimeters of height on her, but he folded down to rest his head on her shoulder. "I... I wrote the documents, the processes, Kira. Calculated the risks, the likely losses. Told everyone what we could do to cut the construction down that far and what it would cost.

"But my god... Three hundred and eighteen people died to build those ships, Kira. *Three hundred* people. Because I worked out how we could save time and what safety protocols we could cut without risking the ships themselves."

She could feel his tears leaking through her dress uniform, and she couldn't bring herself to care if the cloth was stained. She held him.

"Every one of them a volunteer," she reminded him. "We lost enough in fighter training. It's a nightmare, Konrad. But what choice did we have? Redward was going to do everything they could whether we helped them or not.

"More people would have died in the fighter training without Estanza and me. I can't help but feel that more people would have died in the construction without you and Labelle...and they'd have lost the ships anyway."

"I... I have to believe that," he admitted. "Not just for my ego, but because... My god. What have we done?"

"We helped the people of Redward give themselves a chance," she told him. "A chance to stand on their own two feet and decide their own fate—and help the Cluster decide their own fate, rather than let the Institute decide that fate for everyone."

"This is the difference between us and them, I guess," he said. "They'd run the numbers, say this many deaths were necessary and move on. Just...leave the people as statistics. As numbers."

"You're an engineer, Konrad. Is it ever just numbers?"

"No. Every number has something behind it," Bueller said. "And these ones... These ones have *blood* behind them." He inhaled shakily and lifted his head, brushing away his tears.

"Are *you* okay?" he asked.

"Better than you, I think, but no," Kira said. "We'll deal with it together, and we'll shove it down the Equilibrium Institute's throat with a few dozen nukes attached. Sound good?"

He laughed. It was a thin thing but no less real for that.

"Sounds good. I'm sticking to water for tonight, but I think I should at least try to join the party," he said. "And you?"

She checked the time in her headware.

"Our aircar is here in five," she admitted. "It's just about time to find out what the Syntactic Cluster has been up to while we've been locked in a box."

"They're going to regret locking these people in," her boyfriend said fiercely. "Keels are being laid for one-twenties tomorrow. They're not planning on rushing them as badly as we did the *Barons*, but they'll have fleet carriers and battlecruisers soon."

"You did that," Kira told him. "The Institute is going to regret ever screwing with you and me, Konrad. Trust me on that."

"I do," he said simply.

43

THE THREE MERCENARY officers were led into the briefing chamber by a uniformed Palace Guard. Kira was surprised by just how large the audience was. Unless she missed her guess, every flag officer and ship or station commander was either physically or virtually present.

So were the Palace Guard. Dozens of the red-uniformed body-guards lined the walls, more of them than Kira had ever seen in one place before. Despite everything, the Guard was taking no chances with the safety of their monarchs, even with their own officers.

Given that eight officers who *should* have been in the room were now in military jail cells thanks to Neha Bradley, Kira approved. The young pilot had handed them the image of Commodore Tiamat Julien, the commander of a monitor squadron…and the woman at the heart of the Institute's operations in Redward.

They'd taken Commodore Julien by surprise aboard her ship, managing to use a military override to keep her from wiping her head-ware memory. Her encryptions had proven insufficient to counteract the fact that she had Redward military hardware in her head, and Redward Intelligence had swept up her network in a matter of days.

The Palace Guard were clearly assuming that they *hadn't* caught everyone, and since eight senior officers had been part of the network, even the RRF's senior officers couldn't be trusted.

Another trio of officers, a Rear Admiral and his aides from what Kira guessed was a planetside administration command, stepped into the room—and the doors slid shut behind them with an audible crash.

Moments later, Kira's headware lost all connection to the outside world. The holographic presences flickered as high-powered encryption locked in. Kira suspected that if they *could* have put everyone physically in the room, they would have, but that would have left the RRF leaderless.

The room was still chilled to silence as the security measures activated, and the King and Queen of Redward stepped onto the stage in that silence.

"Thank you all for being here," Larry said calmly. "As many of you have guessed, the couriers we sent out to make contact with our allies returned home yesterday.

"We now have several covert mapped nova points around Redward that we can use to circumvent the blockade. Using any of those points for civilian shipping is impractical, but they have allowed us to reach out to the rest of the Cluster and establish an update on what is going on.

"Very little of that news is good," he warned them.

A map of the Syntactic Cluster appeared above the King. Red spheres enveloped several of the familiar stars, and Kira shivered. Not just Ypres and Redward were blockaded, it seemed.

"As expected, Bengalissimo has assembled blockading forces preventing anyone from entering or exiting the Ypres and Redward Systems," Larry told them. "For the moment, they have ignored our new protectorates in the former Costar Clans Systems, but that may not last. They have moved against several of our older allies in New Ontario and Exeteron, though the forces involved there are minimal. No one outside of us, Ypres or Bengalissimo is going to be a major factor in what happens now."

The map zoomed in on Ypres and Redward, both marked with red spheres.

"With Ypres under blockade, no significant traffic has entered or exited the Syntactic Cluster for roughly three months," the King noted. "Not only is Redward cut off from the Cluster, but the Cluster is also cut off from the galaxy at large. Our enemies have struck not only at Redward but at the entire Syntactic Cluster under the pretense of striking at us."

He shook his head.

"Unfortunately, the story they are telling of our aggression enables just that pretense," he admitted. "We have contacted the other systems in the Cluster in the hopes of leaning on old alliances and the Free Trade Zone agreement. We have received soothing words and no promises of actual support."

Angry mutters filled the room, and Larry held up his hands.

"I do not blame them," he barked. "They have corvettes and destroyers at best. What help can they be against a fleet of cruisers backed by Meridian money and Fringe mercenaries? In our isolation, they see their defeat. And in Queen Rossella's claims, they see an excuse for their surrender.

"Bengalissimo claims we have refused to negotiate. That even their most reasonable requests have been denied." Larry shook his head. "We have received no requests. No communications. Not even a demand for our unconditional surrender.

"Bengalissimo paints us as aggressors and conquerors, using the Ypres Federation and our seizure of the Costar Clans Systems as evidence. Our silence in the face of their blockade is only more proof of our plans and our guilt."

The room was angry now and Larry slapped his hand down on the lectern.

"Again, I do not blame our allies," he snapped. "What could they do? Bring a handful of destroyers against the cruisers and nova-fighter carriers that blockade Redward? We cannot ask them to die for us. We cannot ask them to fight without hope of victory.

"And that brings us here." He gestured around the room. "For hidden among those soothing words were other messages. Messages our allies could not *dare* risk Bengalissimo knowing they'd sent."

The map above Larry's head shifted. The trade-route stops around

Redward and Ypres were now highlighted—and numbers and icons appeared next to them.

"None of our information on Bengalissimo's military positions can be taken as gospel," Queen Sonia told the gathered military officers, "but we have data and reports and estimates on the strengths of their positions and the locations of their vessels as of eleven days ago.

"We know the Bengalissimo Fleet's doctrines and protocols," she continued. "We know their officers and their objectives. We don't know the mercenaries supporting them as well, but many of their choices will be shaped by their employer.

"That means that we believe we have identified key points in the blockade structures around both Redward and Ypres. *Not*, I must warn everyone, *weak* points. *Key* points. Logistical support fleets, guarded by the core nodal forces of the blockades.

"If those fleets and their defenders are destroyed or captured, it will be very clear that there *is* a chance of victory," Sonia told them all. "With a chance of victory, our allies will again gather around us and we will be able to drive Queen Rossella's forces back to Bengalissimo— a defeat that will enable those who question her coup d'état to move against her in both the streets and the Parlamento.

"If you can clear the path from Redward to Ypres and deliver a demonstration convoy while shattering their strongest positions, we may be able to force Bengalissimo to sue for peace."

"And even if we fail in that, we will have halved their cruiser strength and gutted their mercenaries," Larry concluded. "We can achieve a far greater concentration of force than they can. We know where our besiegers are positioned and can choose our moment to strike."

He shook his head and looked out at the officers.

"I won't pretend this will be easy. It is war. True interstellar war, such as the Syntactic Cluster has never seen before and I pray will never see again. I put my faith in the officers and ships of the Redward Royal Fleet against any enemy.

"Our allies in the Cluster have delivered us the keys to victory. It falls to you to open the door."

44

BY THE TIME Kira's shuttle was on approach to *Deception*, the entirety of the intentionally misnamed Seventh Fleet had taken up formation. The two big mercenary ships were at the heart of the fleet, still the largest nova ships available to Redward.

Deception was at the center of the forward echelon, the armored spearpoint that would crush any opposition before them. *Baron* and *Duke*, the two new cruisers, were positioned on her flanks—and inside her defensive umbrella.

The two seventy-five-kilocubic cruisers were flawed ships in many ways. So far as Kira understood, none of those flaws affected their immediate combat efficiency, but keeping them shielded by *Deception* was probably wise.

Beyond the two *Baron*-class ships were Redward's older, sixty-kilocubic cruisers, *First Crown* and *Guardian*. Combined, the five cruisers presented the closest thing to a true battle line the Syntactic Cluster could muster—one that was respectable even by the standards of the Apollo-Brisingr war.

Following behind the cruisers was the destroyer flotilla. Five *Serendipity*-class destroyers, Redward's now *second*-most modern ships, formed the core of the flotilla, supported by three older RRF ships,

Commodore Shang's three mercenary ships, and Commodore Shinoda's two Yprian vessels.

Bringing up the rear, intermixed with the logistics detachment to potentially help disguise them, was the carrier fleet. *Conviction* anchored it, obviously, with *Theseus* directly behind her. The four new freighter conversions, forty-five kilocubics apiece, formed a rough square around the bigger carriers.

The logistics detachment was a mix of sixty-kilocubic and forty-five-kilocubic ships, the types that had been converted into *Theseus* and the *Flame*-class carriers respectively.

Twenty-three warships and ten freighters. It wasn't much of a fleet to hang the fate of sixteen inhabited systems on, but it was what Redward had—and it was, by any metric Kira could apply, truly a fleet.

"We're on final approach, sir," the pilot reported. "Commander Tamboli has provided clearance."

Given that the Commodore, the Captain, the executive officer, the chief engineer, and the Commander, Nova Group were all aboard the shuttle—if sharing those titles across a mere three bodies—the deck officer had been forced to take on acting command of the cruiser for about a day.

Since *Deception* was still in one piece and in her place in the formation, Kira figured Tamboli had done okay.

"Take us in, pilot," Kira ordered. "That's a lot of metal floating in space that I do *not* want held up on my account!"

There wasn't much risk of that. Their shuttle was one of dozens still swarming toward and around the fleet as crew, officers and new-fledged nova-fighter pilots were brought aboard.

For all of its apparent readiness, Kira's briefings expected another twenty-four hours before Seventh Fleet commenced its sortie.

"*DECEPTION*, ARRIVING."

The announcement was mostly automated. There wasn't even anyone in the shuttle bay paying attention to the arriving spacecraft.

Most of the techs who would normally be there were probably on the flight deck, dealing with new fighter pilots.

"Welcome home," Zoric said, looking at the other two. "You've both been missed, I have to say. Everything has ticked along, but I wouldn't have wanted to nova anywhere without you two."

"Well, we're back," Kira replied, glancing over at Bueller. He seemed on a bit leveler of a keel today, but she could still see a shadow behind his eyes. She wasn't sure that would *ever* go away, and it hurt to see.

What they'd done had been necessary. More people would have died *without* Konrad Bueller—everyone involved she'd spoken to had agreed on that—but he'd been the man making the call on which safety protocols they could stretch and how far.

Like the seven pilots who'd died in her training program, those deaths would haunt him for a long time.

"I need to get to the bridge," Zoric said after a moment of silence. "I'd suggest you two take it a bit easy to get back into the swing of things, but we are shipping out *fast*."

She studied Kira and Bueller for a moment more, then shrugged.

"You both know this drill as well as I do," she admitted. "Konrad, ship's officers briefing tomorrow morning at oh eight hundred sharp. Should be in your calendar already."

"It is," he murmured. "I'll be caught up by then."

"I'll probably drop in as well," Kira promised. "Sounds like a good way to catch up on *Deception* after I'm up to date on the nova group."

"Speaking of the nova group, I know Tamboli has a surprise waiting for you," Zoric said with a surprising grin. "I think you'll like it, but we haven't trusted any data on it to coms outside the fleet."

"Okay, now I'm curious," Kira admitted.

"Go check it out," Bueller told her, a small smile on his own face. "I have some tachyon-static discharge systems to review. Dinner in your quarters?"

"Twenty-one hundred sharp," she promised. "Sorry, Kavitha, but we'll skip the Captain's mess tonight."

"No apologies," Zoric told her. "It is absolutely not my place to suggest that my CEO and my XO make sure to fuck like bunnies before we go to war, and that is the only reason I haven't done so."

———————

BY THE TIME Kira made it to the flight deck, the slight blush from Zoric's pointed not-suggestion had faded. The two sections of *Deception* designed to receive and launch spacecraft were as far apart as the structure allowed, since the flight deck could easily handle shuttles and, in an emergency, the shuttle bay could handle fighter retrieval.

The first thing she did on the flight deck was check in on her own Hoplite-IV. Apparently, someone had warned the flight crew that she was coming back—the fighter was positively *gleaming*...and half-hidden behind a massive banner proclaiming WELCOME BACK COMMODORE!

The rest of the interceptor's bay was filled with paper streamers, though Kira's trained eye picked out where the streamers had been pinned to keep them out of the way of the bay's functions—and the way they'd been attached to each other to allow for easy removal.

She still had to stand there in front of the fighter for a full minute, just chuckling and basking in the fact that her deck crew appeared to like her.

"There you are!" Tamboli declared, the dark-haired officer barging up on her with a wide grin on their face. "As the sign says, sir, welcome home."

"Thanks, Commander," Kira said. "After the last two months, it's good to be back."

"I'm not going to thank you for the quartet of greenies you've handed me," they replied. "They're better than I was afraid of, but they still squeak when they turn."

"We were all there once," she told them. "Any particular problems?"

"No problems, just new-pilot friction as they learned how to work in our systems," Tamboli replied. "We pulled most of our pilots off *Conviction*, so I figure you picked the best for us."

"I did," Kira agreed. "Watch Bradley for me, Dilshad?" she asked.

"She may have handed Redward the counterintelligence coup of the decade, but she *was* an Institute agent. More than that, she's... Well, she's good at the job, but she's got a kid to go home to. She's not going to be a long-hauler."

"Not all of them can be," Tamboli said philosophically. "We all know our parts and our jobs. Though..."

"You have a surprise for me," Kira told the officer. "Kavitha warned me. I'm guessing it wasn't this"—she gestured at the streamers —"so, what is it?"

"Follow me," the deck officer said, gesturing for Kira to fall in behind them.

Curious, Kira did. Tamboli led her down to the two hangar bays at the very back of the flight deck and gestured widely at the nova fighters occupying those bays.

She stared at the spacecraft in a mix of awe and horror.

"Uglies," she said quietly. The two fighters weren't built to any clear design, assembled from off-the-shelf components and partial fabrication schemes for the three types of fighter *Deception* carried. Except... "*Big* Uglies."

"They're our Screwballs," Tamboli confirmed. "Most of the core frame is from the Weltraumpanzers, but we had to bake in components from the PNC-One-Fifteens to get everything lined up the way we needed.

"They're Uglies, but they're Ugly *bombers*, sir, and we have twenty of them across the fleet."

Kira whistled softly.

"How many torps?"

"Ten. The internal support is a jury-rig; we didn't want to risk more than that," Tamboli said. "The Harrington coils are balanced *enough* and the nova drive works, but...none of it's perfect. But they work."

"And you built twenty of them?"

"*Deception* built two," they corrected. "*Conviction* built twelve, *Theseus* built six." They shrugged. "*Conviction* kept six and sent the rest to *Theseus*. The RRF has a two-squadron hammer just *waiting* to take someone by surprise."

"That might be the best news I've had today," Kira told Tamboli. "And nobody knows?"

"Unless they're on a ship with the Screwballs, they don't have a clue," the deck officer confirmed. "My understanding is that Hoffman has some of the best of the old Darkwings slotted to fly the ones on *Conviction* and the RRF basically has every vet that isn't commanding a squadron sticking a bomber."

"Give them to Yamauchi's squadron," Kira ordered. "Or am I saying the obvious?"

"You're saying the obvious, sir," Tamboli agreed. "We replaced the two Weltraumpanzers we lost against the Clans with the Screwballs. "

"Good call," Kira said. She looked over the misshapen fighter and shook her head. Ugly as it was, if it could put ten torpedoes on target while the rest of the fighters escorted it, the Screwball was going to be worth its weight in gold.

45

KIRA WATCHED from *Deception*'s flight control center as ship after ship pulled into a waiting zone "behind" Seventh Fleet. The call had gone out announcing that the RRF was punching a hole in the blockade and inviting the civilians to join the convoy they were escorting out.

The core was a humanitarian aid convoy destined for Ypres, but her eyeball estimate put it at just over fifty freighters, ranging from tiny ten-kilocubic ships up to civilian-owned sixty-kilocubic bulk freighters to rival the largest of Seventh Fleet's military colliers.

"Countdown is set," Zoric said in her headware, the Captain keeping the announcement quiet for the moment. "Seventh Fleet novas in an hour. We're hoping to get ahead of any warning reaching the target."

"No real way to stop that," Kira admitted. "We haven't told the convoy exactly where we're jumping yet, have we?"

"That's with Admiral Remington," her subordinate said. "I don't think so. On the other hand, every ship in Seventh Fleet now has that data."

"Hopefully, they got all of the military spies at least," Kira said. "Going to be a hell of a few days."

She blinked away a tiny scrap of sleepiness—following Zoric's recommendation, she and Konrad had not slept as much as they should have the prior night—and considered the situation.

"Is there a briefing planned for the ship Captains?" she asked Zoric. "I haven't heard anything myself."

"We just got a data dump of everything Redward Intelligence has on the target," the Captain replied. "Sending to you. I presume we'll have a briefing called in the next few minutes, before the Fleet goes to battle stations."

Kira's headware told her she'd received the file and she nodded.

"I'll go through it while I have time, I suppose. I need to brief the nova group." Kira had full responsibility for all of the two hundred and ninety nova-fighter pilots in Seventh Fleet, a marker of the degree to which the RRF no longer really regarded *Conviction* or *Deception* as mercenaries.

"Remington's doing everything she can, but don't rely on her giving you enough time for that," Zoric warned. "They're not used to fighters being quite as critical as they're going to be for this."

"I know," Kira agreed. "I'll brief the pilots at T minus twenty. Hopefully, the Admiral will give us the spiel before then. If not, well." She skimmed the data dump. "At least she just sent us the main plan."

No one was going to rely on the digital version of the ops plan. Only after a proper virtual briefing where people could ask questions and clarify problems would Seventh Fleet truly be ready to make their move.

Even if they'd gone over every piece of the plan before—a dozen times—they still needed to see how it all came together.

"PILOTS, WE ARE READY," Kira told her people forty minutes later. "The Admiral has briefed everyone." The briefing hadn't been as extensive as she'd expected, but then, they were still trying to maintain data security.

"You know what you're doing," she continued. "But most of you have never flown in combat before. We're novaing directly into a fight and we're going to be launching the *moment* the carriers stabilize.

"Our job at this stage is not to engage enemy capital ships. Intelligence says we're taking five cruisers against three. I don't care if they're all the big shiny new ones Bengalissimo built, because they're not making up those odds.

"So long as it's a cruiser duel, the BF is fucked. We're here to make sure that it stays a cruiser duel—we know there's mercenary destroyers, gunships and nova fighters in the blockade, and we're hitting their main fuel depot.

"They're going to go at the cruisers with everything they've got. Our destroyers will handle their destroyers at first, and we take the fighters and the gunships. Once the battlespace is clear of anything smaller than a destroyer, we hit the merc destroyers.

"By the time we and the destroyers have cleaned up the escorts, *Deception* and the Redward cruisers should have turned the BF's big hitters to scrap."

She paused, letting that all sink in.

"Some of you—you know who and why—won't be launching today unless things really go sideways," she noted. The Screwballs were staying aboard their carriers unless there were a *lot* more cruisers than expected—or they had a shot at one of Cobra Squadron's carriers.

"Now. Like I said, this is the first run into combat for far more of you than I like," she said grimly. "So, I'm going to say a few things I wouldn't normally bother with.

"First, realize right now it isn't going to go according to plan. And once things come apart, there'll be no one to give you updates, no communications to tell you where to go.

"Stick with your wingmen, follow your squadron leaders. Remember the one-light-minute rendezvous point and remember that you have a far better chance of getting a laser link to a carrier than to another fighter," she told them.

"Second…" She looked at the rows of faces in front of her, most of them virtual. "Some of you aren't going to come home. Remember that you have ejection pods and we'd rather save you and the class two drive over just about anything else.

"When everything goes to hell, remember that you are nova-fighter pilots and there is one instinct I hope we've managed to train into you: when things are getting too hot for you…be somewhere else.

"You have more FTL maneuverability than anything else on the battlefield. *Use* it. Today, at least, the cruisers will do the heavy lifting. Stay alive and do your jobs."

Kira looked across the faces again.

"We have five minutes before you need to be in your fighters. If you have any last-minute questions, now is the time."

KIRA RAN her fingers along the hull of her Hoplite. The smooth, painted metal was a familiar feeling, an old friend. This wasn't the Hoplite she'd taken into the war against Brisingr—if nothing else, she'd spent most of that war flying a Hoplite-III—but it was one she'd taken into one nightmare after another there in the Syntactic Cluster.

"Everything tests green," Tamboli told her. The deck chief sounded pleased with themselves. "Every fighter tested out green, even the Screwballs. If it could go wrong, we replaced it. They'll be as reliable as the day they were built, sir."

Kira chuckled.

"The Hoplite-IV has some particular issues with the manufacturer's parts, actually," she pointed out. "If you replaced the parts that might go wrong, she's *more* reliable than the day they built her."

While many of their fighters were clones built in the fabricators aboard *Conviction* and *Deception*, her Hoplite was one of the originals she'd dragged out from Apollo with her.

"She'll serve you well, as she always has," Tamboli said firmly. "And I see my cue to go find something interesting somewhere else on the flight deck."

Kira turned to see the enby deck officer vanish off with surprising speed—and Konrad Bueller standing next to the bay.

"Time to go?" he asked.

"I've got about…three minutes," she told him. "Shouldn't you be in Engineering for the nova?"

"For the fight, but the nova will handle itself," he said. "Wanted to see you off. The way these things go…yeah."

"Fair."

He crossed the deck to her with that implicit permission, wrapping her in his arms and then kissing her.

"I'll be fine," she assured him. "You just make sure *Deception*'s here when I get back."

"What did you call her once? The biggest, baddest warship in the sector?" he asked. "You weren't wrong then and it hasn't changed. I'm not worrying about *Deception*. I might be worrying about her CNG, but I know that that's beyond my control."

She squeezed his hands.

"This is what I do," she said. "There's nowhere I can have a bigger impact on this fight than in the cockpit. There've been times that hasn't been true, but this time it is."

"I know," he agreed. "And I'm not here to stop you." He kissed her forehead and Kira shivered warmly.

"I'm here to wish you luck and your enemies damnation," Konrad Bueller told her. "If I had a favor to give you as you fly into battle, my brave knight, I would, but the thought only just occurred to me."

He smiled. There was still the shadow behind his eyes, but this was the man who'd been growing on her.

"So, the only thing I can send with you to keep you safe is my love," he murmured softly, using a word they had very carefully *not* used up to that moment. "I love you, Kira Demirci. May that be the shield that brings you back to me alive."

And while she was still processing that, the rotten bastard kissed her on the forehead and strode away purposefully toward his own duty station.

"Hey!" she shouted after him. He turned and smiled back at her. She glared at him, well aware that the entire flight deck crew could hear her now.

"I love you too, you arrogant grease monkey," she told him loudly. "Now keep my ship intact while I go win this battle for *your favor*."

Bueller laughed and threw her a textbook-perfect salute.

46

IT HAD BEEN a long time since Kira had novaed in this close to the enemy—but then, it had been a long time since she'd flown off a cruiser that was part of a real battle line. She had a clear vision of the Bengalissimo logistics depot at maybe half a million kilometers before everything around Seventh Fleet vanished into their own jamming.

"Deck has the ball," Tamboli recited in her headware. "Launch on the ball, launch on the ball. Stand by…" There was a pause as the first sets of fighters launched into space, and then the deck boss switched to her. "Basketball, launch."

The "ball" was the control of her fighter, and Tamboli's people had it. Systems aboard both her fighter and the cruiser flared to life, and her Hoplite was flung out into space, the last of the eight-ship Memorial-Alpha squadron.

Three more launch waves followed as Kira brought her fighter into formation above *Deception*, linking laser coms to the cruiser. She wouldn't have coms for long, but she'd use them while she had them.

"Target analysis downloading to your fighter," Davidović told her. "Heavier than we hoped, lighter than we feared. We're making it three cruisers, five destroyers and fifteen light ships. No carriers on the scopes.

"Battle line is advancing."

"Network established," Cartman murmured in Kira's ear. "All fighters online. That won't last."

"No, it won't," Kira agreed, taking advantage of the moment to link to all two hundred and seventy nova fighters under her command. "All nova fighters, mark the range at four hundred and fifty thousand kilometers. RV is in your computers and lock in your targets.

"First sweep is the lighter warships. I don't want anything smaller than a destroyer left, pilots, but hang on to your torpedoes. The cruisers may yet need our help."

She paused, considering what final words she could give the people she'd trained or the people she'd fought alongside. There wasn't really anything.

"Seventh Fleet Nova Group," she said calmly. *"Nova and attack."*

The world flashed around her as it always did, and her Hoplite dove into chaos around the enemy formation. Even if the enemy hadn't brought up their own jammers, it didn't matter. Every fighter novaed with their multiphasic jammers online.

Without a prepared laser network, the Bengalissimo Fleet and their mercenaries' communications were hashed. That moment of confusion was key—that moment of confusion was where nova fighters lived and died, on the ragged edge of violence and speed.

The freighters weren't their target yet, and Kira picked her own prey in a moment—a corvette trying to pull away from a fueling tanker. It was vulnerable but on the far side of the Bengal formation from her formation.

Harrington coils flung her through the enemy formation, dodging around the scattered flak that the warships were starting to put out, and she lined up on her prey—and proceeded to disobey her own orders, firing the single torpedo her nova fighter carried directly at the corvette while opening fire with her guns.

The corvette did *exactly* as she hoped, dodging away from her cannon fire and directly into the path of the torpedo blast. The impact flung the dying ship backward into the fuel tanker itself, tearing a massive hole in the side of the vessel and bringing enough oxygen to ignite a massive portion of the tanker's hydrogen cargo.

A short-lived jet of flame covered Kira as she flipped back into the fleet, searching for prey. There wasn't much. The gunships were gone, swarmed under by ten times their numbers of nova fighters. Long-range plasma fire was already beginning to lace the empty void around the Bengal cruisers as Seventh Fleet closed, but the BF was forming up in good order.

Kira's people would have to deal with the destroyers next, but for now...her sixty seconds was up.

She novaed to the rendezvous point and left the enemy to the cruisers.

KIRA COULDN'T HELP but hold her breath as nova fighters appeared at the rendezvous point and dropped their jammers. Two hundred. Two hundred forty. Two fifty. Two sixty. Two...sixty-six.

Some of the pilots had taken almost forty seconds longer than they should have to get out, but only four were missing. She'd have preferred *no* missing pilots, but she'd take it.

"All fighters, escorts are clear and it's down to the big boys," she told them. "We *could* play it nice and safe and go after the destroyers, clear the way for our battle line."

She let that hang in the air as she considered the weight of metal in the battlespace they'd left behind. The Bengals and their mercenaries were badly outnumbered, and if they were smart, they'd focus their fire on Seventh Fleet's cruisers to try and even the odds.

"We're not going to do that," she said. "They have three cruisers, and we have a hundred and twenty fighter-bombers and heavy fighters. I'm dropping targets by squadron, but I want a hundred torpedoes on each of those big bastards.

"Interceptors, dance and weave. Your job is to make the bastards' gunners lose your big sisters," she told them. "And then we send them to the damn fire. Even the new pilots know the steps.

"Let's dance. Nova and attack!"

She suited her actions to her commands and led Seventh Fleet's fighters back into the chaos. They came out of nova almost fifty thousand kilometers from the cruisers and were immediately back in the fray.

The torpedoes needed to get closer, and Kira's heavier fighters were the key.

The battle lines had closed, spitting fire at each other from about the same distance the fighters had appeared at. There were ships missing on both sides, but Kira couldn't take the time to ID them. One of the Bengal cruisers was badly battered by the fire from *Deception* and the others, but she couldn't even redirect the fighters she'd assigned to it.

Everything came down to getting her fighters into and out of the enemy's defensive fire—and she led a chaotic swarm of over two hundred and sixty nova fighters into the teeth of the enemy formation.

Plasma flashed in every direction, but it took the Bengals and their mercenaries a critical few seconds to realize the threat. Last time her birds had swept through, they'd only targeted the lightest ships and they hadn't used torpedoes.

By the time the cruisers identified the fighters in the jamming and realized what was going on, Kira's people were almost in torpedo range. The defensive fire was late and wide, and her fighter-bombers and heavy fighters launched their torpedoes in massive waves.

It wasn't the synchronized fire of a more-practiced force, one that wouldn't *need* the communications they didn't have, but it was more than enough. The more-practiced force would have intentionally sequenced their fire, stressing the dispersal networks even if they couldn't overload them.

The scattergun fire from Kira's nova group achieved the same result by accident. Two cruisers vanished in a blaze of fire. They might be more replaceable now, but those ships still represented a massive investment on the part of their owners.

The last cruiser was reeling, and Kira had enough time to watch the focused fire of *five* cruisers tear into her before her sixty seconds were up again and she novaed to safety a second time.

IT WAS over by the time the nova fighters returned to the battlespace for the third time. Less than ten minutes had elapsed since Seventh Fleet had arrived, and the blockade force was gone. A third of the freighters that had made up the logistics depot were still in place, under the Fleet's guns as assault shuttles swarmed them.

The other two-thirds were gone, and Kira doubted they'd all been destroyed.

She keyed off her own multiphasic jammers as she set her course for *Deception*. Seconds ticked away as her fighters followed suit, but she had a laser-com link with her cruiser.

"Zoric, where are we at?" she asked.

"Two destroyers and sixteen freighters novaed," the cruiser Captain said instantly. "Admiral Remington is trying to keep people from declaring victory just yet, but it's pretty clear."

"Depends on where those destroyers and freighters went," Kira said grimly. "There *probably* aren't more cruisers in the blockade, though, so..."

She considered, looking at her fighter squadrons as the last of the multiphasic jamming shut down.

"I'm sending the heavies in to refuel on *Deception*," she told her subordinate. "Sending in fighter-bombers and heavies in across the board, in fact. Interceptors will stay out for now."

It took her a moment to pass those orders on. She was down eleven fighters now, though she hoped they would find the survival pods from those planes. Some of those pilots would fly again—and if they got the *full* pod, with the class two drive included, so would the fighters. In spirit, at least.

New alerts pinged across her dash and headware as Remington called an all-senior-officers conference.

"Well done," Remington said immediately. "We did good today, people, but we got burned more than I would have liked. All five cruisers require some in-place repairs, and we lost two of the RRF's destroyers and eleven fighters.

"First wave of the convoy should be joining us in an hour," she continued.

One of Kira's responsibilities had been to send a fighter back to warn them off if the battle was lost. That, thankfully, hadn't been necessary today.

"We will hold here for forty-eight hours to complete quick repairs and see out the civilians who aren't coming with us to Ypres," Remington told everyone. "Watch for counterattack. There was no way to stop Bengal forces escaping, which means the rest of the blockade knows we're here.

"Hopefully, they'll recognize they're outgunned and withdraw quietly. I refuse to hang the fate of this fleet on *hopefully*."

"We are maintaining a full interceptor patrol," Kira reported. "Our most likely counter-act is a fast nova strike, with bombers if they have them, in an attempt to take out one or more cruisers."

"Agreed," Remington said. "All ships are to prepare to repel nova bomber strikes. Mostly, though…that will be on Commodore Demirci and our fighters."

"We are ready," Kira promised. "In their place, I'd give us some time to relax. An hour or two, potentially. And they won't nova the carrier in within easy detection distance. They'll want her drive cooled down before they send in the nova fighters—but if she's only novaing a light-year from another blockade post, they could be as little as five hours."

"I'm afraid it's going to be a long day for you, Commodore," Remington said. "We'll trust your judgment here."

47

EIGHT HOURS LATER, Kira wasn't sure she trusted her *own* judgment. She was cycling nova fighters through her fleet patrol, but she'd remained out in her Hoplite except for a short stop to refuel.

She'd figured that Cobra Squadron likely had one of their carriers supporting the Redward blockade. Everything they'd seen except the cruisers themselves had been mercenary ships, so she'd suspected that the Institute had put their hands all over the blockade.

"No contacts within range," Zoric told her. The Captain had stood down the cruiser to ready status, along with the rest of the fleet. "We might have actually scared them off."

"You realize saying that might have jinxed it?" Kira replied. "Two-thirds of my pilots are asleep, and I've only a hundred fighters in space."

The patrol was also busy assisting in search-and-rescue. They'd pulled six of their missing pilots from the wreckage, along with three copilots. Kira had still lost as many people today as in the entire training program, but nine had lived despite losing their ships.

Civilian shipping was also everywhere now. The official convoy to Ypres was twelve ships on its own, and at least four times that many had now arrived at the trade-route stop. Once people were certain the path had been secured, there appeared to be a small exodus of non-locals who'd been trapped.

Kira could sympathize. She liked Redward well enough, but she could guess how it would have felt if she'd been planning on going back to Apollo.

"Most likely, Commodore, they had an accurate enough feel of the Fleet's strength that they're retreating to Ypres with the news," Zoric told her. "How long are you going to maintain the nova group at this level of readiness?"

"Until we're under the guns of somebody's fortresses," Kira replied. "One-third in space, two-thirds on the carriers."

"Fine. When are *you* coming back aboard?"

Kira checked the clock.

"Call it four more hours," she told the cruiser Captain. "If they haven't hit within twelve hours, they're playing a longer-term game than I was expecting. I just want to make sure we don't get *another* eight-bomber strike landed on *Deception*.

"I still feel bad about the last one."

"Better us than anything else in Seventh Fleet," Zoric said philosophically. "I mean, if you could keep it down to a *six*-bomber strike or even a *one*-bomber strike, I'd be happy, but we can live through eighty torpedoes."

Kira felt as much as saw Zoric's grimace.

"Once," the other woman admitted. "Which is once more than anyone else in the damn fleet."

"I'll make sure to send the Bengals in your dire—"

"Multiple nova flare!" a voice interrupted. Kira hadn't even seen it yet—but Neha "Backstab" Bradley had. The young woman had hit the alert command, and every ship in the fleet got the warning at the same instant—as forty individual nova signatures flashed into the middle of the fleet.

There was no time for more conversation. The newcomers' multiphasic jamming tore apart the communication, and Kira prayed her people knew that most ancient of navigation tools—just as critical in the age of the nova-fighter as in the age of sail.

Sail to the sound of the guns.

THE ENEMY KNEW the odds they were facing. Kira had a hundred fighters in space, half-and-half interceptors and fighter-bombers—there was little to really distinguish the Hoplites and PNC-115s from their RRF clones—against forty.

It took her less than five seconds to determine the real problem: there was a nova bomber wing in the heart of the formation. It was the same trick they'd pulled against *First Crown* months earlier—and Kira had made sure *everyone* in Seventh Fleet knew about it.

She wasn't even the first pilot there. A squadron of Hoplites from *Conviction* blazed into the enemy formation within seconds of the jamming going up. Even without knowing who they were, Kira figured it had to be Hoffman.

No one else was good enough to cause as much confusion as those six fighters caused. She swore that she saw one of the mercenary interceptors shoot another mercenary fighter.

These were the Veles-4s, Crest-built ships comparable to the Hoplites and their Dexter clones. Their only hope had been complete surprise, and Kira had been waiting for them.

At least two squadrons' worth of fighters had coalesced behind her before she slammed into the front half of their formation, dodging around the interceptors and ignoring their fire as she hunted the Ugly bombers at the heart of the formation.

Like the Screwballs aboard her own ships, the enemy bombers were a crude but effective solution to needing to kill real capital ships without real bombers. These ones had sacrificed enough maneuverability that they needed the escorts, but Kira left those interceptors to the second wave of her own fleet as over twenty of her fighters slashed in on ten nova bombers.

It was over in seconds and the Veles-4s scattered in shock. The squadrons that had charged in had been the best Kira had, the ones commanded by her Apollo veterans and made up of the veterans from both *Conviction* and the RRF.

The interceptors scattered away from them and collided with Kira's trainees. Her former students might not rank up with the veterans of a dozen battles that had broken the mercenary formation, but they could handle taking on that broken formation at two-to-one odds.

Nova flashes announced the end of the attack, and Kira smiled coldly as the computers projected the enemy course.

They'd headed right for *Conviction*, trying to punch out the weaker of the two big mercenary ships. Unfortunately for them, some of the best pilots in the cluster called that ship home, and Joseph Hoffman, it seemed, *really* liked his new bunk.

The jammers stayed up for a few more minutes as her fighters orbited back out. There were still four hours left on patrol...and victory against this wave didn't meant there wasn't another one.

There was only one real good piece of news out of this to her: if they'd *only* thrown the Crest-equipped mercenary squadrons at her, there were no other fighters around. Cobra Squadron was somewhere else.

Kira was damned certain they weren't making it to Ypres without colliding with Estanza's old colleagues-in-arms, but she'd take every chance she could get to blood her new pilots before then. Every scrap of combat experience they could accumulate would save lives when they went up against those veteran Institute pilots.

And she was going to bring as many of her people home as she could.

48

"VICTORY IS A HELL OF A DISEASE."

Kira looked up from the status reports she was reviewing in the office attached to her quarters. She was *supposed* to be sleeping, but her nerves were on edge. Seventh Fleet was preparing for the next nova along the route to Ypres. She had a plan for everything and there was nothing she could do…but it was hard to sleep.

Konrad had knocked on her door an hour earlier with a similar complaint. Now he was reviewing engineering reports on a virtual projection from his headware while she poked at fighter status reports at her desk.

"What do you mean?" she asked. The first fight of the campaign had gone better than they could have hoped. The loss of a destroyer and over a dozen fighters wasn't *nothing*—and neither were the two hundred and eighty-six officers, pilots and spacers who wouldn't be going back to Redward.

"Confidence is good," he said slowly, waving away whatever virtual image he'd been looking at to focus on her. "But I'm coordinating with a lot of people as *Deception*'s XO right now, and they're feeling *very* confident.

"Maybe overconfident. It's hard to be sure."

"There was only one of the Bengal's new cruisers here," Kira said. "And Cobra Squadron and their godawful fighters weren't here either. This was the easy fight—and I'm glad for it."

"You wouldn't be able to tell that from the conversations on the fleet admin channels," Konrad warned her. "They think this is in the bag. Your pilots?"

"My pilots know that, for us, Cobra Squadron is the big fight," she said. "I hammered that in as hard as I could. If they're smart, the Crest mercs are out of the game—given the casualties they took going after the King and Queen in Redward, they're now over a hundred percent losses in the last three months.

"That carrier has a few guns but not enough to be worth putting her into a fight alongside the cruisers." She shrugged. "We're down *a* carrier, but the other bunch of Rim mercenaries were never the fear."

"No. The Fringe mercs and the Bengal cruisers are the key, and those are still ahead of us," Konrad agreed.

He sighed.

"Never been an XO before, so this is taking some getting used to," he continued. "But the tone of the fleet worries me. Too many of the RRF officers were jumped to their current positions. Too many of their spacers are fortress and monitor crew who've never served on a nova ship before.

"They needed a confidence boost, but…I worry."

"Do you ever not?" Kira asked with a smile.

"Sometimes," he argued. "I'm not a *permanent* downer, I swear. But it serves an engineer well to be conservative, even a little pessimistic."

"It serves most military officers well, too," she said. "So long as the crew doesn't pick up on the pessimism."

"I know *that* much," Konrad said. He stared blankly at the wall. "*Deception* is ready," he promised her. "And it's not my place to run down morale on other ships; that's for sure. But I have a sinking feeling about how far out of our depth Seventh Fleet actually is."

"We evened the odds a lot yesterday," Kira told him. "That makes a lot of difference."

She closed her files and joined him in sitting on the bed. Her nerves weren't easing, but she did need to at least *try* to sleep.

"We're both buzzing like someone fed us spark," she told him. "We need to stop worrying over the rest of the fleet and get the rest we both need."

She considered him for a moment, then grinned.

"Let's say I rub your back and we see where it leads?"

49

KIRA WAS *MUCH* MORE relaxed as she linked into the senior officers' conference six hours later. A slew of Commodores from two navies and their attached mercenaries filled a virtual table, all looking at Admiral Remington at the head as they waited for their orders.

"All ships have reported in that we've completed what repairs we can," the head of both the RRF and Seventh Fleet told them all. "Commodore Demirci, the fighters?"

"We've received replacement fighters and pilots from the fortresses in Redward," Kira reported. "I'd worry about cohesion in the squadrons...but I was already worried about cohesion in the squadrons.

"Everyone is too green for this, Admiral. We'll do what we can."

"That's all I can ask," Remington told her. The old Admiral looked around the room, holding each virtual hologram's eyes intently for several seconds.

"We have successfully evened the odds, people," she finally announced. "Bengalissimo went from seven cruisers to four overnight. We now have the edge in numbers there, though the evidence from yesterday also drives home that their new cruisers are superior to everything in our line of battle except *Deception*.

"We do not believe Bengalissimo has deployed any significant numbers of nova fighters of their own, but all evidence continues to suggest that the Cobra Squadron mercenaries are securing the Ypres blockade."

She let that sink in.

"Cobra Squadron is legendary, people, and for good reason," she said quietly. "Captain Estanza? You served with them once. Your interpretation of what they will do next?"

"Cobra Squadron traditionally relies on a major individual superiority on both a skill and technology level," *Conviction*'s Captain said. "The Manticore-Sevens are modern *Fringe* fighters. We have modern *Rim* fighters, and the differential is as stark as you could possibly fear.

"Cobra Squadron's fighters will be more maneuverable than ours, carrying heavier guns than ours, and be equipped with torpedoes with a longer range than ours," he laid out. "Their pilots will be experienced veterans who served with distinction in their home forces before they were ever recruited by Cobra Squadron.

"Almost as importantly, every last one of them is a fanatic believer in the ideology and mission of the Equilibrium Institute," Estanza said quietly. "Like I was, once. They will leverage every advantage they have.

"With the warning they will have received, the real question is who is in command at Ypres."

"Captain?" Remington asked. "Could you clarify?"

"Officially, Cobra Squadron is under contract to the Bengalissimo Fleet. It is...unlikely that Lars Ivarsson is in overall command of the Yprian Blockade, but it is possible. Without intelligence on who is in charge, I can't make a guess as to what their plan will be."

"Bengalissimo is unfamiliar with nova-fighter tactics," Kira pointed out. "Given that so much of their firepower is under Ivarsson's command, they may have put him in charge."

"And they may not have," Remington agreed. "As Captain Estanza noted, our intelligence gives us a good idea of what forces are present at Ypres...but not who is in command."

She gestured and images of ships took place amid them.

"The current estimated strength of the blockade fleet is all remaining *Tabby*-class cruisers, all three Cobra Squadron carriers, eight destroyers and thirty lighter vessels."

New vessels appeared alongside those icons as she spoke.

"It is a reasonable assumption that the remaining forces of the Redward blockade will fall back on Ypres, providing the BF with another six destroyers and twelve light vessels," Remington told them. "Fourteen destroyers and forty-two corvettes and gunships are more than enough to even the odds between the two cruiser fleets.

"Even more critically, however, is that the combination of the lighter warships and the nova-fighter strength means that our core mission can very easily be thwarted without defeating Seventh Fleet. The convoy is highly vulnerable, even if accompanied by the fleet. If we fail to deliver the convoy, this breakthrough loses much of both its propaganda and actual value."

The conference was silent.

"We can't move the convoy forward with the fleet," Commodore Shinoda said quietly. "Ypres is going to need the supplies we're protecting."

"I agree, Commodore, which is why I've come up with a slight modification to our plans," Remington said. "Your destroyers will attach themselves to Captain Estanza's *Conviction*, and all three ships will remain with the convoy."

Kira blinked.

"Sir, that pulls a lot of our fighter strength out of the fight," she noted quietly. "It seems risky."

"It is risky," Remington said bluntly. "It also provides us with a reserve that Cobra Squadron might miss. We can, if necessary, spare a single nova fighter to bring Captain Estanza's force forward.

"We will move forward in a leapfrog fashion," she continued. "The convoy will follow Seventh Fleet six hours after we nova—unless they are told not to by one of our fighters. We will wait until the convoy's drives have cooled down before advancing to the next trade route. That will allow Captain Estanza and Commodore Shinoda to nova to our assistance if needed—or for the entire convoy to nova to us to escape an attack."

Remington gestured, clearing the images of the various enemy ships.

"There are only two officers we believe Rossella Gaspari would trust with this mission," she noted. "I know them both. Neither would be willing to concede authority to a mercenary without direct orders from the Queen herself. They will factor Cobra Squadron into their own operational plans, most likely by using Ivarsson's fighters to attack the convoy simultaneously with an attack on Seventh Fleet with their battle line.

"I expect them to retain some fighters for their own defense but, in the main, to see the fighter part of this conflict as secondary. We have an answer for that," Remington said grimly. "Commodore Demirci, does that make sense?"

Remington probably shouldn't have been quite as accommodating of Kira's concerns—but on the other hand, Kira was the Fleet CNG. The plan would put sixty of her fighters—over a fifth of her strength—away from the main point of contact.

She didn't know *any* of the officers in play. Remington did—and Kira figured she was right. Redward had given her command of the nova group, but she and *Conviction*'s crew had spent a long damn time earning that level of trust, and she was still subordinate to Remington.

No one was going to put Ivarsson, an unknown mercenary, in command of an entire blockade.

"It makes sense, sir," she admitted. "But…Captain Estanza, you knew Ivarsson. How cooperative is he likely to be with the Bengal commanders?"

"I knew Ivarsson thirty years ago as one of the most junior pilots in Cobra Squadron," Estanza admitted. "He was aggressive to a fault but had the skill to make it stick. Even within that, he followed orders better than most nova pilots. I'd guess unless he really thinks they've screwed it up, he'll follow the orders.

"He might be Institute to his core, but he's also a mercenary and under contract to Bengalissimo. Rossella is signing the checks and he'll do what she says, so long as it doesn't put his people in active danger."

"It's settled, then," Remington declared. "Seventh Fleet novas in one hour. Estanza—I'm designating your group Task Force Seven Point

Two and putting you in command. Is that acceptable, Commodore Shinoda?"

"I have two destroyers and he has a carrier," Shinoda pointed out with a chuckle. "It's fine."

"Good. TF Seven Point Two will nova in seven hours, which will give you time to get the convoy in order and following instructions."

"You underestimate how annoying merchants can be," Estanza said. "But we'll make it work."

"Good." The Admiral looked around again. "People, this is for it all," she told them. "I *have* to believe that the Institute is running out of resources they can throw at our distant end of the galaxy. If we can drive the Bengalissimo Fleet back to their home system, we will be able to reestablish our King's Free Trade Zone and move forward with our lives.

"I, for one, am very done with a bunch of coreward intellectuals fucking with my home cluster. So, let's go burn off the Institute's fingers, shall we?"

50

YPRES WAS JUST over twenty-six light-years from Redward. The actual *trip* between the two systems was closer to twenty-nine, but that was normal enough. The nova from Redward to the trade route was four light-years, followed by twenty-four light-years in four standard novas along the route, then a one-light-year nova to finish the trip.

Of the five stops along the way, Seventh Fleet had known they were going to hit a fight at the first one with the Redward blockade...and they knew they weren't going to make it to the last trade route stop without the fight they were waiting for.

The first nova along the route went without incident. As the fighters gathered back aboard the carriers for the second trade-route nova, the third of the trip, Kira even relaxed enough to be in Flight Control for the jump instead of in her fighter.

Her squadron couldn't make the initial launch after *every* nova, not without clearly distrusting Cartman and Yamauchi, after all.

"Count down to nova. Sixty seconds," Zoric's voice echoed through the room. "Fleet is synchronized."

"I'm glad I'm not the one syncing this many ships to one nova," Tamboli told Kira. "Navigation is *not* my strong suit."

"Any nova-fighter pilot could do it in their sleep," Kira replied. "If I'm syncing a full fighter strike, even leaving *Conviction* behind, that's two hundred and thirty planes."

"A year ago, I ran a shuttle maintenance facility for an orbital transfer company," Tamboli reminded Kira, their voice dry. "We handled an average of eighteen shuttles at once, but that was because the company rented us out to do maintenance for anyone who needed it. They only owned twenty themselves.

"So far as I knew then, the only nova fighters in the sector were on the mercenary carrier that hung around the system, soaking up the fleet's budget. Wouldn't have even conceived of a two-hundred-fighter formation, let alone that I'd be involved."

Kira chuckled.

"And yet when I posted for someone to run nova-fighter maintenance, you jumped at it."

"Sounded like a challenge, something new that not many others could do that would stretch my skills and maybe show me more of the galaxy." They shrugged. "I wasn't wrong, was I?"

"You were the best-qualified candidate," Kira said. "I'm glad to have you. I prefer not to worry about my fighter falling apart around me."

A moment of tension rippled through the ship as *Deception* novaed.

"Excuse me," Tamboli told Kira, stepping away to take up their station. "Memorial-Bravo squadron, Deck has the ball," they announced.

Kira turned her own focus to the tactical display. Whichever one of Admiral Remington's officers was coordinating the novas was doing a *damn* good job. The fleet had emerged in perfect formation, something not even her old Apollo colleagues had always managed.

Given the disparate components of the fleet, that was impressive. They might have split off the Yprian detachment, but there were still four mercenary ships in the fleet, and the newer ships had small but subtle differences in the nova drives, too.

A squadron of fighters launched from each carrier and *Deception*, putting thirty-six fighters into space in a breath. A few moments later, the carriers followed up with a second wave. Sixty-six nova fighters fell into their patrol patterns, sweeping for threats as the fleet's sensors strained into the darkness.

"We're clear," Davidović reported from the cruiser's bridge. "I was half-expecting trouble."

"Two more trade-route stops after this *and* the buggers are watching for us," Kira replied. "They don't know where we are at any given moment unless someone sees us and novas."

"Well, there aren't even any civilians here," Zoric said. "I guess there wasn't much call for Redward-Ypres traffic with a fleet on both ends."

"And every trade route leading out of the cluster runs past Ypres to provide a place for people to rest and discharge static," Kira agreed. "I doubt the Bengals were letting people leave the Cluster, either."

"You saw the intel," Zoric said. "They've locked down everything. Only freighters leaving the Cluster this way fly Bengalissimo flags. Quite the economic incentive."

"There are other routes out," Davidović pointed out. "They're just not as commonly used because they don't head directly to anywhere of value. Going through Ypres, you're on a direct course for Crest's sector with only one discharge stop along the way."

"They got three blockades for the price of two," Zoric concluded. "But it won't last."

"Don't get too confident, Kavitha," Kira warned, remembering Konrad's comments. "*Deception* may outgun everything they've got, but the *Tabbies* outgun everything else Redward is bringing to the party."

That was what the Screwballs were for, but Kira was hesitant to put too much faith in the Ugly bombers.

"I know," Zoric conceded. "When are you up on patrol?"

"Assuming no one ambushes us, six and a half hours," Kira replied. "Four patrols on each nova stop. Everyone else on standby, even the ones that are sleeping. I think a lot of us are going to be exhausted when this is over, no matter how much sleep we supposedly get."

"Get what rest you can, Commodore," Zoric told her. "I'm swapping with Bueller in a few hours. We'll be ready for whatever comes up, I promise."

"I know."

HOURS PASSED IN NERVOUS SILENCE. By the time Kira took her fighter out from *Deception*'s flight deck, her people had swept everywhere within half a light-day of the fleet. Nothing. The trade route was *dead*.

Some of that was just the Syntactic Cluster itself, she knew. There just weren't enough freighters out there, even considering the hundred-plus that Redward and the other more successful powers each had registered, to have traffic in every trade route at every time.

But if there were any trade-route stops in the Cluster that would normally have had multiple ships, it was the line between Redward, Ypres and the rest of the galaxy. Two of the richest systems in the Cluster and the access to the rest of human space? Someone was always going to be traveling that line.

Except that Bengalissimo had cut the line off and everyone knew it. For ten weeks, Redward had been quiescent, waiting behind the blockade while they desperately assembled ships and fighter squadrons to make this breakout.

Watching her people patrol the area, Kira resisted the urge to fire off quick corrections to her former students. It was their wingmen and squadron COs who would do that now, fixing the thousand and one minor gaps in the knowledge and skill of the pilots she'd trained.

They'd managed to give those kids a solid foundation in sixty days, and that was a *miracle*, as far as Kira was concerned. Somehow, they'd pulled off the impossible.

And, thankfully, long-distance patrol-flying was a *good* place for the pilots to get rust knocked off safely—or as safely as they could ever fly an overpowered plasma-cannon delivery system.

"Backstab, tuck in your vector two degrees for me," she said over her radio. Neha Bradley was now part of her squadron, one of the handful of the new pilots aboard *Deception*. Where Kira could keep an eye on her.

And since she was in Kira's squadron, it fell to Kira to point out when the new pilot got sloppy.

51

"FLEET IS SYNCHRONIZED; the count is on. Sixty seconds."

Kira was in her fighter this time, which meant she was getting the count from Tamboli. She was starting to wonder if her flight deck officer ever slept, which was a point she was going to have to raise with them.

Once she was back aboard ship, anyway. The eight fighters of Memorial-Alpha were ready to go, and her screens told her the other squadrons of the fleet patrol were also standing by.

Seconds were ticking on both her dash and her headware, and Kira tensed. She knew some of Seventh Fleet's officers weren't expecting to run into the Bengals until the very last trade-route stop—and that was part of why she was expecting to see the enemy here.

"Nova...now."

Reality rippled and Kira's hands tensed on the controls.

"Memorial-Alpha, Deck has the ball," Tamboli announced. "Basket-ball, I've got you. Launching now."

The Hoplite-IV flashed into space, three of Kira's fighters gathered around her. Backstab was one of the four, and Kira grinned as she saw that the new pilot was already holding her position better.

Bradley might have ended up trapped by the Equilibrium Institute, but she learned quickly and had a gift for the job. She'd be a great pilot someday, assuming she lived through the next few days.

"Zone is clear," Konrad Bueller's voice echoed in her ears. "No contacts on the scopes; all regions clear."

"Thanks, XO," Kira replied, keeping her own tone professional. "Commencing patrol."

Icons and lines took shape ahead of her in response to a series of mental commands. There was very little she had to actually change beyond confirming squadron assignments, but she checked it all over in a few seconds before sending it out.

"Memorial-Alpha, form on me," she ordered. "Patrol route should be downloading to your computers. We've got outside patrol today; stand by for nova."

Outside patrol meant they were the ones doing the sweep at one light-hour, looking for people trying to be sneaky. The trade-route stop might be dead to everyone's eyes and sensors right now, but distance degraded accuracy.

A starship couldn't hide its heat signature at less than a light-minute or so but *could* hide at longer distances. It depended on tech, of course. Both *Deception*'s sensors and her emission-control systems were superior to anything else in the cluster.

"Nova coordinates locked in," Kira said. "Everyone good?"

A chorus of affirmations answered her, Bradley's a noticeable moment later than the rest. That was fine. The kid was learning.

"Nova on my mark. Three. Two. One. Nova."

They flashed across space and Kira grimaced. Without the adrenaline distraction of a fight, the kick in the stomach of a fighter's less-protected nova rivaled her worst cramps. It lasted a few moments after the nova itself was complete, an old worry she tended to notice less while battle was going on.

"Commence scan sweep," she ordered. "We'll follow this route for twenty minutes, then nova to waypoint two."

The nature of the drive imposed the time frames. A one-light-hour jump required a twenty-minute cooldown for a nova fighter's class two drive—versus thirty-seven for a class one. It wasn't just the minimum distances where the class two had an edge, though the class one took the edge at anything beyond a light-day.

"Let's see what we find, everyone." She smiled thinly. "I'm *hoping* for nothing, but the only way we keep finding nothing is if the Bengals decided to run all the way home without a fight."

She didn't need to tell the seven pilots accompanying her that *that* wasn't likely.

WAYPOINT ONE WAS MUCH what Kira had expected—nothing, nothing and more nothing. The trade-route stops were in deep space, at least a light-year from the nearest star with even the tiniest gravitational fluctuations mapped a thousand times for safety.

Novaing away from or toward a gravity well was simple enough. It was the side vectors that were dangerous for longer novas, even at practically undetectable levels. All of that could be handled and accounted for, so long as it was known. That was the point of the heavily mapped trade routes, to make sure that even small gravity fluctuations were known.

But it also meant that there was literally *nothing* out there. In the Fringe and the Rim, the outer eight hundred light-years or so of human space, there were only occasionally even space stations at trade-route stops. Closer in to the Core, interstellar rest stops became more common, but out here?

Nothing. Just empty space for as far as their sensors could see.

"Stand by to nova to waypoint two," she told her people. "Confirm your coordinates."

"Coordinates confirmed," Bradley said instantly, a moment *ahead* of everyone.

Kira grinned, taking one last look around the sweeping expanse of *nothing* around them.

"Anyone see a threatening speck of space dust I missed?" she asked.

That got her the expected chuckle.

"All right. Nova on my command," she told them. "Keep an eye for that dust, though. You never know when it's going to produce a knife!"

Her pilots were still chuckling as they novaed away.

———

WAYPOINT TWO WAS MORE of the same, but the hairs on the back of Kira's neck were prickling. They were orbiting around at one light-hour from the fleet, which meant that anyone in the points they were visiting wouldn't have even *seen* Seventh Fleet yet.

"Any anomalies?" she asked her pilots. "Anything look out of the ordinary at all?"

"It's a lot of black, sir," Swordheart told her. "I don't even see the fleet."

"That's the point, I guess," Kira said. "We're here before anyone here would see the fleet." She checked the timer. They'd leave waypoint two after twenty minutes, hitting waypoint three forty-three minutes or so after the fleet had arrived.

"Keep your eyes peeled," she ordered. "How's everyone's paranoia?"

"Finely honed after years of diligent practice and heavy exercise," Scimitar replied, Colombera barely getting the crack out before he chuckled at his own humor. "The last year especially."

"If we're very lucky, paranoia is all this is," Kira murmured. "But we're not the only squadron out here and we need to keep our eyes open."

There was even the possibility that Seventh Fleet was *already* under attack and they wouldn't know until they'd completed their cooldown at waypoint three. Hoffman had orders to send fighters to recall the outer patrol if he could spare them—but the four fighters needed to recall those four squadrons could easily make the difference in a critical fight.

"Waypoint three, here we come," Scimitar said. "I've got the same itch on my neck, Basketball. We're being hunted."

"We knew that," Swordheart replied. "Haven't you lot been hunted since you left Apollo?"

"Yes, but that's different," Kira said. "Assassins can be a pain in the ass, but carrier fleets are a bit more problematic."

She checked the cooldown status.

"My fighter is clear. Report in," she ordered.

Confirmations of similar status rippled back from the others. Kira shook away the vagaries of her fears and synchronized their systems.

"Nova to waypoint three on my mark," she ordered. "Three. Two. One. Mark."

If the nova itself hadn't punched her in the gut, she might not have realized they'd moved. Empty space was empty space, after all.

"Sweep."

Her own sensors reached out, soaking up every scrap of data they could. The void was dark and cold, and that was good. Empty void didn't have ships in it—on the other hand, waypoint three *shouldn't* have been empty.

"Got the rogue," Backstab reported, Bradley still sounding very young. "Eleven-point-six-kilometer ferro-carbon asteroid, exactly as the mapping says. Heat signature is as expected."

Which meant that the chunk of iron and carbon was barely above absolute zero, roughly four to five Kelvin versus the normal average in space of a bit below three.

The asteroid was big enough to have a gravity impact on the trade route, so its course was mapped and predicted for the next hundred years. It was still the only hiding spot within a light-year or so in any direction.

"Hit the rock with active sensors," Kira ordered. "We'll orbit and scan for anomalies. We have the time."

That was simple enough to do, the mostly iron rock giving up all of its secrets in a matter of minutes—not that it turned out to have any.

"Take a look at that," Jowita "Lancer" Janda observed. "One-seventy-by-eighty-six, people. That's what home looks like from a light-hour away."

Kira snorted, keeping most of her focus on the scan of the asteroid as the light from Seventh Fleet's arrival finally caught up with them.

"Stop checking your hair in the long-range scanners, Lancer," she told Janda with a chuckle. "What's around us is a lot more critical."

"There's nothing here, sir," Lancer replied. "Just empty space."

"I'd rather be paranoid and wrong than optimistic and dead," Kira replied grimly. "Keep the sweep."

Nothing. Her own sensors were showing nothing and she grimaced. Maybe she was just being paranoid.

"Nothing can hide in space," Swordheart pointed out. "Cooldowns complete here, sir. I think we're done."

"Nothing can hide in space *forever*," Kira corrected. "We couldn't, but Apollo and Brisingr both had special-purpose vessels that could pull assorted tricks. We'd learned all of each other's tricks by the end of the war, but we both pulled some nasty surprises thanks to stealth scouts...and Cobra Squadron has *Fringe* tech."

"Sir," Backstab interrupted. "I've got something."

"If you have something, everyone else would have something," Lancer said.

"Show me, Backstab," Kira said sharply, the rebuke intended for Lancer, not the green pilot.

"It *looks* like a nova signature, but it's spread over a massive area about two light-minutes closer to the fleet than we are," the young woman said quietly. "Almost... A ten-thousand-cubic-meter ship can't spread its nova signature across twenty thousand square kilometers, could they?"

"Filament dispersal net," Kira said, each word a curse in her mouth. "Apollo tried the theory but we couldn't pull it off—we couldn't refine the nova extension that neatly. If Cobra's suppliers *did*, then yeah.

"That's a ten-thousand-cubic ship where half of its volume is a spiderweb of radiators eight thousand kilometers wide."

The squadron channel was silent and Kira stared at the kid's data. It wasn't conclusive. Even if it *was* a dispersal net, it should have been clearer than that...but she didn't know what tech the Institute had access to.

"We're changing your callsign, Backstab," Kira decided aloud.

"Because even *I* was going to miss that. You might have just saved the fleet!

"All fighters, set your course for Seventh Fleet. Nova home, people. The enemy is coming."

52

COMMODORE KIRA DEMIRCI'S *worst* fears weren't realized. Her squadron returned to Seventh Fleet to find the fleet intact and peaceful. They weren't already under attack, but Kira was running worst-case numbers in her head.

Assume a fleet was being kept a few light-months away. They wouldn't wait for the scout to cool down its drive, but they would need time to wake everyone up from readiness and get ready to nova.

Maybe five minutes, maximum. How long after that depended on whether the first wave was fighters or cruisers. Cruisers would arrive in five minutes. Nova fighters would take a few more minutes because the carriers would nova to within a few light-minutes to save the class two drives.

Everything remained quiet, but that didn't last.

Kira hit a mental command, sending alerts to every ship in the fleet.

"Fighters, scramble, scramble, scramble," she barked onto the main command channel. "All ships to battle stations. Incoming enemy strike, ETA three to seven minutes."

She watched Seventh Fleet's response and cursed the inexperience of the green crews. Her fighters were moving, but the warships were taking too long.

"What the hell is going on, Demirci?" Remington snapped. "You shouldn't be calling the fleet to battle stations."

"There's no time, Admiral. There was a stealth ship at one light-hour. They novaed just over five minutes ago. Expect imminent contact."

Nova fighters were spilling into space from the RRF carriers. All of *Deception*'s fighters were already in space.

"All nova fighters, defensive formation six," Kira barked, setting her own course into position above Remington's flagship, the cruiser *Duke*. "Contact imminent."

"I've repeated the battle stations order," Remington told her. "Turrets should be spinning up across the fleet. If you're wrong, Commodore..."

"Then I'm paranoid and we had a lovely readiness exercise," Kira snapped. "But if I'm no—"

"Nova flare!" she heard someone shout on Remington's channel. "Multiple nova flares, multiple flares—no number estimate, *no number estimate.*"

"Jammers up."

That order was the last Kira heard from the RRF Admiral before the universe dissolved into chaos—but she'd seen the nova flares too. *Dozens* of them, which could only mean a fighter strike.

And that meant Cobra Squadron.

WITH THE MULTIPHASIC jamming in place, Kira's visibility was trash and she barely had coms with her own squadron. Watching a hundred and twenty modern fighters flash into Seventh Fleet's formation, she didn't even get to hang on to that.

"Memorial-Alphas, break and attack," she ordered calmly.

Her own focus dropped onto the central strike force of the enemy formation. Thirty nova bombers—*not* the Uglies the Crest mercs had used but honest-to-goodness Fringe-built bombers, more modern than anything she had—were heading toward the cruiser line.

But even as she charged toward them, a pit formed in her stomach.

It had been a *long* time since she'd seen a professional force fight. Despite the harsh training she'd put her people through to keep their skills up, this wasn't something her trainees were going to stand up to.

Nova fighters cycled around the bombers in a swirling dance that prevented her getting a clear line of fire. If any of the Manticore-Sevens were carrying torpedoes, it didn't show in their maneuvers—though they had enough reserve maneuverability that they could probably dance circles around her people, even carrying the heavy weapons.

"Not today," she muttered to herself, arming her guns and locking in on the closest interceptor.

If she couldn't get to the bombers, she could try to clear a path for the *other* fighters to get to the bombers.

She twisted her Hoplite around incoming fire as two *other* Manticores tried to scare her off her target. The closer she got, the more intense the fire grew, but she made her own range and opened fire.

Her target dodged her first burst, twisting their own ship around to return fire. There were now three fighters focused on Kira, and she felt the weight of the lack of training of her new pilots on her shoulders.

They could risk the focus because they'd kill most of her people in seconds with that kind of concentration.

But *she* was not a fresh graduate of a compressed training program. She dodged around the incoming fire and lined up her target again. This time, the pilot didn't manage to evade in time. Her fire tore through the midsection of the fighter and ripped it into several pieces.

Then Kira realized that she'd been drawn away from the bombers. She tried to turn her course back toward the fighters to clear a path, but her two remaining pursuers filled the space around her and focused her attention.

Nobody made it to the bombers before they reached the end of their run. The focused salvos of fire from the cruisers and destroyers took out several of them, but twenty-five survived to ripple-fire the dozen torpedoes each carried...and then they novaed out, taking their nova fighters with them.

Kira watched in horror as Commodore Shang's entire destroyer squadron vanished, along with half of his RRF counterparts. When the explosions cleared, only two *Sensibility*-class destroyers remained to escort the RRF cruisers...and *that* was when the Bengalissimo Fleet arrived.

Like the RRF, they'd decided to keep the corvettes and gunships out of this fight. They still arrived with two of the modern *Tabby*-class cruisers and fourteen destroyers. It might not be enough, not against five cruisers, but the odds still stank to Kira.

She didn't even need to give the order. *This* was what they'd held the Screwballs back against. Even as the Bengal cruisers opened fire, *Theseus* and *Deception* cycled one last fighter launch—and put fourteen of their own bombers into space.

DETAILED ASSESSMENTS and communication were impossible. The risk of misidentifying a friendly as a hostile was minimal—so far, at least—but was definitely present. Right now, though, the biggest concern was that Kira couldn't give orders to her people.

It was absolutely critical that the bomber strike get through, but a third of her nova fighters had novaed to safety during the dogfight and hadn't returned yet. Even the hundred-plus fighters that remained were out of reach, incommunicado through the chaos of the multi-phasic jamming.

All Kira could do was lead by example. Her Hoplite blazed toward the two bomber squadrons, dropping in around them as she maneuvered in a pattern she'd learned long before—one that added even more confusion to the signatures of the bombers.

More fighters joined her. Only her Apollo veterans knew the drill, though. The others, even the veteran RRF pilots, had never flown cover for a bomber strike before. Even for Kira and her Three-Oh-Three vets, though, this was different.

Most of the tactics were built around keeping *fighters* away from the bombers, and Cobra Squadron wasn't back yet. They had another thirty seconds to complete the strike before the fighters returned.

Kira led the way, weaving her way through the hail of fire crossing the void between the two fleets. *Deception* and the RRF cruisers outgunned their Bengal counterparts, but the destroyers were making up the difference. That was the cruel logic of the Cobra Squadron strike —a logic Kira didn't have the command-and-control loop to duplicate.

The plan was to go after the *Tabbies,* and that was the course the bombers set. More fighters joined the swarming formation as they drove across the empty space—but fighters were dying as well. A cruiser's heavy plasma cannon weren't designed to kill fighters, but they carried secondary guns for just that reason.

A bomber died.

Then another. Then another. Kira watched their alpha strike evaporate around her. She watched as a Weltraumpanzer took a hit intended for one of the bombers, one of *her* pilots vaporized in an instant.

And then contact. There were no bombers in the second strike, but there were still over eight Manticore-Sevens—and against the crudely bashed-together Screwball bombers, a more-advanced interceptor was the deadliest tool the Bengals could have.

Kira abandoned the bombers, sending her fighter hurtling directly toward the Manticores. She couldn't directly protect the bombers—but she *could* distract the other interceptors.

Other pilots followed. In moments, she had at least a hundred fighters charging eighty—and if the quality of the planes and pilots had been equal, it would have been well in her favor.

Instead, it was a massacre. Kira dodged around the enemy fire, doing her damnedest to close with the Manticores and kill them to protect her trainees, but she could *feel* the destruction around her. The Cobras worked in slick teams, groups of three focusing on a single Redward fighter for a few seconds and then moving on after they'd destroyed their target.

Three came after her and she twisted around, her fire gutting the central fighter and sending it spinning away. Skill still mattered, and good as Cobra's pilots were, Kira was *better.*

Her trainees weren't. They were dying by the dozen around her... and then her computer informed her of torpedo detonation. Multiple torpedoes, *dozens* of torpedoes—nine of the Screwballs had survived to volley ninety torpedoes into one of the *Tabby* cruisers.

Seventh Fleet's heavy fighters were right behind them, sending fifty torpedoes into the other. Fire washed over both of the big ships and only one emerged, half of its turrets offline and visible gouts of flame getting sucked out by vacuum.

Against five other cruisers, the ship never stood a chance—but Kira and her fighters were still being swarmed. A second group of three was now targeting Kira, which meant *five* fighters were coming after her—and even *she* wasn't that good.

She hit the preprogrammed nova command and the battle around her vanished.

53

THERE WAS a continual cascade of fighters in and out of the rendezvous point. For the first time since Kira had retired from the Apollo System Defense Force, she actually had a fighter group with enough fighters to *not* have her entire force out there.

Theoretically, the cycle was by squadron. In practice, the chaos of a multiphasic-jamming battlespace meant that even smaller formations got shredded. She still sent the ping out to see if her squadron was there.

"Memorial-Alpha, report in. All other fighters, report by squadron," she ordered.

"Backstab reporting in," Bradley reported immediately. "Been clinging to your wing the whole way." She paused. "Think I'd be dead if I'd done anything else."

"Lancer here," Janda joined in. "Was just behind Backstab. And I agree, boss; the kid needs a new callsign."

"Can we argue about that after we've finished kicking Bengal ass? Swordheart here," Asjes reported.

"Of course, Scimitar is here, boss," Colombera added. "I don't have visual on the other three, though. Not here...and not in the battlespace."

"Understood." Kira checked her headware and her fighter's systems. Each fighter pilot that cycled through passed their reports on to the fighters remaining. It gave her a surprisingly detailed view of the battle—probably a better one than Admiral Remington had right now.

"Did anyone see Condor nova for *Conviction*?" she asked. "I don't see him in the rec... *Fuck*."

She'd found him. Condor—one of the trainees flying off of *Theseus* and the designated courier to inform Captain Estanza of what was going on—had been the first victim of the Cobra Squadron strike.

There'd been secondaries...but they were either dead or there. A ball had been dropped and *everybody* was fucked.

"None of the Screwballs made it out, sir," Colombera told her quietly. "There's still a ton of destroyers in the fight, but it's Cobra Squadron that's fucking us."

"They need to rearm their bombers. That's a ten-minute process minimum for us. Seven, *maybe* six for them, but we still have time..."

"To do what?" Lancer asked. "They're massacring us to clear a path for when the bombers rearm. The Fleet can't run..."

"We find the carriers," Kira replied. A chill ran down her spine as she gave an order that might doom Seventh Fleet.

"All fighters, this is a hold order," she barked as her own cooldown ticked past fifteen seconds left. "Nobody novas back into the fight without an order from me. Hold positions and assume formation by squadron."

"Sir, that..."

"The interceptors are a threat to our capital ships but not a big one," Kira told Scimitar quietly. "The *bombers* are the key and that means the *carriers* are everything."

She knew everything that was within ninety light-seconds or so of their rendezvous point. She *didn't*, thanks to the multiphasic jamming, know what was around the fleet and the actual battlespace.

The carriers weren't within her time bubble, which limited where they could be. Not perfectly. Not enough to launch a strike, but enough...

"All fighters, I am transmitting three sets of nova coordinates," she informed her people. She had sixty fighters, a bit over half Hoplites or Sinisters with a single six-ship squadron of Escutcheons.

It wasn't enough…but it had to be.

"Designating locations to each of you. It's a ninety-light-second jump; you have an eighty-second cooldown. Secondary rendezvous is *here*." She pinged a location one light-minute from each of her scouting zones.

"Do not engage the enemy at your waypoint except in self-defense," she ordered. "We cannot lose a single second here. Nova on my command…

"Nova!"

THE THREE POSITIONS Kira had selected were very specifically *not* likely positions for the Cobra Squadron carriers. Instead, they were three points where the light reaching them over the preceding few minutes would fill the holes in her time-lagged visibility sphere and give her complete data over the likely location of Cobra Squadron's support fleet.

Which meant, of course, that the point she'd picked for her own squadron was only ten light-seconds from the three ships she was hunting. She had a perfect view of the converted Meridian-built freighters—and in ten seconds, they'd *know* she did.

"I have never been so glad that the carriers themselves can't nova," Kira muttered. "All fighters, stand by for incoming. They're going to send whatever interceptors they have after us."

"Jammers?" Scimitar asked.

"Negative, let them jam—I want clear coms and clear data for as long as I can," Kira replied. She studied the Cobra ships as carefully as she could.

It was clear that the ships were from two different sources. Two were seventy-kilocubic ships with a smooth grace to them she'd rarely seen replicated out there in the Rim. Despite that grace, they were also pockmarked with decades of repairs and wear and tear.

The *third* ship was a problem. Kira had assumed—as had John

Estanza—that Cobra Squadron was going to stick with their standard of picking up advanced freighters and co-opting their cargo-handling systems to launch fighters.

The third ship probably only carried the same fifty fighters as the other two, but where the converted freighters were barely less vulnerable now than in their original state, the third ship *loomed* with armor and weapons. At ninety kilocubics, it was barely smaller than *Deception* and was at least as well armed as Redward and Bengal's new cruisers.

"That is an assault carrier," Scimitar said grimly. "Griffon-built?"

"I'm guessing it came with the fighters," Kira replied. "Helps pick the bomber target, doesn't it?

"Scimitar, Backstab, Lancer. It's on you—as soon as you're cooled down, don't nova to the rendezvous. Get to *Conviction*. Dump all the data you've scanned to Estan—"

The channel screamed at her as it dissolved into jamming. They were out of time as a dozen Manticore-Sevens burst out of nova to charge them.

THE *GOOD* NEWS, to Kira's mind, was that they'd drawn away the defensive carrier patrol. The bad news was that Cobra Squadron was as on the ball as any force she'd ever met. They'd detected her force, identified them as a threat, and sortied in under ten seconds.

With the ten-second lightspeed delay, that meant she had fifty-five seconds to keep her people alive. Hoping that her wingmen had received *enough* of her orders, she charged the Manticores again, fire spitting from her guns as she targeted the center of the formation.

Again, the Cobras were working in groups of three—a tactic Kira was going to incorporate into her training going forward!—to neutralize her people one at a time. This time, though, she had twenty fighters to their eighteen...and harsh as the day had been, the surviving pilots were either lucky or good.

Unless she missed her guess, Bradley made ace in the first pass, punching out her second Manticore and her third hostile overall while Kira supported.

Kira nailed a fighter of her own, leaving only a single pilot of the trio that had been focusing on Lancer. The disadvantage of their team-work showed as the pilot clearly panicked for a moment—and a moment was more than enough for Scimitar to empty a series of plasma pulses into the Cobra pilot's engines.

Her people were still dying, but for the first time since Cobra Squadron had attacked Seventh Fleet, they were giving as good as they got. As her own squadron tore three Manticores to pieces without losses of their own, the Redward squadrons with them traded five Sinister fighter-bombers for another three-fighter strike team.

And then the timer hit zero and Kira hit the button. Another battle-space flashed away and a *new* rendezvous point was around her.

From there, they could actually see the Cobra Squadron carriers. Her fighters flickered in around her, short the three pilots she'd sent to *Conviction* and the losses against the Cobra carrier patrol.

"Report in fuel and ammo status," she ordered. "Does *anyone* have torpedoes left?"

Reports flickered in and Kira let them wash over her as the counter ticked down. Four Hoplite-IVs. Twenty-three Dexters, so twenty-seven interceptors. Six Escutcheon heavy fighters. Eighteen Sinister fighter-bombers.

And not a single torpedo across fifty-one starfighters.

"All right, people," she told them grimly. "We can take down the junk carriers with plasma guns. Easiest for the Escutcheons, but we don't know how many of their fighters they'll be able to recall to cover for the carriers—and that assault carrier is almost certainly built to gut a fighter strike with flak.

"We go in hard and fast, target the two conversions with everything we've got," she continued. "We have ninety seconds, people. Maybe less. Maybe more. But if we can take down even *one* carrier before they get their bombers back up, we might just save a cruiser. Take down all three? We might just save the whole damn fleet.

"They didn't count on us having bombers, so we got Bengal's cruis-ers. The destroyers can't take our cruisers alone, so they *need* their own bombers.

"We're not going to let them have them, people. This is it. These voidborn assholes have wrecked the peaceful lives of a dozen sectors and a hundred star systems in obedience to some godawful math that none of them even *understand*.

"It ends today. Cobra Squadron ends *today*."

The timer was at five seconds and Kira bared her teeth, hoping her mood made it across the line. Hoping that Captain Estanza made it in time with the last bombers *Kira* had.

Hoping against hope that she wasn't about to lead fifty people she'd trained to their deaths.

"Seventh Fleet Combat Group," she said formally, watching the timer count down. "*Nova and attack!*"

54

THERE WAS no question about the jamming this time. Fifty-one multi-phasic jammers flared alive in the same moment that the starfighters plunged back into reality, shredding any communication the carriers had with each other or anyone else.

Kira counted it as a blessing that there were no escorts. Even a handful of corvettes or gunships would have been a major complicating factor. As it was, the fact that she only saw *five* fighters in the carrier patrol was concerning enough.

They'd left six behind when they'd novaed away, which meant one had novaed to the rendezvous point for the rest of their fighters—and, as if in answer to her fears, another twenty Manticore-Sevens emerged from nova in that instant.

She couldn't give any more orders. All she could do was charge forward to engage the fighters, relying on the rest of the interceptor pilots to follow her. A Hoplite swung in on her left flank and another on her right—the design of the fighters assuring her that they were from *Deception* but not telling her *which* of her pilots were with her.

The heavy fighters did as they'd been ordered, charging toward the two freighter conversions under cover of the rest of the fighter wing—but the junk carriers understood their vulnerability as well as Kira did.

They'd pulled in close to the assault carrier, and Kira's worst fears about the Griffon-built ship were realized as she opened fire.

The assault carrier probably had antiship weaponry, but the vast majority of the cubage not dedicated to her fighter wing was clearly dedicated to armor and rapid-tracking flak cannon like the Rim couldn't even *build*.

She had eighty seconds left before the earliest the bombers could launch, and she could already tell they were in trouble.

Cobra interceptors flashed forward, almost disregarding her attempts to slow them as they targeted the heavy fighters. Kira tore into the side of their formation, plasma flashing both ways as she tried to protect her heavies from the enemy interceptors—and the enemy interceptors tried to protect their carriers from her heavies.

And then the next wave of novas arrived. *Conviction* slammed into the system like a belly-flopping whale, the Cherenkov radiation pulse of her arrival blinding already jamming-frazzled sensors.

But across from her were twenty more Manticore interceptors, and Kira began to wonder how badly they'd misestimated the capacity available to Cobra Squadron. She'd *seen* over a hundred and thirty fighters and bombers now.

Fighters were spilling out of *Conviction*'s deck as the carrier plunged forward to a range she had *never* been intended to fight at.

Kira couldn't do *anything*. All she could do was hope that the orders *Hoffman* had given before launching his group were the same as the ones she would have—and she threw her rough collection of interceptors back at the Manticores.

More interceptors joined her, including one that slotted in under her wing that *had* to be Bradley. With *Conviction*'s fighters, they now had over a hundred nova fighters—and, critically, six bombers.

The assault carrier, unfortunately, *did* have antiship weapons, and those turrets opened up as *Conviction* closed. The old escort carrier's pair of recently installed turrets returned fire, but she was outclassed—and the Cobra interceptors had recognized the bombers.

There was a swirl of death as Kira led the Hoplites against the Manticores. The pilots clinging to her switched in and out in the chaos, but she still had eight left when she hammered into the center of the

Cobra formation. Three of the advanced starfighters died under her wing's guns...but dozens more made it through, and a stone dropped through Kira's stomach as a single squadron—*maybe* six Manticore-Sevens—caught up with the Screwballs.

The bombers burned like paper in a wildfire, and the deaths of all six Manticores a moment later as the Darkwing squadrons hammered into them didn't relieve Kira's fear. What was left of her heavy fighter strike was falling back, missing at least two-thirds of their numbers.

They'd battered one carrier badly and Kira guessed the conversion was no longer able to launch fighters, but there were still two carriers left—and only maybe forty seconds before they redeployed the bombers.

The bombers would nova out the moment they were clear of their carriers. Their fighters would get a tithe of them at best, leaving more than enough to shatter the cruiser fleet. Cobra Squadron might not *win* this battle, but they could wreck the force Redward needed to win this *war*.

And then *Conviction* fired her ace in the hole. Kira had *forgotten* about the array of torpedo launchers they'd rigged up for her previous operations, two dozen single-shot launchers that gave her the fire-power of a heavy cruiser for a single salvo.

That was a salvo more than the undamaged escort carrier could take. The converted freighter broke apart under the pounding—but Kira's attention was on the assault carrier now as the Darkwings charged toward it.

The PNC-115 fighter-bombers carried three torpedoes apiece, and they were the only hope she saw of finishing this battle in time. They were down to *seconds*—and the Manticores threw everything they had at the PNC-115s.

And Kira brought everything *she* had against the interceptors. The Cobra fighters swarmed her people in trios—and she smiled grimly as she saw that over half of her own people were returning the favor, even recently graduated trainees working in groups.

She was certain the two on her wing were Bradley and Colombera, not that she had any way to know. The two synchronized their fire with hers, hammering one of the Manticore-Sevens to pieces as she tried to clear a path for the fighter-bombers.

A new set of novas announced the arrival of the last fighters from the original main battle, and Kira was forced to dodge away from her attack run as new threat vectors opened up. With *Conviction*'s fighters in play, the numbers were about even now—but the Cobra fighters were just plain *better*.

Her numbers were evaporating and her people were being forced to break off. She cursed as she led her trio of fighters in a dance around the incoming fighters and realized they couldn't do it.

Cobra Squadron had formed too effective a defensive formation and had too much of an edge in maneuverability and firepower. Even the fighter-bombers were being forced back, unable to press their attack against the enemy.

They were past her worst-case estimate of the bomber launch time. Cobra Squadron hadn't launched them yet, but it could only be seconds. There was *nothing* Kira could do—given time, they *might* be able to wear the defenders down with hit and run attacks, but there was no time to nova away and reconsolidate.

Once the bombers launched, it was over. They'd have gutted Cobra Squadron—they already *had* gutted Cobra Squadron—but those nova bombers would gut Seventh Fleet in turn.

She held another Manticore in her sights for a few deadly moments as Backstab and Scimitar helped her tear it to shreds, but the victory was ash in her mouth.

And then something moved in the battlespace. A Manticore that was lining up on Backstab didn't dodge fast enough and was blasted out of space by one of *Conviction*'s flak cannons, the plasma bursts tearing through the defensive formation as the carrier charged.

The old ship's two antiship turrets didn't have the firepower to take out the remaining Cobra carrier—but it was only when *Conviction* started shedding escape pods that Kira realized John Estanza's intention.

Ivar Larsson didn't realize it in time—and the hundred-and-sixty-eight-year-old escort carrier slammed into her enemy at literally world-shattering velocities.

Debris sprayed in every direction as the two nova ships came apart, highlighted a moment later when *Conviction*'s fusion reactors intentionally overloaded.

For a few seconds, the battlespace seemed frozen—and then the remaining Cobra Squadron fighters vanished as a single body.

55

JOHN ESTANZA LOOKED PERFECTLY calm at the center of *Conviction*'s bridge. Red lights flared across a dozen panels, warning signs of closing fighters, incoming fire, and active damage alike.

"The fighters aren't going to break through, sir," Mwangi reported, the executive officer managing to seem equally calm, almost diffident, as the carrier wove her way through a battle she'd never been designed for. "Our torpedoes nailed Cobra Bravo, but Alpha is beyond our weapons.

"By Demirci's calculations, we're five seconds from bomber launch."

"I know. Sound abandon ship and get to the bridge pod," Estanza ordered.

"Sir?"

"There's no time," Estanza snapped. Alert lights started flashing around the bridge. "I can only give you twenty seconds, Akuchi. *Go.*"

The XO cursed—but gestured for the bridge crew to follow him as he ran for the attached escape pod.

Estanza remained in his chair, presumably taking control of the ship's systems from there, and smiled calmly at empty air.

"You can all hear me," he told his scattering crew. "I know some of you aren't running. You've guessed what's happening and chosen to *make* it happen. Thank you.

"This is my responsibility, not yours. A duty owed to a past life to finish what I left behind. But to all of you who are clearing the ship and all of you who are staying alike, thank you."

In answer to a silent command, every display on the bridge darkened. They were replaced with a single hologram showing the two ships, with every piece of vector and engine-thrust data available overlaid in familiar patterns.

"It has been an honor," John Estanza said into the channel. None of the crew would have heard him by then, Kira realized—every escape pod had launched and they had the same limits in the battlespace as anyone else.

The hologram showed the course of the two carriers, and Estanza rode it like the big carrier was his old starfighter—and it was *very* clear that Ivarsson had never seen what was coming.

The moment before impact, Kira paused the recording. She sighed, then turned it off and turned to Akuchi Mwangi. The Black officer looked back at her levelly, just as dispassionate as he had been when the battle had been going to hell around *Conviction*.

"How many made it out?" she asked. She had no idea how the contracts and structure of *Conviction*'s legal existence were going to fall out in the end, but she'd take responsibility for Estanza's people for now.

That was the least she could do.

"Two hundred fifty-six," Mwangi said crisply. "With the fighters already in space...just over two-thirds of the people aboard." He paused. "The senior officers made it, except for Labelle. They stayed to rig the reactors. I'm not sure that was part of John's plan."

"I'm not sure it would have worked without it."

Kira shook her head. They were back on *Deception*, the big cruiser anchoring the search-and-rescue efforts through the debris of the strike on the Cobra carriers.

"It might not have. That was one tough voidborn of a ship with some tough voidborn pilots. John... Well, he saved *Deception*, most likely."

"And Redward." Mwangi bowed his head. "I didn't hear his entire speech until now."

"He knew the bridge recorders would get it," Kira said, looking back at where the hologram of *Conviction*'s bridge had hung. "He knew everyone would see it—and everyone *will* see it, Akuchi. We'll share it to everyone from *Conviction* who made it off."

"What do we do now, sir?" Mwangi asked.

"*Deception* was the focus of everyone's fire yesterday," Kira admitted. "She's tough, but she's taken a beating. *Baron* is hanging out with us because we're one solid knock from falling apart."

Deception also now had a capital-ship kill count to terrify small children. The price of it all, though...

"Once we're finished search-and-rescue here, we'll move to Ypres to rendezvous with Seventh Fleet," she told Mwangi. "*Deception* is in no shape to continue operations." She snorted. "Most of Seventh Fleet isn't, in truth, but I suspect they'll fake it at best they can.

"I'll talk to Remington in Ypres and see what the plan is. If nothing else, she's got over half of our fighters and pilots."

Deception had a mismatched collection of twenty nova fighters aboard; there were twenty-five more *Conviction* planes tucked away on one of the RRF's junk carriers. The chaos was such that Kira wasn't even sure who was alive or dead yet.

She had her fears, though.

"Until we officially stand down the corporation or...whatever happens next, I'll stick with you, sir," Mwangi promised. "My understanding is that I answer to Zoric now, anyway. And she reports to you."

"Focus on keeping *Conviction*'s crew sane," Kira told him. "I don't need them to help out around *Deception*, but I suspect helping with repairs and S&R will make them feel better."

"Almost certainly, sir. I will make it happen."

"Work with Kavitha and Konrad," she said. "I trust the three of you. Let me know what you need."

"And you, sir?"

"I'm responsible for search-and-rescue at two battlespaces," Kira pointed out. "I'll be busy."

THE SEARCH-AND-RESCUE SHUTTLE came into the flight deck very, very slowly. It had a pair of large retractable manipulator arms that were currently extended beneath it, holding the wreckage of a familiar-looking fighter.

More accurately, *half* a fighter. Kira stood and watched as an emergency crew rushed to the Hoplite-IV, but she knew the truth, looking at the mangled wreckage. The emergency pod had been trapped by the way the hull had warped, preventing the nova fighter from ejecting the pilot and the class two drive.

Dinesha Patel stood at her right side and she was torn between pretending to have hope and facing reality. Finally, a choked sob from the younger pilot made up her mind.

She turned and pulled him into a hard hug, holding him as he dissolved into tears—which thankfully kept his head against her shoulders and his eyes covered as the emergency team emerged from the wreck with a body bag.

Kira could guess what Joseph Hoffman looked like now. She'd seen enough burnt and mangled bodies pulled from starfighters over the years. She hadn't even *seen* Longknife die.

Patel had flown on his lover's wing, though, and had to have seen the hit. He'd still managed to handle himself through the battle, leading a rapidly changing wing of fighters into the heart of the enemy formation again and again.

"I'm sorry, Dinesha," Kira told him. "He didn't make it."

"I knew," Patel whispered. "I just... I just didn't want to admit it."

Kira looked up as Mel Cartman stepped over, wrapping her own arms around the young man.

"I'm not sure it helps, but we just got an update from one of *Baron*'s shuttles," Cartman told Kira as she gently transferred Patel to cry into her shoulder instead. "They found Michel. She's...not in great shape, but she's alive.

"They're rushing her to *Baron* because she's closer."

Kira grimaced.

"That bad?" she murmured.

"Worse," Cartman admitted. "From what they said...they had to leave about half of her behind in the wreckage to extract her."

"*Starfires*," Kira swore. "And then there were five."

They'd made it this far without losing any of the original six, but the nature of their job meant that could never have lasted.

"What do we now, boss?" Cartman asked.

"We go on," Kira said grimly. "We hold a giant fucking wake when we get back to Redward and mourn our dead. I *think*—I hope—that Bengalissimo is the Institute's last play here in the Cluster, and we've destroyed them.

"They've got one cruiser left. I doubt Redward is going to try the impossible and invade a system, but they can certainly return the blockade favor on Bengalissimo."

"Good," Patel ground out. "I want these voidborn assholes dead."

"Cobra Squadron *is* dead, Dinesha," Kira told him. "They had three carriers and a hundred and thirty fighters and bombers. They've got *maybe* twenty-five fighters left. No carrier. No bombers. And we are going to tell the *galaxy* how Cobra Squadron ended, my friend.

"Hoffman may have died at the hands of a legend, but that legend is *over*. I don't believe in revenge...but he is well avenged."

"I do believe in revenge," Patel snarled, then exhaled a long breath. "But...you're right."

"You haven't slept since the battle. Go rest, Dinesha," Kira told him. "I *will* make it an order and have a doctor knock you out if I have to."

"I think... I think..."

"I'll take care of him," Cartman promised. "You've got a lot going on."

THE SHUTTLE that arrived twelve hours later was smaller than the search-and-rescue ships, painted white with red crosses in the ancient symbol of its purpose.

Kira hadn't ordered an honor guard for their wounded, but she found herself surrounded by one anyway as she met the medical transfer ship. A file of surprisingly gleaming armored mercenaries flanked the ramp as medical pods were rolled down.

"Our people deserve respect," Milani murmured as they joined her. "We won, right?"

"That's the theory," Kira agreed. There were seventeen medical pods coming aboard *Deception* and thirty-two going the other way. Most of the ones going to *Baron* were prisoners. Kira's people weren't equipped to handle interrogation and long-term detention of conscious people, let alone prisoners.

All seventeen of the pods coming her way were pilots, but it was the sixteenth pod that she crossed to meet.

"She's in an induced coma," the tech accompanying the pod told her the moment she arrived. "We've stabilized her, but without artificial life support, she..."

"We have the best systems here," Kira promised. "Everyone will get the best treatment. Evgenia won't get better care than anyone else, but she'll get the best care. She's just special."

"She needs major regeneration. Planetside," the med tech warned Kira, but stepped back to let Kira look inside at the young woman. Michel was even shorter than Kira, with an extremely petite build. She looked fragile *normally*—and Kira had to swallow down a moment of nausea when she realized that Evgenia Michel currently ended about three centimeters below her belly button.

"She'll get it," Kira said firmly. "Whatever it takes."

"Always hard dealing with a case like this," the tech admitted. "We can save them, but rebuilding them is hard and not all of them come back...mentally intact, sir."

"She has four of the best friends in the galaxy to watch over her," Kira told the young man. "Thank you for everything you've done. Without you and your colleagues, we'd have lost more than we did."

"We're picking up a bunch of people who should be in RRF uniforms," the tech replied with a sad smile. "I think the honors are about even."

56

YPRES HADN'T CHANGED MUCH on the surface. Political unification hadn't yet made any major changes to the positions of stations and shipping. It would, Kira was sure, but it had only been a few months and most of those under blockade.

Baron and *Deception* were arriving at Dikkebus, the most heavily populated and industrialized planet in the system. Not much had changed there, though Kira could pick out the signs of new shipyards as her ship slid into position flanking *Duke*.

The Federation had been busier than she'd thought. From what Commodore Shinoda had said, the two nova destroyers they'd given him for the Coalition Fleet had been half of the nova warships his people possessed.

Now *eight* Yprian destroyers orbited with the Redward cruisers. There were even a few lighter warships from other systems—the week since the battle had been enough for the balance to fully shift.

"Admiral Remington sends her regards, Commodore," Zoric told Kira as the pilot surveyed the cruiser's bridge. "You're invited to join her aboard *Duke* at your convenience."

"You think she really means my convenience?" Kira asked dryly. "She *is* an Admiral."

There were few ways an Admiral could request someone to visit them that *didn't* translate as "right now."

"And we're the people who saved the damn Cluster," her Captain replied. "I think she might just. But I guess we don't have much else to do."

"We've still got some of their people on board, and they've still got some of our people on Seventh Fleet's carriers," Kira noted. "Can you coordinate that swap, Kavitha?"

"Easily," Zoric promised. "When do I start getting replacement armor and dispersal networks? Or *turrets*, for that matter?"

Sixty-two of *Deception*'s crew were dead, killed when four of her heavy turrets had been blasted clean off her hull by particularly ballsy Cobra pilots. Fixing *that* damage was going to take a while.

"When we're back in Redward, I think," Kira said. "We're not doing that work here. And that assumes you even still work for me."

"That's up to me, I'm pretty sure, which means I still work for you," Zoric told her. "It's... It's what John would have wanted."

"Thank you," Kira replied, closing her eyes for a moment. "I guess I need to go catch a shuttle."

ADMIRAL VILMA REMINGTON'S office aboard her cruiser was sparser than Kira might have expected. At the very least, she'd figured the old Admiral would have an "I love me" wall of certifications and decorations.

Instead, it was completely standard-issue. One desk. One ceiling-mounted hologram projector. Bare walls except for where the flag of Redward—a stylized red mountain behind a castle—was enameled onto the wall behind her.

That was it. The holoprojector was doing yeoman's work, however, with a full display of the Syntactic Cluster hanging in the air above Remington's desk as the woman studied it.

"Admiral Remington," Kira greeted her. "You requested me."

"I'd have Estanza too, if I could," Remington said. "That man and I spent half a decade arguing everything from contract pricing to intergalactic politics to quantum physics. If I was remotely inclined toward men, I'd have dragged him to bed years ago.

"The absolute ass."

The room was silent.

"But here we are," Kira finally said, internalizing her own grief.

"So we are." A bottle of something appeared on the desk and Remington poured two generous glasses. "Bengalissimo sherry," she said, sliding the glass across the table. "The system produces a few nice things along with assholes and warships."

"To John Estanza," Kira toasted before sipping the smoothly sweet fortified wine. "And the mess he left me."

"Do you know what happens to the mercenary company's assets and people?" Remington asked.

"*Deception* is mine but a bunch of her crew were John's," Kira admitted. "I'll offer them contracts to transfer over once things quiet down. Right now, we're limping along emotionally as well as physically."

"The contract does include provisions for compensation in case of loss of hardware," Remington told her. "I don't think either of us expected it to be quite this messy, but it's still covered."

"Good to know, Admiral."

"Em Demirci, unless you plan on taking *Deception* and leaving the Cluster right this moment, you and I are going to be working together for a while yet," Remington told her. "Call me Vilma."

"If you insist, Vilma," Kira said.

Remington nodded firmly and gestured to the map.

"The good news is that I don't need *Deception* right now," she said. "While the best tactical and operational plan would be to move on Bengalissimo right now, before their allies send them more ships and tech, that would be contrary to our *strategic* objectives."

"You want the rest of the Cluster involved," Kira guessed.

"Exactly. Even if it's only a token commitment from our allies, we *need* this to be a shared Free Trade Zone operation," Remington confirmed. "I'm going to hold here in Ypres with Seventh Fleet until I am reinforced by those allies.

"While I would *prefer* to hang on to *Deception*, your ship is also the worst damaged after that affair. I presume you would like to repair her?"

"I would, yes," Kira agreed.

"I'll acknowledge your contract to support Seventh Fleet on our breakout and breakin as complete," Remington told her. "I'll leave valuing *Conviction* to the analysts on Redward, but I will sign off on a full compensation for her loss in principle and provide partial immediate compensation."

"Immediate compensation, Vilma?" Kira asked with a raised eyebrow.

"We started this mess with five carriers and two hundred and ninety fighters," the Admiral reminded her. "I still have four carriers... but there are only eighty RRF fighters aboard them. On the other hand, *Deception* can't haul forty-five planes."

A new hologram appeared, a familiar one.

"I know our freighter conversions aren't worth a tenth of what *Conviction* was in a fight, but one would let you take your fighters back to Redward with you. *Raccoon* is currently carrying all of your fighters as it is, so transferring her crew and the couple of RRF fighters she still has aboard to another ship will be easy enough.

"She's yours. Well, Conviction LLC's, I guess," Remington noted, "but it gives you a starting point. I hope you retrieved some useful gear from *Conviction*'s wreckage."

"Angel Waldroup insisted," Kira said with a sad chuckle. "We got three-quarters of her fabricators eating up *Deception*'s limited cargo space."

"You can move them onto *Raccoon* or, well, do whatever you want," the Admiral told her. "The ships are yours. The fighters are yours. The money is yours too, if that's any consolation."

"I lost dear friends in this mess," Kira replied. "It's not much of one, no."

"I didn't think it would be." The ship vanished from the hologram. "I was never under the impression that you or John—or Shang Tzu, for that matter—were *just* mercenaries."

Remington studied the map of the Cluster with the single baleful red icon of Bengalissimo glowing on it.

"There'll be work for your people, however it all shakes out," she promised. "But *Deception* needs repairs."

"And escorts, I think, if I'm going to play this game," Kira replied. "I don't suppose I can get a sign-off from you allowing us to buy *Serendipity*-class destroyers?"

Remington chuckled.

"Kira, right now, you could get a sign-off from me to let you buy one of our fucking *asteroid fortresses*," she replied. "We wouldn't have survived without *Deception* and *Conviction*. I know the worth of the 'mercenaries' who stood by my side in the darkest hour of my people and our system.

"The messages I've sent to my King and Queen reflect that, Kira. You and your people may be mercenaries. You may have been born in a dozen star systems across a thousand light-years, but know this: you are Redward's now. We know our own and you will *always* have a home and a place under my King."

57

PRIAPUS SIMONEIT LEANED back in his chair, looking even older than he normally did. His hands trembled as he laid a formal paper envelope on his desk, looking at Kira and Zoric as they sat across from him.

"John's will was updated roughly three months ago," he told them in a weary voice. "I went through it all with him."

Simoneit had been an old friend of Kira's boss—and Estanza's fellow ex-Cobra—Jay Moranis, who'd traveled with the pilot but settled much farther out. He hadn't been John Estanza's lawyer when Kira had arrived, but he'd handled all of Jay Moranis's affairs—and then Kira's, including the establishment of Memorial Squadron, her mercenary company.

"I thought John had another lawyer," Zoric asked.

"Em Legault actually retired a few months ago," Simoneit told her. "At Em Estanza's instructions, we'd been transferring the entire Conviction LLC file over to Simoneit and Partners Law from Legault LLP over that time.

"The will was done separately, though the main asset involved is Conviction LLC itself."

The lawyer shrugged.

"John Estanza reinvested most of his wealth and profits back into the company and the ship," he told them. "One of the reasons for needing to rewrite the will was that it was previously structured so that Daniel Mbeki inherited most of the corporation.

"Given that Em Mbeki's death returned his twenty percent share in Conviction LLC to John Estanza, many adjustments were required. His final request was that both of you be present for this," Simoneit concluded.

"This is hard, Pree," Kira admitted. "I think we all kind of thought he was immortal."

"Believe me, old men know how immortal they're *not*," Simoneit said drily. "Are you aware of the ownership structure of Conviction LLC, Kira?"

"I assumed Estanza owned it, actually," Kira admitted.

"Not all," the lawyer said. "Em Zoric here"—he gestured to Zoric—"owns a twenty percent share. She and Daniel Mbeki were awarded those shares two years ago as part of Em Estanza's succession planning, according to Em Legault."

"That's correct, yes," Zoric said quietly.

"At his death, John Estanza owned eighty percent of Conviction LLC and approximately forty million kroner in assorted liquid financial assets," Simoneit told them. "His desire was quite straightforward, actually.

"Everything he owned is split evenly between the two of you except for the shares in Conviction, which are split seventy-five-twenty-five in Em Demirci's favor."

Kira blinked and did the mental math. Twenty million Redward kroner was about five million Apollon new drachmae. Estanza had been wealthier than he'd pretended. The major item, though, was the shares of the mercenary company.

That would give her a sixty percent share in Conviction to Zoric's forty percent...but Conviction didn't really *own* anything.

"I see his logic," Kira said. "But I'm guessing he assumed *Conviction* would survive him."

"Most likely. If I may make a suggestion?"

Kira made a go-ahead gesture.

"With the ownerships and contract questions around *Raccoon* and the personnel of Conviction LLC—not to mention the cash assets of both the Memorial Squadron and Conviction corporations—a merger of the two entities into a new organization may be the wisest course.

"I'd need to do the math, but I believe that you, Em Demirci, would retain control of the combined entity, with Em Zoric as the second-largest shareholder, nearly matched by Em Patel now that he has inherited Em Hoffman's shares in Memorial Squadron."

Kira exhaled.

"That would make things easier, wouldn't it, Kavitha?" she asked the other woman. "I'll need to run by it by the Memorials, but you and I can sign off for Conviction right now."

"It makes sense, but what do we even call it?"

"*Not 'Raccoon,'*" Kira argued. "I'll keep that carrier as long as we have to and not one bloody minute more."

The junk carrier was *exactly* what she'd expected it to be.

"Memorial still, I think," Zoric said slowly. "We're not just remembering your dead from Apollo anymore, though. For Estanza and Labelle and Hoffman and everyone else."

"Agreed."

"Very well," Simoneit told them. "I can get the paperwork while you get sign-off from the other shareholders of Memorial Squadron." He paused. "That is, of course, assuming that you wish to continue operating a mercenary company, ladies.

"Thanks to Jay Moranis and John Estanza, you are both quite wealthy now. And I think we all just received a clear reminder of the mortality rate of your business."

"I don't have it in me to sit on a beach and sip margaritas, Pree," Kira told the lawyer. "And the Equilibrium Institute is still out there. We might have finally stopped them here, but we still have work to do."

"I'm with Kira," Zoric agreed. "If nothing else, I've spent so long on ships, I don't think I even *could* live on a planet. I know what I do and I know I do it well."

"Very well. I look forward to assisting you in your future endeavors, then, officers.

"Good luck."

58

THERE WAS STILL GOING to be at least *one* beach. Redward wasn't a planet known for its tourist destinations, but very few human-habitable planets couldn't find at least *one* spot with decent sand and warm water.

Kira had rented the entire resort and brought *everyone* down. She had a good idea of what the bill at the end of the weekend was going to be, and she did *not* care.

Especially not as she stood on the beach and watched twenty-one of Milani's troopers, in armor for the only time all weekend, assemble into a line and raise their rifles to the sky.

Plasma bolts lit into the sky. Again and again and again, once for each member of the mercenary company that hadn't made it back from the battle.

"The yards say the repairs are going to ta—"

"No, Konrad," Cartman cut Kira's lover off. "No work, not tonight."

Kira chuckled. She'd been about to elbow Konrad. Since she was leaning against his legs as he sprawled in a beach chair, it wouldn't have taken much to move.

Evgenia Michel was still in hospital, and she was the only one of the key members of the new mercenary company—simply Memorial Force LLC—missing from the group gathered at the center of the beach.

"Hard to avoid it," Colombera said. The youngest pilot was clearly suffering for the lack of his usual partner in pranks, but they were all tired. "Too many of the folks in charge gathered around here right now."

"True," Cartman said with a laugh. The last echoing salvo of blaster fire ended, and she rose to her feet. "I think, then, that we need to split ourselves up for our own good.

"Akuchi, may I have this dance?"

She offered her hand to the dark-haired officer, now *Raccoon*'s Captain, and pulled him to his feet as he laughed and took it.

Patel and Colombera shared a look. Both looked far too tired and sad to Kira to do *anything*, but Colombera dragged the other man to his feet, and they followed Cartman and Akuchi off toward the music.

"Well, that went quickly," Zoric observed, swallowing back her own drink as, suddenly, they were only three. "Think everyone has caught up to being millionaires yet?"

"My pilots have been millionaires since they got to Redward," Kira admitted. "I'm not sure they've realized it yet."

The cruiser Captain chuckled, rising to her feet with a vague, unsteady sway. "I'm going to get another drink. Want anything?"

"Sure, refills?" Konrad asked from behind Kira.

"I know what you ordered," Zoric confirmed. "Keep your clothes on, you two. Or if you can't, go back to your room. The crew doesn't mind if you lovey-dovey, but fucking on the beach might be going too far."

"*Might*," Kira echoed with a chuckle as she patted Konrad's thigh. "Go on, Kavitha; we'll be here when you get back."

Redward's sun Wardstone was setting, sending rays of light across the water. Some of her people were actually swimming, and a few more were wading through the shallows. If she'd wanted, her headware would have let her identify them—but she had over five hundred people at the resort that night.

She'd allow them their anonymity.

"No work, Konrad," she warned her lover. In response, he bent forward and kissed the top of her head, sending a shiver down her spine.

"I try to only make the same mistake once, my love," he told her. The label sent *another* shiver through her back, and she looked up at him with a grin.

"Be careful with that word, my love," she replied. "It has great power. First time you used it, we broke the Institute in the Cluster."

"Perhaps I should be more of sparing of it, then," he agreed. "But it would be hard. I love you, Kira Demirci. Wherever we go, whatever we do, I want to do it with you."

His grin widened and should have made his head fall off.

"And I've been thinking about that whole 'favor' business," he continued. "What I'm planning is half a favor, half a good luck charm, but I'd like you to put it in your fighter. Superstitious, definitely, but I want to do what I can to bring you back to me."

"Tearing apart those Manticores is probably more useful," Kira noted, but she waved away her own cynicism. "No. Whatever you give me, love, I'll take it. And, well."

She leaned her head against his leg and looked at the last dregs of the sunset.

"Wherever we go, whatever we do," she confirmed. "I'm going to bring some friends for *most* of it, but we'll go together. Take on the whole damn galaxy."

Konrad leaned forward to kiss her head again.

"They're never going to know what hit them," he promised.

JOIN THE MAILING LIST

Love Glynn Stewart's books? To know as soon as new books are released, special announcements, and a chance to win free paperbacks, join the mailing list at:

glynnstewart.com/mailing-list/

ABOUT THE AUTHOR

Glynn Stewart is the author of *Starship's Mage*, a bestselling science fiction and fantasy series where faster-than-light travel is possible–but only because of magic. His other works include science fiction series *Duchy of Terra, Castle Federation* and *Vigilante*, as well as the urban fantasy series *ONSET* and *Changeling Blood*.

Writing managed to liberate Glynn from a bleak future as an accountant. With his personality and hope for a high-tech future intact, he lives in Kitchener, Ontario with his wife, their cats, and an unstoppable writing habit.

VISIT GLYNNSTEWART.COM FOR NEW RELEASE
   UPDATES

f facebook.com/glynnstewartauthor

OTHER BOOKS
BY GLYNN STEWART

For release announcements join the
mailing list or visit **GlynnStewart.com**

STARSHIP'S MAGE
Starship's Mage
Hand of Mars
Voice of Mars
Alien Arcana
Judgment of Mars
UnArcana Stars
Sword of Mars
Mountain of Mars
The Service of Mars
A Darker Magic (upcoming)

Starship's Mage: Red Falcon
Interstellar Mage
Mage-Provocateur
Agents of Mars

Pulsar Race: A Starship's Mage Universe Novella

DUCHY OF TERRA
The Terran Privateer
Duchess of Terra
Terra and Imperium
Darkness Beyond
Shield of Terra
Imperium Defiant
Relics of Eternity
Shadows of the Fall
Eyes of Tomorrow (upcoming)

VIGILANTE
(WITH TERRY MIXON)
Heart of Vengeance
Oath of Vengeance

**Bound By Stars: A Vigilante Series
(With Terry Mixon)**
Bound By Law
Bound by Honor
Bound by Blood

TEER AND KARD
Wardtown
Blood Ward

CHANGELING BLOOD
Changeling's Fealty
Hunter's Oath
Noble's Honor
Fae, Flames & Fedoras: A Changeling Blood Novella

ONSET
ONSET: To Serve and Protect
ONSET: My Enemy's Enemy
ONSET: Blood of the Innocent
ONSET: Stay of Execution
Murder by Magic: An ONSET Novella

FANTASY STAND ALONE NOVELS
Children of Prophecy
City in the Sky

Lightning Source UK Ltd.
Milton Keynes UK
UKHW011848080421
381670UK00001B/83